Flavours & Colours
of Mauritius

PREFACE: GUY SAVOY

RECIPES: RICHARD EKKEBUS

PHOTOGRAPHS: CHRISTIAN BOSSU-PICAT

EVASION

Preface

I love Mauritius and its enchanting and peaceful landscape, its warm and friendly hospitality, and my friends here are very dear to me.

I love the Royal Palm, one of those magical places where quality and elegance go hand-in-hand with simplicity.

I also love the cuisine of Richard Ekkebus, who has matched his skills as a chef to this exceptional environment. He uses his perfect mastery of technique and gives fresh value to the riches that nature has bestowed on this island, too often associated with produce from outside.

I particularly appreciate his judicious use of spices and the delicious way in which he uses fish from the Indian Ocean previously unknown to us, producing recipes of real individuality.

Through his professionalism, his creativity and immense talent this alchemist has been able to develop a genuine style incorporating all the culinary traditions of this island, which was even at one time known as "Isle de France".

For all these reasons, and others as well, I am particularly happy to render homage to the exceptional chef and friend that Richard is, and I am sure he will continue to innovate and surprise us to the delight of one and all.

En toute amitié.

Famous French Chef, Guy Savoy with Richard Ekkebus during one of his visits at the Royal Palm.

Guy Savoy

EDITOR: TORIDEN CHELLAPERMAL

TEXT: TIBURCE PLISSONEAU DUQUESNE - TORIDEN CHELLAPERMAL

PRODUCTION: FLORIAN GROSSET - GERARD DESVAUX DE MARIGNY - SHAMS MUSTUN - SEAN CHAN

ENGLISH VERSION: MICHAEL BOOTLE - JANE MARY RIVIERE - FARHAD KHOYRATTY

Flavours & Colours
of Mauritius

"Creation gives shape to being; colour gives life. This is the divine touch that brings creation to life."

DENIS DIDEROT

CONTENTS

The **red** of the flame trees...	*20*
The **blue** of the southern seas...	*62*
The **yellow** of the sandy beaches...	*100*
The **green** expanse of sugarcane fields...	*144*
Recipes	
Red	*185*
Blue	*205*
Yellow	*223*
Green	*245*
Basic recipes	*263*

Flavours and Colours of Mauritius

"More a people than a race, our loyalties to East, West and Africa merge into a kind of melting-pot. Difficult certainly, but necessary, enriching our daily lives...

"Our ancestors all came from somewhere else; we have to carry on that exile in a place that has become our native country."

EDOUARD MAUNICK

Mauritius

Mauritius is often called the rainbow nation, a way of underlining the diversity of the population, the mixture of beliefs, the racial mix and the many faces of the country.

The meeting ground for civilizations from Africa, the East and the West, the Mauritian nation is built on a kind of balance, certainly precarious, but which has survived the test of time, despite the occasional faux pas.

Whilst its ethnic diversity could have led to conflict, over the years and centuries Mauritian society has learnt to transcend its differences and to control the contradictions which, elsewhere, are sources of discord, division and interminable conflicts.

Whatever may divide them, the country's religions and cultures, united by historical accident, live and blossom in the midst of mutual respect, demonstrating a remarkable commitment to shared aims.

Like the colours of the rainbow, whilst the various ethnic groups of the country exist side-by-side in harmony and brush up against each other in everyday life, they do not often mix. Religious feelings, probably exacerbated by exile, are strongly impregnated in the different communities, which, even if they display extreme tolerance, do not, unfortunately, share their social lives.

Still, if there is an area where intermingling has become a consummate art, it is that of the kitchen. Whatever his origin, a Mauritian can appreciate foie gras or Creole rougaille as much as Chinese chop suey, Moslem biryani or an Indian curry.

As if the taste buds are sometimes more daring...

But, perhaps because of his insularity, the Mauritian also enjoys foreign produce, even to the detriment of that found locally.

Flavours and Colours of Mauritius

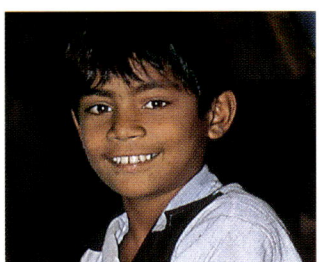

Flavours and Colours of Mauritius

Richard Ekkebus' greatest merit is to have brought not only a new dimension to the intermingling of the different culinary traditions of the country, but also to have brought alive the flavours of the country and of the Indian Ocean, combining originality with refinement. He dares to make unusual marriages, unexpected and even astonishing associations, capable of causing a few surprises.

Is it an irony of history that it should be a Dutchman - for many Mauritians, the Dutch are synonymous with the extinction of the Dodo - who should come and encourage us to stray from the beaten track and to be more imaginative?

Our local chefs will certainly find here an unlimited source of inspiration, to encourage them in this direction, towards the emergence of an authentic Mauritian cuisine.

"Flavours and Colours of Mauritius" is an invitation to a wonderful culinary adventure…

The Royal Palm

The Royal Palm first opened its doors for Christmas 1985 and rapidly became the most prestigious address in the Indian Ocean region.

Built on the finest beach in Grand Baie and repeatedly restored and renovated, the Royal Palm, which became one of "The Leading Hotels of the World" in 1990, has eighty four suites, including three presidential suites, a penthouse, and a Royal suite.

Flavours and Colours of Mauritius

15

Flavours and Colours of Mauritius

They are all carefully adorned with antiques and objets d'art, whilst precious wood and ornamental columns add to the distinctiveness of the hotel, harmoniously reflecting the oriental and western traditions to be found in Mauritius.

The Royal Palm is the natural choice for the discerning traveller who, used to excellence and the traditions of luxurious hotels, finds here the elegance, intimacy and simplicity of the stately home.

It has become a special refuge for leading figures, who appreciate its distinguished welcome, where elegance mingles with the natural grace and the charm of the islands. The renown of the Royal Palm is closely linked to the excellence of its service.

Flavours and Colours of Mauritius

The publication of Richard Ekkebus' book is an opportunity to render vibrant homage to someone who combines talent and intelligence, and who has become an inextricable part of the hotel's success. The way his cuisine transforms such a variety of flavours is magical, turning each meal into a veritable feast.

Let us hope that this book will be the prelude to his consecration as one of the greatest living chefs.

Jean Pierre Chaumard

Flavours and Colours of Mauritius

"Just as one climbs a mountain, the sea's horizon rises into the heavens... its silky surface transforms the Indian Ocean into a mirror of the heavens... civilization is far away and we find ourselves close again to the freedom of Mother Nature. The flowering flame-trees broadcast the advent of summer in an orgy of brilliant red colour, in answer to the hints of the litchi trees... and we humans, hovering between the sea and the sky, deep inside we can feel the urge both to float on earth and sea and to fly into the heavens."

ROBERT EDWARD HART

Flavours and Colours of Mauritius

Vegetable samossas

with Rodriguan red chilli sauce

I love chilli, whether it is red or green, fresh or dried. There are more than two hundred different varieties around the world. Small chillies are reputed to be the hottest, such as the one known in Mauritius as "piment pétard" (banger chilli). Some people have difficulty in appreciating their hotness, but it is a taste that can be acquired gradually. That is why it is preferable to start with mild dishes and gradually move on to spicier ones. My favourite is the red chilli from Rodrigues, which has a subtle and delicious flavour. I often use it instead of pepper, because it brings out the flavour in some vegetables and adds zing to a salad. Chillies are very popular in the warmer regions of the planet, as they increase perspiration and thereby lower body temperature. Fresh chillies are also a good source of vitamin C.

RODRIGUAN RED CHILLI

Chilli is mentioned for the first time in 1493, during Christopher Columbus' second voyage to the Americas. Chilli was in common use amongst American Indians and was the main seasoning used by the Aztecs and Incas. It was imported into Europe in 1514, before spreading to other parts of the world. It is an acquired taste, to be tried in small doses to start with… but worth acquiring. It does not need to overwhelm other flavours but is added to bring out the basic flavour.

Recipe page 187

Shrimps marinated in tandoori massala

and green salad with mango and bean sprouts

A multi-racial country, Mauritius continues to be one of my principal sources of inspiration. The possibilities, as yet unimagined, of a great hybrid cuisine lurk within this country. Unfortunately, the chefs, mostly trained in Europe, tend to favour what they have learnt abroad, instead of drawing on the rich variety of produce and flavours to be found locally.

SOYA BEAN SPROUTS

Used particularly in Chinese cookery, bean sprouts originate in India. They are obtained by soaking dried Mung beans for three to four days. Bean sprouts are eaten raw, lightly blanched, or fried so that they remain crunchy. In Mauritius, bean sprouts always accompany the famous fried noodles (mines).

Recipe page 188

Flavours and Colours of Mauritius

25

Creamy faye-faye crab flavoured with sherry

garnished with a green vegetable salad

Coin de Mire and Mahébourg are the main places where faye-faye or giraffe (spanner crabs) are caught, especially during the main summer fishing-season. This crab, with its ten claws, is considered one of the finest shellfish in the Indian Ocean region. It has a reputation as an aphrodisiac, as it contains phosphorous and phosphates propitious, as one might say, for romantic alliance.

FAYE-FAYE (SPANNER) CRAB

The beauty of the Creole language: to create a superlative, repeat the same word twice, or even three times - but what does "faye" really mean? It does not appear in a single encyclopaedia… but that does not matter! Savour this deep-sea crab that will remind you of the taste of the fleshier spider crab.

Recipe page 189

Flavours and Colours of Mauritius

Flavours and Colours of Mauritius

Chinese chicken and shrimp salad

with sesame bread

Although it has its origins in harsh and poor everyday life, paradoxically Chinese cuisine has become one of the world's most inventive. For a long time, this has been the favourite salad at our Beach restaurant. It is refreshing, with a variety of textures and flavours that blend well together. The small shrimps and the grilled chicken are a perfect match, whilst the sweet and sour sauce tempers the chilli. The slices of sesame-flavoured bread complement the tasty mix, which is best appreciated when the weather is very hot.

CHEVRETTES DE MER

It's surprising they do not appear in Gulliver's Travels. These tiny shrimps would have been at home in the land of the Lilliputians!

Recipe page 190

Crispy sweet potato layers

with pan-fried duck foie gras, cep mushrooms and chestnut shavings

The excellent flesh of the sweet potato, whose taste is reminiscent of chestnut, immediately seduced me. I have used it in my own way, by putting the emphasis on contrasting textures, going from the smoothness of foie gras, through the crisp feuillantines, before reaching the firmness of the ceps. In this dish, I particularly like the delicious blend of sweet and salty.

SWEET POTATO

Charming and delicious Ipomoea: they can be used in all potato recipes but add a slightly nutty flavour that makes them so popular, from Africa to Asia as well as in the American tropics.

Recipe page 191

Flavours and Colours of Mauritius

33

Whisky-flavoured urchin bisque
with fennel and herb ravioli

"Should ever your beauty fail to gain you admission to Paradise, dear lady, here is a bisque which will find favour with the Father Almighty himself."

ÉMILE ZOLA

All the chefs who have worked with Guy Savoy have been greatly influenced by his cuisine, especially by his creamy cappuccino-style soups, which are amongst his specialities. The technique is very simple, because the thickening process incorporates air, leading to a considerable reduction in the fat content. His former pupils, such as my friend Miles James at his "James at the Mill" restaurant in Arkansas in the USA, Gordon Ramsey in London or Eyvind Hellstrom in the Bagatelle restaurant in Norway, use the same method.

SEA URCHIN

"The egg of the world", as Pliny called it, protects itself in its spine-covered shell, violet or white according to the latitude. A fine, strongly iodised delicacy, the orange-coloured insides can be savoured with a small teaspoon.

Recipe page 192

Pan-fried red mullet

with pink peppers and home-made curry in salted Queen Victoria pineapple-butter sauce

The use of spices in French cookery often provokes controversy. Some consider that hybrid cooking and spices are in the process of destroying the very nature of French cuisine. Such an argument appears exaggerated to me, as we should not forget that the spices found in today's French cuisine - pepper, cloves and nutmeg - came mostly from abroad, particularly Indonesia. Could we imagine, even for a moment, traditional French cooking without these exotic products? Hybrid cooking is far from being a new phenomenon. Between 1884 and 1890, Auguste Escoffier had been inspired by the virtuoso chef, Amia Dilip Kumar, personal cook to the Maharajah of Baroda. Escoffier was so fascinated by the Indian cook that he spent a long period of time studying his methods and habits, so much so that he ended up creating his own curry recipe.

ROUGET (RED MULLET)

The rouget is a kind of red mullet, and comes to us from the dawn of time. There isn't a chef who hasn't created at least one recipe for it or an author who hasn't described its tastiness. Fished in pots woven from bamboo, it simply longs to leap into a pan of hot oil or to join other fish in a soup. The fish is also caught with a rod and the start of the season each year is the stuff of folklore.

Recipe page 193

Flavours and Colours of Mauritius

Rock lobster in tandoori massala

with sweet potato fondant and coriander pesto sauce

A feast for the eyes, this dish is a marvellous mix of three colours: red, green and white. It was during my apprenticeship with Pierre Gagnaire in Saint Etienne that I started to use the tandoori spices prepared by Thiercelin in France. After my arrival in Mauritius, I created my personal tandoori massala recipe, which can be used with fish, shellfish and white meat.

TANDOORI MASSALA

Pakistani, Indian and Mauritian cookery lead us into an extremely sophisticated spicy universe, as the dishes, commonly referred to as curry, are prepared with a great number of different spice mixtures. The word "curry" is not even Indian but English, from the word, "kari", which in the Madras region originally described a spiced vegetable dish. Moreover, there is no one curry, but dozens of spice mixtures called massalas. Often mild and wonderfully aromatic, it gives a characteristic touch to a dish, blending together black pepper, cumin, cardamom, cloves and cinnamon. Tandoori refers to food cooked on live charcoal in the small, traditional, mud oven called Tandoor. It is all a matter of nuance, regional and family traditions, sleight of hand and inspiration.

Recipe page 194

Shrimp curry

with coconut and banana buds

In Mauritius, spices are generally sold by weight in the market or at a spice shop. They are packed in glass jars or in plastic sachets, and, being in regular demand, are generally fresher than those found in the West. Whenever possible, it is better to buy spices whole. Ground spices do not produce the same flavour, except in Asian shops where they are more freshly ground. See if you can locate an Asian spice shop or a specialist shop, so that you can find authentic ingredients and spices. It greatly enhances the pleasure.

BANANA BUDS

The leaves of the banana buds are used in Thailand to make small boats decorated with banana leaves. Launched in the rivers and propelled by the current, they carry away bad luck and regrets of the past year. More prosaically, Mauritians eat them in a curry.

Recipe page 195

Flavours and Colours of Mauritius

Rack of cochon marron

roasted in five spices and glazed with Rodriguan honey

"Cooking skills can be acquired; roasting is a skill with which you have to be born."

JEAN-ANTHELME BRILLAT-SAVARIN

Leaving to stand: this exercise, which consists of allowing meat and poultry to stand before cutting, greatly improves their flavour. All the juices seep back inside the joint. If you cut the meat straight from the oven, the inside may be tender but the outside will be dry. In leaving the joint to stand, you let the juices spread evenly.

COCHON MARRON

Descended from the domestic pig, freed into the wild by the Dutch in the 17th century, it has developed characteristics close to those of the wild boar. The best specimen weighs no more than 80 kg, but the ideal weight is about 30 kg. This is excellent game, at its best in late summer, during the wild guava season. At this time, the meat is tender and slightly sweet.

Recipe page 196

Flavours and Colours of Mauritius

Potato and cauliflower curry

with perfumed Basmati rice and green mango pickles

What we call curry, Indians call massala, which means a mixture. The best-known is Madras curry, which is spicier than most. Curry enthusiasts claim that the best curry is that prepared on a curry stone (a rectangular slab with a rough surface) and its "baba" (a stone grinder). The curry stone is used to crush the various spices (turmeric, ginger, cumin, cinnamon, chilli and so on). Connoisseurs claim that a curry prepared this way, has a unique taste.

TURMERIC

Fresh turmeric (safran vert) is crushed on the grinding stone into a peppery, spicy paste. Turmeric is also used in the preparation of food for many Hindu ceremonies, especially weddings. During the Safran ceremony, the bride and groom-to-be are adorned with an ointment made from turmeric, which is considered a sacred plant.

Recipe page 197

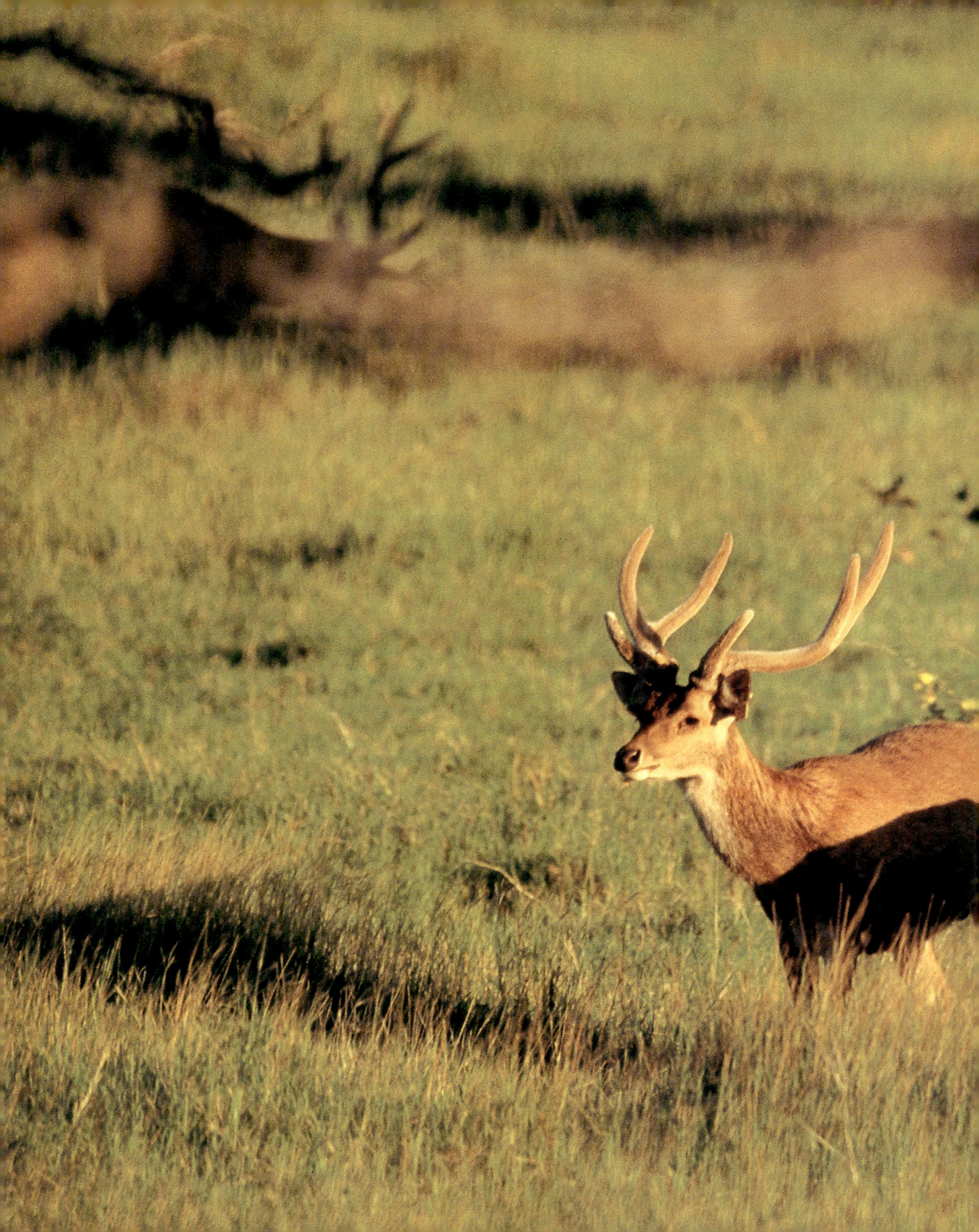

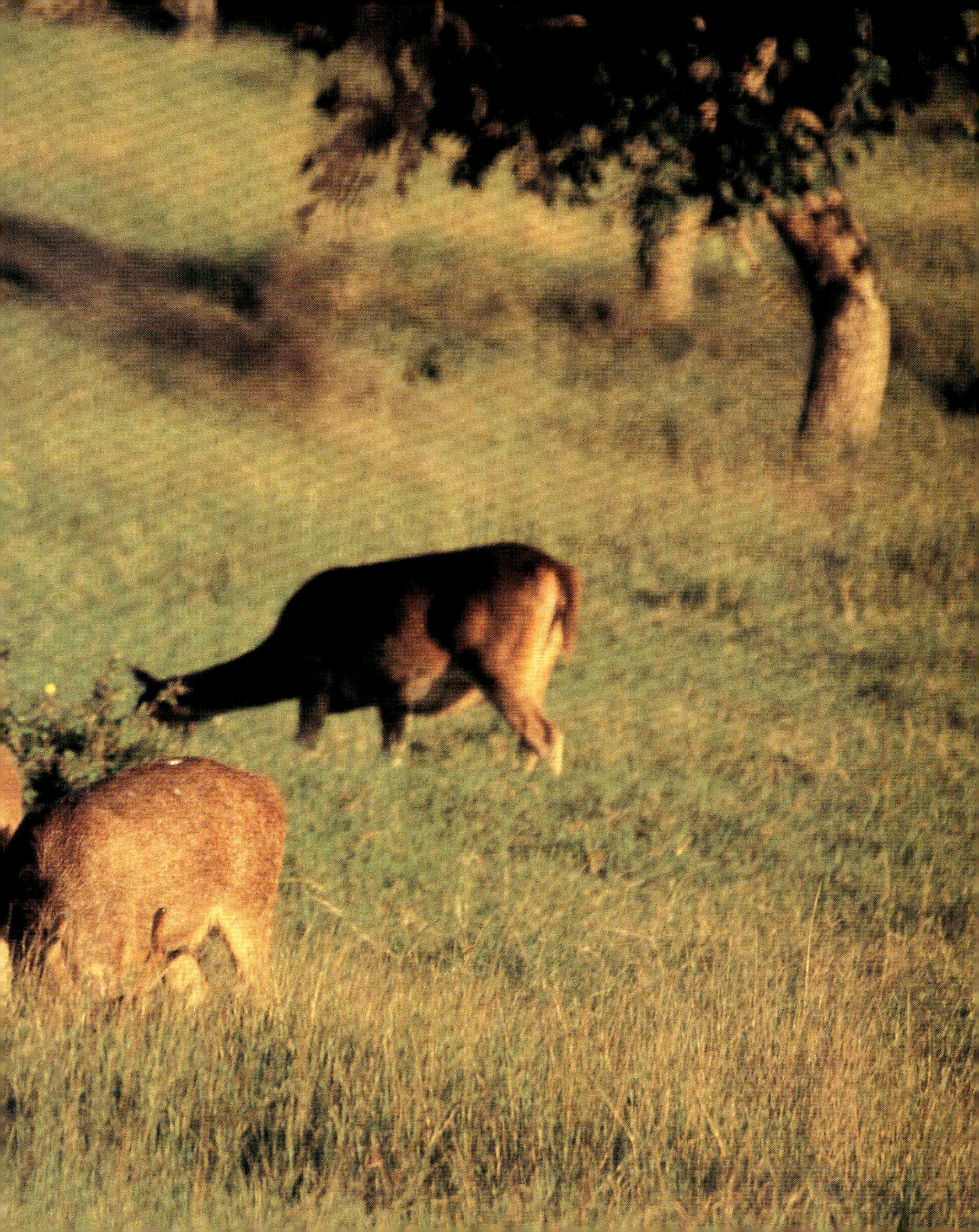

Java deer roasted in sweet spices

with goyaves de Chine sauce and arouille violette purée

Robert Kranenborg used to say: "A chef has to learn to play with fire and to control the heat perfectly." I learnt a great deal about the techniques of cookery from him, and not least precision and discipline, as well as respect for the individuality of each ingredient. Robert Kranenborg is undoubtedly the finest chef in the Netherlands. His wide knowledge and his organisational skills have always been an example to me, and, indeed, it is thanks to him that I went to France.

CINNAMON

The oldest of the spices to come from Asia. The Queen of Sheba even offered some to Solomon. Cinnamon was considered a luxury, and was used to flavour wines and for its numerous medicinal and aphrodisiac qualities.

Page 46: The Java deer, the most popular game animal in Mauritius, was also introduced by the Dutch.

Recipe page 198

Flavours and Colours of Mauritius

Asian-style poached and glazed lamb shank
with brèdes Tom-Pouce, confit tomatoes and shii-take mushrooms

"I hate people who are not serious about their food."

OSCAR WILDE

I have always felt that preparing vegetables is the most interesting part of cooking. Temperature control is all-important. In it, I rediscover the pleasure of the alchemist, knowing how to pass the frying pan over the flame without damaging the particular produce, controlling the flame so that the essence does not evaporate, making sure that the texture and colour are not affected. Vegetables provide an enormous and amazing range of complex textures and flavours, as well as an extraordinary variety of shapes and colours. Here I work with a dozen small, market gardeners. Young vegetables, pumpkins and green beans come from Gilbert Margéot, whose garden lies at the back of La Salette Church in Grand Baie. Mr. Dookhun in Quartier Militaire provides the herbs and edible flowers, Mr. Suresh from the village of Cottage supplies the lettuce, whilst the palm hearts come from the Ferney hills. The success of our kitchen owes a great deal to these people, who supply fresh produce to the Royal Palm every day.

BRÈDE TOM-POUCE

Variously called baby bok-choy or pak-choy, this is one of the most popular Chinese greens in Mauritius, where they are nicknamed "Tom Pouce" (Tom Thumb), probably because of their small size and their squat, white stems. It is eaten lightly sautéed or as a side dish with red or white meat, shellfish or fish.

Recipe page 199

Roast duck breast

with cinnamon kofta in a ti-chinois sauce

Small farmers provide the best vegetables and fruits in Mauritius. In Europe, you tend to buy a vegetable for its look. Here carrots, for example, have sometimes very odd shapes and are in fact quite ugly, but, as the soil is still uncontaminated, the flavour is excellent.

TI-CHINOIS

You might call it orangequat, and you would not be completely wrong… only the colour of its skin is different. It is something Mauritians have enjoyed since 1760 - and not just Mauritians of Chinese origin.

Recipe page 200

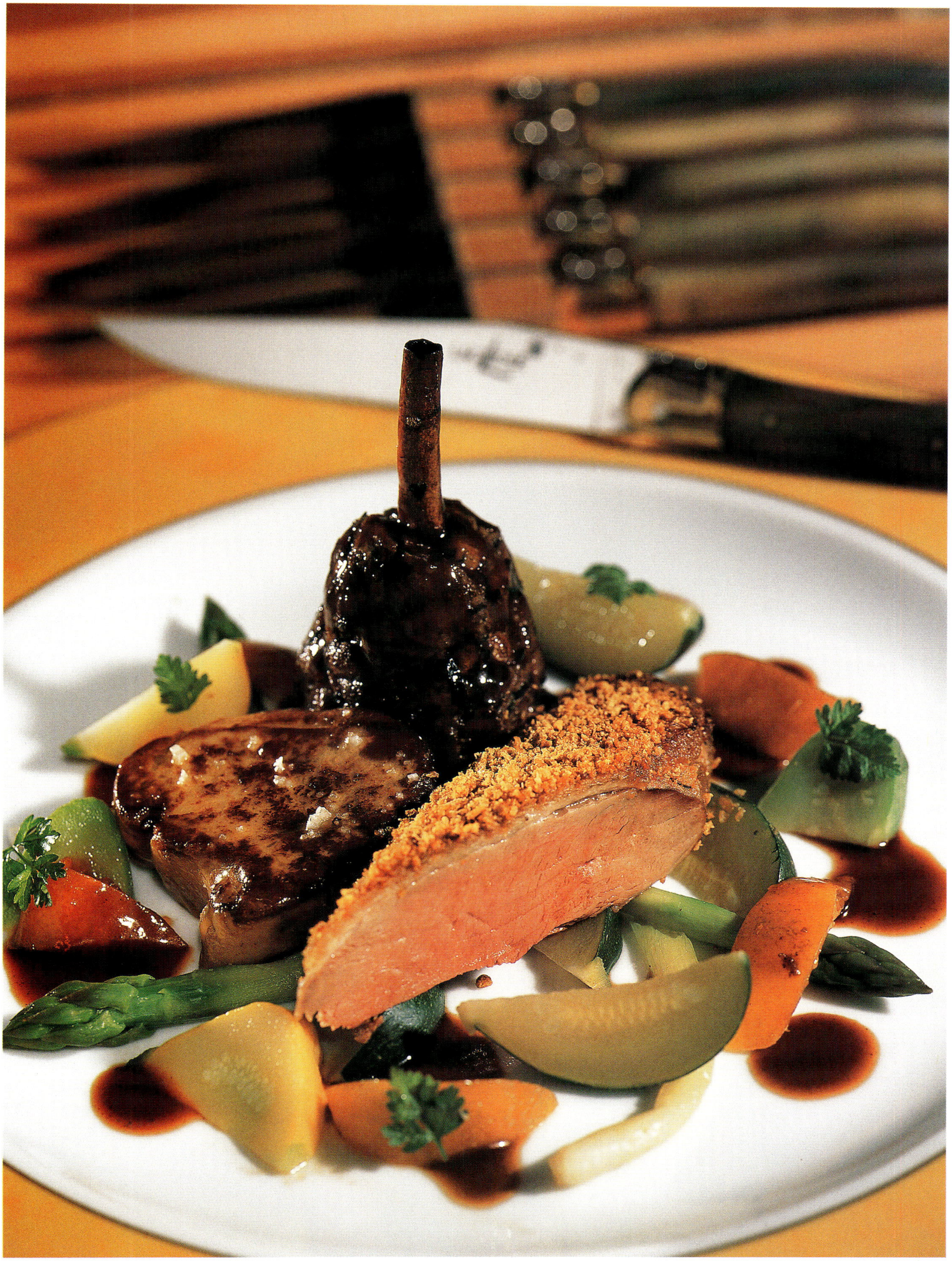

Flavours and Colours of Mauritius

Warm goyaves de Chine

in red wine and pepper-flavoured ice-cream

Each year, the goyaves de Chine (wild guava) season is special in Mauritius. Whole families set off, especially to the areas of Plaine Champagne and Chamarel, to pick this delicious fruit, which the cochons marrons (wild boar) also greatly appreciate. Mauritians eat the wild guavas with salt and chilli, but the fruit is also very good for aspic and jams.

GOYAVE DE CHINE

This wild guava is the curse of botanists, for it invades and kills all other vegetation. Guava picking (casse-goyave) in the higher plateaus is almost a ritual for Mauritians. In their enthusiasm, they don't wait for the fruit to ripen fully. The colour of wine sediment, gorged with sunlight, their heady scent fills the air. Contrary to what its name indicates, it is native to Brazil, but it grows widely in tropical countries.

Recipe page 201

Panna cotta scented with Fragrans vanilla

and sweet tomatoes

Vanilla is America's best-known and most important contribution to the world of flavourings. Its importance in chocolate making is well known, but it is also an aphrodisiac and a restorative, as well being used to cure poisonous bites. The belief in its aphrodisiac qualities dates back to 1529, and a specialist in the flora of the Antilles even went so far as to state that vanilla was "a strong source of genital stimulation, not advisable for ardent and easily aroused youngsters".

VANILLA

Vanilla is native to Central America, and grows wild in trees up to a height of forty feet. Pre-Columbian civilizations have probably used it for millennia. Vanilla appeared in Europe towards the end of the sixteenth century and was introduced in Mauritius and Reunion Island in 1827. Professor C. Morren was the first to understand the need for the manual fertilisation of the flowers, but it was a slave in Reunion Island, Edmond Albius, who discovered and propagated the technique of manually pollinating vanilla. He had the idea of using a lemon thorn to raise the small membrane separating the male from the female organs of the flower, thus allowing fruit to form and the development of vanilla cultivation. Vanilla is gathered into bunches and packed in tins. Make sure you buy vanilla pods, which is vanilla at its best. It is a guarantee of quality and authenticity.

Recipe page 202

Flavours and Colours of Mauritius

57

Flavours and Colours of Mauritius

Vanilla-flavoured rice pudding

covered with caramelised mango and kumquat sauce

If there is one dessert that reminds me of my childhood, then it is the rice pudding found in Thailand and the Philippines, where mango slices, with sticky rice, sweetened with coconut butter, are considered the best of all desserts. The texture and taste of the fruit mix perfectly with milk products. This is a very tasty version: the grains of Arborio rice blend with the slices of caramelised mango and produce a very pleasant and complementary mix of texture and taste.

KUMQUATS

An orange for a Barbie doll's tea party… round or in the shape of an olive, preserved or crystallised, it is a like a pill full of vitamins and minerals. You are sure to like them.

Recipe page 203

Mauritian vanilla crème brûlée

with crispy coconut tuiles

Royal Palm's regular guests consider this crème brûlée recipe one of our best desserts. There is a degree of confusion about crème brûlée, which some people believe should be served cold. They are wrong because, on the contrary, it should be served slightly warm! The crème should be soft, not dry and solid! You can prepare it the day before and refrigerate it. Before serving, you just need to heat it in the oven at no more than 150° C before coating it with caramel. It is then that you can obtain the perfect balance between the soft crème and the crunchy caramel.

COCONUT

The existence of coconut palms in the Indian Ocean region was confirmed by the first navigators who sailed up and down the coasts of the various islands. Plantations were encouraged along the coastlines and on outlying islands to make copra. Coconut is an extremely useful fruit. "Sweet coconut water" (the liquid of the young, green coconut) is very refreshing and Mauritians like to mix it with their rum. The flesh of young coconuts is very soft, so that it can be eaten with a teaspoon. The milk is used to make liqueurs and desiccated coconut is used in pastry making. Once it is dry, the nut, cut in half, is used in Mauritius as a floor polisher and the stems to make brooms and even ropes.

Recipe page 203

Flavours and Colours of Mauritius

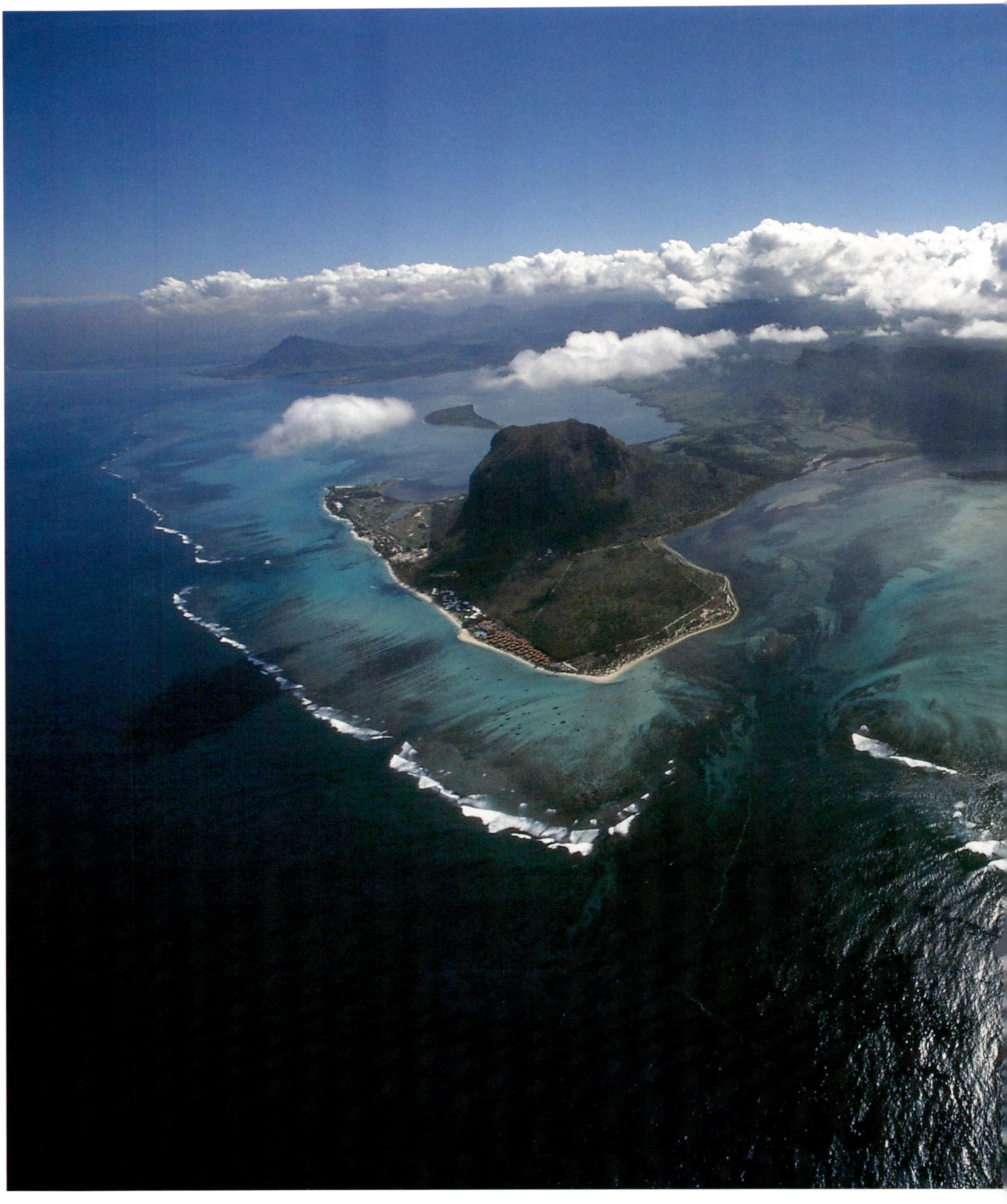

*"They say the island
is small enough to hold
in the palm of your hand...
but the island
reverberates to the splashing
and returning waves
stretches through the sugarcane
fields and rises to its striking
mountain tops."*

RAYMOND CHASLE

Brèdes Tom-Pouce broth

with cateau bleu fish-balls and ginger-flavoured shrimps

My parents are great enthusiasts of Asian food and I was initiated into Chinese, Thai, Japanese and Indonesian cuisine when I was still very young. As a child, it was a treat to travel through the kitchens of faraway countries. My taste for travelling and my passion for cooking probably date back to those years. I admit I am still attracted to the simplicity, contrasting flavours and variety of textures of Asian cuisine.

BLUE-BARRED PARROTFISH (CATEAU BLEU)

There are several varieties of cateaux or parrotfish, the parrots of our lagoons! The Creole imagination, or perhaps the need to name fish varieties never seen by scientists, has transposed to this fish the name of the shimmering bird from Sri Lanka, cousin of the parrot. Both are equally colourful - apple green, blue and red spots - and share a parrot's beak. Vivid, like a drawing in a child's colouring book, the Parrotfish is a feast for the eyes, but also makes a feast of a meal.

Chinese cuisine tends to make it into fish-balls for soup but it can be prepared in all sorts of ways. It is known by many different names, a charming roll-call of Creole terms : Difé, Bosse, Dents rouillées, Goémon, Mordé vert, Arc en ciel and many others.

Recipe page 207

Flavours and Colours of Mauritius

Rock lobster medallions
in iced consommé flavoured with ginger, salted lemon and green salad seasoned with red chilli

"A weakness for good food: an honourable and exquisite pleasure."

BAPTISTA PLATINA

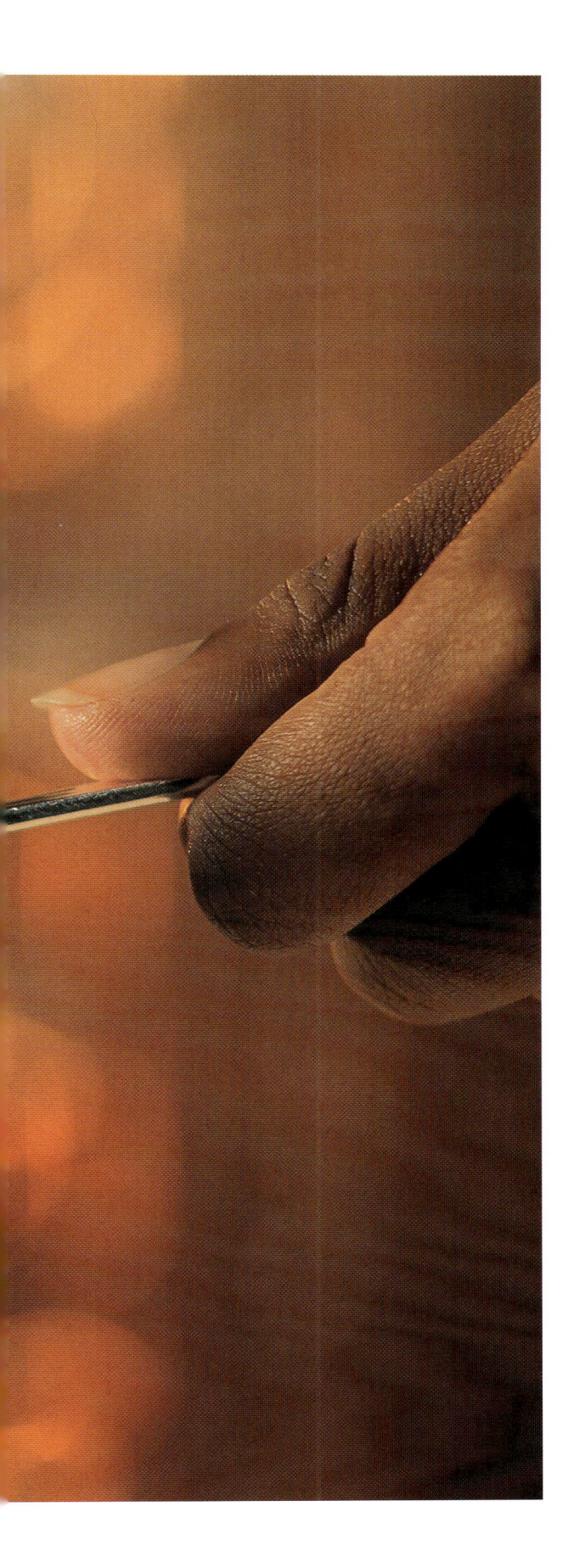

Creating a recipe begins in my head: I conceive the mixture of flavour, texture and aroma. I first need to identify the nuances in the ingredients I intend to use and imagine the dish's impact. An idea may gestate for several months in my head before I decide to try it out in the kitchen with my team. So I spent several weeks considering how I could produce an iced consommé, something simple, a light broth, flavoured with ginger, with crisp lobster medallions, with salted lemon peel, trimmed with lettuce, spiced with chilli. This is how this sunshine first course was born, a perfect lunchtime meal on a summer's day.

ROCK LOBSTER

It walks, it has ten feet or claws, and is nicknamed "The Runner". Its larva sheds its skin more than twenty times before reaching its maximum size of about 25 centimetres. Rock lobster is fished in pots and is eaten grilled, poached or cooked on charcoal, wrapped in aluminium foil. It is also called crawfish, but should not be confused with crayfish.

Recipe page 208

Creole-style octopus salad

with chilli, onion and coriander

In Japan, the most well thought of sushi restaurants are located close to the harbours. The Japanese are very particular about the quality and freshness of their seafood. Being located on the beach, the Royal Palm is superbly placed for supplies of fish and shellfish. The fishermen bring their day's catch directly to the doors of the hotel. When the fish arrives at the Royal Palm, it has been out of the water for less than eight hours. Being so close to the source of supply is a real delight for the chef, who wants his clients to forget the twelve-hour flight that has brought them to this superb island.

OCTOPUS OR RODRIGUAN OURITE

It is the small cousin of the far-northern creature, Captain Nemo's nightmare! A very close relative that blushes with modesty to be classified within the cephalopod family. It is too much honour, she says, nibbling on a winkle and resigning herself to being skewered on the spear of the "piqueuses d'ourites", before being impregnated with a thousand and one flavours and making you melt with pleasure.

Recipe page 209

Flavours and Colours of Mauritius

Ginger-flavoured sacréchien tartar
and green salad with roasted sesame seeds

"Disputes are only properly resolved over the dining table."
ALEXANDRE GRIMOD DE LA REYNIÈRE

In Mauritius, the fishermen go to sea at dawn, and it is not until the afternoon that they return. Rod fishing is mainly within the lagoon. The palangre - a rope to which are attached a large number of hooks - is also part of the Mauritian fisherman's equipment. Luck, experience and a knowledge of the local waters is also crucial. It is Madeven and Coco Parsuramen who go up and down the coast from Grand Gaube to Pointe aux Piments, from Le Morne to Mahébourg, passing through Trou d'Eau Douce, to bring fresh fish to the hotel.

SACRÉCHIEN

It you are told that they belong to the lutjamidaes family, you will be in trouble with your Latin, or what little Latin you remember. Anyway, lutjamidaes or not, this red or white fish with yellow stripes haunts the great deep. Its flesh is fine and delicate, to be eaten when it is just cooked, as soon as the flesh turns opaque.

Recipe page 210

Flavours and Colours of Mauritius

Coneau-coneau shellfish salad

Rodriguan-style

Rodrigues, which lies a few hundred miles north-west of Mauritius, is where I first encountered the Coneau-coneau on the opening of the seine-fishing season. The day is a major event for the island, given the importance of fishing there. After our return from the fishing expedition, we stopped at a small restaurant in the capital, Port Mathurin. The owner, a delightful lady, suggested we try this shellfish salad. It was unforgettable. Her oven-baked sausages, another Rodriguan speciality, were a further great culinary experience.

CONEAU-CONEAU

Also known as the sea snail, this beautiful, brown shellfish, shaped like a tulip, is plucked at low tide from the rocks to which it sticks. Its flesh is used in the preparation of a soup, much sought-after for its aphrodisiac properties.

Recipe page 211

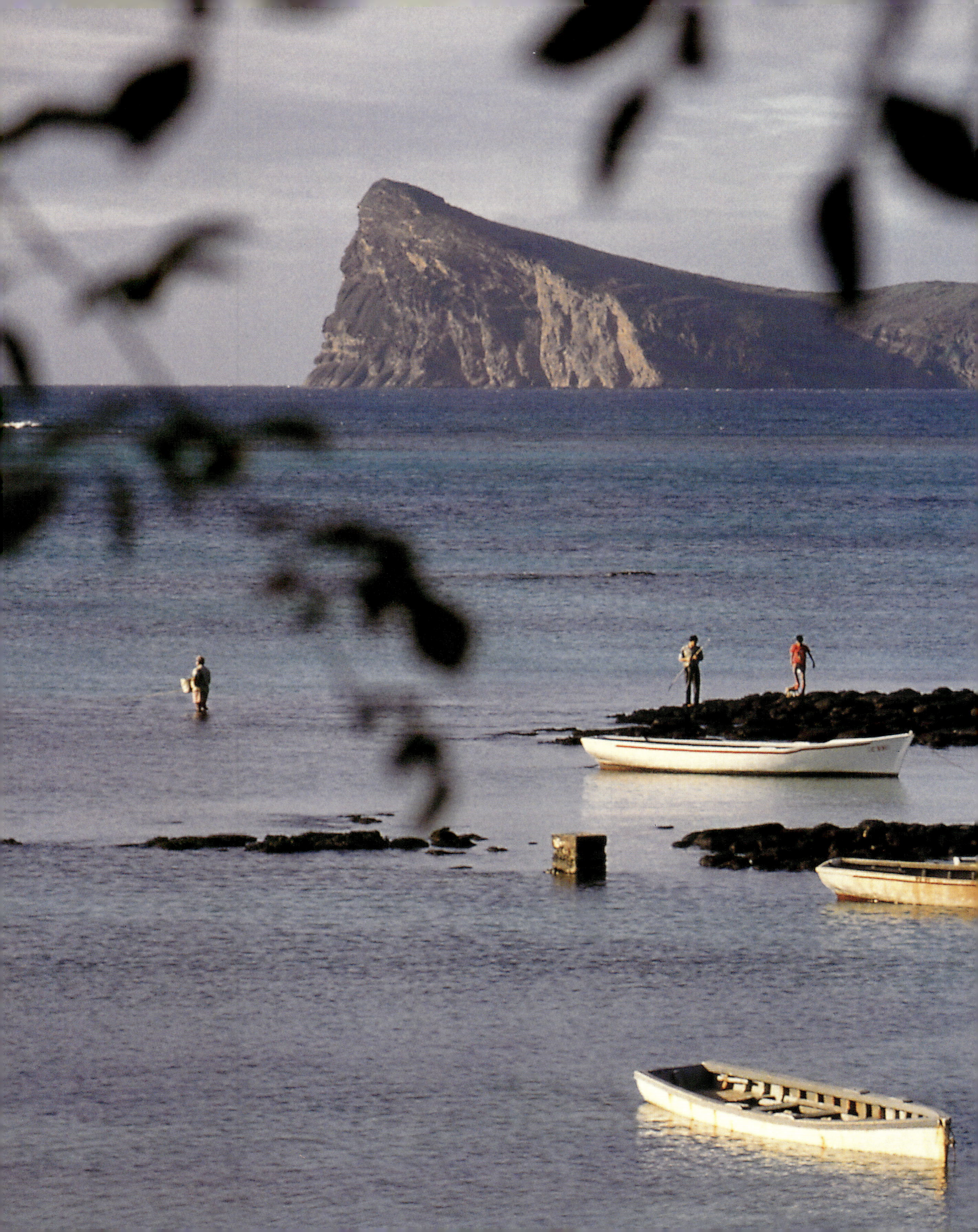

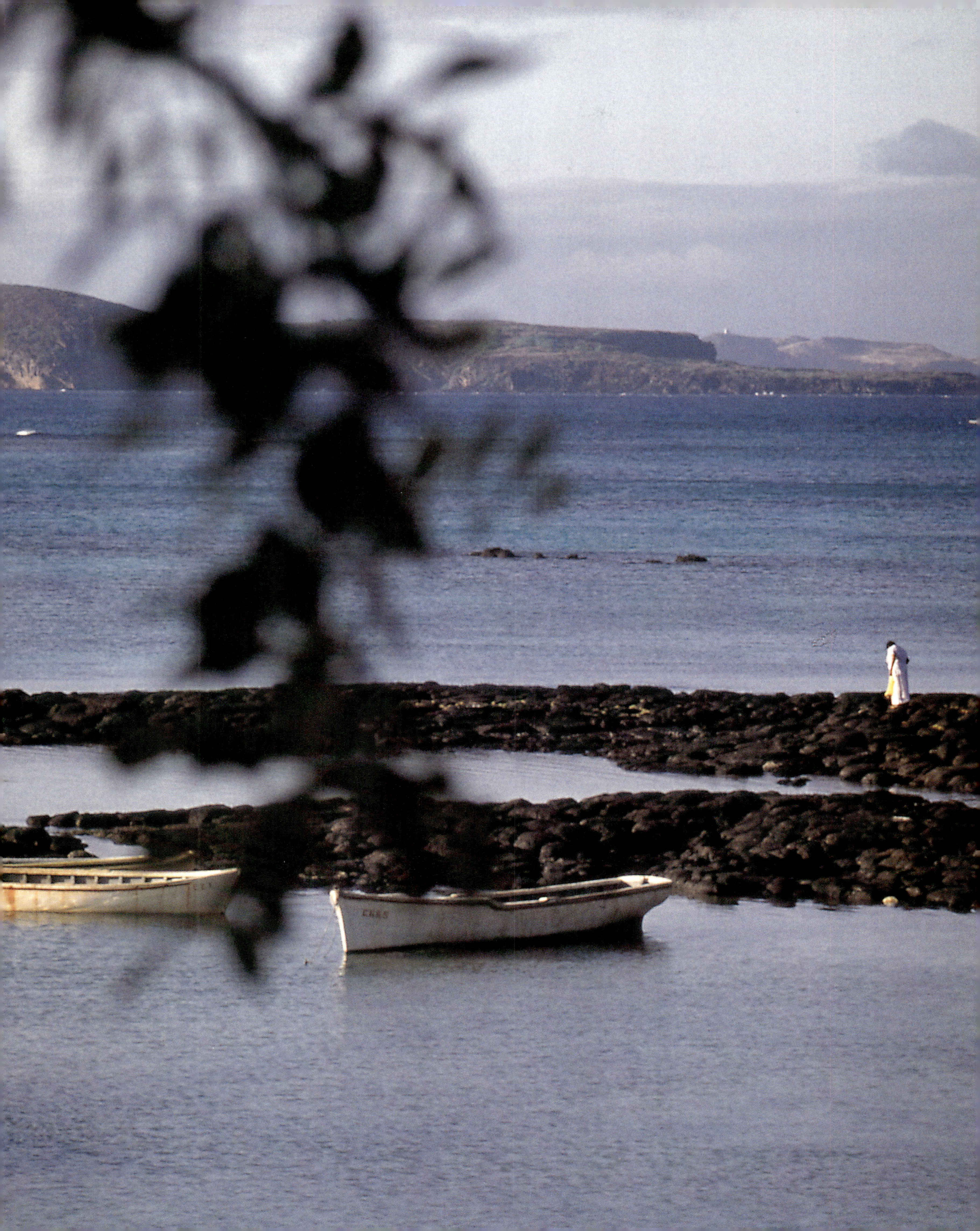

Thin slices of smoked blue marlin

with herb salad and shallots

Marlin, swordfish, the mako shark or Spanish mackerel are marinated in coarse sea-salt, cane sugar and ground black pepper. Then they are cold-smoked over a mix of choice wood, such as oak, apple or cherry wood. The smoking technique is a speciality of the region where I was born, Zeeland, which is in the south-west of the Netherlands. They use old barrels to smoke various fish such as eels and mackerel. When I arrived at the Royal Palm, I asked the maintenance department to transform a barrel for smoking food. In time, the barrel was replaced with a proper smokehouse.

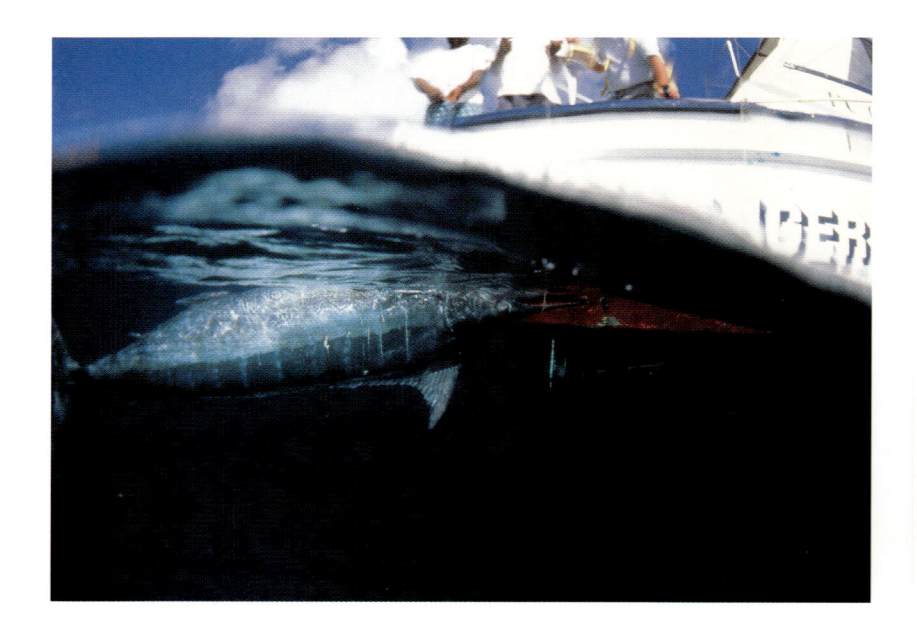

MARLIN

A warm-water fish, the marlin is a migratory fish that travels thousands of miles on currents of warm water. They are born male and become female when they reach five hundred kilos. There are four varieties of marlin in the Indian Ocean: blue, black, striped and sailfish. The ultimate feat, for everyone who fishes for sport, is to haul in a marlin.

Recipe page 211

Flavours and Colours of Mauritius

Flavours and Colours of Mauritius

Grand Gaube clams

in tomato, ginger and tamarind

The sea at Grand Gaube is a unique habitat for shellfish, especially clams. The fishermen use rakes to gather these molluscs. Collen and Dario have learnt to recognise the rhythm of the tides. They patiently await low tide to rake their catch of clams from the mud-banks. This recipe is to some degree a tropical version of mussels cooked in beer, a speciality of my hometown.

TAMARIND

Superstitions abound! In certain regions of India, Hindus eat the fruits of the mango tree only after having mixed it with tamarind. For the Burmese, the tamarind tree is the home of the god of rain. The sourest variety of tamarind is used in all sorts of preparations: soups, a number of fish dishes and curries. Jam, juice, syrups and sweets are made from the pulp of the sweeter varieties. In Britain it is used to make sauces, of which Worcester sauce is the best-known. Elephants are made to drink it in Malaysia and in Thailand, not only to cure their aches and pains but also to calm them down, almost tranquillise them. Finally, tamarind juice is very effective for cleaning all sorts of metal, including copper!

Recipe page 212

Lagoon bouillabaisse

Fish soup is one of the local specialities in every country where there is a major fishing village. There are many examples including French bouillabaisse, American chowder, Chilean "Caldillo de Congrio" and Belgian "Waterzooi". This recipe is a local adaptation of traditional French bouillabaisse. The great variety of fish found in the Mauritian lagoons allows plenty of variation. I have added chilli and coriander, and the thickening of this broth is done with local squashes. Family and friends are happy to gather around this delicious dish.

LAGOON FISH

The calm, warm waters of the lagoon that surround the island are a favourite habitat for the great variety of fish that live there whilst reproducing. Some species remain in the lagoon for much of their young lives. However, fishing within the lagoon has been strongly discouraged for some time now to enable fish stocks to grow.

Recipe page 213

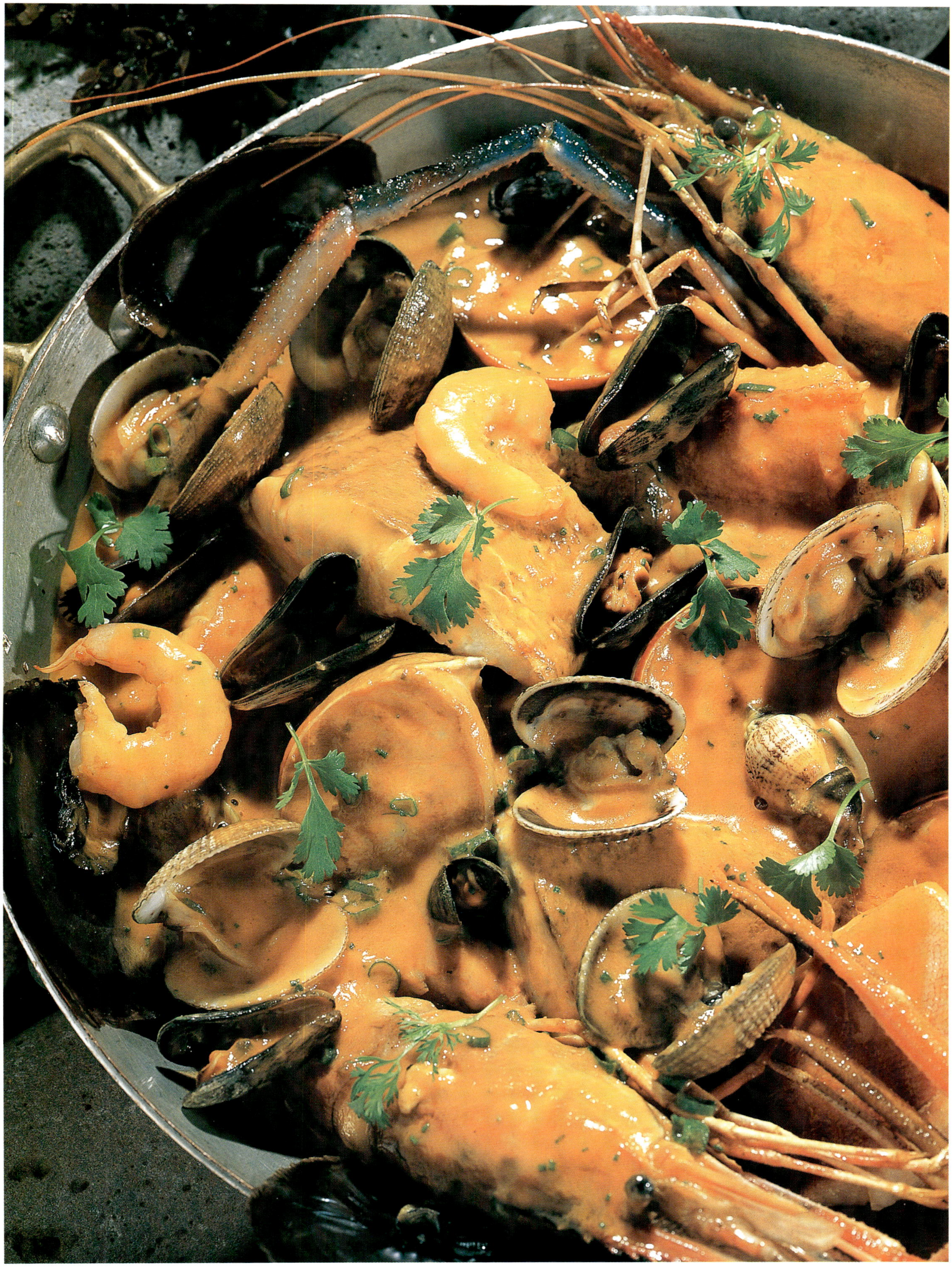

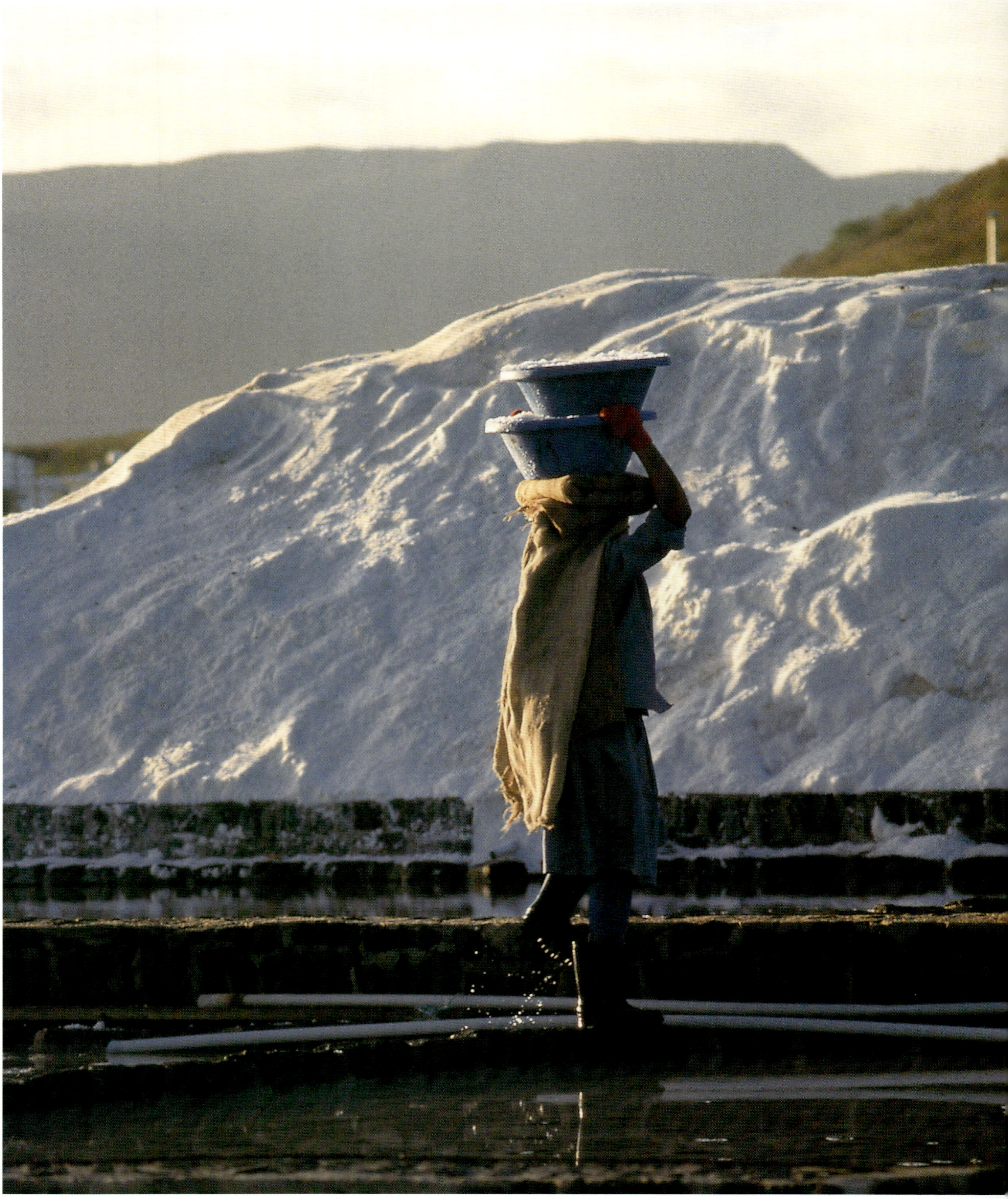

BLACK RIVER SALT

The first salt-pans in Mauritius date back to the time it was a French colony, when salt was very important, particularly to salt meat for use on board ships. The salt works have existed for many decades and the method of making salt has changed very little over the years. So, from June to December, from dawn onwards, women sauniers can be seen moving around the salt farms, carrying straw baskets full of salt on their heads.

Sacréchien

cooked whole in a Black River sea-salt crust with Taggiasche oil and black pepper

One of the Royal Palm's classic dishes. In my opinion, this recipe is a subtle and exquisite way to cook fish. The taste of the sea is retained because the fish is cooked in its skin. Fresh sacréchien fillets cooked in salt, have a superb shine and an extraordinary softness. To avoid damaging the flavour of the fish, use a good virgin olive oil and add a little ground black pepper and a dash of lemon. To accompany the dish, serve good bread or simple mashed potato.

Recipe page 214

"Everything belongs to the one who improves it."

BERTOLT BRECHT

Flavours and Colours of Mauritius

Shrimp rougaille

and coconut-flavoured okra fricassée with Basmati rice

This is one of my favourite Mauritian dishes. To make a success of the recipe, the rougaille sauce needs to be well spiced. Guests are greeted by the range of colours of the various side-dishes as they move to the dining table for this typical Mauritian meal: okra that melts in the mouth, a range of pickles (chatinis) and the chilli paste present a palette of colours fit for an artist.

OKRA

The most surprising of vegetables! You may be fooled by its original viscous consistency, as it will explode your taste buds as soon as the first impression has passed. To appreciate its quintessence, it should be steamed and seasoned with a strong vinaigrette. A good initiation for the less brave would be to eat them fried or as fritters. Those who shy away from trying something different and who are afraid to swallow these pyramid-shaped capsules should try them as a soup, like inhabitants of the West Indies and Louisiana, who have made the soup a "national" dish. However, if all this puts you off, remember that okra is from the hibiscus family, whose flowers you love. So, hesitate no longer and eat lalo flower fritters!

Recipe page 215

Roast young rabbit

with spicy orange powder and chou-chou in a clear gravy

Rabbit is one of my favourite meats because of its taste. It can be prepared in a number of ways: the loins can be pan-seared, the legs make excellent confit and a rabbit stew is delicious. However, you have to make sure that it is not over-cooked, as rabbit meat is very lean. If you are not careful enough, you can end up with flesh that is dry and overcooked. The dish I suggest here is elegant and perfumed, perfect for a summer dinner. If you do not particularly like rabbit, you can use the recipe for poultry instead. The combination of flavours will not be dissimilar.

CHOU-CHOU

Found throughout the warmer climes, there are two main varieties of this climbing cucurbitaceous, one with white skin and the other green. Called chou-chou in Mauritius, it is also known as christophine, chayote or chouchoute. "Cho-Cho" tends to be the name used in English. Its white and even flesh is sweet. Some enthusiasts eat it as a raw salad, like grated carrots, but the majority prefer it cooked, again served as a salad with a strongly-seasoned vinaigrette, or more often can be puréed and cooked au gratin. The skin makes an original receptacle in which to serve it.

Recipe page 216

Flavours and Colours of Mauritius

Flavours and Colours of Mauritius

Madras lamb and jackfruit curry

with ginger-flavoured giraumon, perfumed Basmati rice and chutneys

When preparing a curry, the method of cooking the spices is the most important part. It helps to reduce the bitterness of the spices whilst releasing the essential oils. This allows you to achieve a balance among the various ingredients, without any particular spice assaulting the taste buds or dominating the other spices.

JACKFRUIT

A beautiful, very decorative tree, the jackfruit can grow to over sixty feet tall, but it is gradually disappearing from our orchards, for its hard wood is very popular with cabinet-makers and carpenters because of its vivid colour. Its use for boat-building has also contributed to its decimation. Its enormous, warty, green fruits, bristling with short hairs, hang directly from the trunk. They really are big, and sometimes weigh as much as 20 kg, making them one of the world's biggest fruits. Each fruit contains many large kernels, with a chestnut-like taste, which are grilled or boiled. When the fruit reaches maturity, the pulp exudes a very strong smell. This far from discourages the real connoisseur of the fruit, who uses it to make a curry.

Recipe page 217

Rasgoula

with a mild spicy syrup and lime sorbet

Travel is not a luxury for a chef, but a necessity. Curiosity, tied to the discovery of new flavours, is essential in our profession. Throughout the world, the outstanding chefs are both open-minded and curious to learn about and discover new produce and ideas.

"And when the Queen of Sheba heard of the fame of Solomon concerning the name of the Lord, she came to test him with hard questions. And she came to Jerusalem with a very great train, with camels that bore spices, and much gold, and precious stones."

1 KINGS 10: 1-2

STAR ANISE

The wood smells like green aniseed and the fruit like bay leaves. This spice is used more in Chinese than in European cuisine, but what would Ricard be without star anise? It has numerous medicinal qualities and is used in making perfumes.

Recipe page 218

Flavours and Colours of Mauritius

Crisp sesame cannelloni

with ginger ice-cream and Queen Victoria pineapple tartar flavoured with combava lime

This dish has all the ingredients needed for success. The marked contrast between the crisp and the smooth is tempered by the refreshing nature of the pineapple tartar, flavoured with combava lime peel. Lightly sweetened, this dessert is easy to digest. One of the nicest compliments that I have received for this recipe came from Gaston Lenôtre. One morning, when he was holidaying with us, he said to me: "Your cannelloni is pretty good. I've feasted on it for the past three evenings." Gaston Lenôtre collaborated with the Royal Palm in developing our in-house viennoiserie. We were delighted with his exceptional involvement.

GINGER

Its therapeutic and culinary qualities have been recognised for at least 2 500 years. Ginger has been used in China and India for millennia and was already used to make sweets in the Middle Ages.

Recipe page 219

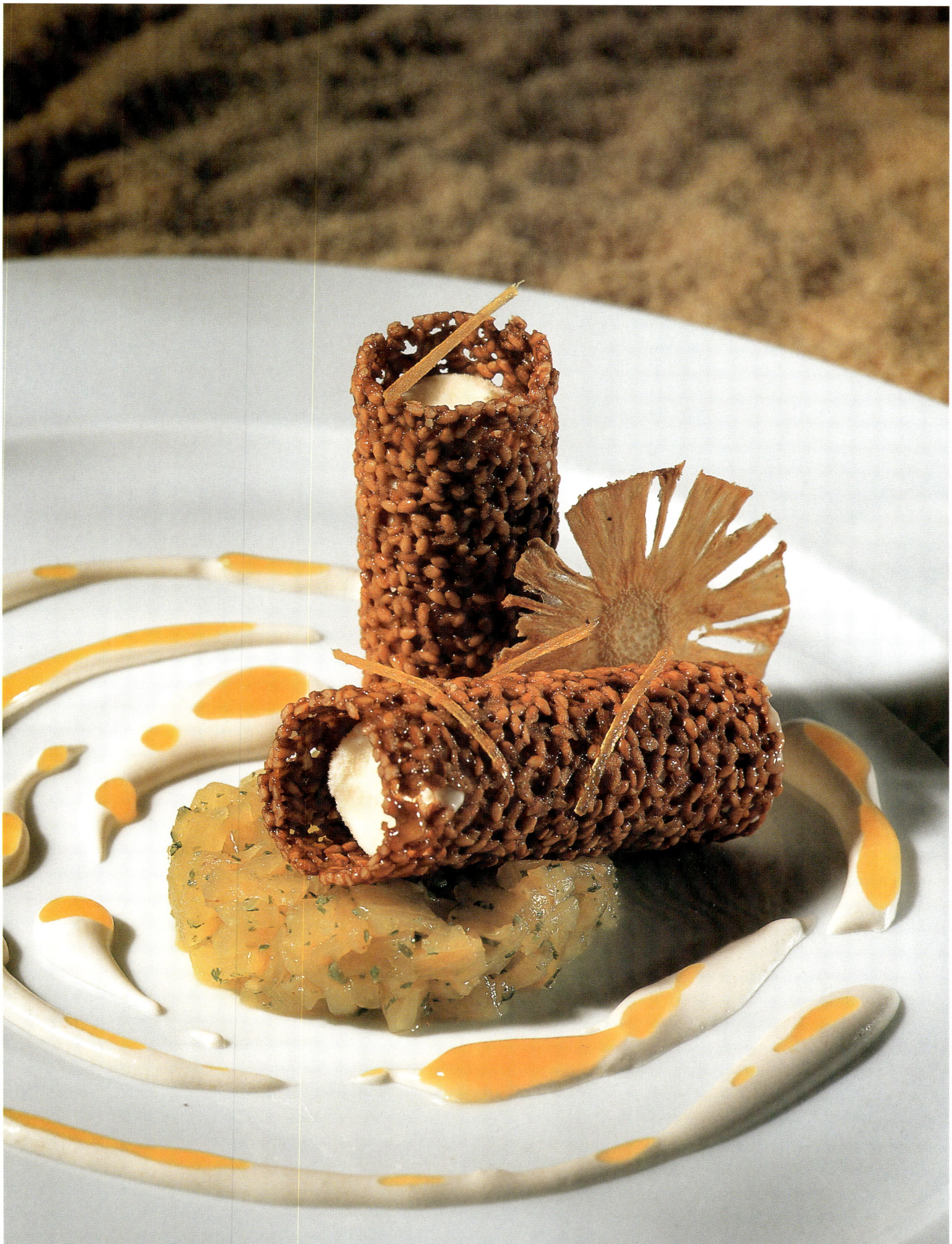

Flavours and Colours of Mauritius

Spring rolls

filled with vanilla-flavoured papaya compote and lime sorbet

Papaya aids digestion, especially of meat, thanks to one of its enzymes, as is true for pineapples. The fruit has many properties, one of which particularly surprised me: it seems that papaya seeds are a very effective remedy for intestinal worms. They can wipe out all kinds of parasites! Is this a possible cure for the Japanese anisakis worm problem?

SOLO PAPAYA

Smaller, fleshier and with a stronger perfume than its cousin, the papaya, it is most often enjoyed either for breakfast or as a dessert, with just a little lime juice, salt, pepper or chilli to bring out its delicate flavour.

Recipe page 220

Iced citrus fruit salad

in saffron-flavoured syrup and vodka-flavoured pineapple sorbet

This dessert is full of freshness and light. This fruit salad was inspired whilst walking in the magnificent Labourdonnais estate, in the north of the country, abundant with citrus trees and plants. The estate manager, Gerard de Fontenay, can talk for hours about farming methods, and he knows everything about the origins and species of plants.

POMELO

Pamplemousse came originally from Malaysia, but has gradually been superseded by the pomelo, most commonly known as pink grapefruit, as in English, and which originates from Puerto Rico. The pink grapefruit is the result of a cross between the original pamplemousse and an orange from China.

Does its more or less dark pink flesh seduce us to the detriment of its ancestor, with its yellow flesh and sometimes more acid taste? The deeper pink it is, the sweeter the taste. Once limited to making fruit juice or for dieting, it has emerged from the role of hors d'oeuvre to blend with mixed salads, to venture into ices, cakes and desserts and is even caramelised under the grill.

Recipe page 221

Flavours and Colours of Mauritius

99

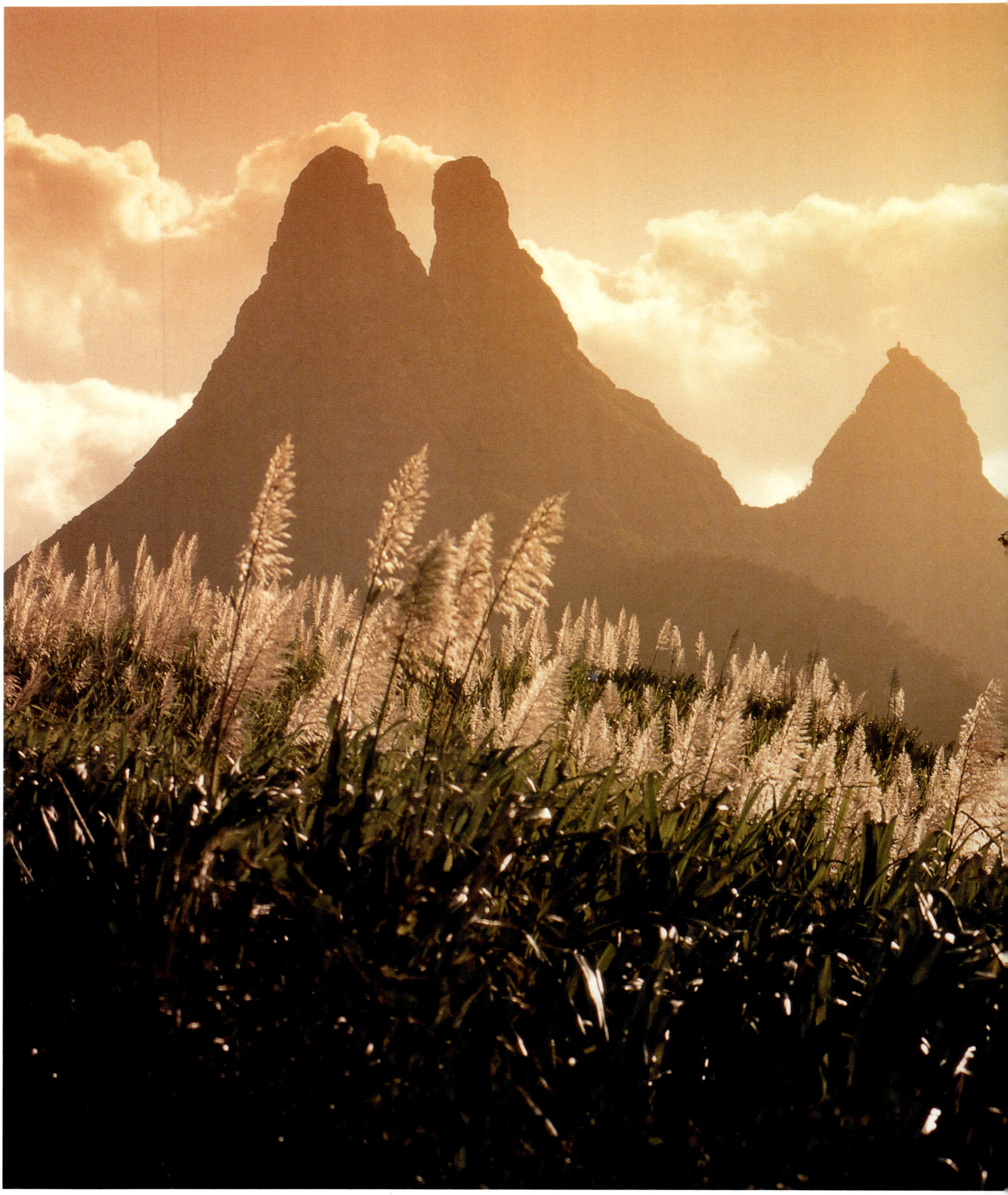

*"As the evening shadows rise
from the fields
and slowly ascend
the slopes of the mountains
Do you remember, sister,
how the two of us used to listen
to those indistinct voices,
the thousand daytime sounds,
surprised by nightfall,
a chirping nest of happiness?"*

CHARLES BAISSAC

Flavours and Colours of Mauritius

Shrimp and curry croquettes

with coriander

This is a speciality of my native country, the Netherlands, and I have made it more exotic by flavouring it with coriander, curry and red chilli. The croquettes can also be served with the aperitif as well as for lunch.

HOME-MADE CURRY

A real curry is mixed on a curry stone according to a well-established ritual. Apart from spices that are traditionally found in a curry, the curry leaf ("carri-poulé" as it is called in Mauritius), with its strong smell, adds a slightly bitter and lemony taste to the curry. The curry stone, together with its stone baba (pestle or grinding stone), has a predominant place in Mauritian cuisine. They used to be found in every back yard. The curry stone is used not only to grind the ingredients for curries but also for chutneys (tomato, coconut and chilli). With the march of time, the famous curry stone is gradually being replaced with more sophisticated equipment. Some purists refuse to set aside this old custom, for it is said that a curry prepared on a stone has a very special taste.

Recipe page 225

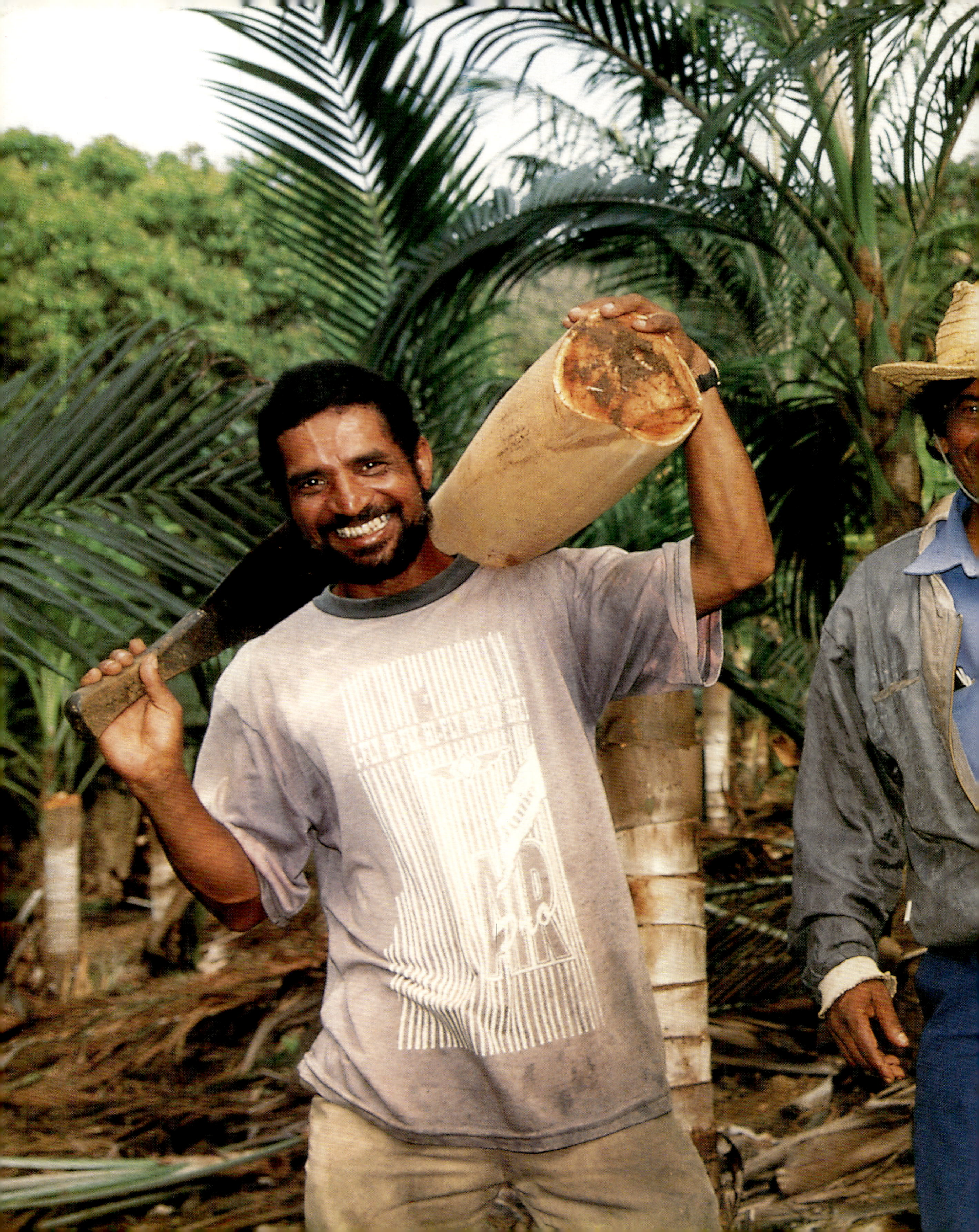

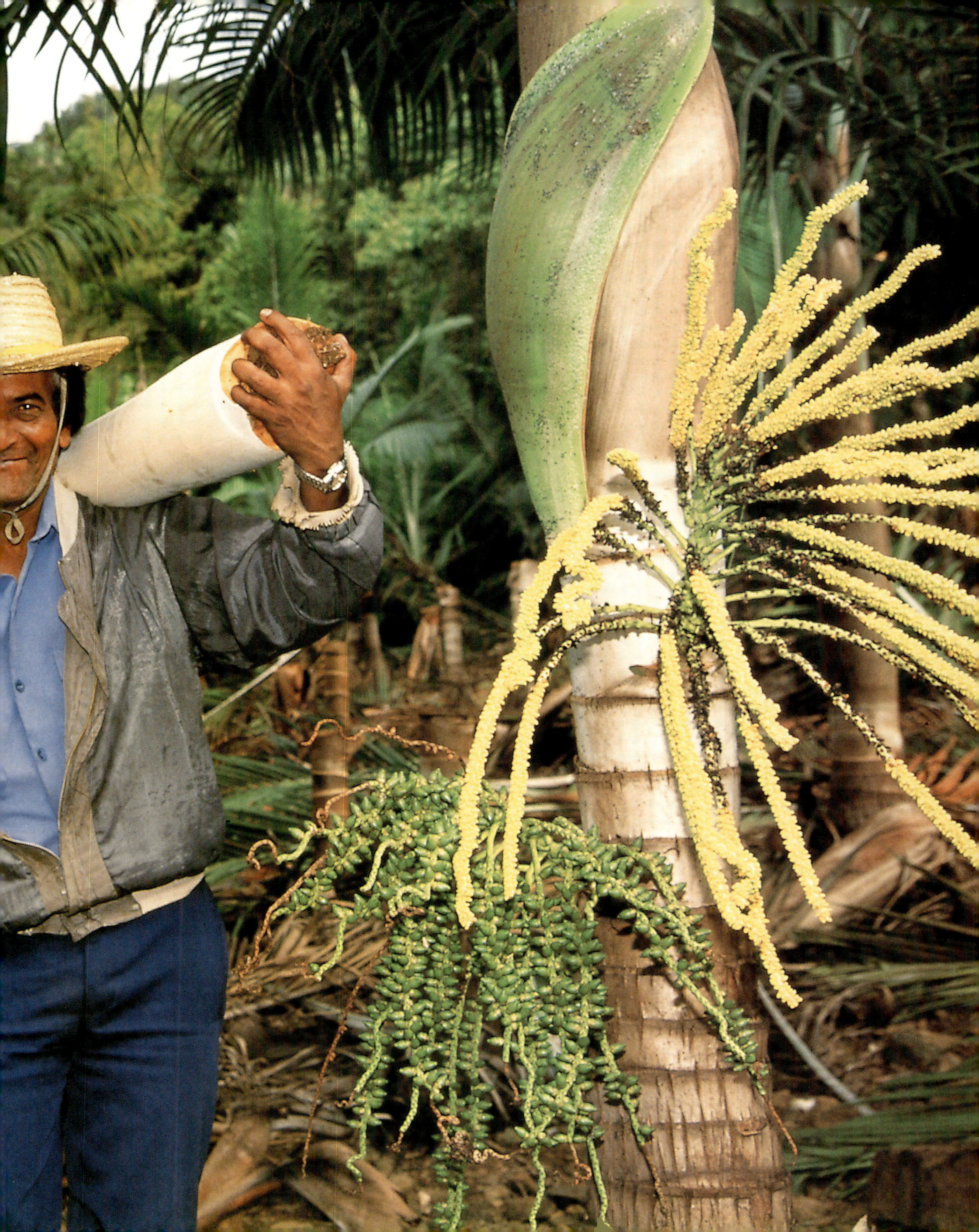

Ceylon coconut palm heart tartar

covered with slices of yellow-fin tuna and osietra caviar

Here, we have renewed the carpaccio of Hemingway's hero by playing on the texture and the flavour of the palm heart as well as the refinement and the slightly salty note of the caviar. Much of the preparation can be done in advance. Serve this dish during an elegant dinner party: the impact is guaranteed.

PALM HEART

"It is called the cabbage, the heart of the tree-trunk, with young leaves and flowers, not yet fully grown. It makes a delicious dish, one of the most pleasant that I encountered in tropical countries. It is white, firm and crunchy, with a nice, delicate taste. It is eaten raw with coarse salt as a salad, boiled, charcoaled, with a butter sauce or with butter like asparagus, fried in sugar and in all sorts of other ways. It is pleasant, and an intelligent cook can use its flavour and shape to good advantage for his table." This is how the naturalist, Boris de Saint Vincent, described the palm heart during a voyage in our region in 1801. He did not know that the plant also makes excellent achards (pickles), a delicacy of Creole cuisine.

Recipe page 226

"They were wedge-shaped strips and he cut them from next to the back bone down to the edge of the belly. When he had cut six strips he spread them out on the wood of the bow. I don't think I can eat an entire one, he said and drew his knife across one of the strips. It would not be bad to eat with a little lime or lemon or with salt."

The Old Man and the Sea

ERNEST HEMINGWAY

Flavours and Colours of Mauritius

Mangrove crab on palm-heart tartar

flavoured with home-made curry and green apple

A plant indigenous to Mauritius and Reunion, the "Distyosperma album" palm was called the White Palm by Bory de Saint Vincent, who visited Mauritius in 1801. According to historians, the Dutch were the first to plant palms and coconut trees, for their hearts. In 1861, Harmansen gave instructions to plant coconut, banana and orange trees in Port Sud-Est. When the Dutch ship, De Nassau, approached the Mauritian coast on 24 December 1628, its crew was suffering from scurvy. They stayed until 16 January 1629, leaving with a cargo of tortoises, dodos, pigs, and goats as well as palm hearts.

CARRELET (MANGROVE) CRAB

Three edible species of crabs are found in Mauritius: the bouillon crab which lives under rocks and which gets its name from usually being used in soups, as it has very little flesh, the faye-faye crab and the carrelet crab, which can weigh as much as 2 kg and whose flesh is excellent. The last is usually caught with a net in the muddy bottom of mangroves at river mouths, hence the name "mangrove crab" in English.

Recipe page 227

Flavours and Colours of Mauritius

Coconut and citronella-flavoured shrimp soup

with sesame toast

Citronella, ginger, coriander and coconut milk give a refined flavour to this magnificent dish. The taste of the shrimps is not masked by the flavours but is rather delicately enhanced.

SESAME SEEDS

"Open Sesame!" the magic formula used by Ali Baba to open the door to the mysterious cave. Does this imply that this seed is symbolically linked to fertility?

Recipe page 228

Six Grand Gaube silver oysters

with a spicy sauce

I love oysters. They arouse in me marvellous childhood memories, when my father and I used to dive near Yerseke, in Zeeland, off fishing boats. I especially remember the delightful moments when, on our way back, the skipper would open large quantities of oysters and mussels cooked in beer. In Mauritius, oysters are small but very tasty and have a strong iodine flavour. There are several varieties of oysters including the small hollow oyster, the small flat oyster, the Manguac oyster and the silver oyster. In this recipe, I use silver oysters but Belon oysters or Portuguese oysters can be used instead. This is quite a straightforward recipe, but the combination of flavours and textures is dazzling.

SILVER OYSTERS

The legendary shell! The aphrodisiac of Casanova and all Casanovas! The patience of oyster farmers who take 4 to 5 years to raise this exquisite flesh that we swallow by the dozen in a few minutes… the first string of pearls that a young lady wears to her first ball… the tenth that confirms her fortune… the black pearl of Tahitian women… the mother-of-pearl of buttons: it is the whole sea that we swallow in a single oyster or in a dozen, when we eat a plate of Mauritian silver oysters.

Recipe page 229

Plantain and coconut soup

with coriander-flavoured spicy shrimps

Contrary to the bananas that we usually eat, the plantain banana (one of the several species of banana) is normally eaten cooked. With its larger size, its coarser flesh and its higher starch content, it can in fact be treated as a vegetable, which is why it works well in a velouté soup.

BANANA

Mention the banana, and you speak of a goldmine for some countries, or a means of political pressure for certain governments, hence the expression Banana Republic.

You are used to eating it ripe. It is also eaten green - sautéed, roasted, boiled, stuffed; it is a staple food in its producing countries. An aftertaste of chestnuts compensates for the somewhat abrasive aspect of this fruit, that can be used like a vegetable.

Recipe page 230

Flavours and Colours of Mauritius

115

Flavours and Colours of Mauritius

Babonne with saffron potatoes and oysters

in a light fennel sauce

A fish with extremely white flesh and a fine and smooth constituency, the babonne's eccentric colours stand out. It is the royal babonne (called Vieille Betilac) that I prefer. This fish can be used in all sorts of dishes: it can be grilled, fried, poached, braised or steamed.

BABONNE

The black-saddled coral grouper is the somewhat lengthy English term for this fish, often found in vivid shades of yellow and red. The exuberance of colours is one of the main attractions of the coral universe and this phenomenon has a very precise purpose. The camouflage provided by their colours, for example, allows fish to go unnoticed in their environment, a warning colour highlights an aspect feared by predators, and finally there are mating colours, with males and females presenting different colours either permanently or for a limited period during the reproductive process.

Recipe page 231

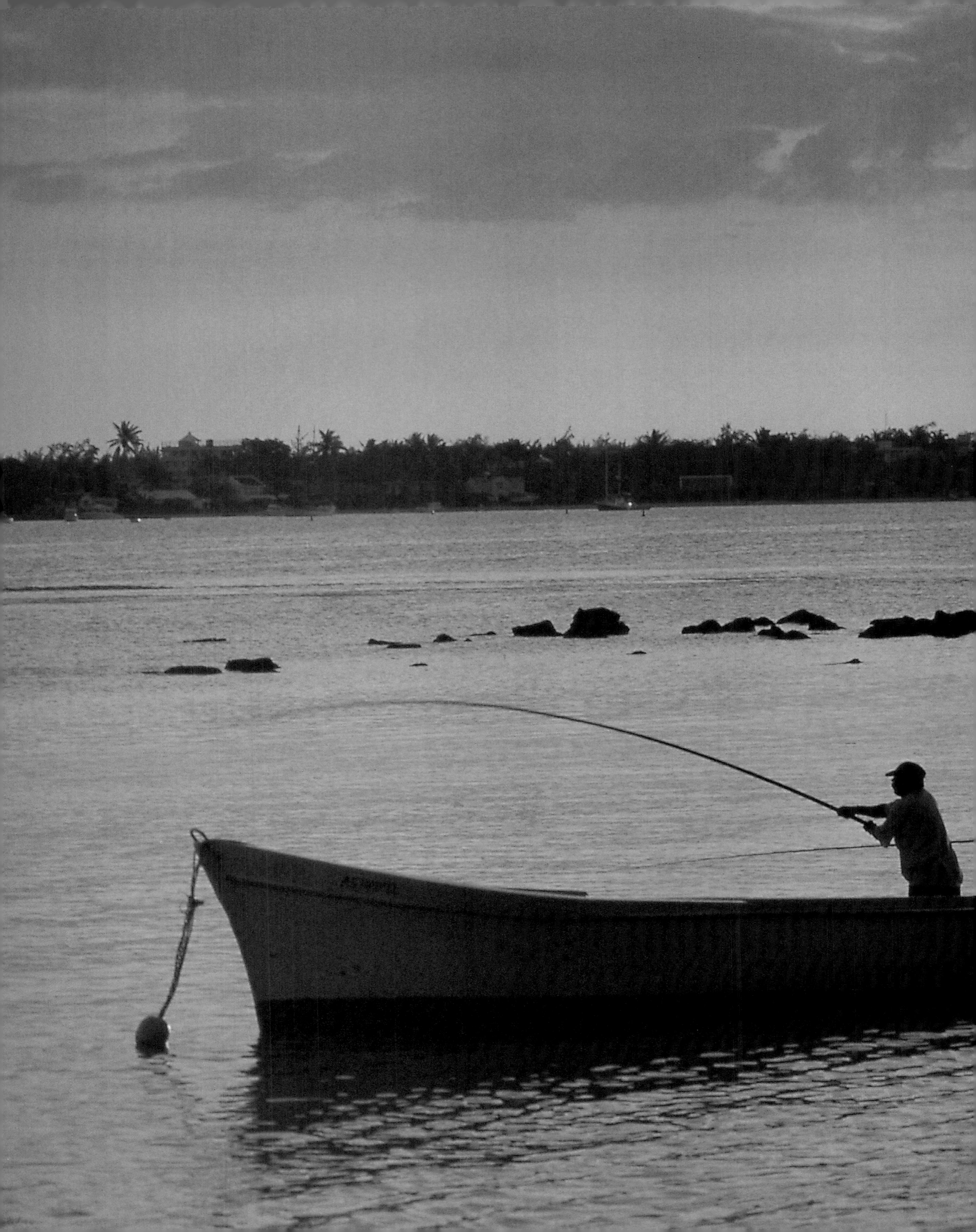

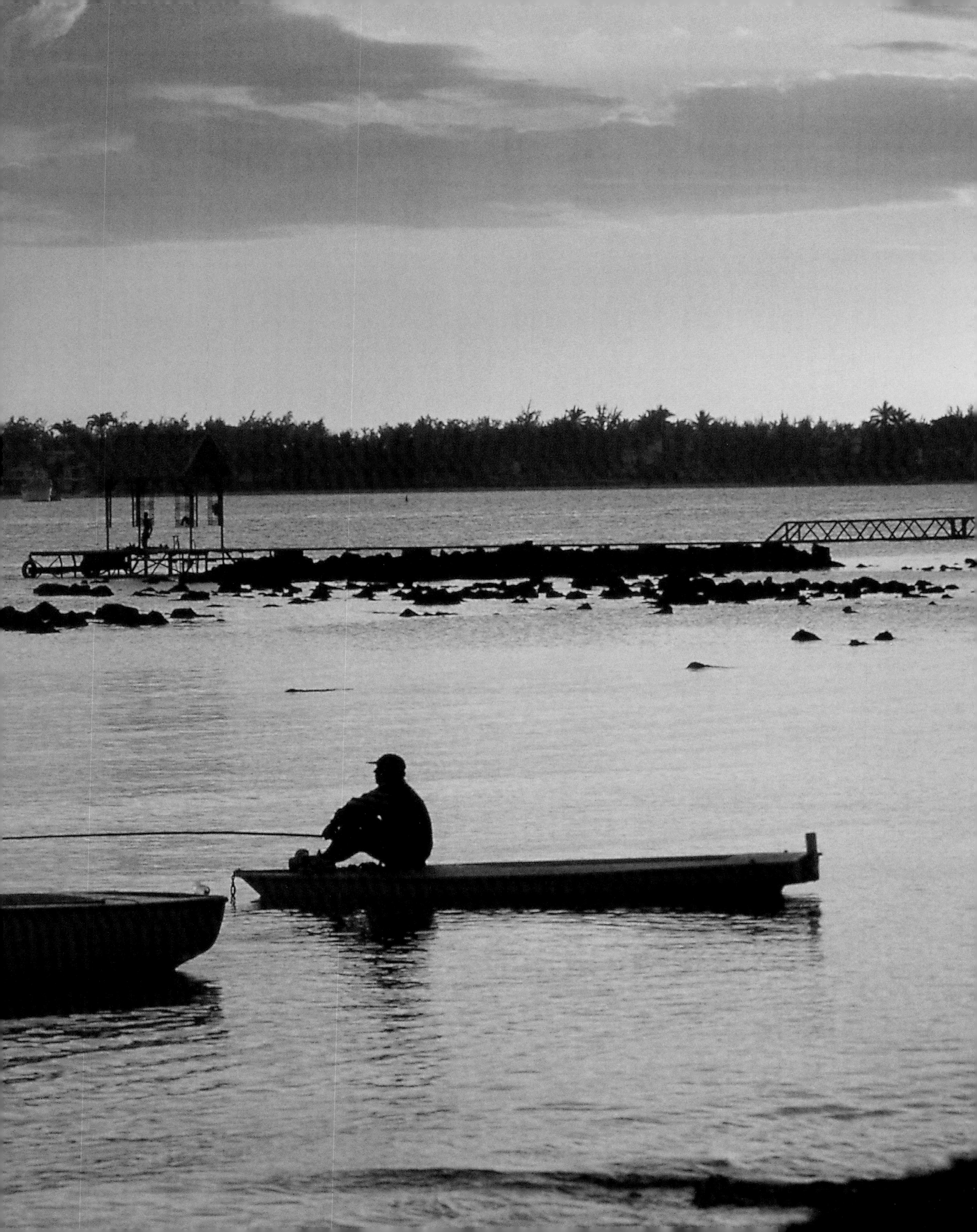

Vieille rouge

simmered with Vadouvan and shii-take mushrooms

Bok-choy (brèdes Tom-Pouce) is regularly found in my dishes because I like its texture and flavour. I like to use it with fish, shellfish and white meat. These greens, slightly tasting of mustard, are one of the favourite vegetables of the Chinese. Bok-choy can be eaten on its own or mixed with other vegetables. I recommend buying the smallest baby bok-choy because they need the shortest cooking time.

VIEILLE ROUGE

This is the black-tip grouper. Ichthyology holds many surprises: why "vieille" (old) in the case of this fish? Rouge (red) is rather more obvious. Try it steamed and whole to appreciate it at its best. But not if its name is "vieille loutre" (greasy grouper), which is inedible! But would you buy a greasy grouper?

Recipe page 232

Flavours and Colours of Mauritius

Flavours and Colours of Mauritius

Sand lobster roasted in its shell

with combava-flavoured curry sauce

Sand lobster looks like rock lobster, with its pretty greenish-brown colour. It also has a strong tail and very fine flesh. Sand lobsters have no pincers but two pairs of antennas including one pair in the form of a palette. They are, alas, becoming increasingly rare.

COMBAVA (KAFFIR LIME)

The Kaffir lime, seems to have been the subject of a spell cast by the wicked fairy: the skin, like a toad's, masks an exquisite, fresh and subtle perfume.

Recipe page 233

Flavours and Colours of Mauritius

Pan-fried grouper

with chicken wings and chicken oysters

In this region of the globe, tropical fish lack iodine. Their flesh is rather bland compared to fish from cooler waters. It is therefore essential to season the fish so that it becomes more interesting. Here I have combined the flesh of the grouper with chicken stock, and confit chicken wings, and the blending of textures gives a unique character to this dish.

THE GROUPER

The grouper belongs to the serranidaes family. There are a lot of different kinds of grouper, and 68 species divided into 12 different types are found in the Indian Ocean region. The serranidaes are sedentary fish, whose size can vary from a few centimetres in the case of the smallest to two metres for the largest.

Recipe page 234

Crispy sesame layers with pan-fried duck foie gras
and mango roasted with the savours of Mauritius

"Unless you are something of a magician, don't bother trying to cook."

COLETTE

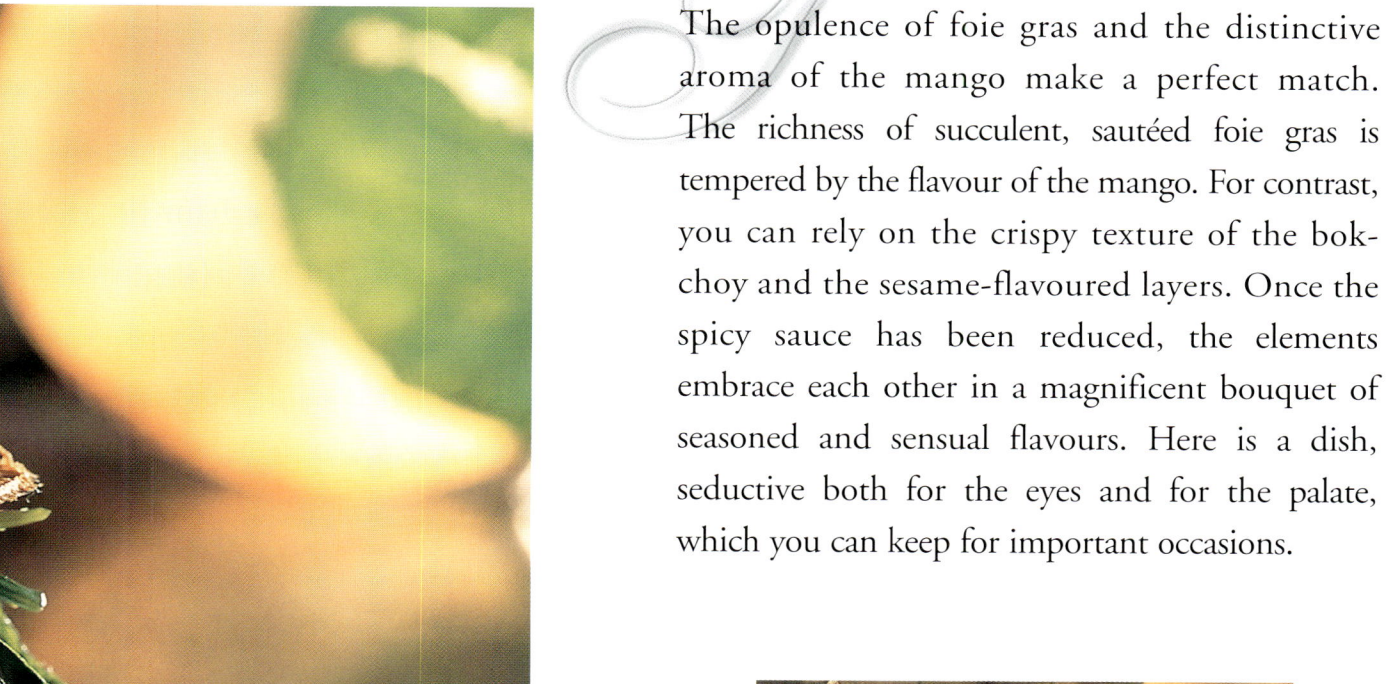

The opulence of foie gras and the distinctive aroma of the mango make a perfect match. The richness of succulent, sautéed foie gras is tempered by the flavour of the mango. For contrast, you can rely on the crispy texture of the bok-choy and the sesame-flavoured layers. Once the spicy sauce has been reduced, the elements embrace each other in a magnificent bouquet of seasoned and sensual flavours. Here is a dish, seductive both for the eyes and for the palate, which you can keep for important occasions.

COURGE

Also called "melon d'hiver" (winter melon) in French, it is known as butternut squash in English. It is often used in Chinese cuisine in soups and stews or steamed.

Recipe page 235

Pumpkin and calabash vindaloo

flavoured with coconut and almonds

Made with pork marinated in wine and garlic (alho), "Vinha d'alhos" is still eaten in Portugal. But, for their part, the inhabitants of Goa felt that this dish lacked bite, so they made it more to their taste by adding extra garlic and spices. The dish has become a classic in Goa. In Mauritius, vindaloo ("vindaye" as it is known locally) is not prepared in the same way. Here vindaloo forms part of a vegetarian thali, a Southern Indian tray of dishes, which includes a great variety of vegetables, with spices, lentils, pickles, rice, bread and bananas as well as a dessert. I ate one of my best thalis at the home of our salad supplier, Mr. Dookun, who had invited me to take part in a religious ceremony. Eaten on a banana leaf and with the fingers as tradition dictates.

VINTAGE KOHINOOR BASMATI RICE

Yes, this is exactly what you read: rice, just like wine, has a vintage: the Kohinoor, of course, which is grown in the foothills of the Himalayas. The main grand crus: Punni, Dehra Sun, Jeera Sali and Ambre Moohu.

Recipe page 236

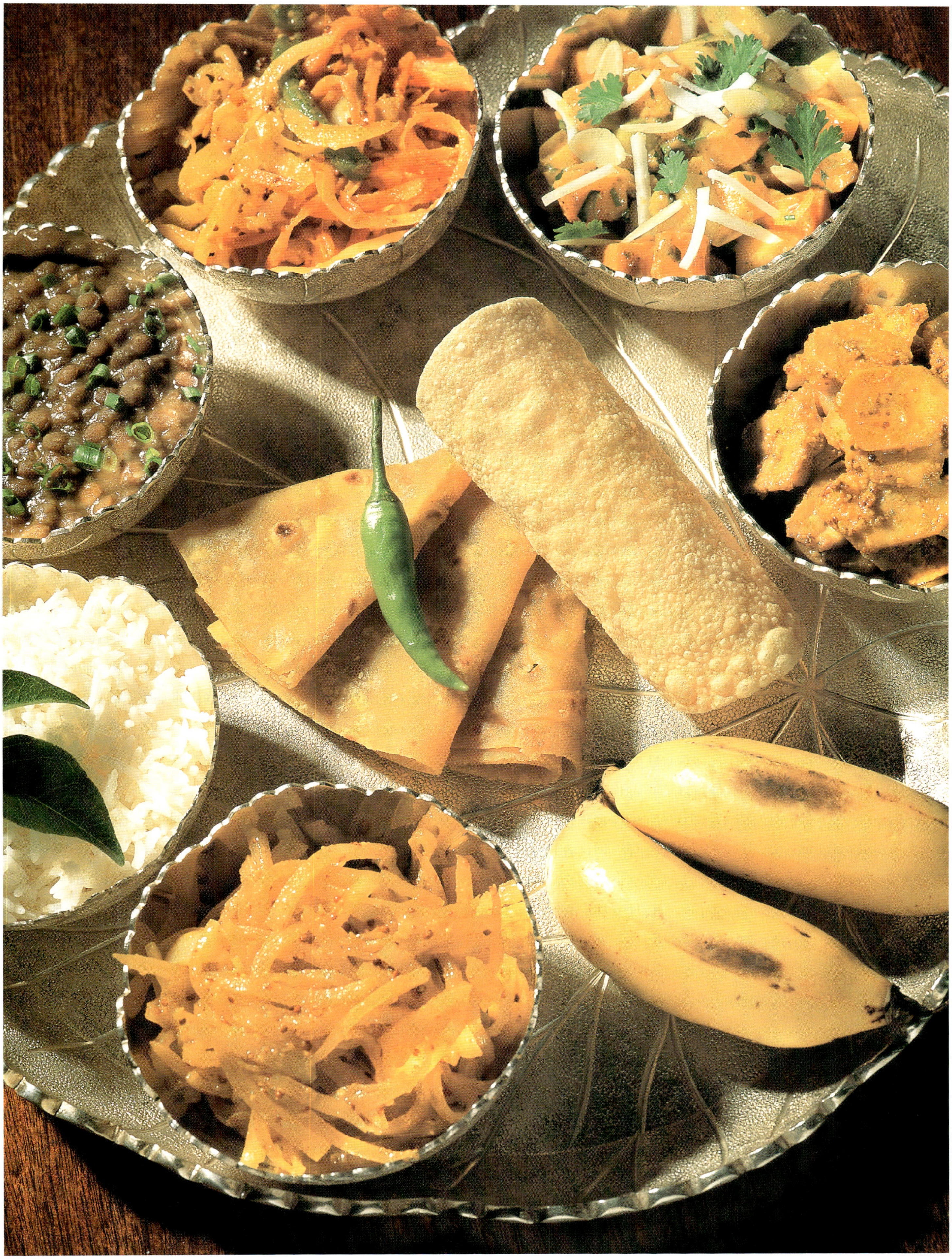

Flavours and Colours of Mauritius

"A refined soul loves fish."

EDMOND DE GONCOURT

With its fruity, woody and piquant perfume, for me black pepper is as indispensable as salt. Lightly roasted for a few minutes in a dry pan before being ground, it spices up good fish fillet, as in this white tuna recipe.

TUNA

Is it a fish or an industry? An economic weapon? The systematic plundering in the waters of countries that have inadequate means of surveillance. Mauritian waters have often been over-exploited by foreign fishing boats. Tuna is good, not only tinned, but also fresh, whether red or white. Delicious Tahiti-style, as carpaccio or tartar. Call me Albacore or Germon; it is so much more elegant.

Recipe page 237

130

Roast white tuna with black pepper
and bonemarrow on garlic-flavoured mashed potatoes

Traditional Moslem chicken biryani

with various chutneys and Rodriguan lime pickle

This typical Northern Indian dish has become a national dish in Mauritius. Essentially a Moslem dish, biryani is traditionally served at weddings and religious ceremonies. It is most often prepared by men, the "Bhandaris".
Biryani is cooked on a wood fire, in enormous, copper pots called "deg" (depending on the size of the pot, the contents can serve from 50 to as many as 400 people). Biryani is usually prepared with chicken or beef.

FREE-RANGE CHICKEN

In Mauritius, chickens are still widely bred domestically and it is not unusual to have to brake to let a mother hen and her chickens cross the street. Chicken curry together with farata is a very common dish in the island and is often eaten during the cyclonic period when the family, taking refuge in the house, waits patiently for nature to calm down. So, by free-range chicken, I mean those that are raised outdoors and fed mainly on corn and produce of plant origin.

Recipe page 238

Flavours and Colours of Mauritius

Spicy cocoa crunch

with ladyfinger banana ice-cream

"Lovers of good food: they have such shining eyes!"

Jean-Anthelme Brillat-Savarin

When you prepare an ice-cream, it is better to serve it as soon as possible, rather than keeping it for any length of time in the freezer. This particularly applies to a sorbet, which loses its quality irredeemably when it is not served straightaway. The balance of flavours is upset, as some flavours weaken whilst others start to dominate. Nothing can compare with the smooth and creamy texture of freshly prepared ice-creams or sorbets.

LADYFINGER BANANAS

Another delicacy for the dolls' tea parties. Its size, shape and fine skin reminds one of a chubby baby's hand. As for its taste, copy Mauritians by saying "sweet, sweet, sweet" instead of our "sugary and smooth as a liqueur".

Recipe page 239

135

Mango and longan fruit salad

with mildly-spiced yoghurt sorbet

LONGANS

Also called Dragon's eye fruit because of the white mark in the form of an eye on the seed of its fruit. Younger brother and close relative of the litchi, less juicy but just as tasty.

Recipe page 240

Flavours and Colours of Mauritius

The marvellous variety of fruits that can be found here is part of the island's charm. Their exquisite sweetness, the incredible variety of their shapes, colours and sizes, as well as their heady aroma, delight tourists as well as local people. The markets sell fruit in season, but fruits such as apples and oranges, are available throughout the year. It is not unusual to see carefully laid-out fruit stalls by the roadside. Hawkers also sell pickled and semi-ripe fruit, mixed with vinegar and sugar and served with chilli.

Pineapple Tatin

with caramel fudge and ice-cream flavoured with oriental spices

No one has the recipe for that tart, hand-written by the Tatin sisters, innkeepers at La Motte Beuvron, at the beginning of the last century. Spiteful gossip has even suggested that this famous dessert owes everything to a servant called Marie. The Tatin tart is cooked upside-down under a pastry cover but served the right way up, that is the pastry at the bottom and the fruit on top. We have created a variant on this great classic, the pineapple Tatin tart. A spiced ice-cream goes very well with this dessert, with a few pieces of candied fruit to emphasise the pineapple taste.

NUTMEG

There is no more beautiful fruit than the nutmeg, especially once it is open. The red mace surrounding the seed is gently removed. The kernel of the stone, which is also called nutmeg, is a delicate spice with a somewhat peppery and nutty taste. To appreciate all its subtlety, you could savour "the tender pieces of ham, from a pig stewed in stock, with the gentle aroma of celery and nutmeg", just like Colette, who mentions them in L"Étoile Vesper".

Recipe page 241

Flavours and Colours of Mauritius

Crispy Grand Cru Caraque chocolate ravioli

with rum-flavoured sabayon, preserved pineapple and cocoa sorbet

Pasta for pudding? Why not? Instead of boiling the ravioli, you fry it to obtain a perfect balance between the smoothness of the chocolate filling and the crunchiness of the pastry. This dessert allows me to offer a nice combination of tastes: chocolate and ginger. I have added pineapple for freshness, cocoa sorbet for its intensity and rum-flavoured sabayon for the final touch. Use small ravioli that can be eaten in one mouthful. The marvellous sensation provided by the association of the smoothness and the crunchiness of the ravioli can be better appreciated this way.

OLD RUM

Multicoloured and shimmering, the world of rum is sure to conjure up the West Indies and its buccaneers. A powerful and impetuous eau de vie, it rivals cognac and armagnac in body and mellowness. To be sipped, to shore up your holiday memories.

Recipe page 242

Flavours and Colours of Mauritius

"The love of good food and a fine wit combine to make a man a fine companion"

ALEXANDRE GRIMOD DE LA REYNIÈRE

141

Rodriguan honey madeleines

"Little pastry shells, so richly sensual beneath their severe and devout folds."

MARCEL PROUST

This exquisite little golden cake in the form of a shell is my real weakness. Not a day passes without my eating one or two. My son, Mathis, is crazy about them. Try these honey madeleines and you will understand why this recipe is so greatly appreciated by our guests.

RODRIGUAN HONEY

The harshness of the Rodriguan climate suits the production of a heavy, almost musky honey, full of aromas. To be spread on bread or toast for breakfast, or indeed over your body if you want to follow a custom of the Egyptians, Greeks and Romans, for whom it was one of the most natural beauty products.

Recipe page 243

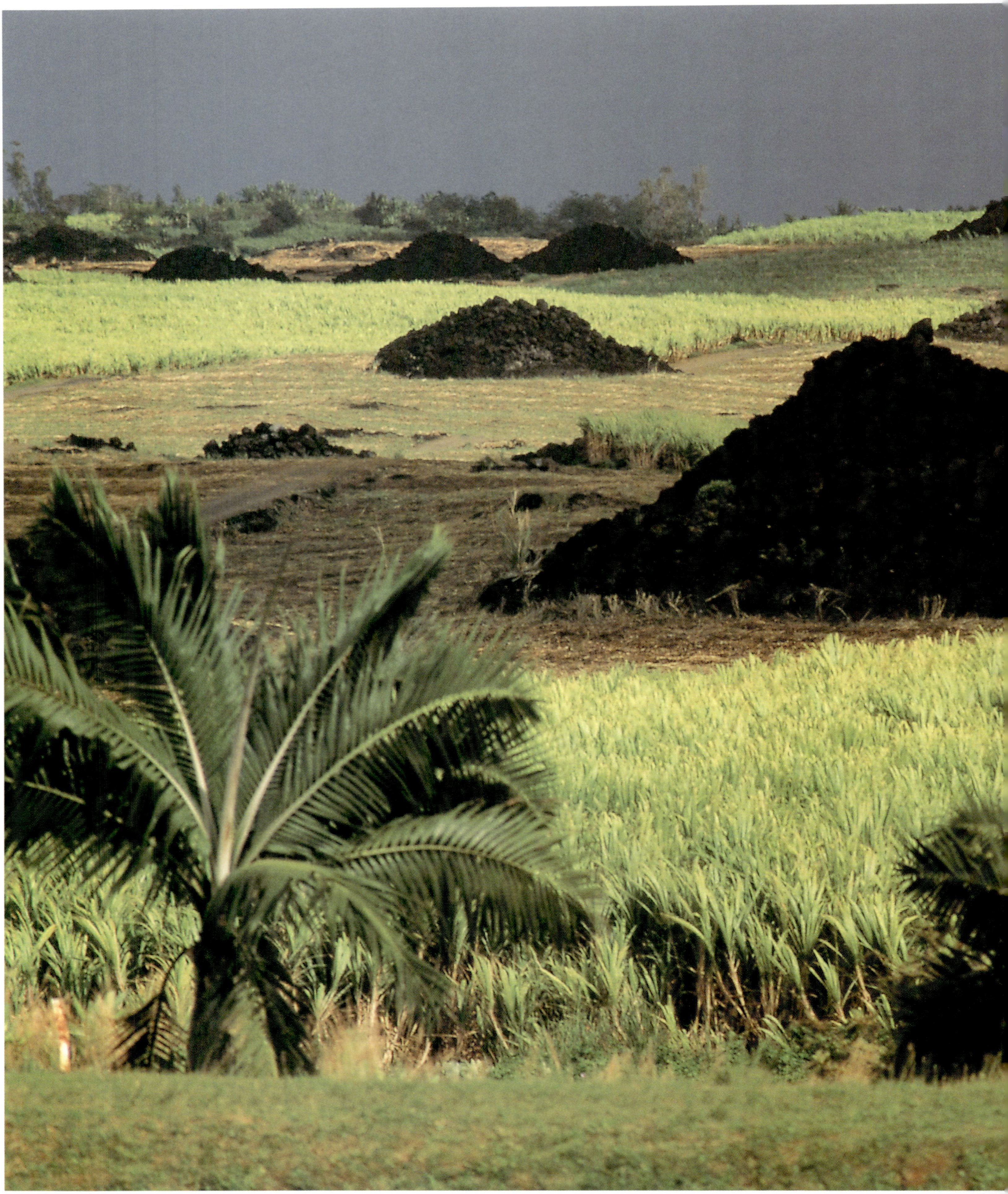

Flavours and Colours of Mauritius

*"Without wandering through
the flowers in May
Running together on the craggy
green slopes
Assailing the lake of dreams
and the deceptive
monoliths of stone
You will never know me
Without knowing the ritual cries
Echoing from the forgotten
watersides
and glimpses of the fins of the
elusive parrotfish
You will never know me
You must have seen the colour
of the sugarcane to know the
essence of the sugar
That criss-crosses our
mountain-sides.»*

ANANDA DEVI

Flavours and Colours of Mauritius

Spiced snapper

on sugarcane skewers

Sometimes very little is needed to set off very simple produce to advantage. In Mauritius, there are many such possibilities and sometimes a chef must dare to make some associations, which are not always obvious at first sight.

BERRI BLANC

White berry - another enigma so far as the origin of its name is concerned. A kind of snapper, this choice fish with its silvery colour, that loves the deep, is very adaptable, even in the hands of the craziest cook.

Recipe page 247

Vegetable terrine

in mazavarou-flavoured Taggiasche oil with garlic crostini

The terrine is a superb and elegant way in which to prepare vegetables. Each prepares it in his own way, but I have chosen this light but tasty version, playing on the colour and appearance of each vegetable. I believe that vegetables should not be served only as side dishes; they have their own importance in a menu. Here the crostini add a crunchy note.

AUBERGINE

"Brinjelle", the Mauritian name for aubergine, already existed in Burma for four thousand years, before arriving in Europe on board Arab ships in about the thirteenth century. Aubergines comes in several varieties but, independently of the colour of its skin, the flesh is always spongy and milky white.

Recipe page 248

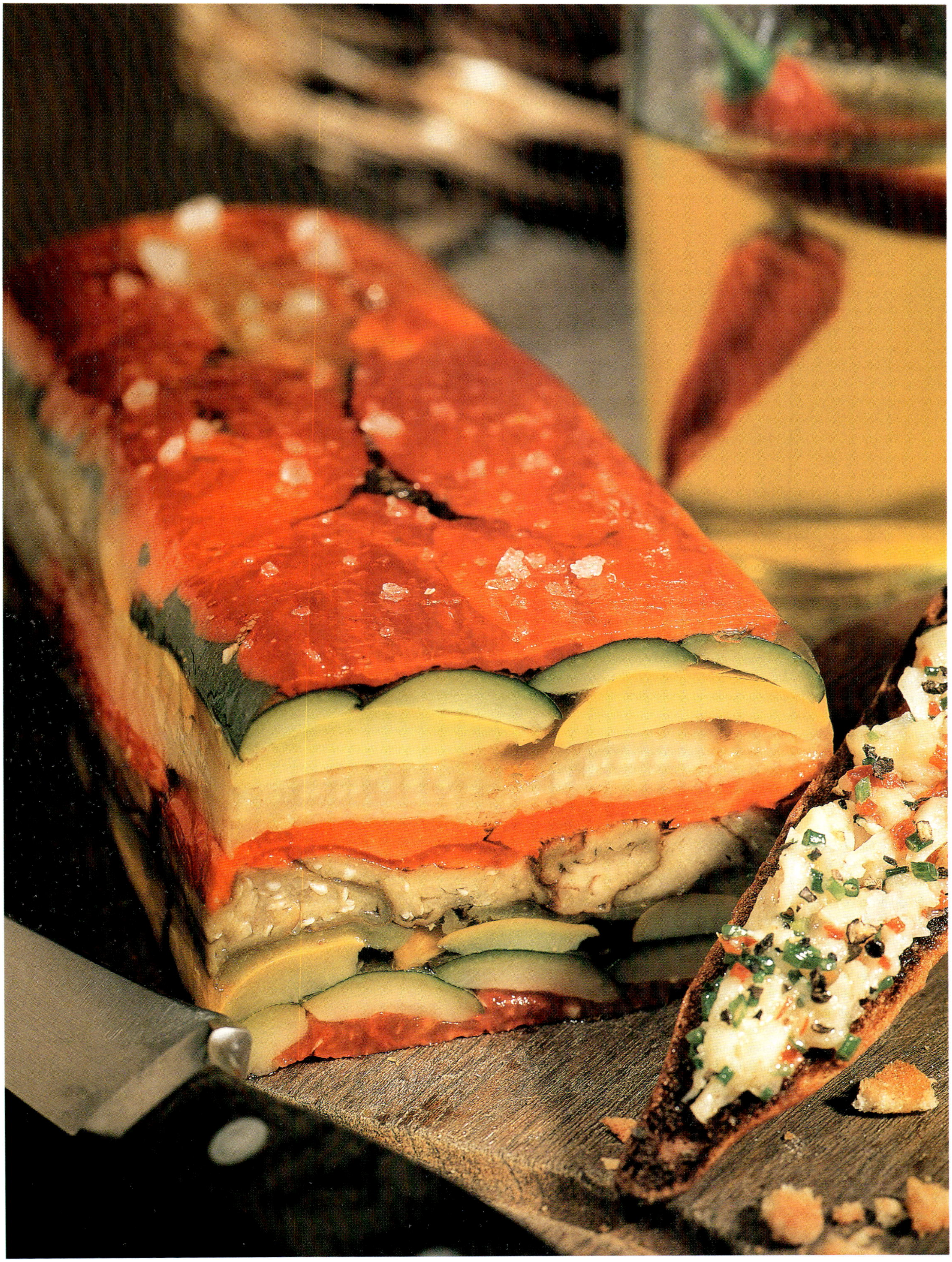

Flavours and Colours of Mauritius

Green pineapple ravioli

with spicy rock lobster fricassée and eucalyptus honey vinaigrette

This recipe is inspired by an Alain Passard speciality, his "Lobster and turnip with honey and sherry vinegar". I trained with this great chef and his simple and intelligent way of cooking, blending technique and elegance, has greatly influenced me. The quality of a chef is also measured by how successful he is in the preparation of simple dishes. This ravioli includes all the components of a perfect first course: simplicity, elegance, visual impact and refined taste are all present. Success is guaranteed with this superb but simple dish.

QUEEN VICTORIA PINEAPPLE

The baby of all pineapples: round, plump, fleshy, smooth, one almost regrets being unable to bite into its skin, the colour of the setting sun.

Recipe page 249

Sea bream carpaccio

flavoured with green lemon and coconut

At the risk of repeating myself, always choose fresh fish to produce a successful carpaccio. When you buy fish, you must make sure it is fresh by using your senses of sight, touch and smell. A few tips to guide you in your choice: fresh fish has firm flesh covered with a viscous liquid, a bulging eye with a vivid and bright pupil, as well as a vivid colour, with an iridescent skin and bright red gills.

GUEULE PAVÉ DORÉ

Mouth of stone - at last, a name that has a clear explanation in the confusing jungle of the underwater world: its strong jaw and big molars help it to crush the shells of the molluscs that it feeds on. It is a kind of sea-bream, the French dorade, the El Dorado that all gourmets seek.

Recipe page 250

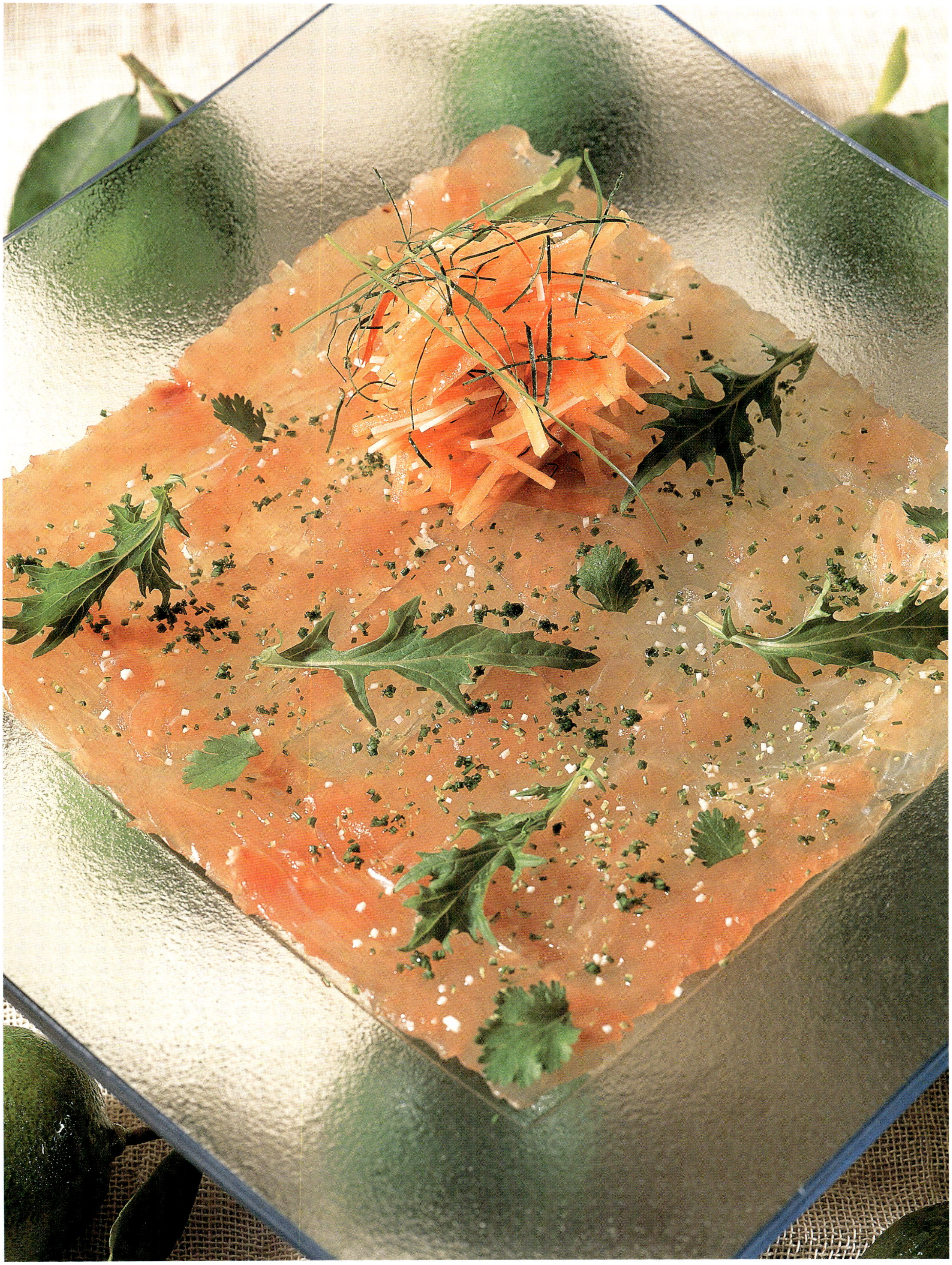

Flavours and Colours of Mauritius

Creamy watercress soup

served as a cappuccino with clams and salted Grissini

I believe I owe my entrance into Guy Savoy's restaurant to my tallness - he is a great lover of rugby. A Flying Dutchman of my size was perfectly suited to the weekly matches we played at the Bois de Boulogne on Fridays, between lunch and dinner. My stay at this great chef's was undoubtedly the best moment of my training in France. Guy Savoy is one of the most genuine people I have ever met. His enthusiasm ("We must have a good time!"), his professionalism and his extraordinary sense of hospitality are and will always be a source of inspiration to me. Besides, it was Guy Savoy who encouraged me to come to the Royal Palm. As a sign of respect and admiration, I have decided to send him the first copy of this cookery book.

POUS-POUS

Sometimes written pus-pus, but don't worry, the spelling is correct enough, for it is definitely not a pousse-pousse (rickshaw). Another iodine tablet from our reefs to flavour our bouillon, as we call our soups or broths, in this case a sea-food soup.

Recipe page 251

Creamy breadfruit soup

with crispy smoked bacon

Unfortunately breadfruit does not receive the attention it deserves in Mauritius. It can be prepared as a vegetable, but it must be picked before it is ripe, when its skin is still green and becoming slightly yellow. Breadfruit tastes good fried in crispy, thin slices and sprinkled with salt, chilli powder or sugar syrup. But I prefer this simple and tasty soup version with a smooth consistency and the taste of grilled lard, which gives richness to this velouté. Pancetta is suggested here, but any salted and smoked lard can be used instead.

BREADFRUIT

Its discovery in the eighteenth century caused a sensation. Who can have failed to have heard of the Mutiny on the Bounty? Whilst it may remind us of potatoes, it has the same nutritional value as bread. Very popular in Polynesia, once fermented it even changes into a vegetarian cheese. The gum of the tree is used to seal the hulls of boats.

Recipe page 252

Flavours and Colours of Mauritius

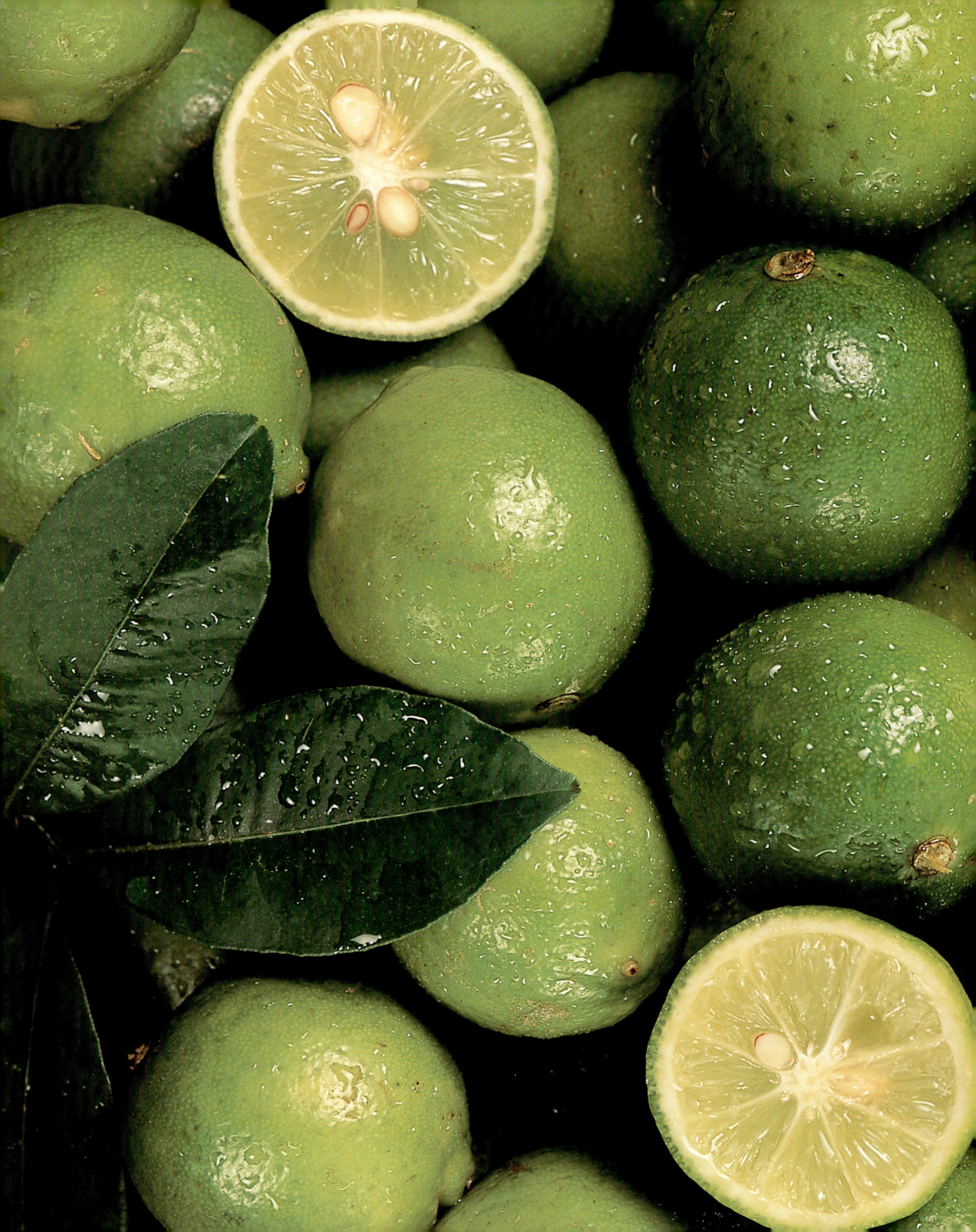

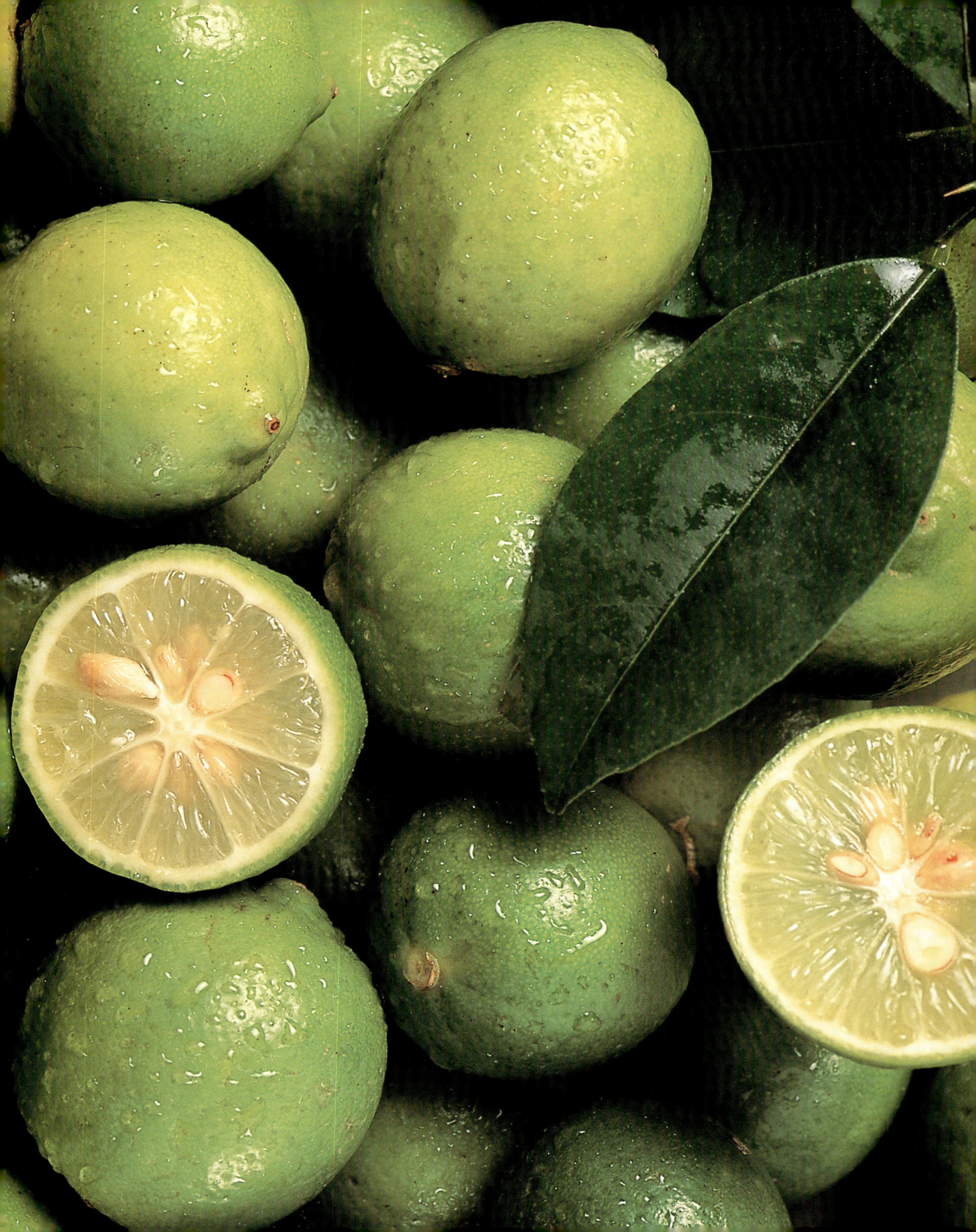

Flavours and Colours of Mauritius

Mildly-spiced camarons

with pineapple and Rodriguan lime chutney

When I was 18, I decided to become a chef. My first cookery book was a Dutch translation of Auguste Escoffier's "Guide Culinaire", written about a century ago and which remains one of the best guides to French cooking. Escoffier was a real genius and many believe that we are indebted to him for the basic elements of modern cookery. It is not really inaccurate to think that practically all dishes have already been invented. Today, we can only improve on certain techniques by using new technologies and in presenting the textures and flavours of ingredients in a new way.

CAMARONS

Fresh water prawns with their large pincers, this shellfish, with its delicious taste, is becoming increasingly rare in its natural habitat. Camarons especially the rosenberghi, a popular variety in Mauritius, is normally bred in prawn farms nowadays.

Page 158: the «ti limon» from Rodrigues is famous for its wonderful scent.

Recipe page 253

Flame snapper and crayfish on vegetables

simmered in dried fruit with a spicy pumpkin-flavoured sauce

In this recipe, I use the pulp of Japanese pumpkin to give a pleasant consistency to the sauce, without having to add butter or cream. This produces a lighter, perfumed sauce, whilst a dash of extra virgin olive oil gives it body. I like to thicken sauces with vegetable purées. Sometimes I also use shallots and onions, squash or carrots that I caramelise beforehand, to bind meat or poultry stock.

GIRAUMON

A member of the pumpkin family, this Japanese pumpkins was grown by the Dutch in Mauritius from 1861, but harvests were destroyed by locusts. However, it survived over the years and remains the most common variety in the island.

Recipe page 254

"After a good dinner one can forgive anybody, even one's own relatives."

OSCAR WILDE

Pumpkin and gourd Vialone Nano risotto

with crispy smoked pancetta

The risotto, a much appreciated summer dish, is not difficult to make. You must have very good quality rice and arm yourself with a lot of patience, for you must be ready to stir the dish for twenty minutes. At the Royal Palm, we use Ferron's Vialone Nano rice. This variety, very popular in the regions of Mantova and Verona, produces large round grains. Do use this type of rice, which enables you to make a smooth and creamy risotto. Black truffle risotto is one of the most popular dishes at the Royal Palm when the tuber is in season.

CALEBASSE

The calabash or gourd is the only vegetable cultivated both in the old and the new world since time immemorial. It is most probably the oldest, nutritional plant grown in the tropics and certainly the most common. The gourd is also used in Africa as a kitchen utensil and to make musical instruments.

Recipe page 255

Flavours and Colours of Mauritius

Flavours and Colours of Mauritius

Pot-roasted farm-raised veal rump

with shii-take mushrooms and ginger-flavoured gravy

It is said that a calf is raised "under the mother" if it is nourished with her milk. Its feeding is completed by milk from other cows and about 10 to 20 eggs per day for breakfast. It provides meat called "white", tender and tasty, with non-oily fat. This superb veal can only be bought at the best butchers.

SHII-TAKE

Also called the black forest mushroom, shii-take has a firm texture. The taste is rich, close to that of meat. It can be grilled, braised, fried or added to a stew. Its medicinal qualities, particularly in lowering cholesterol levels, have been confirmed by Western scientists.

Recette page 256

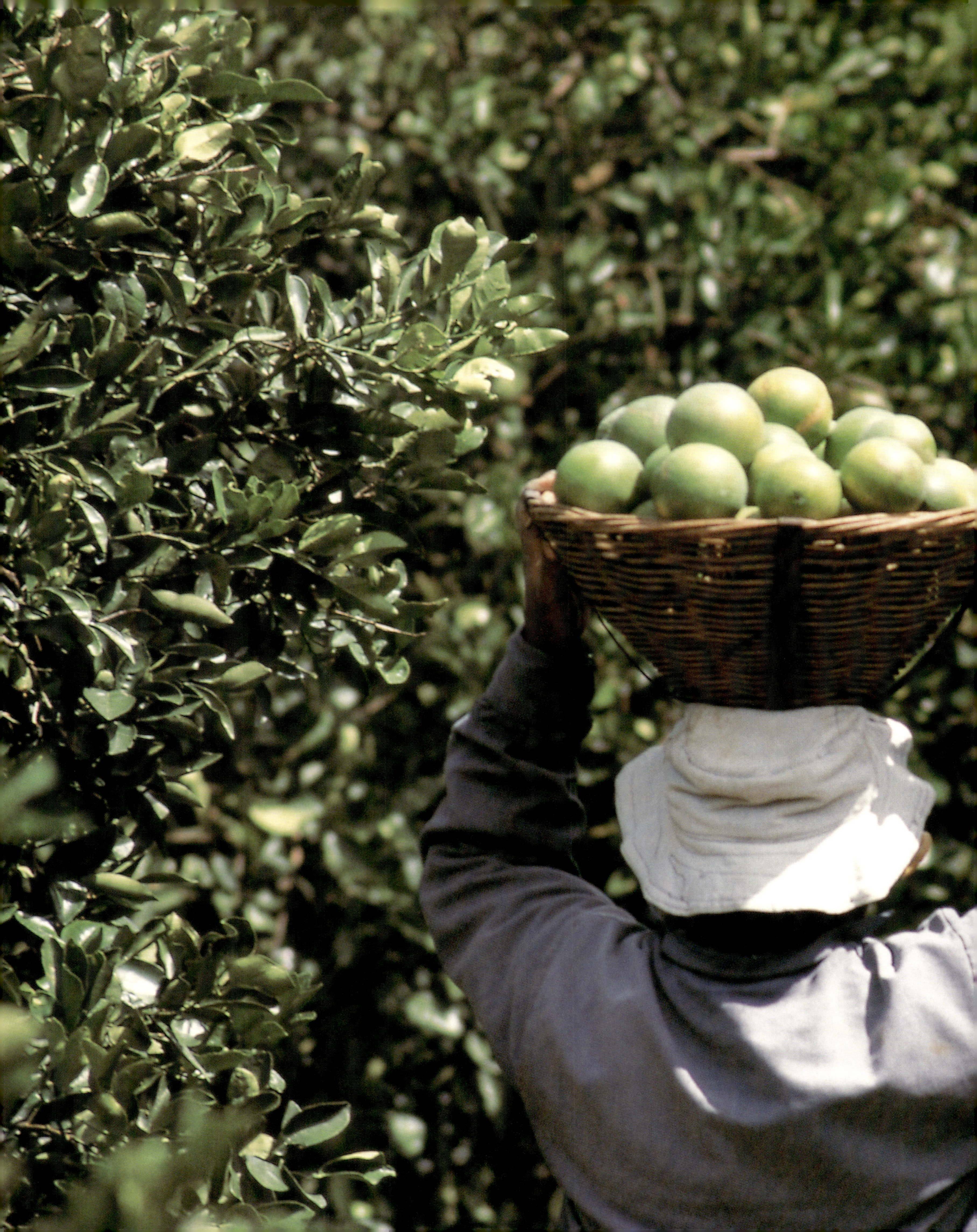

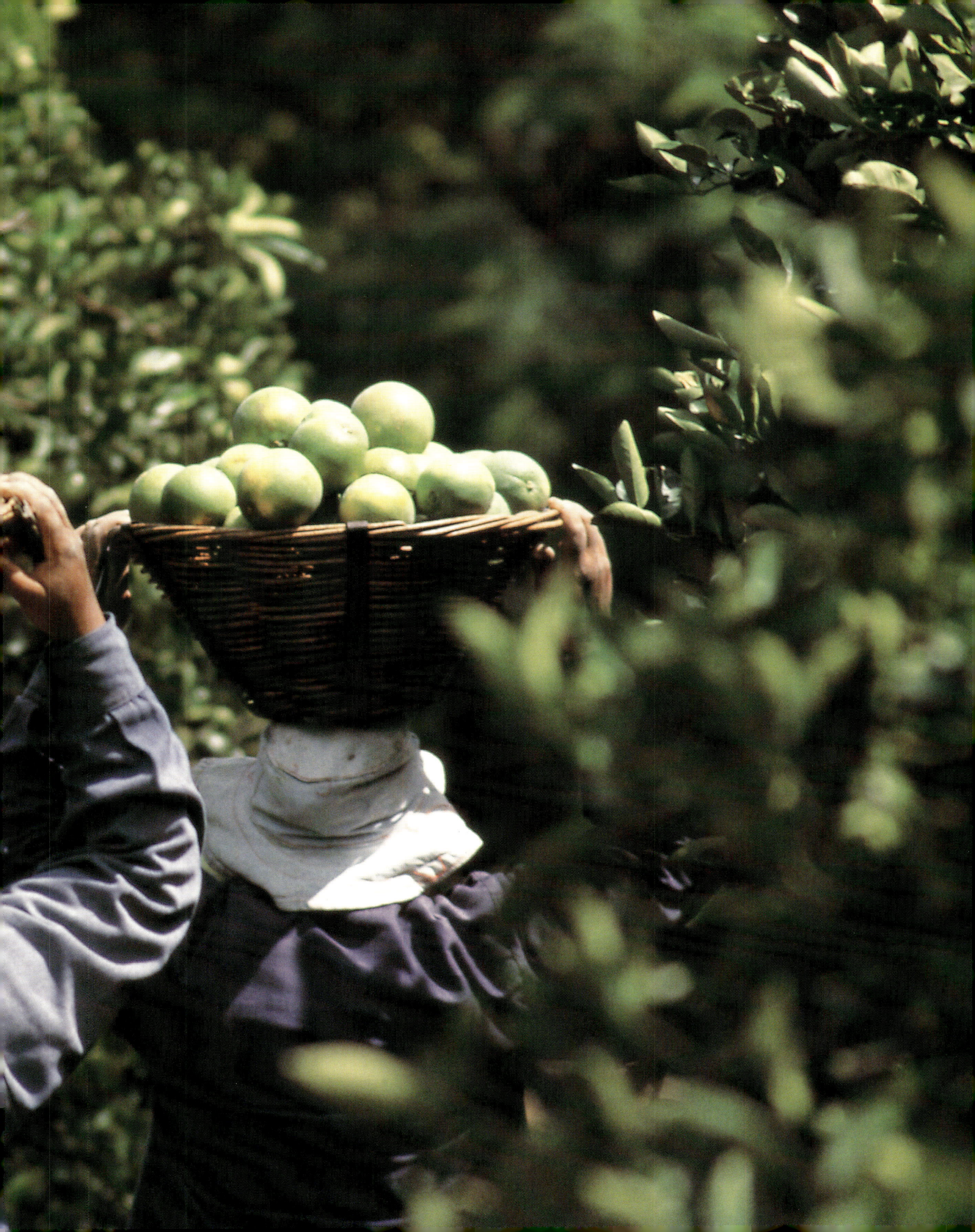

Spit-roasted free-range chicken

served with citronella-flavoured gravy and crispy cassava straws

My favourite method of cooking chicken is what the French call "poached-grilled". The chicken is poached whole in a good chicken stock to half-cook it before it is roasted in the oven. In this way, the chicken flesh remains succulent and its aroma is more intense. The citronella placed under the skin transmits its delicate freshness to the chicken and the vegetable stuffing gives it an additional flavour, while preventing its flesh from drying out.

CITRONELLA

The discreet charm of Tonkin and Indochina. An old-fashioned suavity, like a novel by Pierre Benoît or Mazo de la Roche. Always present in Vietnamese or Malaysian cooking, it is timeless and versatile, finding a place both in pharmacy and perfumery. Lemon grass, as it is more commonly known, is used in infusions and the oil is rubbed on the skin to repel mosquitoes.

Recipe page 257

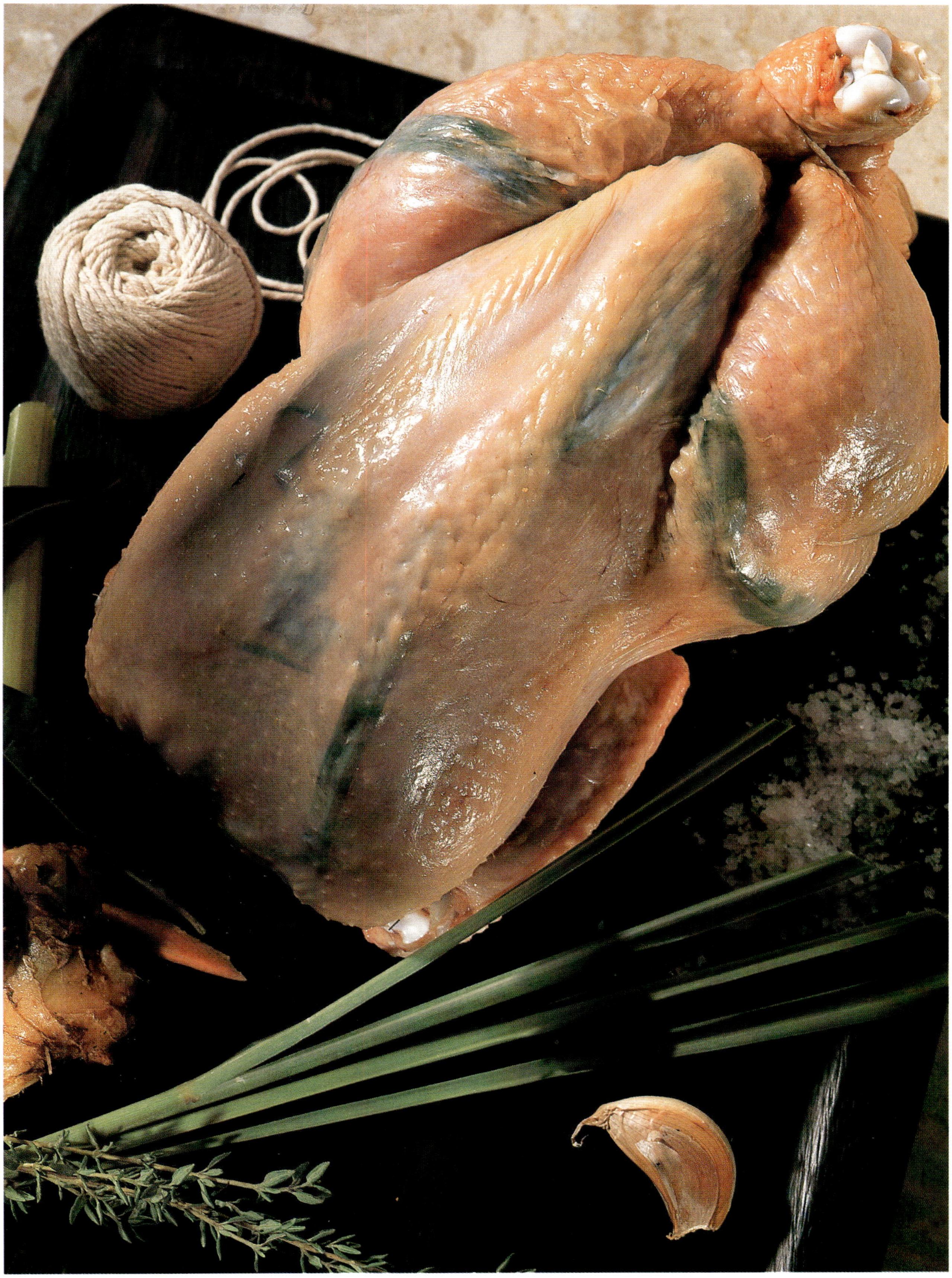

Crème caramel

with rum-flavoured raisins

Here is a classic dessert reinvigorated by the play of textures and flavours. To the smoothness of the cream, we add the raisins and the matured rum, whose taste admirably blends with that of raisins. Try using coconut milk instead of cow's milk, use half an egg, and you will obtain a surprising result. You will quickly appreciate this real island-style crème renversée.

CANE SUGAR

"The reed that secretes honey". Choose the least refined raw sugar; its strong fragrance makes it almost a pudding in its own right.

Recipe page 258

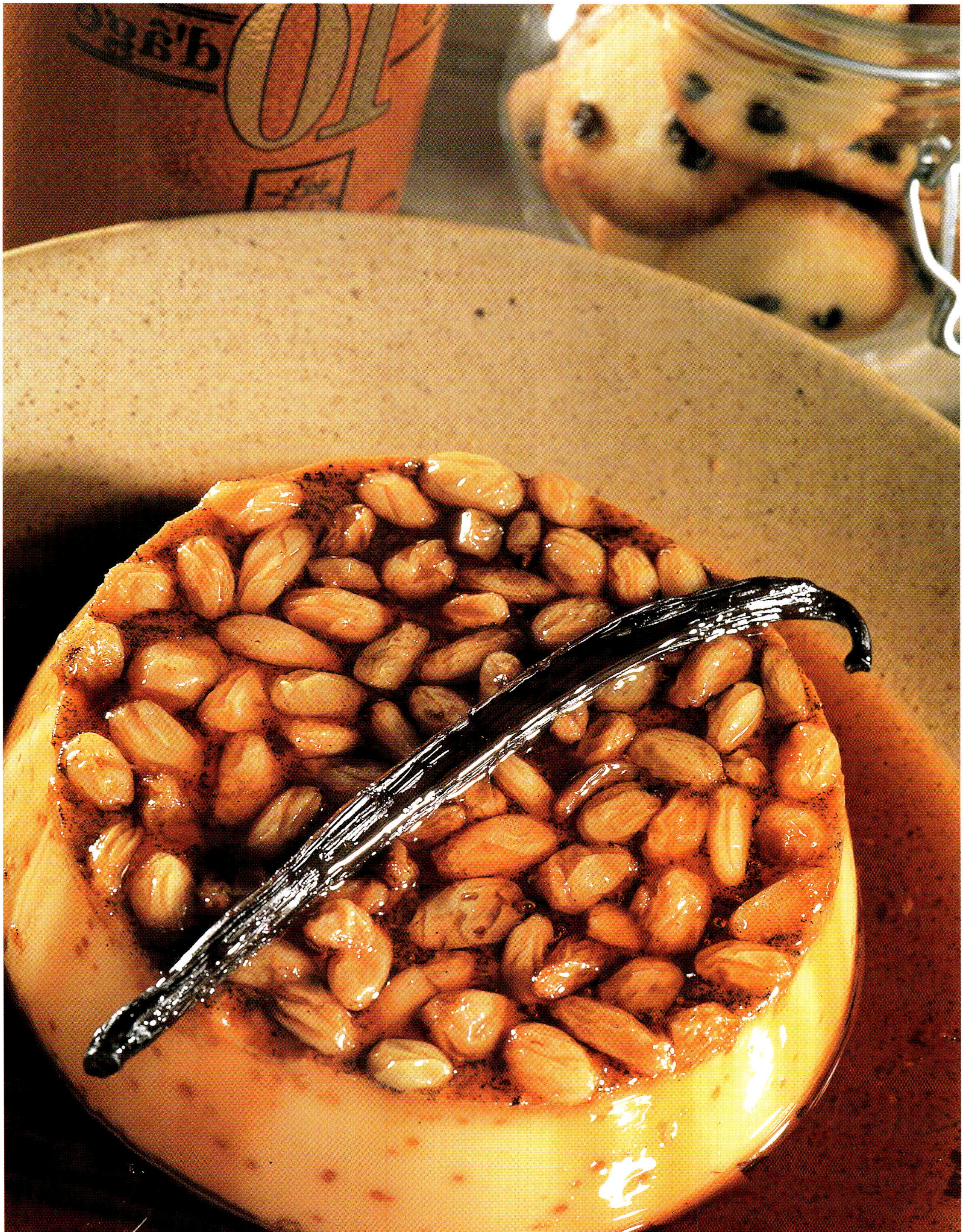

Flavours and Colours of Mauritius

Queen Victoria pineapple

baked in Sichuan pepper and caramelised with cane sugar, served with citronella ice-cream

Combining hot and cold, sweet and sour, in a clever mix of flavours; the sweetness of the fruit and the perfume of the pineapple with the peppered orange peel; the rich harmony of the ice-cream and the citronella: this magnificent dessert is even better when it is prepared several hours in advance. It just needs heating up before it is served.

SICHUAN PEPPER

The dried seed of the fagara, Sichuan pepper is very popular in this Chinese province and adds a spicy note to dishes. The reddish-brown berries are often roasted slowly in a pan until they become crisp, then ground. Sichuan pepper is excellent for seasoning fried chicken.

Recipe page 259

Mango baked in Fragrans vanilla

with diplomat cream and crispy pistachio-flavoured philo

My whole stay in Mauritius has been notable for the strong bonds that I have formed with the island and its inhabitants. The country has given me an unbelievable opportunity to express myself freely, drawing on its rich culinary diversity.

MANGO

Few other fruits have such a distinguished past. Alexander the Great came across it in the Indus valley, it blossoms in all tropical countries, refuses methodical classification and is impossible to recognise from one place to another. The only common denominator, apart from its delicious flesh, is that mangoes introduce you to the most charming young ladies: Adèle, Rosa, Agnès, Orphée, Amélie, and Julie, to name but a few!

Recipe page 260

Flavours and Colours of Mauritius

Flavours and Colours of Mauritius

Guava jam

Soon after I arrived in Mauritius, I realised that the hotels tend to serve jams such as apricot and raspberry, fruits that are not grown in Mauritius. I found this quite incongruous in a country with such a wealth of succulent and exotic fruit. I therefore sought the help of Jacques Sulem, a tremendous professional, and we produced thirty sorts of jam such as Victoria pineapple, coconut, maison rouge mango, passion fruit, Rodriguan lime and ti-chinois…

These jams are so full of fruit (up to 70%) that you could almost call them compotes. For example, for kumquat jam we buy organic kumquats from a small local grower, cut them into fine slices, before cooking them, without boiling, in a copper preserving pan. Nothing is added. There's nothing better to get the day off to an auspicious start!

"The world would be a sadder place without the pleasing smells of preserves and jams."

GEORGES DUHAMEL

GUAVA

The guava is a large berry with a strong aroma, a sweet and slightly acid flavour, with a pale yellow or yellowish green skin when ripe. Depending on the species, its granular white or pink flesh contains either a lot of seeds or none at all. Rich in vitamins A and C, as well as potassium and calcium, the guava also contains a lot of pectin, very useful in making delicious fruit spreads, jellies and jams. In tropical countries, the guava plays the same role in baking as the apple does in temperate regions, and is also used to flavour ice-cream and fresh drinks. The guava tree produces an excellent wood for charcoal and its bark is used in dyeing silk and in tanning.

Recipe page 261

Caramel-flavoured ladyfinger banana samossas
with coconut sorbet

Flavours and Colours of Mauritius

"Those who enjoy fine food are fortunate; we are in ignorance of their delight."
MONTESQIEU

"If I were to create a sweet samossa ..." thus was this dish born in my imagination. With my staff, we first tried pineapple and then mango, before finally ending up with the banana. This fruit needs little sweetening and the contrast between the crisp pastry and the tender banana is simply divine. We are already trying out another variation: samossa Guanaja "Grand Cru" chocolate, coffee semi-freddo and puffed rice caramelised with cardamom. The coffee is arabica from Chamarel.

CARDAMOM

A highly perfumed spice, also called "Paradise seed". Of the same family as ginger, cardamom is said to take its name from the Cardamone mountains in the west of Cambodia, where it is grown. Cardamom is used in the preparation of sweets and sweet dishes, in all spice mixtures, and to flavour hot drinks. An essential element in Asian rituals, it opens the door on to a world of luxury.

Recipe page 262

Flavours and Colours of Mauritius

Richard EKKEBUS

Red Recipes

Vegetable samossas with Rodriguan red chilli sauce	187
Shrimps marinated in tandoori massala and green salad with mango and bean sprouts	188
Creamy faye-faye crab flavoured with sherry, garnished with a green vegetable salad	189
Chinese chicken and shrimp salad with sesame bread	190
Crispy sweet potato layers with pan-fried duck foie gras, cep mushrooms and chestnut shavings	191
Whisky-flavoured urchin bisque with fennel and herb ravioli	192
Pan-fried red mullet with pink peppers and home-made curry in salted Queen Victoria pineapple-butter sauce	193
Rock lobster in tandoori massala with sweet potato fondant and coriander pesto sauce	194
Shrimp curry with coconut and banana buds	195
Rack of cochon marron roasted in five spices and glazed with Rodriguan honey	196
Potato and cauliflower curry with perfumed Basmati rice and green mango pickles	197
Java deer roasted in sweet spices with goyaves de Chine sauce and arouille violette purée	198
Asian-style poached and glazed lamb shank with brèdes Tom-Pouce, confit tomatoes and shii-take mushrooms	199
Roast duck breast with cinnamon kofta in a ti-chinois sauce	200
Warm goyaves de Chine in red wine and pepper-flavoured ice-cream	201
Panna cotta scented with Fragrans vanilla and sweet tomatoes	202
Vanilla-flavoured rice pudding covered with caramelised mango and kumquat sauce	203
Mauritian vanilla crème brûlée with crispy coconut tuiles	203

Vegetable samossas with Rodriguan red chilli sauce

Recipe

Prepare the samossa dough in the bowl of a food processor. Place the flour and salt in the bowl, switch on the processor, and then add the water little by little until the dough is thoroughly mixed and forms a smooth ball. Wrap the dough in cling film and leave it to stand in a refrigerator. The longer it stands, the easier it will be to roll out. Cut the dough into 40 g pieces. Shape into balls and then roll out into circles. Brush each piece generously with oil, and stack six circles on top of each other, then roll out this stack to a thickness of 3 mm. Cook slowly in a non-stick pan until each side is golden. Separate the 6 layers whilst they are still hot. Cut the samossa dough into strips, 5 cm wide and 15 cm long.

To prepare the stuffing Wash and peel the potatoes and dice them into small pieces (macédoine). Place them in a small 14 cm wide saucepan with a lid, and cover with salted water. Cook on moderate heat for 10 to 15 minutes: the tip of a knife inserted into a potato cube should come out easily. Drain as soon as they are cooked.

Meanwhile, wash and peel the carrot, and then cut it into macédoine. Fill a large pan with iced water. Separately bring 2 l. of water and half a handful of salt to the boil. Dip the carrots in the boiling water and then transfer them immediately into the iced water to cool. Shell the peas and meanwhile bring a further 2 l. of water and half a handful of salt to the boil. Dip the peas in the boiling water and immediately cool them in the iced water. Peel the French beans by breaking off the two tips between the thumb and forefinger, then string them. Cut the beans into 5 mm slices, wash in cold water and drain them in a colander. Bring 2 l. of water and half a handful of sea salt to the boil and add the beans. Cook for a few minutes only (the beans must remain green and crisp). Drain, dip into iced water, and drain them again.

Peel the ginger and the garlic, removing the green germ, and then crush in a mortar. Peel and cut the onion into very thin slivers. Clean the coriander, discard the stalks and snip up the leaves. Cut the chilli into two, remove the seeds and dice into thin brunoise. Clean the leek, wash it thoroughly and cut into thin slices.

Cook the leek, onion, garlic and ginger in peanut oil in a thick-bottomed saucepan for a minute or two, without letting them brown. Then add the curry powder, turmeric, chilli, thyme and curry leaves. Cook for one minute and then add the macédoine (carrots, potatoes, peas and beans). Simmer for 5 minutes, check seasoning, remove from the stove and leave to cool down completely.

To prepare the paste Mix the flour and water to obtain a very liquid paste.

To fill the samossas Place small heaps of the stuffing near the edge of the strip of dough. Fold into the shape of a triangle. Continue to fold, keeping the triangular shape. Brush the edges of each strip with the paste so that the samossas do not open during cooking. Lay the samossas side by side on a clean tea towel and place them in the refrigerator.

To prepare the sauce Peel the ginger and garlic (removing the germ) and slice thinly. Cut the chilli into two, remove the seeds and cut into thin brunoise. Heat the oil in a 15 cm wide frying pan, add the ginger, garlic and red chilli, sweat until translucent and then add the tomato purée and ketchup. Next add the vegetable stock, simmer slowly for 10 minutes and thicken with cornflour. Remove from the stove. Leave to stand for 15 minutes before filtering. Cool rapidly, cover with cling film and refrigerate.

Last minute

Pour the oil into a large 5 l. pan or into a deep fryer. Heat to 180° C. Fry the samossas in the boiling oil, in batches of 8 to 10, for 5 or 6 minutes. When they are golden and crisp, use a skimmer to remove them from the oil and drain them, and place on kitchen paper. Add salt to taste. Serve straightaway, accompanied by the red chilli sauce served in a small dish.

Alternative

250 g of sautéed and chopped shrimps can be added to the stuffing or the chilli sauce replaced with a raita sauce (see the recipe for shrimps marinated in tandoori massala on page 188).

To make 25 samossas

Ingredients

Dough

250 g	Flour
2 to 3 dl.	Water
5 g	Table sea salt
6 tbsp	Peanut oil

Stuffing

2	Large potatoes
1	Carrot
1	Leek
50 g	French beans
50 g	Peas (shelled)
1	Onion
15 g	Ginger
3 cloves	Garlic
1 sprig	Thyme
4	Carri-poulé (curry) leaves
2 tbsp	Home-made curry powder *
1 tbsp	Turmeric powder
1	Small red chilli
1/4 bunch	Coriander
	Table sea salt
3 tbsp	Peanut oil

Sauce

1/2 l.	Vegetable stock *
40 g	Cane sugar
5 g	Table sea salt
1 dl.	Rice vinegar
5 g	Ginger
1 clove	Garlic
1	Red chilli
1/2 tbsp	Tomato purée
4 tbsp	Ketchup
1 1/2 tbsp	Cornflour
2 tbsp	Peanut oil

Paste

20 g	Flour
2 dl.	Water

Oil for frying

3 l.	Peanut oil

* see basic recipes

Shrimps marinated in tandoori massala and green salad with mango and bean sprouts

Recipe

To prepare the shrimps Make a shallow incision of 0.5 cm long at each end, to reach the intestinal vein. Gently take hold of the vein and remove it. Keep in a cool place.

Peel the shallot, garlic (removing the germ), and ginger. Cut the chilli into two and remove the seeds. Wash the coriander, discard the stalks and chop up the leaves. Blend the shallot, garlic, ginger and chilli in a mixer. Next mix them with the yoghurt, tandoori massala and chopped coriander in a bowl. Mix the shrimps into the tandoori marinade and leave to marinate for 1 hour in a cool place.

To prepare the salad Wash the salad leaves and drain them. Sort through the bean sprouts and sear them rapidly in a dash of olive oil. Peel the mango and cut into thin slices (julienne). Sort through and wash the coriander, chervil and mint, and then drain them.

Last minute

Pour 2 tbsp olive oil into a very hot pan and maintain on high heat. Add the shrimps. Without stirring, wait until they become lightly golden on one side, then turn them quickly and repeat the process. Place on kitchen paper and move on immediately to the garnish.

Pour the vinegar into a salad bowl and add the oil, salt and pepper. Whisk the ingredients together. Put the salad leaves, herbs, bean sprouts and mango slices into the bowl, mix with the vinaigrette and check seasoning. Arrange the shrimps in a circle on each plate, the round side towards the edge, with a small heap of salad in the centre. Finally edge with the raita sauce.

Alternative

There are several ways of preparing raita sauce. For example, a Granny Smith apple can be used instead of cucumber.

Serves 4

Ingredients

800 g	Large shrimps (shelled)
2 tbsp	Olive oil
1/2 clove	Garlic
1/2	Shallot
10 g	Ginger
3 tbsp	Yoghurt
1/2	Red chilli
1 tbsp	Tandoori massala *
1/2 bunch	Coriander
	Table sea salt

Raita sauce

70 g	Yoghurt
1	Cucumber
	A few leaves of mint
1 pinch	Cayenne pepper
	Table sea salt

Salad

1/4	Curly endive
1	Lettuce heart
50 g	Mizuna (Japanese green salad)
50 g	Tat-soy or young spinach leaves
100 g	Bean sprouts
1	Mango
1/4 bunch	Coriander
1/4 bunch	Chervil
1/4 bunch	Mint

Vinaigrette

2 tbsp	Banyuls vinegar
6 tbsp	Taggiasche extra virgin olive oil
	Table sea salt
	Freshly ground white pepper

* see basic recipes

Creamy faye-faye crab flavoured with sherry garnished with a green vegetable salad

Recipe

To prepare the crabs Cook the crabs in *4 l.* of sea water or vegetable stock with a pinch of Cayenne pepper for 15 minutes. Remove the water and leave to cool a little. Use nutcrackers to break the shells and remove the flesh. Put the crabmeat to one side. Prepare the consommé (see the shellfish consommé recipe). Soak the 3 sheets of gelatine in cold water to soften them and then drain them. Melt the gelatine in a *1/2 l.* of hot crab consommé. Check seasoning, and stand the jelly to one side.

Whisk the cream in a bowl in ice to obtain a very thin whipped cream, whilst gradually incorporating the lemon juice. Soak the gelatine sheet in cold water to soften it, then drain. Dissolve the gelatine in a bowl using half of the hot concentrated crab coulis (see the basic recipe for shellfish coulis), then add the remaining sauce, sherry, olive oil and curry powder. Gently mix in the crabmeat. Add the whipped cream, and salt and pepper to taste.

Take 4 round plastic or stainless steel moulds, 5 cm wide and 3.5 cm high, put the mixture in a piping bag with a nozzle and fill the moulds to 3 cm. Leave in the refrigerator for at least 6 hours. Then add a layer of about 3 mm of crab jelly to each mould and chill in the refrigerator for a further 2 hours.

To prepare the vegetables Wash the brèdes, separate the stalks from the leaves and whittle the stalks into petal shapes using a sharp knife. Remove the tip of the cucumber and cut it, unpeeled, into 5 cm slices. Cut into 6 and shape them as for the brèdes stalks. Peel the green asparagus, wash in cold water and cut each asparagus diagonally into three equal parts. Remove the tips of the courgettes and cut diagonally into 1 cm slices. Peel the gourd and cut it into slices, 5 cm long. Slit the slices in the middle and remove the seeds with a teaspoon. Twist each gourd to give it the shape of a petal. Cut the chou-chou into two and peel them. Use a spoon to scoop out balls of chou-chou. Discard the green part and roots of the leeks, and then rinse the leeks thoroughly in lukewarm water and bunch them together with trussing string.

Fill a large pan with iced water, and fill another large pan with water and bring it to the boil. Salt and add the brèdes, and stir. Cook for about 2 minutes (the leaves must remain green and slightly crisp). Drain the brèdes, dip them into the pan of iced water, and drain them again. Cook all the other vegetables in the same way in the pan one after the other (leave the leeks till last), then cool them in the iced water and drain them.

Wash the fresh herbs, remove the stalks and chop up half the leaves of each. Leave the rest of the leaves.

Last minute

Mix the green vegetables, seasoned with the Royal Palm vinaigrette, in a bowl, adding the chopped herbs. Check seasoning. Place the creamy crab moulds in the middle of 4 very cool dishes, then gently remove the moulds. Place the green vegetable salad around and sprinkle with the uncut herb leaves. Serve immediately accompanied by the toast melba.

Alternative

Faye-faye crabs can be replaced by spider crabs or common crabs. A lettuce salad could be used instead of the vegetable salad.

Serves 4

Ingredients

2	Faye-faye (spanner) crabs, weighing 500 g each
4 dl.	Sea water or vegetable stock *
1 pinch	Cayenne pepper

Creamy crab

60 g	Faye-faye crab meat
16 cl.	Dry sherry
16 cl.	Taggiasche extra virgin olive oil
66 cl.	Crab (shellfish) coulis *
	Dash of lemon juice
1 sheet	Gelatine
1 pinch	Home-made curry powder *
160 g	Crème fraîche
	Table sea salt
	Freshly ground pepper

Crab jelly

1/2 l.	Crab (shellfish) consommé *
3 sheets	Gelatine

Green vegetable salad

1	Chou-chou (cho-cho)
2	Brèdes Tom-Pouce (baby bok-choy)
1/2	Green cucumber
9	Green asparagus
6	Young leeks
4	Baby courgettes
1/2	Snakegourd
1/2 bunch	Flat-leaved parsley
1/2 bunch	Chervil
1/2 bunch	Tarragon
1/2 bunch	Dill
1/2 dl.	Royal Palm Vinaigrette *

Served with

8	Toast melba *

* see basic recipes

Chinese chicken and shrimp salad with sesame bread

Recipe

Remove the skin from the chicken breasts. Salt and pepper. Brush them with 3 tbsp of olive oil. Set the grill to high. Grill the chicken breasts on both sides. Remove from the grill and leave them to cool down. Cut the chicken breasts into thin slices.

To prepare the shrimps Make a shallow incision at each end, 0.5 cm long, to remove the intestinal vein. Pour 3 tbsp olive oil into a very hot pan and maintain on high heat. Add the shrimps. Do not stir them but wait until they become slightly golden on one side, then turn them quickly and continue to cook on the other side. Place them on kitchen paper.

To prepare the vegetables Remove the tips of the French beans by breaking them off between the thumb and forefinger. String them, wash in cold water and drain them in a colander. Fill a large pan with iced water. Fill another large pan with water, bring it to the boil, add salt and then the French beans. Cook for about 4 minutes (the French beans must remain green and crisp). Drain, dip them into the iced water, rinse under cold water and drain them again.

Peel the peppers, remove the seeds and the white parts found inside, then cut them into sticks, 7 cm long and 0.5 cm wide. Heat 2 tbsp peanut oil in a pan on moderate heat. Add the peppers and fry for 2 to 3 minutes, until tender. Add salt and pepper. Place them on kitchen paper.

Sort through the bean sprouts. Cut the chillies into two, remove the seeds and slice them into thin julienne. Snip up the chives.

Pour the peanut oil into a deep-fat fryer and heat it to 180° C. Fry the cashew nuts, leaving them for 2 to 3 minutes in the boiling oil. When they are golden, drain them in a colander and place them on kitchen paper. Add salt.

Wash the coriander, discard the stalks and make small bunches with the leaves.

To prepare the sesame bread Heat the sesame seeds in a frying pan to dry them out. Remove them from the pan when the seeds are golden.

Cut 4 slices, 7 mm thick, from the loaf. Spread salted butter on the slices and sprinkle with roasted sesame seeds. Cut into fingers, 8 cm long and 2.5 cm wide.

Last minute

Put the chicken slices, sautéed shrimps, the peppers, beans, sprouts, red chilli, cashew nuts and chives into a salad bowl, mix them with *1¹/₂ dl.* of Chinese vinaigrette and check seasoning. Line a large salad bowl with banana leaves cut into circles. Place the salad on the leaves, and decorate with the fresh coriander leaves. Serve straightaway.

Alternative

Ordinary shrimps or small scampi can be used instead of the chevrettes de mer.

Serves 4

Ingredients

2	Chicken breasts (weighing a total of about 350 g)
8 tbsp	Olive oil
350 g	Chevrettes de mer shrimps (peeled)
80 g	Bean sprouts
150 g	Red peppers
150 g	Green peppers
150 g	French beans or snowpeas
1	Red chilli
20 g	Chives
1/2 bunch	Coriander
2 dl.	Peanut oil
30 g	Cashew nuts
1	Banana leaf (optional)
1¹/₂ dl.	Chinese vinaigrette *
	Table sea salt

Oil for frying

1 l.	Peanut oil

Sesame bread

	Wholemeal loaf of bread
20 g	Salted butter
50 g	Sesame seeds

* see basic recipes

Crispy sweet potato layers with pan-fried duck foie gras cep mushrooms and chestnut shavings

Recipe

To prepare 12 feuillantines Wash the sweet potatoes. Cook them unpeeled in salted water for 30 to 35 minutes on moderate heat. Use a sharp knife to check whether they are cooked; it should be able to pierce and come out of the potato fairly easily. Drain and peel them quickly, whilst they are still hot. Mash through a sieve.

Put the purée in a pan and add 2 egg whites, 25 g soft butter, salt and pepper, then mix vigorously with a rubber spatula. Using a tablespoon, place small scoops of the mixture onto a non-stick tray. Gently flatten the purée into 1 mm thick layers about 90 mm across, using a spatula that has been dipped in cold water. Cook in an oven preheated to 160° C. The feuillantines take 2 to 3 minutes to cook. Once they are golden, remove them from the oven, let them cool down and then keep them in an airtight container.

To prepare the garnish Scrub the ceps, clean the stalks thoroughly, cut them into thick slices and put them to one side on a clean cloth. Wash the cep trimmings and put them to one side for the sauce. Wash the chervil, discard the stalks, and thinly snip up the leaves. Cut the chestnuts with a mandoline into forty or so thin shavings.

To prepare the sauce Peel the shallots and cut them up thinly. Heat 1 tbsp olive oil in a small thick-bottomed pan, add the shallots and the cep trimmings. Stir for 2 minutes on low heat, until they are golden. Add the sugar and caramelise for 5 minutes on very low heat, stirring continuously. Add the vinegar and let it evaporate. Add the duck stock. Reduce the sauce to concentrate the taste, making sure to remove any scum. Filter through a muslin conical-shaped sieve, check seasoning and keep hot.

Last minute

Remove any traces of gall that might remain on the foie gras, cut it diagonally into 8 slices of 70 g each and keep in a cool place.

Heat the sweet potato jam and keep it covered.

Heat the olive oil in a 30 cm wide pan, place the cep slices in the pan, colour them on each side and add the chervil. Salt and pepper.

Meanwhile, season the foie gras slices with salt. Cook them in a very hot frying pan, without adding any fat, for 2 minutes on each side, making sure not to burn them. Sprinkle with fleur de sel.

To serve Take 4 pre-warmed plates. Put a small knob of sweet potato jam in the middle of each plate on top of 1 feuillantine. Make a small bed (about 80 mm across) in the jam, and place half of the fried ceps and chestnut shavings in the middle. Then add a slice of hot foie gras and a second feuillantine with a small knob of sweet potato jam, and make another small bed in the middle of that. Garnish it with the other half of the ceps and chestnut shavings. Add a second slice of foie gras and the third feuillantine. Pour sauce around the bottom of the plate and serve straightaway.

Note In all recipes, crushed course sea salt can be used instead of fleur de sel, if necessary.

Serves 4

Ingredients

600 g	Landais duck foie gras
	Fleur de sel
	Table sea salt
	Freshly ground white pepper

Sweet potato layers (feuillantines)

500 g	Sweet potatoes
2	Egg whites
25 g	Echiré butter (softened)
	Table sea salt
	Freshly ground white pepper

Garnish

250 g	Ceps (porcini mushrooms)
1/2 bunch	Chervil
3 tbsp	Olive Oil
8 to 10	Vacuum packed chestnuts
6 tbsp	Sweet potato jam *

Sauce

75 g	Shallots
40 g	Cep trimmings
1 tbsp	Olive oil
1 tbsp	Cane sugar
3 tbsp	Old red wine vinegar
3 dl.	Duck stock *

* see basic recipes

Whisky-flavoured urchin bisque with fennel and herb ravioli

Recipe

To prepare the urchins Ask the fishmonger to open the urchins or open them yourself (wearing gloves) from the soft part that surrounds the mouth, with pointed scissors: cut round to mid-height and after removing the crown, remove the digestive track. Detach the roe with a teaspoon and set aside 150 g for the butter and the rest of the roe in their filtered juice for the garnish. Crush the urchin shells in a pan.

To prepare the urchin butter Crush the 150 g of urchin roe with a fork in a bowl, then mix into a paste with the softened butter. Sieve the mixture. Place this butter into a plastic container with a lid and keep in the refrigerator. When set, cut into small, 1 cm cubes.

To prepare the bisque Peel and cut the shallots and leeks into small, even pieces (mirepoix). Heat the oil in a 30 cm frying pan and drop in the crushed urchins. Sweat dry before adding the garnish of shallots and leeks. Combine for 5 minutes. Pour in the whisky and then the white wine, letting them evaporate and reduce until "dry". Pour the urchin juice and vegetable stock into the frying pan. Add the bouquet garni and crushed black pepper.

Simmer slowly for 30 minutes, removing any scum. Remove from the stove. Leave to stand for 10 minutes before filtering the stock through a muslin conical-shaped sieve. Add the cream, bring to the boil and reduce. Season to taste (the urchins will have salted the bisque slightly already).

To prepare the dough Use the bowl of a food processor to prepare the ravioli dough. Place all the ingredients (semolina, rice and wheat flour, and eggs and egg yolks) into the bowl, switch on the processor and run until the dough forms a smooth and even ball. Wrap the dough in cling film and refrigerate. The longer it stands, the easier it will be to roll out.

To prepare the stuffing of fennel and herbs Rinse the fennel and dice into thin brunoise. Rinse the herbs, pat them dry, and chop them up thinly. Cook the fennel in butter in a hot frying pan. Stir in the herbs when the fennel is cooked, and season with salt and pepper. Remove from the stove and leave to cool down.

To prepare the ravioli Roll out the dough thinly with a rolling pin and place a strip of dough on the lightly floured work surface. Use a pastry cutter to cut out circles of about 5 cm diameter. Place a teaspoon of stuffing in the centre of each circle and with a brush moisten the edge of half of the circle of pastry with water. Holding the circle in the palm of your hand, fold one side onto the other to close in the stuffing. Pinch the edges to stick them together. Place the ravioli to dry on a clean cloth, keeping them apart so that they do not stick together.

Last minute

Cook the ravioli in boiling salted water. They are ready when they float to the surface. Place them into hot soup bowls and surround them with urchin roe. Boil the bisque, stirring briskly and mix in the urchin butter (the bisque must not boil anymore or it will lose its urchin roe taste). Pour the frothy bisque into the bowl and sprinkle with herbs (dill, parsley, chives, chervil and tarragon).

Note The best urchins are flat and are 6 to 8 cm. They are greenish brown or very deep purple verging on black, and bristle with long moving spines.

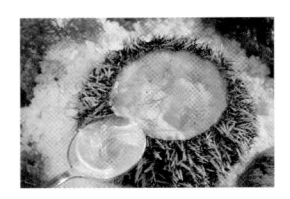

Serves 4

Ingredients

15	Large sea urchins
40 g	Leeks
60 g	Shallots
3 tbsp	Olive oil
1 dl.	Dry white wine
4 tbsp	Malt whisky
1	Bouquet garni *
1 tbsp	Crushed black pepper *
2 l.	Vegetable stock *
3 dl.	Urchin juice (the liquid from the urchins)
1 1/2 dl.	Crème fraîche
1/2 cup	Herbs (dill, parsley, chives, chervil and tarragon)
	Table sea salt

Sea urchin butter

150 g	Urchin roe
150 g	Echiré butter (softened)

Ravioli stuffing

350 g	Fennel bulbs
20 g	Butter
50 g	Chopped herbs (parsley, dill, chervil, tarragon and chives)

Ravioli dough

250 g	Italian semolina flour
100 g	Rice flour
50 g	Wheat flour
240 g	Egg yolks
2	Eggs

* see basic recipes

Pan-fried red mullet with pink peppers and home-made curry in salted Queen Victoria pineapple-butter sauce

Recipe

To prepare the fish Remove the scales, and then the heads and innards. Rinse them under cold water. Detach the fish fillets. Carefully remove the small bones with a pair of tweezers or ask your fishmonger to remove them. Place in the refrigerator.

To prepare the pineapple butter Heat a small knob of butter in a small, thick-bottomed pan, add the peeled and thinly chopped ginger, and sweat on high heat for 30 seconds. Add the pineapple juice and reduce to *250 ml.* to concentrate the taste. With a hand-held mixer, whip with butter and check seasoning. Add the juice of one lemon and then sieve. Place on one side but make sure it stays warm.

To prepare the garnish Dice the pineapple into small 7 mm brunoise and cook in butter. Lightly season with salt. Cut the courgettes into 5 mm thick strips and cook in a dash of olive oil. Season with salt and pepper. The pineapple and courgettes need to be cooked just before serving.

Last Minute

Sprinkle the fish fillets with sea salt and freshly ground white pepper. Heat the oil over a hot flame in a large non-stick pan. When the oil is very hot, add the rouget fillets, skin-side down. Three quarters of the way through cooking, turn the fish, lower the heat and then add the home-made curry powder, the slightly crushed pink pepper and 1 tbsp butter. Braise for a few seconds, then remove from the stove. The flesh of the fish should be opaque but still supple and moist. Place the strips of courgettes on 4 pre-warmed plates and place the fish on top. Top each fillet with 1/2 tbsp of the cooking juice from the pan, and sprinkle with fleur de sel. Surround with the shimmering hot pineapple brunoise and the nasturtium petals. Heat the salted pineapple butter and make it frothy with a hand-held mixer, arrange round the fish fillets and serve straightaway.

Alternative

Rouget de roche is one of the many varieties of goatfish, and resembles red mullet. Gilt-head bream (dorade Royale) can be used as an alternative.

Serves 4

Ingredients

2	Rougets de roche (each about 700 g)
1 1/2 tbsp	Pink pepper
1 tbsp	Home-made curry powder *
1 tbsp	Butter
	Table sea salt
	Fleur de sel
	Freshly ground white pepper

Pineapple butter

1 l.	Victoria pineapple juice
	Juice of 1 Meyer lemon or Tahiti lime
5 g	Ginger
125 g	Echiré butter

Garnish

1/4	Queen Victoria pineapple
4	Nasturtium flowers
8	Courgettes
3 tbsp	Olive oil

* see basic recipes

Rock lobster in tandoori massala with sweet potato fondant and coriander pesto sauce

Recipe

To prepare the rock lobster Wash the lobsters and twist off the tails. Cut the shell with a pair of scissors, carefully remove the meat and lightly trim the ends. Lay flat on a plate, belly-side down. Make a shallow incision, about 0.5 cm long, at each end in order to reach the intestine. Gently take hold of the intestine and remove it. Leave to stand in a cool place.

To prepare the sauce Peel and chop the shallot, celery, fennel, coriander and the white part of the leek into thin mirepoix. Crush the lobster heads as thinly as possible in the bowl of a food processor. Heat the oil in an 18 cm frying pan, add the heads and brown slightly before adding the aromatic garnishes cut into mirepoix. Stir for 1 minute. Pour in the wine, let it evaporate and reduce until "dry". Pour in water to cover, add a pinch of salt, simmer for 30 minutes and then remove from the stove. Allow to stand for 10 minutes, then filter the coulis through a muslin conical-shaped sieve, pressing the crushed lobster well to extract all the juice.

Heat a small knob of butter in a small thick-bottomed pan, add the peeled and thinly chopped ginger and the curry powder. Sweat for 30 seconds on high heat, then add the coulis and reduce to concentrate the taste. Add the cream and further reduce to $2^{1/2}$ dl. Whip into a butter with a hand-held mixer, check seasoning, then sieve. Keep the sauce warm.

To prepare the garnish Wash and peel the sweet potatoes. Cut into 12 round slices, 3 to 6 mm thick. Brown in a pan with a knob of butter and cover halfway with the chicken stock. Salt and pepper. Cover with a piece of greaseproof paper and cook slowly for 6 to 7 minutes, until the sweet potatoes are tender. Use the tip of a knife to check that they are done. Correct seasoning.

Use a sharp knife to cut off the bottoms and the conical core (about 0.5 cm) of the brèdes. Wash them carefully with water, spreading out the stalks to remove all the soil, and slice them into two lengthwise. Fill a large pan with iced water. Fill another large pan with water, bring it to the boil, add salt and then the brèdes. Cook them for about 6 minutes (they should remain green and slightly crisp), remove with a skimmer, dip in the iced water and drain them.

To prepare the pesto Clean the coriander leaves and discard the stalks. Peel and chop the ginger. Peel the garlic clove, cut it into two and remove the germ. Rinse the chillies, remove the seeds and mix all the ingredients in the bowl of a food processor together with the olive oil. Salt. Process until all the ingredients are blended together into a liquid paste. Put the mixture in a bowl, in the refrigerator.

Last minute

Sprinkle the lobster tails with salt and pepper. Heat the oil on moderate heat in a small 16 cm non-stick pan. Add the shelled lobster tails once the oil is hot. Halfway through cooking, turn them over and lower the heat. Add the tandoori massala, 1 tbsp butter and braise for a few seconds. Remove from the stove. The lobster must be firm, soft and still moist. Heat the brèdes in a frying pan, using 2 tbsp olive oil and 1/2 tbsp butter. Season with salt and pepper.

Arrange the brèdes in 4 large, pre-warmed soup dishes, along with the hot sweet potato rounds, and place the lobster tails on top. Dress each tail with 1/2 tbsp of the cooking butter from the pan and sprinkle with fleur de sel. Heat up the sauce and make it frothy with a hand-held mixer. Edge the lobster with the sauce and use a teaspoon to add a few drops of the coriander pesto over the sauce. Serve immediately.

Alternative *Brittany lobster can be used instead of rock lobster. Rock lobster is also known as crawfish (not to be confused with crayfish).*

Serves 4

Ingredients

4	Rock lobsters (each 500 g)
3 tbsp	Olive oil
1 tbsp	Tandoori massala *
1 tbsp	Echiré butter
	Fleur de sel
	Table sea salt
	Freshly ground white pepper

Sauce

125 g	Echiré butter
2 tbsp	Crème fraîche
1/2 dl.	Dry white wine
1 tsp	Home-made curry powder *
1	Shallot
1 stick	Celery
1/2	Leek
1/2	Fennel bulb
5 g sprigs	Coriander
10 g	Ginger
1 piece	Leek

Garnish

500 g	Sweet potatoes
1 1/2 tbsp	Butter
3 dl.	Poultry stock *
8	Brèdes Tom-Pouce (baby bok-choy)
2 tbsp	Olive oil

Pesto

100 g	Fresh coriander
5 g	Ginger
1 clove	Garlic
1/4	Red chilli
1 1/2 dl.	Taggiasche extra virgin olive oil

* see basic recipes

Shrimp curry
with coconut and banana buds

Recipe

To prepare the prawns Make a shallow incision in each shrimp, 0.5 cm long, at each end to reach the intestinal vein. Gently take hold of the vein and remove it.

To prepare the banana Remove the outside leaves surrounding the banana bud and take off the flowers until the pinkish-white heart appears. Use an oiled knife to cut the bud into four lengthwise. Remove the hard stamen at the centre of each flower as well: it is a delicate but necessary operation. After preparing the bud, slice and blanch it in lightly salted water.

To prepare the curry Cut the chillies into two, remove the seeds and dice into thin brunoise. Peel the ginger and the garlic (removing the germ) and grind in a mortar. Peel and slice the onion. Wash the coriander, remove the stalks and chop up the leaves. Snip up the chives. Remove the core from the tomato. Dip the tomato in 2 l. of boiling water. Remove it after thirty seconds and dip it immediately into iced water. Peel the tomato, cut it into two, remove the seeds and chop it up.

Using a thick-bottomed casserole dish, heat 3 tbsp olive oil on moderate heat and add the thinly sliced onion. Sweat for 3 to 4 minutes, then add the garlic, ginger, chilli, chopped tomato and all the spices (except the powdered turmeric), stirring continuously.

Add the thyme and the carri-poulé leaves. Add the fish stock and cook slowly for 20 minutes, stirring from time to time. Then add the coconut milk and blend it in carefully with a spatula. Check seasoning.

Last minute

Season the shrimps with table sea salt and sprinkle them with powdered turmeric. Pour 3 tbsp olive oil into a hot pan at high heat. Add the shrimps and cook on both sides without stirring. Use a skimmer to drain the shrimps. Add them to the curry sauce, together with the blanched banana buds and flowers and simmer for 5 minutes. Sprinkle with chopped coriander and chives. Serve straightaway on pre-heated plates, with the white basmati rice, fricasséed lentils and the various chutneys.

Alternative

The shrimps may be replaced with giant prawns (gambas) or fresh-water prawns.

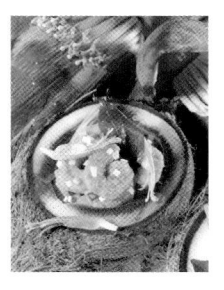

Serves 4

Ingredients

800 g	Shelled shrimps
4 dl.	Coconut milk
1	Banana bud
3	Onions
5 cloves	Garlic
10 g	Ginger
4	Carri-poulé (curry) leaves
1 sprig	Thyme
1/2 bunch	Coriander
1/2 bunch	Chives
1	Vine tomato (ripe)
1	Red chilli
5 tbsp	Home-made curry powder *
1/2 tsp	Powdered turmeric
1 pinch	Ground cumin
1/2 piece	Cassia cinnamon
6 tbsp	Olive oil
4 dl.	Fish stock *
	Table sea salt

Served with

4 portions	Basmati rice *
4 portions	Black lentil fricassée *
4 portions	Various chutneys *

* *see basic recipes*

Rack of cochon marron roasted in five spices and glazed with Rodriguan honey

Recipe

Sprinkle the rack of pork with 1 tsp of the five spices mixture and *1 dl.* olive oil, making sure the spices stick to the meat. Leave to marinate for 12 hours.

To prepare the vegetables Sort through the bean sprouts. Peel the onion and chop it thinly. Rinse and drain the chives and snip them up thinly. Cut the chou-chou into two, peel and slice, and cut into sticks. Do not discard the central kernels. Heat the oil in a 30 cm pan. Add the chou-chou sticks, sauté for 3 minutes on moderate heat, add the thinly sliced onion and bean sprouts and sweat for 2 more minutes, stirring with a wooden spatula. Add the Kikkoman soy sauce, pepper, chives, and the sliced chou-chou kernels. Keep warm. Prepare the confit shallots, as in the basic recipe.

To prepare the wild boar Preheat the oven to 180° C. Heat 3 tbsp olive oil and a knob of butter in a large 30 cm oven-proof pan. Remove the rack from its marinade and sprinkle with salt. Brown for 4 minutes on each side, then put it in the oven for 12 minutes, basting frequently. Heat the honey and sugar in a small 12 cm saucepan. Deglaze with rice vinegar and let it evaporate a little. Remove from the stove. Take the meat out of the oven, place on a rack over a dish, to let the juices drain, and keep it warm. Discarding the fat, pour the cochon marron stock into the saucepan and reduce. Filter through a thin conical sieve, check seasoning and keep hot.

Last minute

Brush both sides of the meat two or three times with the honey glaze and return it to the oven to caramelise. Slice it into cutlets and sprinkle with fleur de sel. Place the chou-chou in the middle of 4 pre-heated plates. Arrange the cutlets in the form of a fan around the brèdes. Add the shimmering hot confit shallots. At the same time, heat the sauce and add the remaining, filtered juices. Pour into a gravy boat and serve straightaway.

Alternative

Good quality farm pork, for example Saint Yrieix pork from Limousin, can be used instead of wild boar or cochon marron.

Serves 4

Ingredients

2	Rack of cochon marron (wild boar)
1 tsp	Five spices *
25 g	Eucalyptus honey
15 g	Cane sugar
1 dl.	Japanese rice vinegar
3 dl.	Cochon marron stock *
	Fleur de sel
	Table sea salt

Vegetables

4	Chou-chou (cho-cho)
1	Onion
100 g	Bean sprouts
2 tbsp	Olive oil
2 tbsp	Kikkoman soy sauce
	Freshly ground white pepper
1/2 bunch	Chives
8 portions	Confit shallots *

* see basic recipes

Potato and cauliflower curry
with perfumed Basmati rice and green mango pickles

Recipe

Peel the ginger and garlic (remove the germ) and grind in a mortar. Peel and slice the onions. Wash the chilli, cut into two, remove the seeds and dice into thin brunoise. Removing the stalks, clean the coriander leaves and chop them up. Snip up the chives. Remove the core from the tomatoes, bring 5 l. of water to the boil, dip in the tomatoes, remove them after 30 seconds and immediately dip them in cold water. Peel the tomatoes, cut them into two, remove the seeds and chop them up. Take the cauliflower, discard the green leaves and soak the rest in water mixed with the vinegar for 10 minutes. Then rinse under running water, remove the stalk and break up into smaller pieces. Pour the oil into a large 4 l. pan or deep fryer. Heat the oil to 150°C. Meanwhile wash and peel the potatoes, and chop them into 2 cm cubes. Add salt and a pinch of turmeric. Fry the cauliflower and the potatoes separately for 3 to 4 minutes in boiling oil. When the potatoes and cauliflower turn slightly golden, use the point of a knife to check that they are cooked, remove them from the oil and put them aside on kitchen paper. Melt the ghee in a thick-bottomed pan on moderate heat and add the thinly sliced onions, cinnamon, cumin, cardamom and cloves.

Sweat for a few seconds and add the crushed garlic and ginger. Then add the curry powder, turmeric, chopped tomatoes and ground mustard. Cook slowly for at least 15 minutes. Pour in the vegetable stock, add the thyme, carri-poulé leaves, chilli and tamarind. Season and simmer. As soon as the sauce thickens, add the potatoes. After cooking for 10 minutes, add the cauliflower and the garam massala. Cook for a few minutes; the cauliflower should remain firm. Finish by sprinkling with coriander and chives, and mix carefully with a spatula. Check seasoning.

Last minute

Arrange the potato and cauliflower curry in a pre-heated dish. Serve with perfumed or Basmati rice and the lentils. The pickles and various chutneys should be served separately in small bowls.

Alternative

The curry can be adapted to personal preferences and to what is available in the market. For example, peas can be added or cauliflower replaced by another vegetable.

Serves 4

Ingredients

300 g	Onions
30 g	Garlic
30 g	Ginger
30 g	Ghee *
1 stick	Cassia cinnamon
5	Cardamom (green)
3	Cloves
1 tbsp	Cumin
2 tbsp	Home-made Curry powder *
1 tbsp	Powdered turmeric
500 g	Vine tomatoes (ripe)
1 tbsp	Garam massala *
	Vegetable stock *
1 sprig	Thyme
1 sprig	Carri-poulé (curry) leaves
1	Chilli
1 tbsp	Ground mustard seeds
1 tbsp	Tamarind pulp *
750 g	Cauliflower
1 tbsp	Vinegar
750 g	Potatoes
2 l.	Peanut oil
1 bunch	Chives
1 bunch	Coriander
	Table sea salt

Served with

4 portions	Basmati rice *
4 portions	Black lentil fricassée *
4 portions	Green mango pickles *
4 portions	Various chutneys *

see basic recipes

Java deer roasted in sweet spices with goyaves de Chine sauce and arouille violette purée

Recipe

To be prepared 7 days in advance Heat the mixture of spices in a hot pan for 3 minutes to bring out the flavours. When it has cooled down a little, grind it in a blender or a coffee grinder and keep in an airtight jar.

Clean, trim and bone the venison, removing the nerves and fat. Do not discard the trimmings but keep them for the gravy. Tie the venison and sprinkle it generously with 2 tbsp of the spices, marinate for 7 days, covered with olive oil and cellophane, in the refrigerator.

The day of the meal In a small thick-bottomed pan, reduce the red wine vinegar, red wine, port, crushed black pepper and the wild guavas cut into quarters. Allow to evaporate and reduce completely, then add the venison stock. Reduce the sauce to concentrate the taste, carefully removing the scum. Filter through a muslin conical sieve, check seasoning and keep hot.

To prepare the garnish Preheat the oven to 180° C. Scrub the beetroot under cold water, but do not peel them. Wrap them in aluminium foil and place them on a layer of salt in a roasting pan. Cook till tender for 50 minutes in the oven. Peel them with a knife, then cut them into rounds, 2.5 to 3 mm thick. Sauté them in a pan with a knob of butter and check seasoning.

Wash and peel the turnips with a knife, giving them a roundish shape. Cut them into slices, 2.5 to 3 mm thick. Blanch them for 1 minute to remove the bitterness. Sauté them in a knob of butter in a pan, and half fill the pan with poultry stock. Cover with a piece of greaseproof paper and cook slowly for 7 minutes until tender. Check seasoning.

Fry the wild guavas with a knob of butter in a pan on high heat. Add a little sugar and caramelise. Keep hot.

To cook the meat Preheat the oven to 180° C. Having left the venison to stand for 7 days, remove it from the marinade. Season the gigot with sea salt. Heat 3 tbsp olive oil and a knob of butter in a 30 cm frying pan. Baste the joint all over. Cook in the oven for 20 minutes, basting often. Ensure it remains pink, so that it retains its taste and tenderness. Leave it to stand at room temperature.

Last minute

Reheat the gigot for 4 minutes in the oven. Cut it into thin slices, 5 mm thick. Serve the meat on 4 pre-heated plates and sprinkle with fleur de sel. Surround the meat with beetroot, turnips, and the shimmering hot guavas. Put the arouille violette purée into a hot dish. Heat the sauce, and after filtering them, add the juices left over from carving the gigot. Pour the sauce into a gravy boat. Serve straightaway.

Note The venison should remain pinkish after cooking, so that its taste and tenderness are not impaired. This recipe will work for most kinds of venison.

Serves 4

Ingredients

1 1/2 kg	Venison gigot (haunch or leg)
1 l.	Olive oil
	Table sea salt
	Fleur de sel

Mild spice mixture

5 g	Coriander seeds
10 g	White pepper
6 g	Black mustard seeds
6 g	Yellow mustard seeds
6 g	Fennel seeds
10 g	Black pepper
20 g	Sichuan pepper
10 g	Cassio cinnamon

Guava sauce

1 tbsp	Red wine vinegar
1/3 dl.	Red wine
1/2 dl.	Port
1/2 tsp	Crushed black pepper *
150 g	Goyaves de Chine (wild guavas)
3 dl.	Venison stock *

Garnish

3	Large beetroot (of even size)
3	Large turnips
3 dl.	Poultry stock *
12	Goyaves de Chine (of even size, washed)
1 tsp	Cane sugar
3 tbsp	Echiré butter
	Freshly ground white pepper

Served with

4 portions	Arouille violette (taro) purée *

* see basic recipes

Asian-style poached and glazed lamb shank with brèdes Tom-Pouce, confit tomatoes and shii-take mushrooms

Recipe

To prepare the meat Remove the nerves and fat, and tie up each piece. Peel and slice the ginger into julienne. Peel and chop the shallots and the garlic cloves (removing the germ). Scrub the mandarins under running water, remove the peel leaving the white pith, and shred the peel lengthwise into thin slices.

Pour the chicken stock into a small 18 cm pan and add the ginger, shallots, garlic, the peel of one mandarin, the soy sauces, sugar, anise and cinnamon, and then add the lamb. Boil slowly for 1¹/₂ hours, being sure to remove any scum that may form. Then use a wire-mesh strainer to remove the meat. Keep the meat warm.

Bring the chicken stock and its seasonings quickly to the boil. Turn down the heat and let it cook slowly, removing any scum, so that the stock is reduced to about *1 l*. Keep hot

To prepare the peel Bring the remainder of the mandarin peel slices to the boil in a pan filled with *4 dl.* of water, and keep boiling for 1 minute. Repeat the process three times, then add 150 g sugar to produce a syrup. Drain and leave to crystallise on low heat.

To prepare the vegetables Peel and slice the ginger into very thin julienne. Cut the chilli into two, remove the seeds and dice into very thin brunoise. Wash the chervil, discard the stalks and snip up the leaves thinly. Remove the outer fennel layer and cut off the tips. Prepare the leeks, cutting off the roots at the bottom of the bulb. Remove the top of the leaves, keeping only one third of green to two thirds of white. Remove the outer leaf. Carefully rinse the leeks under running water, separating the leaves to remove any soil more easily. Whittle the stalks of the brèdes into a football-type shape. Trim and rinse the shii-take mushrooms, drain them and keep them whole.

Take an 18 cm pan with a lid. Put in the olive oil and the butter, ginger julienne, red chilli and half the chicken stock. Heat slowly. Add the fennel. Salt and pepper. Cover and cook slowly for 5 minutes. Add the leeks and continue cooking for another 5 minutes, until the vegetables are tender. Keep an eye on the vegetables and shake the pan from time to time to prevent the vegetables from browning. Then add the shii-take, confit tomato quarters and the confit garlic and continue to cook for 1 or 2 minutes. Add the snipped chervil at the end.

Last minute

Place the lamb in a 24 cm pan with *6 dl.* of the reduced stock and allow it to glaze for at least 20 minutes in an oven at 180° C, basting frequently. Serve the meat on 4 pre-heated plates. Surround it with the hot confit vegetables. At the same time, heat the cooking juices and whisk in one tsp sesame oil. Check seasoning. Top the meat with a little of the juices, add a few candied mandarin julienne and sprinkle them with fleur de sel.

Note Use the shanks of the back legs as they are bigger.

Serves 4

Ingredients

4	Lamb shanks (unboned, of about 450 g each)
3 l.	White chicken stock *
25 g	Ginger
10 cloves	Garlic
3	Shallots
30 dl.	Light soy sauce
1 tbsp	Kikkoman soy sauce
50 g	Cane sugar
2	Star (Chinese) anise
3 sticks	Cassia cinnamon
2	Clémentines or mandarins
150 g	Cane sugar
1 tsp	Sesame oil
	Table sea salt
	Fleur de sel

Vegetables

1/2	Red chilli
10 g	Ginger
4	Brèdes Tom-Pouce (baby bok-choy)
20	Confit tomato quarters *
4	Small fennel bulbs
12	Young leeks
250 g	Shii-take mushrooms
12 cloves	New garlic confit *
25 g	Echiré butter
3 tbsp	Olive oil
3 dl.	White chicken stock *
1/2 bunch	Chervil

* *see basic recipes*

Roast duck breast
with cinnamon kofta in a ti-chinois sauce

Recipe

To prepare the ducklings Remove the feathers, singe and clean out the ducklings, putting the giblets (liver, gizzard and heart) to one side. Remove the wings, neck and lower legs and cut them into small pieces. Take off the two thighs, discarding the skin and bones, and keep them in a cool place; they will be used later for the kofta. Trim and remove the fat from the liver, heart and gizzard. Keep them cool.

To prepare the duckling koftas Peel and chop the shallots and ginger. Rinse the mushrooms, dry them and chop them thinly. Melt a knob of butter in a 16 cm frying pan on moderate heat and sweat the shallots and ginger. Add the chopped mushrooms, salt and pepper. Raise the heat to evaporate the water from the mushrooms and then put them in the refrigerator. Dice 200 g of the meat of the chilled duckling thighs, mince very finely together with the duckling giblets as well as the duck foie gras. Add the mushroom mix (duxelle) from the refrigerator, the cream and mild spices, and season with salt and pepper.

Use this stuffing to create 4 koftas, giving each the shape of a knuckle of ham (each about 60 g). Pierce them with the cinnamon sticks and leave them in a refrigerator for about 30 minutes.

To prepare the sauce Wash the ti-chinois quats thoroughly, cut them into four and remove the pips (keep the juice). Heat the sugar in a small pan to make a thick caramel and deglaze with the wine and the vinegar, then reduce to a syrup. Add half the ti-chinois (keep the rest for later) and some ginger julienne and simmer for 1 minute. Moisten with *3 dl.* duck stock and reduce, simmering slowly for 20 minutes, without letting it boil. Sieve the sauce through a muslin conical sieve, add 1 tbsp of ti-chinois juice, mix with a spatula, check seasoning and keep warm.

To prepare the vegetables Wash the fennel, remove the outer layer and cut off the ends. Peel the carrots and turnips. Discard the stalks from the baby courgettes and the patissons, wash them and cut them into two lengthwise. Take the chervil, discard the stalks, and snip up the leaves.

Take an 18 cm pan with a lid. Add the olive oil and the butter, together with the chicken stock. Heat slowly. Add the fennel. Salt and pepper. Cover and cook slowly for 5 minutes. Add the carrots and turnips and cook for a further 5 minutes, until the vegetables are tender. Keep an eye on the pan, and shake it from time to time, to prevent the vegetables from browning. Then add the patissons and the baby courgettes and continue cooking for 3 to 4 minutes more. Check seasoning. Finish by adding the chopped chives.

To prepare the ti-chinois confit Bring the ti-chinois to the boil in a saucepan containing *4 dl.* water, and keep boiling for 1 minute at even temperature. Repeat the operation 3 times. Place the ti-chinois in a small 14 cm pan, add *4 dl.* water and the sugar, and cook slowly, stirring carefully with a wooden spatula. Continue cooking until the ti-chinois are tender. Keep warm.

To cook the ducklings Preheat the oven to 180° C. Heat 2 tbsp olive oil in a roasting pan and add the ducklings, breast-down. Place in the oven and baste frequently. After 8 minutes, remove the ducklings and sprinkle with the citrus fruit powder (mixture of orange and lemon powder) and simmer for 2 minutes, basting regularly.

To cook the koftas Cover the cinnamon sticks with aluminium foil to prevent them from burning and then cook the koftas in an oven-proof pan with 2 tbsp olive oil and brown on all sides at high temperature. Remove the fat from the pan and deglaze with *2 dl.* duck stock. Finish cooking the koftas in the oven at 160° C for 10 minutes, basting frequently with the duckling juice. Keep warm.

Last minute

Cut the foie gras into 2 cm thick slices and season them with fleur de sel. Cook the foie gras slices, without any added fat, in a very hot frying pan for 2 minutes on each side, without burning them. Place them on kitchen paper and sprinkle with fleur de sel and ground pepper. Reheat the ducklings for 3 minutes in the oven. Cut off the duck breast fillets (magrets) and carve them into slices. Serve the meat on 4 plates and sprinkle with fleur de sel, then add the koftas and the foie gras. Surround them with the hot ◊

Serves 4

Ingredients

2	Barbary ducklings (each about 1.6 kg)
120 g	Duck foie gras
7 g	Orange peel powder *
3 g	Lemon peel powder *
2 tbsp	Olive oil
	Table sea salt
	Fleur de sel
	Crushed black pepper *
	Freshly ground white pepper

Kofta

4 sticks	Cassia cinnamon (6 cm long)
5 g	Shallots
5 g	Ginger
50 g	Mushrooms (champignons de Paris)
40 g	Duck liver
25 g	Duck heart
25 g	Duck foie gras
25 cl.	Double cream
2 g	Mild spices for meat *
1 knob	Echiré butter
2 dl.	Duck stock *
2 tbsp	Olive oil

Ti-chinois sauce

100 g (8)	Ti-chinois (orange quat)
10 g	Ginger
1 1/2 dl.	Red wine
1/2 dl.	Red wine vinegar
2 tbsp	Cane sugar
3 dl.	Duck stock *

Ti-chinois confit

100 g (8)	Ti-chinois (orange quat)
100 g	Raw sugar

Vegetables

4	Small yellow patissons (custard marrows)
4	Small green patisson
4	Young fennel bulbs
8	Small turnips
8	Baby carrots
4	Baby courgettes
2 tbsp	Olive oil
25 g	Echiré butter
1/2 dl.	White chicken stock *
1/2 bunch	Chervil

* see basic recipes

vegetables. Heat the sauce, filter the juices left over from carving the meat and add them to the sauce. Top the duckling slices with this ti-chinois sauce, add the ti-chinois quarters and serve.

Alternative

Any good farm-raised duck can be used instead of Barbary ducklings, and kumquats can replace the ti-chinois.

Warm goyaves de Chine in red wine and pepper-flavoured ice-cream

Recipe

To prepare the ice-cream Bring the milk to the boil in a 30 cm wide pan. Add the pepper and the leaves. Allow to infuse for 3 minutes, then add the cream. Blend the yolks and the sugar, then whisk the mixture until it becomes whitish. Gradually add the flavoured milk. Return the pan to the stove on low heat and stir constantly with a spatula until the cream starts to thicken. Remove the cream from the stove, continue to stir for 10 seconds and pass it through a muslin conical sieve into a bowl within a bowl of ice (bain-marie). Allow it to cool down, then put all the ingredients into an ice-cream maker and turn it on. When the ice-cream is almost set, put it in an ice-tray in the freezer.

Last minute

Wash the guavas after removing the stalks. Heat a 20 cm wide pan and add the oil. Add the guavas, sauté for 30 seconds and add the butter. Then sprinkle with the sugar and allow to caramelise a little. Add the wine and let half of it evaporate, then add the pepper and simmer slowly. The fruit should remain whole. Add the raspberry sauce and cook for 2 to 3 minutes, until the fruit softens. Remove from the stove and divide the fruit into 4 bowls. Top them with the sauce in which they were cooked, add a scoop of pepper-flavoured ice-cream and decorate with a small piece of shortbread sprinkled with icing sugar.

Alternative

The guavas can also be served with vanilla ice-cream.

Serves 4

Ingredients

500 g	Goyaves de Chine (wild guavas)
1 tbsp	Olive oil
2 tbsp	Echiré butter
75 g	Brown sugar
1 pinch	Freshly ground black pepper
75 ml.	Red wine
100 ml.	Raspberry sauce *

Ice-cream infused with black pepper

500 ml.	Skimmed milk
500 ml.	Double cream
200 g	Cane sugar
1 g	Crushed black pepper *
6 g	Pepper plant leaves (optional)
9	Egg yolks

Served with

4	Shortbread biscuits *

* see basic recipes. For the shortbread, use the shortcrust pastry recipe.

Panna cotta scented with Fragrans vanilla and sweet tomatoes

Recipe

Confit tomatoes Wash the orange and lemon thoroughly. Remove the peel, working from top to bottom on a chopping board. Use a sharp knife to remove the bitter white pith. Slice the fruit into thin julienne. Bring the water, sugar, orange juice, orange peel and the split vanilla pod to the boil in a 20 cm diameter pan, and then remove from the stove. Bring 2 l. water to the boil in a 15 cm wide pan, remove the tomato cores, dip the tomatoes in the water, remove them after 30 seconds and dip them immediately into cold water. Peel them, cut them into two and remove the seeds. Cut them again into quarters and add them to the syrup. Simmer slowly for 1 hour, until the tomatoes are preserved (confites). Take two thirds of the syrup, strain through a muslin conical sieve, return it to the stove and reduce to a thick syrup. Leave it to cool down.

To prepare the panna cotta Soften the gelatine sheets in iced water. Heat the cream, split vanilla pods and sugar in a 20 cm wide pan, but do not boil. Remove from the stove, add the drained gelatine sheets and whisk. Pass the cream through a sieve and fill 4 moulds, 90 mm wide, with the cream. Leave it to set in the refrigerator.

To prepare the brunoise of dried and candied fruit Peel the pineapple and dice it into thin brunoise, 5 mm thick. Sweat the brunoise in a small 15 cm pan, caramelise a little with 1 tsp brown sugar, and season with the clove powder, anise and the inside of a vanilla pod. Chop the pistachio nuts and almonds into large pieces. Dice the orange peel and candied lemon into thin brunoise. Chop up the mint leaves. Mix all the ingredients with $1^{1/2}$ dl. of the tomato syrup and 2 tbsp of lemon juice.

Last minute

Turn out the panna cotta from the moulds onto chilled plates and place 3 tomato quarters (petals) on each panna cotta. Place the mixture of dried and candied fruit around the panna cotta. Top the tomatoes with a little of the syrup in which they were cooked and serve.

Notes For best results, it is important to have firm, plump, shiny and ripe tomatoes. Vine tomatoes are available all year round from France and Sicily. Fragrans is a variety of vanilla found in Mauritius.

Serves 4

Ingredients

Confit tomatoes

4	Vine tomatoes (ripe)
400 ml.	Water
100 ml.	Orange juice
75 g	Cane sugar
1/2	Orange (organic)
1/2	Lemon (organic)
1 pod	Fragrans vanilla

Panna Cotta

500 m	Double cream
100 g	Cane sugar
2 sheet	Gelatine
5 pods	Fragrans vanilla

Garnish

1/2	Pineapple (medium-sized)
25 g	Currants
25 g	Sicilian pistachio nuts
25 g	Almonds
20 g	Candied orange peel *
20 g	Candied lemon peel *
10 g	Garden mint
2 tbsp	Meyer lemon or Tahiti limejuice
1 pinch	Clove powder
1 pod	Fragrans vanilla
2 pinch	Star anise powder
1 tsp	Brown sugar

* *see basic recipes*

Vanilla-flavoured rice pudding covered with caramelised mango and kumquat sauce

Recipe

To prepare the rice pudding Cook the rice slowly with the milk, split vanilla pod, a pinch of salt and the orange peel in a thick-bottomed pan. Stir the rice frequently with a spatula so that it does not stick to the bottom of the pan. When the rice is almost cooked, add the sugar, mix thoroughly and continue to cook. As soon as the rice has absorbed all the liquid, turn off the heat. Remove the vanilla pod and the orange zest. Soften the gelatine in iced water, drain well and add to the hot rice, then blend with a spatula. Mix in the egg yolk and leave it to cool down.

Bring the water and sugar to the boil in a 15 cm wide pan and then leave it to cool down a little. Peel the mangoes and remove the stones. Cut them into 2 mm thick slices and put them into the syrup for 2 minutes. Drain them. Line 4 dome-shaped moulds, 50 mm wide and 30 mm high, with cling film. Arrange the mango slices in the moulds, slightly overlapping them. Use a tablespoon to press down rice around the edges. Cover with cling film and leave to set in the refrigerator for at least 3 hours.

Last minute

Turn out the moulds, sprinkle the domes with brown sugar and put them under the grill for 1 to 2 minutes. Place them in the centre of the dishes, top with kumquat sauce and serve.

Alternative

Camargue or Spanish round rice can be used instead of Arborio rice.

Serves 4

INGREDIENTS

Rice pudding

1 1/2 cl.	Full-cream milk
60 g	Cane sugar
60 g	Arborio round-grain rice
1 pinch	Table sea salt
1 pod	Fragrans vanilla
1	Egg yolk
1/2 sheet	Gelatine
1/2	Orange
500 ml.	Water
50 g	Brown sugar
3	Mangoes (ripe but firm)
	Kumquat sauce *

Mauritian vanilla crème brûlée with crispy coconut tuiles

Recipe

Preheat the oven to 100° C. Slowly heat the milk and the split and scratched vanilla pods in a 20 cm wide pan, then turn off the stove and leave to infuse for 15 minutes. Whisk the yolks and 100 g sugar in a bowl for 1 minute. Whisk in the flavoured milk and then the liquid cream. Pass through a muslin sieve, pour into 4 shallow oven-proof bowls, 10 cm wide, and place in the oven. Cook for 30 to 40 minutes, until the cream sets. Remove the dishes from the oven and leave them to cool down to room temperature. Cover with cling film and refrigerate for two hours before serving.

Last minute

Just before serving, turn on the oven grill. Take the crèmes from the refrigerator and remove the cling film. Sprinkle them with cane sugar and place under the grill until the sugar has caramelised. Serve straightaway with the crispy coconut tuiles.

Alternative

The basic crème brûlée can be made with many other flavours: for example, infuse the milk with Cassia cinnamon, Mancha saffron, jasmine or citronella.

Serves 4

INGREDIENTS

4	Egg yolks
175 g	Cane sugar
3 pods	Fragrans vanilla
400 ml.	Double cream
260 ml.	Milk

Served with

12	Coconut tuiles *

* see basic recipes

Blue Recipes

Brèdes Tom-Pouce broth with cateau bleu fish-balls and ginger-flavoured shrimps — 207

Rock lobster medallions in iced consommé flavoured with ginger, salted lemon and green salad seasoned with red chilli — 208

Creole-style octopus salad with chilli, onion and coriander — 209

Ginger-flavoured sacréchien tartar and green salad with roasted sesame seeds — 210

Coneau-coneau shellfish salad Rodriguan-style — 211

Thin slices of smoked blue marlin with herb salad and shallots — 211

Grand Gaube clams in tomato, ginger and tamarind — 212

Lagoon bouillabaisse — 213

Sacréchien cooked whole in a Black River sea-salt crust with Taggiasche oil and black pepper — 214

Shrimp rougaille and coconut-flavoured okra fricassée with Basmati rice — 215

Roast young rabbit with spicy orange powder and chou-chou in a clear gravy — 216

Madras lamb and jackfruit curry with ginger-flavoured giraumon, perfumed Basmati rice and chutneys — 217

Rasgoula with a mild spicy syrup and lime sorbet — 218

Crisp sesame cannelloni with ginger ice-cream and Queen Victoria pineapple tartar flavoured with combava lime — 219

Spring rolls filled with vanilla-flavoured papaya compote and lime sorbet — 220

Iced citrus fruit salad in saffron-flavoured syrup and vodka-flavoured pineapple sorbet — 221

Brèdes Tom-Pouce broth
with cateau bleu fish-balls and ginger-flavoured shrimps

Recipe

Peel the onions and shallots, and cut them as well as the mushrooms and leeks into fine pieces (mirepoix). Crush the bones, heads and trimmings as finely as possible. Take a 35 cm wide frying pan and sweat them dry in the peanut oil. Add the vegetable mirepoix, sauté them on high heat without browning and then add the coriander seeds. Add the water and poultry stock and a pinch of table salt.

Bring quickly to the boil, frequently skimming off the scum. Simmer for 30 minutes, without stirring. Leave to stand for 10 minutes before filtering the stock through a muslin conical sieve, pressing the bones firmly to extract all the liquid. Reduce the stock slowly to 3 l., to concentrate the flavour. Cool rapidly.

Clarification Grind the fish trimmings and the shellfish carcasses as finely as possible. Use a whisk to mix them with the egg whites. Incorporate this clarification into the cooled stock, place on moderate heat, cook and reduce, stirring very often with a spatula, until the ingredients of the clarification float to the surface and form a sort of frothy hat. Reduce the heat and stop stirring for 30 minutes (the liquid must simmer without boiling), so that the clarification is properly cooked. Pass what has become a consommé through a conical sieve lined with damp cheesecloth, transferring it gradually with a ladle, taking care not to disturb it too much. Keep it warm.

To prepare the garnish Ask the fishmonger to fillet the parrotfish and remove the bones. Mince the fish and then use a blender to obtain a smooth mixture. Slowly start to incorporate the cornflour and soy oil, stirring vigorously to make the stuffing smooth and light. Add the finely chopped red chilli, chopped coriander and fish sauce. Shape it all into small 2.5 cm balls.

Separate the leaves of the brèdes from the stalks. Cut the stalks into fine julienne and the leaves into thin strands.

Trim and wash the shii-take mushrooms, drain and leave them whole. Prepare the shrimps: make a shallow incision, 0.5 cm long, at each end, to be able to reach the black intestinal vein. Gently take hold of the vein and remove it. The shrimps should be kept cool. Peel and slice the ginger thinly into julienne. Snip up the chives.

Last minute

Cook the balls in salted water, keeping them separated. Heat the consommé to a temperature of 85° C and poach the shrimps, the brèdes stalks and the ginger julienne. Add the shii-take mushrooms and continue to cook for 1 to 2 minutes. Place 5 shrimps, 3 fish-balls, 3 shii-take and some brèdes julienne in each consommé cup. Adjust the seasoning with a few drops of fish sauce. Add a few drops of sesame oil to the very hot consommé. Sprinkle with chives, coriander leaves and the strands of brèdes leaves.

Alternative

Lemon sole can be used instead of parrotfish.

Note If you do not use the broth immediately, freeze it in *1/2 l.* portions to be able to use it later.

Serves 4

Ingredients

1.5 kg	Fish bones, heads (without the gills) and trimmings
50 g	Onion
50 g	Peeled shallots
100 g	Leeks
50 g	Mushroom stalks
3 tbsp	Peanut oil
1 tsp	Coriander seeds
	Table sea salt
1 1/2 l.	Poultry stock *
1 1/2 l.	Water
20 g	Ginger

Clarification

100 g	Raw white fish (parrotfish trimmings)
250 g	Shellfish carcasses
5	Egg whites

Fish balls

1 kg	Cateau bleu (blue-barred parrotfish)
1/2 tsp	Cornflour
2 tbsp	Coriander
1	Red chilli
1 tbsp	Thai fish sauce
1 tbsp	Soya oil

Garnish

20	Large shrimps (shelled)
1/2 bunch	Chives
1/4 bunch	Coriander
4	Brède Tom-Pouce (baby bok-choy)
12	Shii-take mushrooms
15 g	Ginger
2 tbsp	Thai fish sauce
	Sesame oil

* see basic recipes

Rock lobster medallions in iced consommé flavoured with ginger, salted lemon and green salad seasoned with red chilli

Recipe

To prepare the spiced oil Slice the chilli and sweat it in 3 tbsp olive oil, without browning, stirring all the time. Simmer for 2 minutes, then add the rest of the oil and leave to infuse for 1 hour at 60° C. Strain through a conical sieve, to collect the oil.

To poach the lobsters Bring the vegetable stock to the boil and drop in the lobsters head first. Cook for five minutes after the stock has begun to boil again. Remove the pan from the stove and leave the lobsters in the vegetable stock for between 30 minutes and 1 hour. During this time, the lobsters will continue to cook but their meat will remain tender. Remove them from the vegetable stock and drain thoroughly. Shell the lobsters, place in a dish, cover with cling film and keep refrigerated.

To prepare the consommé Prepare the lobster consommé as per the basic recipe for shellfish consommé. During the clarification, add the peeled and finely shred ginger. Stand the gelatine in cold water to soften it. Drain it and melt it in 1/2 l. of very hot consommé. Check seasoning, then refrigerate.

To prepare the garnish Remove the core from the tomato, dip it in boiling water for 30 seconds, cool it immediately in cold water, peel, quarter, and remove any water and the seeds. Then cut the quarters lengthwise into thin julienne. Wash the chilli, cut it into two, remove the seeds and slice into very thin julienne.

Sort and wash the lettuce and drain them. Sort through and wash the coriander, chervil and mint and drain them. Cut the chives into 4 cm long sticks. Sort through the bean sprouts and sweat them in 1 tbsp olive oil. Place 80 g on one side for the stuffed lettuce. Peel the snakegourds and cut into thin julienne. Prepare a large pan with iced water. Fill another large pan with water, bring it to the boil, add salt and then the snakegourds. Cook for about 1 minute (the snakegourds must remain green and slightly crisp). Drain them with a skimmer, dip in the iced water, drain again and stand on kitchen paper. Keep all the vegetables in the refrigerator. Cook the lettuce leaves in the same pan and water. As soon as they boil, make sure the leaves are all soaked, so they are easier to shape. Remove immediately and dip into iced water. Drain and place them on a tea towel.

Remove the peel from the brined lemon, without removing the white pith, cut the peel thinly lengthwise and keep it in the refrigerator.

Peel and finely slice the shallots. Wash the coriander, remove the stalks and chop up the leaves. Heat 1/2 tbsp olive oil and 1/2 tbsp sesame oil in a small frying pan. Put in the Chinese dried mushrooms and the sliced shallots. Sweat rapidly for 2 minutes. Pour in 1 dl. of water, let it evaporate, then reduce completely. Cool rapidly. Take the spinach, discard the stalks, wash the leaves thoroughly and drain. Peel the clove of garlic. In a pan, heat 1/2 tbsp olive oil and 1/2 tbsp sesame oil with 1/2 a clove of garlic, slightly crushed. When the oil begins to smoke, add the spinach leaves, salt and cook on high heat until all the leaves have become soft and the water has reduced completely. Stir with a wooden spoon.

As soon as the spinach is ready, remove it from the stove and cool rapidly. Carefully blend the spinach with 80 g of bean sprouts, the dried mushrooms and the snipped coriander. Salt and pepper. To stuff the lettuce (4 portions) take 2 small lettuce leaves and put them one on top of the other crosswise; use one leaf only if they are large. In the centre of each portion, place a ball of the spinach mixture and close the leaves around the ball to form a small packet. Place in the refrigerator.

Cut each lobster tail into ten slices. With the tip of a small knife, remove the intestine, which runs as a black line through the centre of each slice. Place a portion of stuffed lettuce in the middle of 4 very cold shallow dishes and arrange the lobster slices around them. Top the slices with the iced consommé, which should have just set. Leave the 4 dishes in the refrigerator for at least 45 minutes.

Serves 4

Ingredients

4	Rock lobsters, weighing 450 g each
5 l.	Vegetable stock *
50 g	Bean sprouts
1	Ripe tomato
100 g	Snakegourd
1	Brined lemon *

Spiced oil

5 dl.	Taggiasche extra virgin olive oil
1/2	Red chilli

Iced Consommé

1/2 l.	Lobster consommé *
35 g	Ginger
1 1/2 sheet	Gelatine

Stuffed lettuce

1	Lettuce (keep the heart for the salad)
100 g	Bean sprouts
100 g	Dried Chinese wood ear mushrooms
250 g	Spinach
1/2 clove	Garlic
1/2 tbsp	Coriander
1 tbsp	Sesame oil
2 tbsp	Taggiasche extra virgin olive oil
1	Shallot

Salad

1/4	Curly endive
1/2	Lettuce heart
50 g	Lambs' lettuce
1/4 bunch	Chives
1/4 bunch	Chervil
1/4 bunch	Coriander
1/4 bunch	Mint
1	Combava (Kaffir lime)
1	Red chilli
	Table sea salt
	Freshly ground white pepper

see basic recipes

Last minute

Surround the stuffed lettuce and lobster with bean sprouts, snakegourd and tomato julienne and brined lemon peel. Mix the herbs, 12 thin slivers of red chilli and the salad in a large bowl and stir with your hands. Grate the peel of the lime, and pour 4 tbsp of spiced oil, the peel and the juice of the lime onto the salad. Add salt and mix carefully but thoroughly so that all the elements are lightly covered with the seasoning. Place little heaps on top of the stuffed lettuce and serve immediately.

Alternative

Breton lobster can be used instead of rock lobster.

Creole-style octopus salad with chilli, onion and coriander

Recipe

To clean the octopus Remove the eyes and the mouth, rinse thoroughly under running water, then drain.

Poach the octopus in salted water in a thick-bottomed, 20 cm wide pan for about 45 to 60 minutes, remove with a skimmer and place on a plate. Use a knife to remove the reddish skin. Cut the octopus into small 1 cm pieces. Keep them in a cool place.

Peel and slice the onion thinly. Take the coriander, discard the stalks, place a few leaves to one side for later, and chop up the rest of the leaves. Remove the cores from the tomatoes, dip them for 30 seconds in boiling water, then cool them immediately in cold water. Peel and quarter them, removing the seeds and any water, then cut the quarters lengthwise into fine julienne. Wash the red chilli, cut it into two lengthwise, remove the seeds and cut it similarly into fine julienne. Snip up the chives. Peel the ginger and cut it into thin slices.

Last minute

Carefully mix the octopus slices with all the ingredients in a bowl. Add the limejuice, season the octopus salad with salt and black pepper to taste, and leave the mixture to marinate for 10 minutes in the refrigerator before serving. Place a banana leaf, cut into a 15 cm wide circle, in the middle of 4 chilled plates, arrange the octopus salad on top and sprinkle with coriander leaves. Serve straightaway.

Alternative

Squid, cut into stick shapes and seared rapidly in olive oil, can be used instead of octopus.

Note Octopus can have a rubbery texture. To avoid this problem, keep it in the freezer for a night before cooking it, to tenderise the flesh.

Serves 4

Ingredients

1 kg	Octopus
3	Ripe vine tomatoes
1	Red onion
1/2 bunch	Chives
1/2 bunch	Coriander
1	Red chilli
10 g	Ginger
	Juice of 2 Meyer lemons or Tahiti limes
10 tbsp	Taggiasche extra virgin olive oil
	Table sea salt
	Freshly ground black pepper
	Banana leaf (optional)

Ginger-flavoured sacréchien tartar and green salad with roasted sesame seeds

Recipe

Ask the fishmonger to fillet the fish and remove the skin and bones. Use a sharp Sachimi knife to dice the sacréchien fillets into 5 mm brunoise and place them in a bowl. They should be kept cool.

Cut the chillies into two, remove the seeds and cut them into very fine julienne. Wash the coriander and chervil leaves. Wash and drain the lettuce. Wash the chives, keep about 20 thin pieces for decorative purposes, and snip up the rest.

Scrub the limes under running water, remove the peel but not the white pith, cut the peel up thinly lengthwise and then dice into very fine brunoise. Squeeze the lemons and keep the juice.

Wash and peel the ginger, cut into slivers, then into fine julienne and chop into tiny pieces. Heat and roast the sesame seeds in a pan. Stop when the seeds turn golden brown.

Last minute

To prepare the tartar Place the diced sacréchien pieces in a basin, along with the snipped chives, chopped ginger and lime peel. Mix in the olive oil, limejuice, salt and pepper, and blend them carefully together with a rubber spatula. Check seasoning.

To prepare the salad Mix the lettuce, red chilli julienne, roasted sesame seeds and the herbs in a salad bowl. Mix in the vinaigrette and seasoning.

To serve Place a mould or a 60 mm pastry cutter in 4 chilled dishes. Fill them with tartar, gently holding the edge of the mould to keep it in place. Add a handful of seasoned green salad on top and a few petals of Japanese sweet and sour ginger. Also add two slices of melba toast. Decorate with the chive stems. Serve straightaway.

Alternative

Sea bass can be used instead of sacréchien.

Note There are a number of varieties of sacréchien, variously called jobfish and snapper in English.

Serves 4

Ingredients

1	Sacréchien (ruby snapper), weighing about 600 g
1/2 dl.	Taggiasche extra virgin olive oil
20 g	Ginger
1/2 bunch	Chives
2	Meyer lemons or Tahiti limes
	Table sea salt
	Freshly ground white pepper

Green salad bouquet

40 g	Rocket lettuce
40 g	Mizuna (green Japanese salad)
1/4 bunch	Coriander
1/4 bunch	Chervil
1	Red chilli
1 tsp	Black sesame seeds
1 tsp	White sesame seeds
12	Japanese sweet and sour ginger petals
1/2 dl.	Royal Palm vinaigrette *

Served with

Toast melba *

* see basic recipes

Coneau-coneau shellfish salad Rodriguan-style

Recipe
Rinse the coneau-coneau thoroughly. Bring some water to the boil and poach the coneau-coneau, cooking for 3 minutes after the water has returned to the boil. Use a skimmer to remove the coneau-coneau and leave them to cool down. Shell the coneau-coneau by holding the back of the shell and tapping it 2 or 3 times against a chopping board; the flesh will come out easily. Remove the tip of the coneau-coneau (it is often green and is inedible) with a sharp knife. Cut the coneau-coneau into two, then finely slice the whitish part lengthwise. They need to be kept cool. Peel and thinly slice the onion. Wash the coriander, discard the stalks, keep a few leaves on one side for later, and snip up the rest.

Wash the red chilli, cut into two lengthwise, remove the seeds and cut into thin julienne. Snip the chives. Peel the green peppers and then cut them into thin julienne, 5 cm long. Peel the ginger with a sharp knife, cut it into thin slivers and then chop it into small pieces.

Last minute
Carefully mix the coneau-coneau with all the ingredients in a bowl, add the limejuice, season the salad with salt and black pepper to taste, and leave to marinate for 10 minutes in the refrigerator before serving. Place a banana leaf, cut into a 15 cm wide circle, in the middle of 4 chilled dishes, arrange the coneau-coneau salad over the leaf, and sprinkle with coriander leaves. Serve straightaway.

Alternative
Whelks can be used instead of coneau-coneau.

Serves 4

INGREDIENTS

20	Coneau-coneau (sea snails)
2	Green peppers
7 g	Ginger
1	Red onion (medium-sized)
	Juice of 1 Meyer lemon or Tahiti lime
1/2 bunch	Chives
1 bunch	Coriander
10 tbsp	Taggiasche extra virgin olive oil
	Table sea salt
	Freshly ground black pepper
	Banana leaf (optional)

Thin slices of smoked blue marlin with herb salad and shallots

Recipe
Sort through, wash and drain the lettuce and salad leaves and herbs. Cut the chives into 9 cm long sticks. Peel the shallot and cut it into very thin slices. Then cut the gherkins into thin julienne.

Last minute
Cut the smoked marlin into thin, almost transparent, slices with a "salmon" knife. Divide the slices evenly over 4 plates, without leaving any space between the slices, and top with virgin olive oil. Sprinkle with crushed black pepper. Mix the herbs, lettuce and salad leaves in a large bowl and toss with your hands. Add the gherkin julienne, capers, and snipped shallots and toss once again. Pour the vinaigrette onto the salad and mix carefully but thoroughly until all the elements are lightly covered with the dressing. Place in heaps in the centre of the marlin slices and serve immediately with toast or slices of rye bread with Echiré butter.

Alternative
Smoked swordfish can be used instead of smoked marlin.

Serves 4

INGREDIENTS

400 g	Marinated smoked marlin
4 tbsp	Taggiasche extra virgin olive oil
	Crushed black pepper *

Salad

50 g	Mizuna (Japanese green salad)
50 g	Rocket lettuce
1	Curly endive
1	Lettuce heart
50 g	Lambs' lettuce
1/4 bunch of each	Tarragon, cress, dill, chervil and flat-leaved parsley
1 bunch	Chives
1	Shallot
3	Gherkins
2 tbsp	Capers
	Table sea salt
	Freshly ground white pepper
6 tbsp	Lime vinaigrette *

* see basic recipes

Grand Gaube clams
in tomato, ginger and tamarind

Recipe

Carefully scrub the clams, wash them several times in plenty of water to remove the small grains of sand which stick to them, and drain them in a colander. Peel and cut the shallot and the garlic (removing the green germ). Wash the red chillies, cut them into two, remove the seeds and cut into thin julienne. Peel the ginger and cut into fine julienne. Wash the coriander, remove the stalks and chop up the leaves. Snip up the chives.

Take the tomatoes, remove the cores, soak them for 30 seconds in boiling water, peel them, cut them into two crosswise, and remove the seeds and any water. Then dice them into brunoise.

Melt the butter on high heat in a suitably large pan. Add the shallot, garlic, ginger and curry powder, sweat for 20 seconds, then add the clams. Deglaze with *1 dl.* white wine and the rum. Bring to the boil, maintaining a high flame. Cover the pan and cook until the clams open (which will take about 4 minutes). Remove the clams as they open. They must not cook for too long. Discard the clams that have not opened. Keep the clams hot and covered. Strain the sauce through a fine conical sieve and reduce to concentrate the flavour. Add the tomato brunoise and the tamarind pulp, season with black pepper and, if necessary, salt, and finish by sprinkling with coriander leaves and chives.

Last minute

Serve the clams in 4 large soup dishes and top with sauce. Serve straightaway.

Alternative

Mussels can be used instead of clams.

Serves 4

Ingredients

4 kg	Clams
1	Shallot
2 cloves	Garlic
20 g	Ginger
200 g	Plum tomatoes (ripe)
2	Red chillies
1/4 bunch	Coriander
1/4 bunch	Chives
6 tbsp	Tamarind pulp *
2 tbsp	White agricultural rum
1 dl.	Dry white wine
1 tbsp	Home-made curry powder *
50 g	Echiré butter
	Table sea salt
	Freshly ground black pepper

* see basic recipes

Lagoon bouillabaisse

Recipe

Ask your fishmonger to scale all the fish and to remove their heads, guts and eyes (N.B. you will need the heads later).

Wash everything in cold water. Keep the heads on one side for the stock. Leave the small rock fish as they are, but cut the bigger fish into 4 cm slices. Shell the Tiger prawns tails, but keep the heads attached. Twist off the heads from the lobsters and crush them in a mortar. Slice the lobster tails into 8 pieces and remove the central intestine.

Scrub the clams carefully, rinse under running water and drain in a colander.

To prepare the stock Peel and slice the onions, shallots and cloves of garlic (removing the germ). Peel and wash the fennel and slice. Wash the tomatoes, remove the cores, and break them up into pieces. Cut the red chilli into two and remove the seeds. Scrub the oranges under the tap, and use only the peel (without the white pith). Mix all these ingredients in a stainless steel bowl with the small rockfish, adding the pepper, coriander seeds and the saffron. Cover with cling film and leave to marinate in the refrigerator for 12 hours.

Wash and peel the squash, and cut it into 1 cm cubes. Heat 2 tbsp olive oil in a 20 cm wide thick-bottomed casserole dish, add the diced squash and cover. Stew for 10 minutes. Then use a mixer to blend it into a smooth purée.

Sweat the marinated items in olive oil in a large, thick-bottomed pan, 30 cm wide. Stew for a few minutes, deglaze with white wine, cover with water, add the tomato purée and bouquet garni. Salt. Simmer and skim off the scum from time to time. After half an hour's cooking, use a skimmer to remove and discard the bouquet garni and peel, blend the rest in a food-mill and filter the stock through a muslin conical sieve, pressing firmly to extract all the liquid. Reduce the stock slowly to *1 l.*, to concentrate the flavour. Thicken the stock with the squash purée, using a hand-held electric mixer. Check seasoning and strain through a muslin sieve. Keep warm.

To prepare the garlic mayonnaise Peel and cut the cloves of garlic into two, remove the germs and grind in a mortar. Add the egg yolks, salt and pepper and whip up with *5 dl.* olive oil as for a mayonnaise.

To prepare the croutons Cut the bread diagonally into slices, 0.5 cm thick, to make about fifty croutons. Place them on a non-stick baking tray, sprinkle with olive oil and toast on both sides in a slow-burning stove or grill them in the oven at 160° C until they are very crisp and golden brown.

Last minute

Heat *3 dl.* of olive oil in a non-stick pan, add a little salt to the fish steaks (darnes), tiger prawns and lobsters. Sear quickly. Place in a dish. Then put the tiger prawns and the lobsters into a 30 cm wide thick-bottomed casserole dish. Cover with the stock and bring to the boil. Add the vieille rouge, rouget and sacréchien and simmer for 6 to 7 minutes on moderate heat to complete the cooking. Meanwhile quickly heat 2 tbsp olive oil in a 16 cm thick-bottomed casserole dish and add the clams. Boil quickly until all the clams open. Drain in a large colander. Check whether the fish and shellfish are cooked. Carefully remove all the fish and shellfish with a small skimmer and arrange them in a hot, large, shallow dish. Take the clams and arrange them in the same dish. Sprinkle with washed and snipped chives. Keep hot. Bring the stock quickly to the boil, pour in the Taggiasche extra virgin olive oil, mixing vigorously with a small hand-held mixer to make it smooth and thick. Pour a few ladles of hot soup over the fish, shellfish and clams, and pour the rest of the very hot soup into a tureen. Serve quickly, with the croutons and the garlic mayonnaise.

Alternative

Indian Ocean rock fish can be replaced with Mediterranean fish such as scorpion fish, John Dory, conger eel, weaver, and gurnard.

Serves 8

Ingredients

2 kg	Rock fish, such as grouper, wrasse, goatfish, bream and mackerel
60 g	Onions
50 g	Shallots
4 cloves	Garlic
80 g	Fennel bulbs
200 g	Vine tomatoes (ripe)
180 cl.	Olive oil
2	Oranges
2 dl.	Dry white wine
1 tsp	Crushed black pepper *
2 g	La Mancha saffron
1	Red chilli
1 tbsp	Tomato purée
500 g	Butternut squash (courge)
30 cl.	Taggiasche extra virgin olive oil
	Table sea salt
	Freshly ground white pepper
	Bouquet garni *

Garnish

1	Vieille rouge (blacktip grouper) of about 750 g
2	Rougets (goatfish or red mullet), each of about 250 g
1	Sacréchien (snapper or jobfish) of about 750 g
8	Large tiger prawns
2	Rock lobsters, each of about 500 g
800 g	Clams
1/2 bunch	Chives

Garlic mayonnaise

3 cloves	Garlic
1	Egg yolk
5 dl.	Taggiasche extra virgin olive oil
	Table sea salt
	Freshly ground white pepper

Croutons

2 stale	French sticks (ficelle)
4 tbsp	Olive oil

* see basic recipes

Sacréchien cooked whole in a Black River sea-salt crust with Taggiasche oil and black pepper

Recipe

Preheat the oven to 220° C. Remove the gills and gut the sacréchien via the gill area, without scaling it. Rinse the fish under the tap inside and outside until all traces of blood disappear. Use a towel to dry the fish.

Mix the coarse salt and egg whites in a basin. Spread an even layer, 3 cm thick, on a baking tray, place the fish in the middle, completely seal the fish from head to tail with the rest of the salt mixture, making sure the fish keeps its shape.

Place the baking tray in the centre of the oven and cook for about 40 minutes (add 5 minutes more for each additional 250 g of fish). Remove the tray from the oven and leave to stand for 10 minutes.

Remove the salt crust from the fish, carefully scrub the skin from the fish on one side and discard. Use a couple of spoons to remove the top fillets and place them on pre-heated plates. Remove the central bone and then the fillets on the other side, and place them on the hot plates. Top generously with the olive oil and crushed black pepper. Serve immediately, with mashed potatoes and slices of lemon.

Alternative

Sea bass or gilt-head bream (dorade) can be used instead of sacréchien and any good-quality coarse sea salt instead of Black River salt.

Serves 4

Ingredients

2 kg whole	Sacréchien (red snapper)
4	Egg whites
3 kg	Black River coarse sea salt

Served with

	Crushed black pepper *
	Taggiasche extra virgin oil
4 portions	Mashed potatoes *
2	Lemons

* see basic recipes

Shrimp rougaille and coconut-flavoured okra fricassée with Basmati rice

Recipe

To prepare the sauce rougaille Take the tomatoes and remove the cores. Bring 6 to 7 litres of water to the boil. Dip in the tomatoes, remove them after 30 seconds and dip them immediately into cold water. Peel them, cut them into two and remove the seeds. Use a knife to chop them into large pieces. Peel and slice the onions, cloves of garlic (removing the germ) and ginger.

Pour 3 tbsp olive oil into a thick-bottomed pan. Heat slowly. Add the onion, garlic and sliced ginger. Sauté gently, then add the tomato purée and the coarsely chopped tomatoes, the sprigs of thyme, the curry leaves and Cayenne pepper. Add salt.

Cook on moderate heat, stirring from time to time with a wooden spatula. When the tomato juice has evaporated, stop cooking and add half the thinly chopped fresh coriander. Check seasoning and keep hot.

To prepare the shrimps Make a shallow incision, 0.5 cm long, at each end to reach the intestinal vein. Carefully take hold of the vein and remove it. Place in the refrigerator.

To prepare the okras Wash and dry the okras. Remove the tips and cut diagonally into 2 cm pieces. Peel the onions and slice them thinly. Peel the garlic (removing the germ) and chop them up thinly. Peel and chop up the ginger. Heat the ghee slowly in a thick-bottomed pan. Sauté the onions, and then add the garlic and ginger and cook for 5 minutes, stirring constantly. Incorporate all the spices (except for the garam massala) and cook for 2 to 3 minutes. Add the okras, cook for another 3 minutes, and then mix in the coconut milk. Salt and bring to the boil. Cover and simmer slowly for 15 minutes, until the okras are tender and soft, and then powder them with garam massala. Sprinkle with chives and keep hot.

Last minute

Season the shrimps with table sea salt and sprinkle with the powdered turmeric. Heat a dash of olive oil in a very hot pan on maximum heat. Add the shrimps carefully as oil may spatter from the pan. Do not stir, wait until they become slightly golden on one side, then turn them rapidly and cook on the other side. Use a skimmer to drain and remove the shrimps. Incorporate them into the rougaille sauce, simmer for 5 minutes and sprinkle with chopped fresh coriander. Serve at once with the okras, Basmati rice and various chutneys.

Alternative

This recipe can also be used for large Mediterranean prawns (gambas) or fresh-water prawns instead of shrimps.

Serves 4

Ingredients

700 g	Shelled shrimps
2 pinch	Turmeric
1 kg	Vine tomatoes (ripe)
2	Large onions
3 cloves	Garlic
30 g	Ginger
8	Carri-poulé (curry) leaves
2 sprigs	Thyme
1 pinch	Ground Cayenne pepper
1 bunch	Coriander
25 g	Tomato purée
75 g	Olive oil

Okra in coconut milk

500 g	Okra (ladies' fingers)
1 tsp	Garam massala *
20 g	Ginger
3	Onions (medium-sized)
2 cloves	Garlic
1 tsp	Ground coriander seeds
1 tsp	Ground cumin
1/2 tsp	Ground Cayenne pepper
50 cl.	Coconut milk (tinned, unsweetened)
3 tbsp	Ghee *

Served with

4 portions	Basmati rice *
4 portions	Various chutneys *

* see basic recipes

Roast young rabbit
with spicy orange powder and chou-chou in a clear gravy

Recipe

To cut the rabbit Remove the livers and kidneys. Trim off the scraps of skin, the feet of the front legs and all the excess bones. Use a knife to cut the body of the rabbit crosswise into three pieces: the front legs with the breast (keep on one side for the stock), the hind legs and the saddle. Cut the fillets from the saddle, then remove the nerves and trim. Cut the 4 rabbit fillets to a length of about 10 cm. Remove the fat from the kidneys and clean the livers. Season with table salt. Pour 2 tbsp olive oil into a very hot pan, on high heat. Add the kidneys and livers. Without stirring them, wait until they are slightly golden on one side then turn them rapidly and cook the second side until golden. Place on a dish and leave to cool down.

Make a small incision along the length of each fillet and insert a kidney and half a liver in each. Roll into shape and truss the fillets. Remove the bones from the legs.

To prepare the rabbit gravy Cut the breast and front legs of the rabbit into pieces. Cut the garlic into two crosswise. Peel the shallots and the carrots. Chop them up, as well as the celery, tomatoes and mushroom stems. Fry the rabbit pieces in the olive oil until nicely golden, then add the chopped vegetables. Salt and pepper. Cook for 5 minutes, making sure that the vegetables do not burn, and then pour in the chicken stock. Add the thyme, garlic, tomato purée and bay leaves. Continue to cook for 3 hours, skimming off any scum from time to time. Use a skimmer to remove the rabbit and discard. Strain the stock through a muslin sieve into a large pan. Bring quickly to the boil. Reduce the temperature and boil slowly, skimming carefully, to reduce the stock to about *2 dl*.

To prepare the vegetables Dice the dried apricots into thin brunoise. Cook the chickpeas slowly in the vegetable stock for about 30 minutes. Drain them and collect the stock. Blend the chickpeas and the saffron in the bowl of a mixer into a smooth and even paste. Now start to incorporate the butter. If the purée seems to be rather dry and heavy, add a little vegetable stock or butter. Check seasoning. Keep hot. Use a paring knife to peel the asparagus, cutting off the hard part of the stalk 12 cm from the tip. Tie up 2 small bunches, with 6 asparagus in each bunch, and cook in very salty water until the tip of a knife easily pierces the stem. Drain. Melt 25 g of butter in a frying pan. Roll the asparagus all over in the butter. Cut the chou-chou into two, peel them, cut into 6 cm long sticks and twist the sticks into large petal shapes.

Remove the outer layer of the fennel and cut off the tips. Braise the fennel and the chou-chou in 25 g butter and *2 dl.* of chicken stock in a small frying pan. Glaze and check seasoning.

Last minute

Heat 2 tbsp olive oil and a knob of butter in a large 20 cm oven-proof pan. Sprinkle the rabbit fillets and legs with sea salt. Sauté them for 2 minutes on each side, then place them in the oven for about 8 minutes (they should remain pinkish to retain their taste and tenderness), basting them often with their fat. Then place them on a rack (to drain) over a plate and sprinkle them with spicy orange powder. Discard the grease from the cooking juices, and reduce the rest. Filter through a muslin conical sieve, check seasoning and keep hot. Preheat the oven to 220° C.

Reheat the fillets and legs for 2 minutes in the oven. Cut the legs into two and the fillets into 3 pieces. Divide over 4 plates and sprinkle with fleur de sel and the apricot brunoise. Surround with the fennel, chou-chou and asparagus. Place a spoonful of chickpea purée on the side of each plate. Finish off the sauce by mixing the rabbit gravy with the cooking juices from the fillets. Heat and filter. Serve in a gravy boat.

Note Farm rabbit is bigger and better, especially if it has been fed on grass and cereals.

Serves 4

Ingredients

2	Whole rabbits (around 1 kg each)
1 tbsp	Spicy orange powder *
4 tbsp	Olive oil
25 g	Echiré butter
	Table sea salt
	Freshly ground white pepper

Rabbit gravy

	Breast and front legs of the rabbits
2 tbsp	Olive oil
1 pinch	Table sea salt
1/2 tbsp	Tomato purée
50 g	Carrots
100 g	Shallots
50 g	Mushroom stems
2	Plum tomatoes (ripe)
1 stig	Celery
1 head	Garlic (small)
1 sprig	Thyme
1	Bay leaf
	Crushed black pepper *
1 1/2 l.	White chicken stock *

Vegetables

12	Green asparagus
4	Young fennel bulbs
2	Chou-chou (cho-cho)
2 dl.	White chicken stock *
2	Dried apricots
80 g	Echiré butter
200 g	Chickpeas
1/2 g	La Mancha saffron
1/2 l.	Vegetable stock *

* see basic recipes

Madras lamb and jackfruit curry with ginger-flavoured giraumon, perfumed Basmati rice and chutneys

Recipe

Peel the ginger and garlic (removing the germ), and grind in a mortar. Peel and slice the onions. Wash the coriander, remove the stalks and chop up the leaves. Snip up the chives. Cut the chillies into two, remove the seeds and cut into thin julienne. Remove the cores from the tomatoes, bring 5 l. of water to the boil, dip in the tomatoes, remove after half a minute and dip immediately into cold water. Peel the tomatoes, cut them into two, remove the seeds and chop them up.

Cut the meat into 2 cm cubes, sprinkle with 1 g of turmeric and add salt. Cut the jackfruit into 4 lengthwise, then use a sharp knife to remove the rough skin, and cut it into 2 cm cubes as well. Let it stand in cold water for 5 minutes. Drain in a colander and sprinkle with 1 g of turmeric.

Heat 2 tbsp peanut oil in a thick-bottomed pan, sear the meat on high heat and keep hot. Repeat the process with the jackfruit in the same pan, until it turns a yellowish, golden colour. Keep hot.

Heat 3 tbsp peanut oil in a thick-bottomed casserole dish on moderate heat and add the thinly sliced onions. Sweat 3 to 4 minutes, then add the garlic, ginger, chilli, tomatoes and all the spices except for the garam massala, whilst stirring constantly. Also add the meat, the thyme and the carri-poulé leaves. Cover with the vegetable stock and cook slowly for 20 minutes. When the meat is half cooked, add the jackfruit and cook for another 25 minutes, stirring from time to time. Finally add the garam massala, coriander and chives and carefully blend them in with a spatula. Check seasoning.

Last minute

Arrange the lamb and jackfruit curry in a hot dish. Serve with perfumed rice and braised giraumon, as well as various pickles and chutneys in small dishes.

Note There are about thirty kinds of lamb. We have a great weakness for Limousin lamb at the Royal Palm. It is available all year round and has quite a strong, almost woody flavour. I prefer the shoulder, as it is tastier than the leg.

Serves 4

Ingredients

1 kg	Shoulder of lamb (boned)
3 tbsp	Peanut oil
3	Large onions
5 g	Turmeric powder
15 g	Home-made curry powder *
20 g	Ginger
2 cloves	Garlic
2	Red chillies
200 g	Vine tomatoes (ripe)
6	Carri-poulé (curry) leaves
1/2 bunch	Coriander
1/2 bunch	Chives
2 sprigs	Thyme
15 g	Garam massala *
5 g	Cumin
1 g	Cloves
2 g	Cassia cinnamon
15 g	Black mustard seeds
2 l.	Vegetable stock *
500 g	Jackfruit (tender and green)
	Table sea salt

Served with

4 portions	Perfumed Basmati rice *
4 portions	Braised giraumon (Japanese pumpkin) *
4 portions	Various chutneys *
4 portions	Cythera pickles *

see basic recipes

Rasgoula with a mild spicy syrup and lime sorbet

Recipe

To prepare the sesame cigars Preheat the oven to 170º C. Spread out the sesame tuile mixture and cut into rectangles 20 cm long and 30 cm wide. Place on a non-stick tray or on cooking paper and cook in the oven for 6 to 7 minutes, until golden. Remove from the oven. When they have cooled down a little, move them to a chopping board. Cut into 8 rectangles, 15 cm long and 2 cm wide. Whilst they are still warm, roll each piece around a wooden skewer lengthwise and press the edges firmly together. Leave to cool for a minute before removing the skewers. Keep them in an airtight tin.

To prepare the rasgoula Mix the flour, powdered milk, baking powder, white cardamom and melted ghee together. Add the milk to form a dough. Leave to stand for 15 minutes, then shape it into 20 small balls, 2 cm wide. Prepare a syrup in a 16 cm wide pan, using *2 l.* of water, the sugar, citronella, cinnamon, pink pepper, star anise, green cardamom and cloves. Cover and leave to infuse for 2 hours, then strain.

Pour the oil into a large pan or a deep fryer. Heat to 170º C. Fry the balls in batches of 10, leaving them for 4 to 5 minutes in the boiling oil. When they are golden, remove them with a skimmer and place on kitchen paper. Bring the syrup to the boil, turn off the stove, drop in the balls and leave them to marinate for 1 hour. Leave them to cool down completely.

Last minute

Take 4 shallow dishes and place 5 rasgoula in each dish. Pour the syrup over them, add 1 scoop of lime sorbet and decorate with the sesame cigars and a leaf of mint.

Alternative

Passion fruit sorbet can be used instead of lime sorbet.

Serves 4

Ingredients

100 ml.	Skimmed milk
300 g	Milk powder
4 tbsp	Flour
1 tsp	Baking powder
5 seeds	White cardamom
4 tbsp	Ghee *

Mild spicy syrup

800 g	Cane sugar
150 g	Citronnella
1/2 sticks	Cassia cinnamon
1 tsp	Ground pink pepper
1	Ground star anise
6 seeds	Green cardamoms
2	Cloves

Garnish

	Lime sorbet *
300 g	Sesame tuiles mixture (see recipe, page 219)
1/4 bunch	Mint

Oil for frying

2 l.	Peanut oil

* see basic recipes

Crisp sesame cannelloni
with ginger ice-cream and Queen Victoria pineapple tartar flavoured with combava lime

Serves 4

RECIPE

To prepare the tuiles Preheat the oven to 170º C. Melt the butter in a small 10 cm wide pan. Mix all the dry ingredients in a bowl. Add the lemon juice and then the melted butter. Mix them all together with a wooden spatula and place in a refrigerator for about half an hour. Spread the sesame mixture out thinly into 4 rectangles, 16 cm long and 18 cm wide, on a non-stick tray and cook in the oven for 6 to 7 minutes until golden. Remove from the oven and leave to cool down. When the tuiles have cooled, place them one after the other on a cutting board. Cut 8 rectangles of 8 cm long and 9 cm wide. While the tuiles are still warm, roll them around plastic tubes of 25 mm diameter lengthwise and press the edges firmly together. Leave to cool for a minute before removing the sesame cannelloni. Keep them in an airtight tin.

To prepare the pineapple tartar Bring the sugar and water to the boil in a 10 cm wide pan. Peel the pineapple, cut into four and remove the heart. Put the pineapple quarters in the syrup and cook slowly for 15 minutes. After cooking, drain and leave them to cool down. Then dice the pineapple quarters into small 3 mm cubes and place in a basin. Use a mandoline to grate the peel of the combava lime, and chop finely before mixing with the pineapple. Place in the refrigerator.

To prepare the ice-cream Heat the milk in a thick-bottomed 10 cm wide pan. Peel and finely chop the ginger, incorporate it into the milk, cover, and leave to infuse away from the stove for 15 minutes. Pass this milk through a fine sieve. Add the cream to the milk and bring it to the boil. Whisk the egg yolks and sugar in a basin. Pouring slowly, whisk the boiling liquid into the sugar mix. Return everything back into the pan and cook slowly, stirring into a custard. Remove from the stove and pour through a muslin sieve into a container standing in ice. When the cream has cooled down again, pour it into an ice-cream maker. Once the ice-cream has set, place it in the freezer.

LAST MINUTE

Place a 50 mm wide plastic circle, such as a pastry cutter, in the middle of each dish, fill with pineapple tartar, and then remove the pastry cutter. Put a cordon of sabayon around it, with a few streaks of mango sauce. Take the cannelloni, remove the ice-cream from the freezer, put it into a piping bag with a nº 8 nozzle, and fill the cannelloni to the brim with ice-cream. Use a sharp knife to remove any surplus ice cream. Stand a cannelloni upright next to the tartar and lay another cannelloni horizontally in front of the other piece. Place a piece of candied pineapple between the two cannelloni. Add a few slices of confit ginger to the cannelloni, and decorate with two chocolate cigars.

Note The combava is the Kaffir lime. Meyer lemons or Tahiti limes can be used instead.

INGREDIENTS

200 g	Chilled rum-flavoured sabayon *
25 ml.	Mango sauce *
15 g	Confit ginger
4	Dried candied pineapple *
8	Chocolate cigars *

Sesame tuiles

100 g	Sesame
100 g	Icing sugar
30 g	Flour
20 g	Lemon juice
80 g	Echiré butter

Pineapple tartar

500 ml.	Water
100 g	Cane sugar
1/2	Pineapple
1/2	Combava (Kaffir lime)

Ginger ice cream

300 ml.	Semi-skimmed milk
300 ml.	Double cream
8	Egg yolks
100 g	Cane sugar
50 g	Fresh ginger

* see basic recipes

Spring rolls
filled with vanilla-flavoured papaya compote
and lime sorbet

Recipe

To prepare the compote Wash and peel the papayas. Dice the papayas into small 1 cm cubes and place them in a 20 cm wide pan. Add the sugar and sliced vanilla pods and cook slowly for 10 to 15 minutes, until the papayas become soft. Place them into a bowl and allow them to cool down, before covering with cling film.

To prepare the rolls Preheat the oven to 230º C. Melt the butter slowly. Cut 8 circles, 18 cm wide, in the rice paper. Brush the edges with melted butter. Garnish the edge (the one facing you) of each sheet with 2 tbsp of papaya compote. Fold the edges from each side into the centre, roll diagonally, seal the edges and coat with melted butter. Place the rolls on a non-stick tray, coat with melted butter and sprinkle with icing sugar. Bake in the oven for 8 to 10 minutes, and then remove from the oven.

Last minute

Place one of the rolls upright in the middle of a plate, and lay another one horizontally next to it. Place a cordon of sabayon around them, with a few traces of mango sauce. Remove the sorbet from the freezer. Use a spoon to mould a scoop of lime sorbet, and place the scoop next to the spring rolls. Then decorate with a few slices of lemon peel.

Alternative

Mangoes can be used instead of papayas, and grappa instead of rum: the result is equally delicious.

Serves 4

Ingredients

Papaya compote

3	Solo papayas
50 g	Cane sugar
2 pods	Fragrans vanilla

Spring rolls

8	Rice paper wrappers
25 g	Butter
	Icing sugar

Garnish

1/2 l.	Meyer lime sorbet *
1	Citrus fruit peel *
8 tbsp	Chilled rum-flavoured sabayon *
4 tbsp	Mango sauce *

* see basic recipes

Iced citrus fruit salad in saffron-flavoured syrup and vodka-flavoured pineapple sorbet

Recipe

Scrub the citrus fruit under running water, remove the orange, lime, and grapefruit peel (but not the white pith), and cut the peel thinly lengthwise. Peel the mandarins, stand them upright and remove the peel by sliding a very sharp knife from the top to the bottom, following the curve of the fruit. Slip the knife blade along each segment to remove the membrane from all sides. Proceed in the same way for each fruit. Place the orange, lime, the various grapefruit and the mandarin segments in a basin. Use the basic recipe to prepare the citrus peel.

To prepare the saffron syrup Bring the water and sugar to the boil in a 20 cm wide pan. Add the saffron, cover and leave it to infuse for 25 minutes. Strain through a conical sieve and leave it to cool down. Then pour the syrup into the basin with the citrus fruit and keep cool for one hour before serving.

To prepare the sorbet Whisk the sugar and the pineapple juice in a bowl, until the sugar is completely dissolved. Put it in an ice-cream maker to make it set. When the sorbet is almost set, add the vodka. Churn for another two minutes, remove the sorbet and put it in the freezer.

To make the philo pastry cigars Preheat the oven to 220º C. Melt 50 g of butter in a small pan and remove it from the stove. Roll out the philo pastry and cut 8 rectangles, each 5 cm long and 3 cm wide. Brush the rectangles with melted butter and sprinkle with icing sugar. Roll the dough lengthwise around wooden skewers and press the edges firmly together. Remove the wooden skewers and place the cigars on a non-stick baking tray. Coat with melted butter, sprinkle with icing sugar and bake in the oven for 3 to 4 minutes, until they are golden. Remove them from the oven, allow them to cool down and keep them in an airtight tin.

Last minute

Place the marinated fruit in 4 chilled shallow dishes. Pour the syrup over the citrus fruit, just enough to cover them. Top with a scoop of pineapple sorbet. Decorate with citrus fruit peel. Add two philo cigars in the shape of a cross and one piece of candied pineapple. Serve straightaway.

Alternative

The contents of the salad can be varied, according to personal preference and availability. For example you could add preserved kumquats, or more oranges or grapefruit.

Serves 4

Ingredients

Citrus fruit salad

3	Navel oranges
1	Pomelo grapefruit
1	Meyer lemon or Tahiti lime
2	Pink grapefruit
2	Ugli (a variety of citrus fruit)
3	Mandarins or clémentines

Saffron syrup

750 ml.	Water
300 g	Cane sugar
1 pinch	La Mancha saffron

Citrus peel confit

	Peel of 1 organic orange
	Peel of 2 organic limes
	Peel of 1/2 an organic grapefruit
500 ml.	Water
150 g	Cane sugar

Vodka-flavoured pineapple sorbet

500 ml.	Victoria pineapple juice
125 g	Cane sugar
20 ml.	Stolichnaya vodka

Philo cigars

1 sheet	Philo pastry
20 g	Echiré butter
50 g	Icing sugar
4 pieces	Dried candied pineapple *

* see basic recipes

Yellow Recipes

Shrimp and curry croquettes with coriander — 225

Ceylon coconut palm heart tartar covered with slices of yellow-fin tuna and osietra caviar — 226

Mangrove crab on palm-heart tartar flavoured with home-made curry and green apple — 227

Coconut and citronella-flavoured shrimp soup with sesame toast — 228

Six Grand Gaube silver oysters with a spicy sauce — 229

Plantain and coconut soup with coriander-flavoured spicy shrimps — 230

Babonne with saffron potatoes and oysters in a light fennel sauce — 231

Vieille rouge simmered with Vadouvan and shii-take mushrooms — 232

Sand lobster roasted in its shell with combava-flavoured curry sauce — 233

Pan-fried grouper with chicken wings and chicken oysters — 234

Crispy sesame layers with pan-fried duck foie gras and mango roasted with the savours of Mauritius — 235

Pumpkin and calabash vindaloo flavoured with coconut and almonds — 236

Roast white tuna with black pepper and bonemarrow on garlic-flavoured mashed potatoes — 237

Traditional Moslem chicken biryani with various chutneys and Rodriguan lime pickle — 238

Spicy cocoa crunch with ladyfinger banana ice-cream — 239

Mango and longan fruit salad with mildly-spiced yoghurt sorbet — 240

Pineapple Tatin with caramel fudge and ice-cream flavoured with oriental spices — 241

Crispy Grand Cru Caraque chocolate ravioli with rum-flavoured sabayon, preserved pineapple and cocoa sorbet — 242

Rodriguan honey madeleines — 243

Shrimp and curry croquettes with coriander

Recipe

To prepare the shrimps Make a shallow incision, 0.5 cm long, at each end to reach the black intestinal vein. Carefully take hold of the vein and remove it. Cut the shrimps into three, sprinkle them with 1/2 tbsp of curry, and marinate for 10 minutes. Keep in a cool place or refrigerator.

Pour 2 tbsp olive oil into a hot pan on high heat. Add the shrimps. Do not stir. Wait for the shrimps to become slightly golden on one side, and then turn them rapidly and cook the other side. Place them on kitchen paper. Wash the coriander, remove the stalks and chop up the leaves.

To prepare the stuffing Wash the chilli, cut into two, remove the seeds and dice into thin brunoise. Melt the butter in a small thick-bottomed pan on moderate heat, add the home-made curry powder and simmer for 1 minute. Incorporate the flour and stir quickly to obtain a smooth mixture, without letting it change colour. Pour in the shrimp coulis (see the shellfish coulis recipe), whisking to avoid any lumps. Salt, and add the red chilli. Cover and cook for 15 minutes, stirring constantly to make sure the various flavours are blended together thoroughly. Add the cream and continue cooking for 5 more minutes. Then add the shrimps and the coriander leaves. Let it completely cool down. Divide the resulting stuffing into 20 g to 30 g portions and give them a cylindrical shape.

To prepare the breadcrumbs Pour the flour into a shallow dish. In a second shallow dish, break the eggs and mix them with the oil. Salt and pepper generously. Put the breadcrumbs into a third dish. Pour the oil into a large *4 l.* pan or a deep fryer and heat to 180º C. Meanwhile, coat the balls of stuffing in flour, shaking them to remove any excess. Then dip them into the beaten eggs, let the excess drain off and then coat them all over with breadcrumbs. Place what are by now croquettes side by side on a clean tea towel. They must all be coated before you start to fry them.

Last minute

Fry in batches of 10 to 15, leaving them for 3 to 4 minutes in the boiling oil. When they are golden and crisp, use a skimmer to remove and drain them. Place them on kitchen paper and serve straightaway.

Alternative

Large Mediterranean prawns (gambas) or even rock lobsters can be used instead of shrimps.

To make 40 to 50 pieces

Ingredients

110	g	Flour
110	g	Echiré butter
3 3/4	dl.	Shellfish coulis *
1/2	dl.	Crème fraîche
1/2	bunch	Coriander
220	g	Shrimps (shelled)
2	tbsp	Olive oil
1 1/2	tbsp	Home-made curry powder *
1/2		Red chilli
10	g	Table sea salt
		Freshly ground white pepper

Breadcrumbs

250	g	Fine flour
2		Large eggs
2	tbsp	Peanut oil
250	g	Fresh breadcrumbs

Oil for frying

2	l.	Peanut oil

* *see basic recipes*

Ceylon coconut palm heart tartar covered with slices of yellow-fin tuna and osietra caviar

Recipe

Squeeze the lemon. Use a knife to remove the peel from the brined lemon, but without removing the white pith, and cut the peel into thin slices lengthwise and then into thin brunoise. Wash and snip the chives.

Cut the palm heart into thin brunoise and coat with lemon juice to prevent it from going dark. Carefully mix the brined lemon peel and chives with the mayonnaise in a basin. Check seasoning.

Last minute

Place an 80 mm wide pastry cutter in the middle of 4 cold dishes. Fill the cutters with the palm heart tartar, holding the edges gently to keep the cutters in place.

Use a sharp Sashimi knife to cut the tuna fillet into very fine, almost transparent, slices. Place the slices on top of the tartar without leaving any space between them.

Brush the tuna slices with lemon vinaigrette. Sprinkle with just a little fleur de sel and carefully remove the cutters. Place a generous scoop of caviar and a sprig of chervil in the centre and serve straightaway.

Alternative

There are many varieties of palm, and others can be used instead of the Ceylon coconut palm.

Serves 4

Ingredients

1/2		Palm heart, from a Ceylon coconut palm
1		Lemon
1	dl.	Olive oil mayonnaise *
1		Brined lemon *
1/4	bunch	Chives
250	g	Yellow-fin tuna dorsal fillet
100	g	Osietra caviar (royal or imperial)
3	tbsp	Lemon vinaigrette *
		Chervil
		Table sea salt
		Fleur de sel
		Freshly ground white pepper

* see basic recipes

Mangrove crab on palm-heart tartar flavoured with home-made curry and green apple

Recipe

To poach the mangrove crabs Bring the vegetable stock to the boil and add the crabs. Cook for 7 minutes, after the stock returns to the boil. Remove the pan from the stove and leave the crabs to stand in the stock for about 30 minutes. Whilst they stand, the crabs will continue to cook and their meat will remain tender. Then remove the crabs from the vegetable stock and drain them thoroughly. Carefully remove the meat from the inside and the claws. Put the pieces of crabmeat in a dish and cover.

To prepare the tartar Heat 6 tbsp olive oil slowly in a 10 cm wide, thick-bottomed pan. Add a teaspoon of home-made curry powder and simmer for about 15 seconds. Remove from the stove, place it in a small container and let it cool down. Keep the oil for later.

Remove any bits from the foot of the celery stick, but keep the top leaves for later. Slice up the stick of celery and dice into brunoise. Blanch in salted water, keeping it crisp, then drain it well. Wash and peel the apple, remove the core and dice into brunoise. Wash the celery leaves and bunch them up. Chop up half the leaves and keep the rest for frying later.

Squeeze the juice from the lemon. Cut the palm heart, discarding the hard parts. Cut the heart into thin brunoise and coat with lemon juice to prevent it from changing colour. Carefully mix the mayonnaise, the infused curry powder, chopped celery leaves, green apple and celery brunoise together in a bowl and check seasoning. Keep in the refrigerator.

To prepare the chatini Remove the cores from the plum tomatoes and dip them for 30 seconds in boiling water. Remove them and cool them straightaway in cold water, peel them, cut them into quarters, remove the seeds and slice them into julienne. Peel the ginger and chop it up thinly. Wash the chives and slice them thinly. Clean the coriander and chop that up thinly as well. Mix all the ingredients in a bowl and season with olive oil, salt and pepper.

Pour the oil into a deep fryer and heat to 160º C. Fry the celery leaves, leaving them for 30 seconds in the boiling oil, drain with a skimmer and place on kitchen paper. Add salt.

Last minute

Place pastry cutters, 80 mm wide, in the middle of 4 chilled plates, and fill them with the tartar. Hold on the cutters to keep them in place. Season the crabmeat with pepper and olive oil and spread over the tartar. Carefully remove the cutters. Place a small heap of tomato chutney in the middle and top with a fried celery leaf. Surround with pieces of candied apple and dribble a few traces of curried oil over the plates. Serve straightaway.

Alternative

Common or spider crabs can be used instead of mangrove crabs.

Serves 4

Ingredients

2		Mangrove crabs, weighing 600 g each
3	l.	Vegetable stock *
4	tbsp	Taggiasche extra virgin olive oil
		Table sea salt
		Freshly ground white pepper

Tartar

1/2		Palm heart
1		Lemon
1		Granny Smith apple
4	tbsp	Mayonnaise *
1	tbsp	Chopped celery leaves
6	tbsp	Olive oil
1	tsp	Home-made curry powder *
25	g	Stick celery
		A few celery leaves

Oil for frying

1/2	l.	Peanut oil

Tomato chatini (chutney)

2		Plum tomatoes (ripe)
4	g	Ginger
1	tbsp	Chopped coriander
1	tbsp	Chopped chives
2	tbsp	Taggiasche extra virgin olive oil

Garnish

20	pieces	Dried candied green apple *

* see basic recipes

Coconut and citronella-flavoured shrimp soup with sesame toast

Recipe

To prepare the shrimps Shell the shrimps, and keep the shells for the stock. Make a shallow incision, 0.5 cm long, at each end to reach the intestinal vein. Carefully take hold of the vein and remove it. Keep in a cool place.

To prepare the stock and the garnish Clean the coriander, discard the stalks, and make the leaves up into small bunches. Cut the shallots and mushrooms into thin mirepoix. Peel and chop the ginger. Crush the shrimp shells as finely as possible in the bowl of a mixer.

Meanwhile, melt a knob of butter in a 26 cm wide, thick-bottomed frying pan and sweat the shallots, mushrooms and ginger for 1 minute. Add the shrimp shells and cook for another 2 minutes. Deglaze with the champagne and bring to the boil. Add the vegetable stock and cook for 10 minutes. Add the citronella, coconut milk and cream. Reduce to concentrate the flavour. Whip in the butter and add half the coriander. Check the seasoning, then strain through a muslin conical sieve and keep the mixture warm.

Meanwhile sort through the bean sprouts. Peel the carrots and cut into thin julienne.

To prepare the sesame toast Clean the chervil, remove the stalks and chop up the leaves. Mix 125 g of peeled shrimps, lemon juice, Tabasco sauce, chervil and salt in a processor. Process until the stuffing is smooth and even, then strain through a conical sieve.

Cut the loaf of bread lengthwise into 7 mm thick slices. Spread the slices with the stuffing and coat with sesame seeds. Cut into 8 sticks, 20 cm long and 1.5 cm wide. Meanwhile pour the oil into a pan or a deep fryer. Heat to 180º C.

Last minute

Heat the butter in a hot, large pan until it is light brown. Still on high heat, add the rest of the shrimps. Do not stir. Wait until the shrimps become slightly golden on one side then turn them rapidly and finish cooking the other side. Remove them from the stove and place them on kitchen paper.

Heat 1 tbsp olive oil in a frying pan and sweat the carrot julienne with salt and pepper. Repeat for the bean sprouts. Keep hot.

Fry the bread in batches of 4, leaving them for 3 to 4 minutes in the boiling oil. When they are golden and crisp, use a skimmer to drain and remove them from the oil. Place the toasts on kitchen paper and serve straightaway.

To serve Place the hot shrimps in 4 pre-warmed soup plates and top with the carrots and bean sprouts. Blend the soup with a hand-held mixer until it becomes frothy and pour it piping hot over the shrimps and vegetables. Finish the soup with fresh coriander leaves and serve with warm sesame toast.

Alternative

Small scampi or prawns can be used instead of shrimps. Those who like their food spicy can add a thinly-sliced green chilli or two to the soup.

Serves 4

Ingredients

1 1/2	kg	Large pink shrimps
2		Shallots
125	g	Mushrooms
40	g	Ginger
1	glass	Champagne
1	l.	White chicken stock *
50	g	Citronella (lemon grass)
1 1/2	dl.	Coconut milk (tinned and unsweetened)
250	g	Crème fraîche
125	g	Echiré butter
1/2	bunch	Coriander

Sesame toast

125	g	Shelled shrimps (to be taken from the 1.5 kg in the main ingredients)
1/2		Lemon
100	g	Stale bread
		Tabasco sauce
1/4	bunch	Chervil
2	l.	Peanut oil

Garnish

1		Large carrot
150	g	Bean sprouts
25	g	Butter
2	tbsp	Olive oil

* *see basic recipes*

Six Grand Gaube silver oysters with a spicy sauce

Recipe

Open the oysters, remove the flesh and put it in a small bowl, with the water from the oysters. Wash the shells and let them drain thoroughly, upside down, on a tea towel. Strain the water from the oysters through a cheesecloth or a very fine sieve.

Peel and finely slice the shallot, ginger and turmeric. Heat a small knob of butter in a 15 cm wide saucepan and add the shallot, turmeric, ginger and spices. Sweat rapidly for 1 minute. Pour in the champagne, let it evaporate and reduce to "dry", and then add the water from the oysters (but keep 4 tbsp of the oyster water for later) and *1/2 dl.* of chicken stock. To concentrate the flavour, reduce to *1/3 dl.*, add the cream and whip into a butter. Check seasoning, add the juice of 1 lemon, then strain through a conical sieve and keep the sauce hot.

Wash the brèdes, separate the leaves from the stalks and cut the stalks into julienne.

Remove the tomato core, dip the tomato for 30 seconds in boiling water, cool immediately in cold water, peel, quarter, remove the water and seeds, and then dice the quarters into brunoise.

Put a knob of butter and *1/2 dl.* poultry stock into a pan and stew the brèdes stalks slowly for 2 minutes. Salt and pepper. Add the brèdes leaves and continue to cook for 1 more minute, until the vegetables are tender. Shake the pan from time to time to prevent the vegetables from browning. Check seasoning and keep hot. Wash and thinly chop up the chives.

Last minute

Fill the bottom of 4 shallow dishes with coarse sea salt, place 6 shells on top and leave them in the oven preheated to 60° C. Warm the oysters in 4 tbsp of the oyster water in a 20 cm wide pan for 1 to 2 minutes, place them on a tea towel to drain and add a little white pepper. Add the tomato brunoise and the chives to the sauce. Arrange a spoonful of brèdes julienne on the bottom of each shell and place an oyster on top. Place a leaf of brède on each oyster. Top with sauce and serve immediately.

Alternative

Belon no. 0 oysters can be used instead of Grand Gaube silver oysters.

Serves 4

Ingredients

24		Grand Gaube silver oysters
4		Brèdes Tom-Pouce (baby bok-choy)
1	tbsp	Echiré butter

Sauce

1	dl.	White chicken stock *
3/4	dl.	Champagne
1		Shallot
4	tbsp	Crème fraîche
3	g	Home-made curry powder *
1	pinch	Cassia cinnamon
2	g	Turmeric (fresh or powdered)
5	g	Ginger
1	pinch	La Mancha saffron
100	g	Echiré butter
1		Lemon
1		Vine tomato (ripe)
1/4	bunch	Chives
		Table sea salt
		Freshly ground white pepper
800	g	Coarse sea salt

* see basic recipes

Plantain and coconut soup with coriander-flavoured spicy shrimps

Recipe

Prepare the soup Peel the plantains under running water and set aside two pieces for the garnish. Cut 10 plantains into 1 cm cubes. Peel and chop the ginger and chop the onion in tiny pieces. Slowly melt a small knob of butter in a 20 cm wide, thick-bottomed pan, then add the ginger and shallots, and sweat for 2 to 3 minutes, without browning. Add the bananas, cook gently for a few seconds, pour in the chicken stock and add a few drops of fish sauce. Cook for 20 minutes. Incorporate the green curry paste, cream and coconut milk and bring to the boil. Remove from the stove and use a hand-held mixer to blend the soup. Strain through a muslin conical sieve, rectify the seasoning with fish sauce, and keep the soup hot.

To prepare the shrimps Shell the shrimps. Make a shallow incision, 0.5 cm long, at each end to reach the intestinal vein. Carefully take hold of the vein and remove it. Keep the shrimps cool.

Cut the chillies into two, remove the seeds and slice into very thin julienne. Wash the coriander, remove the stalks and bunch the leaves together.

Open the coconut by breaking it with a hammer or rolling pin and remove the liquid. Use a paring knife to cut out the coconut pulp, and dice it into fine brunoise with a sharp knife. Cut the two remaining plantains into thin brunoise.

Last minute

Pour 3 tbsp olive oil into a very hot large pan and add the red chilli julienne and the plantain brunoise. Maintain on high heat and add the shrimps. Without stirring, wait until the shrimps become lightly golden on one side, then turn them rapidly and finish cooking the other side. Add the coconut brunoise and add salt. Remove from the stove immediately and place all the ingredients on kitchen paper.

Place the shrimps, plantains and coconut on the bottom of 4 pre-warmed soup bowls. Mix the soup with a hand-held mixer until it becomes frothy. Pour the very hot soup onto the shrimps and sprinkle with fresh coriander leaves. Serve immediately.

Serves 4

Ingredients

12		Plantain bananas (ripe)
1		Small onion
25	g	Ginger
1	tsp	Green curry paste *
1	l.	Poultry stock *
2	cl.	Double cream
3	cl.	Coconut milk (tinned and unsweetened)
		Thai Fish sauce
120	g	Echiré butter

Garnish

600	g	Shrimps
5	g	Red chilli
1/4		Coconut
3	tbsp	Olive oil
1/4	bunch	Fresh coriander

see basic recipes

Babonne with saffron potatoes and oysters in a light fennel sauce

Recipe

Ask the fishmonger to fillet the babonne, and remove the skin and bones. Divide the fillets into 4 portions of about 160 g each. Keep in the refrigerator.

Open the oysters. Remove the flesh and place in a small bowl. Strain the water from the oysters through cheesecloth or a very fine sieve. Keep the oysters and water separately in the refrigerator.

To prepare the garnish Remove the stalks, ends and outer layer from the fennel, wash them in plenty of water and then slice them into thin julienne. Keep the trimmings for the sauce.

Use a paring knife to cut off the roots from the leeks, very close to the bulb. Shorten the tips of the leaves, keeping only one third of green to two thirds of white. Remove the outer leaf. Wash the leeks carefully several times, changing the water each time, and then under running water, separating the leaves to eliminate any soil more easily. Bunch the leeks and tie them firmly with two to three twists of string at the top and the bottom, then tie in the middle.

Fill a large pan with iced water. Fill another large pan with poultry stock and bring it to the boil. Add salt and the bunch of leeks. Cook for about 10 minutes (the leeks should remain green but become tender). Drain the leeks with a skimmer, dip them into the iced water, drain again, cut them diagonally into 3 cm slices and keep them cool.

Peel the potatoes. Sauté them in 1 tbsp butter for 1 minute in a 14 cm wide, thick-bottomed pan. Add 5 dl. poultry stock, saffron and salt. Cook for about 15 minutes. The tip of a knife pushed into a potato should come out easily. Keep hot.

Clean the flat-leaved parsley, remove the stalks and then snip the leaves up thinly. Repeat for the dill.

To prepare the sauce Peel and slice the shallot and the fennel trimmings. Heat a small knob of butter in a small, thick-bottomed pan, add the shallot, the star anise and fennel, and sweat rapidly for 5 minutes. Pour in the white wine and vermouth, and let them evaporate and reduce to "dry". Add the fish stock and the oyster water and reduce to concentrate the flavour. Add the cream and reduce to $2^{1/2}$ dl., whip up with butter with a hand-held mixer and check seasoning. Add the lemon juice, then strain through a muslin conical sieve, pressing the vegetable pulp well to extract all the sauce. Keep hot.

Last minute

Melt 25 g butter slowly in a 14 cm wide pan with a lid. Add the fennel, sweat rapidly, then cover and cook slowly for 2 to 3 minutes. Make sure the fennel does not brown by shaking the pan from time to time. Salt and pepper. Add the dill.

Sprinkle the babonne fillets with sea salt. Heat 3 tbsp oil on moderate heat in a large, non-stick pan. When it is very hot, add the fillets. When the fillets are half-cooked, turn the fish, lower the heat and add the parsley and 1 tbsp butter. Cook for a few seconds and remove from the stove. The flesh of the fish must be opaque but still supple and moist.

Sauté the slices of leek in a frying pan with 1 tbsp olive oil and 1/2 tbsp butter. Season with salt and ground white pepper. Heat a knob of butter on moderate heat in a small, non-stick pan. When it is hot, add the oysters and braise for a few seconds, add pepper and remove from the stove. The oysters need to be kept slightly warm.

Place the fish fillets in the middle of 4 pre-warmed plates and sprinkle with fleur de sel and crushed black pepper. Surround the fish fillets with the slices of leek, potatoes and oysters. Add the slivers of fennel. Heat the fennel butter, add the juices from the oyster pan, and use a hand-held mix to froth it up. Dribble traces of this sauce around the edge of the babonne fillets, add a few dill leaves and serve straightaway.

Alternative

Most kinds of grouper fish can be used instead of babonne.

Serves 4

Ingredients

2		Babonnes (black-saddled coral grouper), weighing 800 g each
		Fleur de sel
		Table sea salt
		Freshly ground white pepper
1/2	tbsp	Crushed black pepper *
4	tbsp	Olive oil
1/4	bunch	Flat-leaved parsley

Garnish

12		Pacific rock oysters
12		Jersey royal potatoes
1	g	La Mancha saffron
6		Leeks
200	g	Fennel bulbs
1		Shallot
1	dl.	Dry white wine
3 1/2	l.	White chicken stock *
130	g	Echiré butter
1/2	dl.	Crème fraîche
1/4	bunch	Dill

Sauce

5	dl.	Fish stock (fumet) *
1/4	dl.	Dry white wine
1/4	dl.	Dry vermouth
1		Shallot
30	g	Fennel trimmings, cut off from the bulbs
1/2		Star anise
1	tbsp	Single cream
120	g	Echiré butter
		Lemon juice

* see basic recipes

Vieille rouge
simmered with Vadouvan and shii-take mushrooms

Recipe
Ask the fishmonger to fillet the vieille rouge and remove the skin and bones. Divide the fillets into 4 portions of about 170 g each. Keep in the refrigerator.

To prepare the sauce Peel and finely slice the shallot and ginger. Heat a small knob of butter in a small thick-bottomed pan, add the shallot and ginger and sweat rapidly for 30 seconds. Pour in the yellow wine, let it evaporate and reduce to "dry". Add the fish stock (keep 3 tbsp to braise the fish) and reduce to concentrate the flavour. Add the cream and reduce to $2^{1/2}$ dl., whip up with butter with a hand-held mixer and check seasoning. Add the lemon juice, then strain through a muslin conical sieve and keep hot.

To prepare the garnish Wash the brèdes, separating the leaves from the stalks and shape the stalks into petals. Keep both the leaves and the "petals". Trim and wash the shii-take mushrooms, cut off the stems but leave the caps whole, then dry them. Use a knife to cut the roots off the leeks, very close to the bulb. Shorten the tips of the leaves, keeping only one third of green to two thirds of white. Remove the outer leaf. Wash the leek carefully several times, changing the water each time, and then under running water, separating the leaves to eliminate any soil more easily. Use string to bunch them together.

Fill a large pan with iced water. Fill another large pan with water and bring it to the boil. Add salt and the brèdes petals. Cook for about 2 minutes (the brèdes should remain green and slightly crisp). Drain with a skimmer, dip in the iced water and drain once again. Cook and drain the bunch of leeks in the same way. Wash the chilli, cut it into two, discard the seeds and dice into thin brunoise.

Last minute
Take an 18 cm wide pan with a lid. Add the olive oil and the 25 g of butter, the red chilli brunoise and *1/2 dl.* of vegetable stock. Heat slowly. Sweat the leeks rapidly, then cover and cook slowly for 2 minutes. Add the brèdes petals and continue to cook for another minute. Make sure that the vegetables do not brown, by shaking the pan from time to time. Salt and pepper. Then add the shii-take mushrooms and the brèdes leaves and continue to cook for 1 to 2 minutes until the vegetables are tender.

Sprinkle the vieille rouge fillets with sea salt and freshly ground white pepper. Heat 3 tbsp oil on moderate heat in a small, 26 cm wide, non-stick pan. When it is very hot, add the fillets. Half way through cooking, turn the fillets, reduce the heat, then add the Vadouvan, the chopped parsley, 1 tbsp butter and 3 tbsp fish stock. Braise for a few seconds and remove from the stove. The meat of the vieille rouge should be opaque but still supple and moist.

Place the brèdes, shii-take mushrooms and the hot leeks in 4 large, pre-warmed soup dishes. Place the fillets on top. Top each fillet with a 1/4 tsp of the cooking butter from the pan and sprinkle with fleur de sel. Heat the sauce and use a hand-held mixer to froth it up, dress it around the fish and serve straightaway.

Alternative
Atlantic redfish or large-scaled scorpion fish can be used instead of black-tip grouper.

Note Vadouvan is a fermented spice mixture of cumin, lentils, mustard seeds, fenugreek, turmeric, curry leaves and onions.

Serves 4

Ingredients

8		Vieilles rouges (black-tip grouper), weighing 375 g each
20	g	Vadouvan
1/4	bunch	Flat-leaved parsley
3	tbsp	Olive oil
1	tbsp	Echiré butter
		Fleur de sel
		Freshly ground white pepper
		Table sea salt

Sauce

5	dl.	Fish stock *
1/2	dl.	Yellow Jura wine
2		Shallots
15	g	Ginger
125	g	Echiré butter
2	tbsp	Crème fraîche
1		Lemon

Garnish

8		Young leeks
16		Shii-take mushrooms
4		Brèdes Tom-Pouce (baby bok-choy)
25	g	Echiré butter
2	tbsp	Olive oil
1/2	dl.	Vegetable stock *
1/2		Red chilli

* see basic recipes

Sand lobster roasted in its shell with combava-flavoured curry sauce

Recipe

To prepare the sauce Peel and chop the shallots and the clove of garlic (removing the green germ). Heat a small knob of butter in a 15 cm wide frying pan, add the shallot and garlic, sweat rapidly for 2 minutes, then add the curry powder and the half lime leaf, chopped up finely. Heat for a further 30 seconds. Deglaze with the white wine and let it evaporate and reduce until "dry". Add the fish stock and reduce to concentrate the flavour. Add the cream and reduce, whip it up with butter and check seasoning. Add the combava limejuice, then strain through a conical sieve. Keep hot.

To prepare the garnish Peel the red pepper, remove the core and cut into four. Remove the seeds by scrubbing inside and cut out the whitish parts. Marinate with a peeled and crushed clove of garlic (having removed the germ), a sprig of thyme, 4 tbsp olive oil and a pinch of salt, for 1 hour. Leave the pepper quarters to turn confit in the oven, heated to 90º C. It will take 30 minutes. Remove the peppers from the oven and cut them into brunoise. Keep hot.

Wash the brèdes, separate the leaves from the stalks and shape the stalks into large petals. Sort through the bean sprouts, and snip up the chives.

Add 1 tbsp olive oil, 25 g butter and 3 tbsp vegetable stock. Heat slowly. Add the brèdes stalks. Salt and pepper. Cover and cook slowly for 3 minutes (the brèdes should remain green and slightly crisp). Add the brèdes leaves and bean sprouts and continue to cook for 1 more minute until the vegetables are tender. Make sure they do not brown by shaking the pan from time to time. Finish by carefully mixing in the chives with a spatula. Check seasoning.

Last minute

Cut the lobsters into two lengthwise and remove the central intestine as well as the sand sack. Heat 3 tbsp olive oil rapidly in a large pan. Sprinkle the lobsters with the rest of the oil. When the oil is very hot, place the lobsters in the pan, colour the flesh well for 3 minutes, then lower the heat. Turn the lobsters, sprinkle with curry powder and braise in the butter. Share them out over 4 pre-warmed plates and sprinkle with fleur de sel. Surround the lobsters with the brèdes, bean sprouts and the shimmering hot red pepper brunoise. At the same time, heat the sauce and use a hand-held mixer to froth it up. Pour into a sauceboat and serve.

Alternative

Britanny lobsters or rock lobsters can be used instead of sand lobsters.

Serves 4

Ingredients

4		Sand lobsters, weighing 600 g each (live)
3	tbsp	Olive oil
1	tbsp	Home-made curry powder *
25	g	Echiré butter
		Fleur de sel
		Table sea salt
		Freshly ground white pepper

Garnish

4		Brèdes Tom-Pouce (baby bok-choy)
1		Red pepper
100	g	Bean sprouts
1	clove	Garlic
1	sprig	Thyme
50	cl.	Vegetable stock *
5	tbsp	Olive oil
25	g	Echiré butter
1/4	bunch	Chives

Sauce

1	tbsp	Home-made curry powder *
2		Shallots
1	clove	Garlic
1	dl.	Dry white wine
1/2		Combava leaf
2	tbsp	Combava (kaffir lime) juice
120	g	Echiré butter
1	tbsp	Crème fraîche
5	dl.	Fish stock *

* see basic recipes

Pan-fried grouper with chicken wings and chicken oysters

Recipe

To prepare the marinade Peel the ginger and garlic (removing the germ) and crush in a mortar. Wash and sort the thyme. Mix all the ingredients in a bowl with a whisk until the sugar is completely dissolved. Add the wings, cover with cling film and place in the refrigerator. Marinate the wings for 24 hours.

To cook the wings Pour the oil into a *2 l.* pan and heat to 90º C. Remove the wings from their marinade and cook slowly for 20 minutes. When they are tender, use a skimmer to drain and place them in a dish to cool down.

To prepare the citronella oil Peel and chop the ginger. Cut the citronella into slices. Sauté the ginger and citronella in 3 tbsp olive oil, without browning them, stirring all the time. Leave to simmer for 2 minutes. Add the remaining oil and leave to infuse for 1¹/² hours at 60º C. Strain through a muslin conical sieve. Keep the oil.

To prepare the fish Ask the fishmonger to fillet the grouper and remove the skin and bones. Divide the fillets into 4 portions of about 150 g each. Keep in the refrigerator.

To prepare the garnish Peel and trim the baby fennel. Braise the fennel in a small frying pan in 25 g of butter and *2 dl.* of white chicken stock until they are tender and glazed. Check seasoning.

Use a sharp knife to cut off the bottoms of the brèdes and remove 1/2 cm from the tops. Remove the outer leaves and wash carefully with water, separating the branches to remove any soil, and cut into two lengthwise. Fill a large pan with iced water. Fill another large pan with salted water and bring to the boil. Add the brèdes. Cook for about 6 minutes; they need to remain green and slightly crisp. Drain them with a skimmer, dip into the iced water, run under cold water and drain them again.

Peel the ginger and slice into thin julienne, using a sharp knife. Peel and chop the garlic (removing the germ). Wash and clean the chervil, discarding the stalks.

To prepare the sauce Heat the poultry stock with the ginger and, once it has come to the boil, simmer for 10 minutes. Salt and pepper. Keep hot.

Last minute

Sauté the brèdes in a frying pan in 1 tbsp olive oil and 1/2 tbsp butter. Season with salt and freshly ground white pepper. Heat 1 tbsp goose fat on moderate heat in a small, non-stick pan. When it is very hot, add the chicken oysters and the confit wings. Turn them halfway through the cooking, add the chopped ginger and garlic, 1 tbsp butter and caramelise for a few seconds. Deglaze with the Kikkoman soy sauce and add pepper. Remove from the stove. The chicken oysters should be tender.

Sprinkle the grouper fillets with sea salt and freshly ground Sichuan pepper. Heat 3 tbsp goose fat on moderate heat in a large, non-stick pan. When it is hot, add the grouper fillets. Halfway through the cooking, turn the fillets to cook the other side and remove from the stove. The meat of the fish should be opaque but still tender and moist.

To serve Place the brèdes on 4 pre-warmed plates and add the shallots and fennel, shimmering hot. Place the fish on top of them. Sprinkle with fleur de sel. Surround them with the similarly hot chicken oysters and wings. Reheat the sauce. Pour a layer around the fillets and use a teaspoon to add a few drops of citronella oil. Add a few pieces of chervil and serve straightaway.

Alternative

Turbot or John Dory fillets can be used instead of grouper fish.

Note The chicken "oysters" are the two tender morsels found in the back of each chicken.

Serves 4

Ingredients

2	Groupers, weighing 800 g each
	Freshly ground Sichuan pepper
4 tbsp	Goose fat
	Table sea salt
	Fleur de sel
	Freshly ground white pepper
12	Chicken wings
12	Chicken "oysters"
1 l.	Olive oil
10 g	Ginger
1 clove	Garlic
3 tbsp	Kikkoman soy sauce
2 tbsp	Echiré butter

Marinade

3 dl.	Kikkoman soy sauce
1 dl.	Rice vinegar
1 dl.	Water
2 cloves	Garlic
20 g	Ginger
1 tbsp	Raw sugar
2 sprigs	Thyme

Garnish

6	Confit Shallots *
4	Brèdes Tom-Pouce (baby bok-choy)
8	Baby fennel bulbs
2 dl.	White chicken stock *
60 g	Echiré butter
1 tbsp	Olive oil
1/2 bunch	Chervil

Sauce

4 dl.	Poultry stock *
5 g	Ginger

Citronella oil

3 g	Ginger
80 g	Citronella stalks
2 1/2 dl.	Taggiasche extra virgin olive oil
	Freshly ground white pepper

* see basic recipes

Crispy sesame layers with pan-fried duck foie gras and mango roasted with the savours of Mauritius

Recipe

To prepare 12 feuillantines Wash the sweet potatoes. Start with cold water in a deep pan and add 5 g of salt. Cook the potatoes for 30 to 35 minutes on moderate heat. Use a knife to check that they are done: it should go in and come out of the potatoes easily. Drain the potatoes and peel them quickly, whilst they are still hot. Mash them with a spatula through a sieve. Put the purée into a saucepan and add 2 egg whites, 25 g softened butter, salt and pepper. Mix vigorously.

Use a tablespoon to put small scoops of the purée onto a non-stick tray and spread them into thin layers about 1 mm thick and not larger than 9 cm across. Sprinkle with black and white sesame seeds. Cook in an oven preheated to 160º C. The feuillantines (crispy layers) take to 2 to 3 minutes to cook. They will be a beautiful golden brown. Once the feuillantines have cooled down, keep them in an airtight container.

To prepare the sauce Sweat the home-made curry powder in butter, then add the rest of the spices and simmer for a few more seconds. Deglaze with *1 dl.* red wine and reduce until dry.

Add *5 dl.* duck stock. Simmer for a few minutes before straining the sauce through a conical sieve. Check seasoning and keep hot.

To prepare the garnish Wash the brèdes, separate the leaves from the stalks and shape the stalks into petals. Use a sharp knife to cut off the roots of the leeks very close to the bulb. Shorten the tips of the leaves. Keep only one third of green to two thirds of white. Remove the outer leaf. Wash the leeks carefully several times, changing the water each time, and then under running water, separating the leaves to eliminate any soil more easily. Wash the chou-chou, peel and cut into four to remove the stones. Cut each quarter into three pieces lengthwise.

Fill a large pan with iced water. Fill another large pan with water and bring it to the boil. Salt and add the brèdes, then stir them. Cook for about 2 minutes (the brèdes should remain green and slightly crisp). Drain them with a skimmer, dip them in the iced water and drain them again. Cook all the other vegetables in the same way, one after the other, in the same pan, leaving the leeks for last. Cool them in the iced water and drain thoroughly.

Wash and peel the squash, remove the seeds and the fibre in the centre, cut them into large scallops before frying them in a knob of butter until they are tender and golden. Lightly salt and pepper. Wash the mangoes, peel them and cut into four so that the seeds can be removed. Cut the quarters into large scallops, and then fry in the same way as the squash.

Last minute

Remove any traces of gall that remain on the foie gras. Cut the foie gras diagonally into 4 slices weighing 140 g each and keep cool. Take an 18 cm wide pan with a lid. Pour in the olive oil and add 25 g of butter and *1/2 dl.* vegetable stock. Heat slowly. Sweat the leeks rapidly; they need to remain beautifully green and white. Cover and cook slowly for 2 minutes. Add the chou-chou and the brèdes and continue to cook for 1 more minute until the vegetables are tender. Make sure the vegetables do not brown, by shaking the pan from time to time. Salt and pepper.

Meanwhile season the foie gras slices with fleur de sel. Cook the foie gras in a very hot frying pan, without adding fat, for 3 minutes on each side without letting it burn. Sprinkle the foie gras with crushed black pepper.

Take 4 pre-warmed plates. Place a feuillantine in the middle of each plate and add the hot mangoes on top, making an 80 mm diametre bed in the middle of them. Place the second feuillantine on top of the mangoes. Place half of the vegetables on this second feuillantine, then a foie gras scallop, cover with vegetables once again and top with the third feuillantine. Pour sauce around the edge of the dish and serve immediately.

Note *We tend to prefer duck to goose foie gras. It tends to go softer more easily when cooked; it has a rich and unctuous texture and its taste is stronger than goose foie gras.*

Serves 4

Ingredients

600 g	Landes duck foie gras
	Fleur de sel
	Table sea salt
	Freshly ground white pepper
	Crushed black pepper *

Sweet potato layers (feuillantines)

500 g	Sweet potatoes
2	Egg whites
25 g	Echiré butter
5 g	White sesame seeds
5 g	Black sesame seeds

Sauce

5 g	Tandoori masala *
2 g	Paprika
10 g	Home-made curry powder *
2 g	Coriander seeds
3 g	Pink pepper
1 dl.	Red wine
1 l.	Duck stock *

Garnish

3	Alphonso or Tommy Atkins mangoes (semi-ripe)
12	Brèdes Tom-Pouce (baby pak-choy)
12	Young leeks
2	Chou-chou (cho-cho)
1/2	Butternut squash
75 g	Echiré butter
1/2 dl.	Vegetable stock *
2 tbsp	Olive oil

* *see basic recipes*

Pumpkin and calabash vindaloo flavoured with coconut and almonds

Recipe

Peel the ginger and garlic (removing the germ) and crush in a mortar. Peel and slice the onion thinly. Clean the coriander, remove the stalks and chop up the leaves. Snip up the chives. Cut the chilli into two, remove the seeds, and dice finely into brunoise. Remove the cores from the tomatoes, bring 5 l. of water to the boil and dip in the tomatoes. Remove the tomatoes after 30 seconds and dip them immediately into cold water. Peel, cut them into two, remove the seeds and use a knife to chop them up.

Peel the pumpkin and cut into two. Remove the seeds and the fibres from the heart. Cut the flesh into 1.5 cm cubes. Prepare the calabash in the same way.

Heat 2 tbsp oil in a 26 cm wide pan, sauté the pumpkin cubes, season with salt and a pinch of curry powder. Make sure that the pumpkin does not brown by shaking the pan from time to time. Repeat for the calabash. Place the calabash and pumpkin separately to one side.

Heat 3 tbsp peanut oil in a thick-bottomed, 26 cm wide casserole dish, add the cinnamon, cumin, clove and cardamom. Sauté them for a few seconds until they give off a good aroma. Add the sliced onion, and the crushed garlic and ginger. After 5 minutes, add the turmeric, the rest of the curry powder and the tomatoes. Sweat for 10 minutes and then add $2^{1/2}$ dl. of vegetable stock and 3 dl. coconut milk. Bring it close to the boil and add the thyme, curry leaves, chilli and salt. Simmer slowly for 15 minutes. As soon as the sauce starts to thicken, first add the calabash, then the pumpkin and the garam massala. Check seasoning.

Open the coconut by breaking it with a hammer or rolling pin. Remove the coconut water. Peel the coconut pulp with a paring knife and cut into thin julienne with a sharp knife.

Soak the whole almonds in lukewarm water, then remove their skin and cut them into small sticks.

Last minute

Place the vindaloo in a hot dish. Sprinkle with chives, chopped coriander, coconut julienne and the almond sticks. Serve the black lentils fricassée and the white rice separately, as well as small dishes of pickles and the various chutneys.

Alternative

There are many varieties of gourds and squashes, and any can be used instead of the calabash and pumpkin.

Serves 4

Ingredients

300	g	Onions
30	g	Garlic
30	g	Ginger
1	dl.	Peanut oil
1	stick	Cassia cinnamon
5	g	Green cardamom
5		Cloves
1	tbsp	Cumin
2	tbsp	Home-made curry powder *
1	tbsp	Turmeric powder
300	g	Vine tomatoes (ripe)
1	tbsp	Garam massala *
2 1/2	dl.	Vegetable stock *
1	sprig	Thyme
1	branch	Carri-poulé (curry) leaves
1		Red chilli
3	dl.	Coconut milk (tinned and unsweetened)
1	kg	Calabash (gourd)
1	kg	Pumpkin
50	g	Almonds
50	g	Coconut
1/2	bunch	Chives
1/2	bunch	Coriander
		Table sea salt

Served with

4	portions	Black lentils fricassée *
4	portions	Perfumed Basmati rice *
4	portions	Various chutneys *
4	portions	Cythera pickle *

* see basic recipes

Roast white tuna with black pepper and bonemarrow on garlic-flavoured mashed potatoes

Recipe

To prepare the marrowbones Remove the marrow from the bones, put the bone-marrow to soak for 24 hours in a container, changing the water several times. Then drain and cut each piece into three parts. Poach the bone-marrow slices in a pan of salted cold water, place on moderate heat and remove as soon as the water begins to simmer. Keep the marrow in its cooking water.

To prepare the mashed potatoes Peel 1 head of new garlic, cut each clove into halves and remove the germs. Blanch the garlic in a pan of salted cold water, bring quickly to the boil and remove after cooking for 1 minute. Change the water, repeat this operation 3 times and then rinse the garlic immediately under cold water. Poach the garlic in a pan of salted cold milk: bring the milk quickly to boiling point and cook slowly for about 30 minutes; the milk must never boil but only simmer. Drain the garlic as soon as it is cooked. Then sieve.

Now start to incorporate the garlic purée into the mashed potatoes, stirring vigorously to make it smooth and light. Check seasoning and keep hot.

To prepare the garlic Remove the outer leaves of the second head of garlic and separate the cloves. Do not peel the individual cloves. Put the cloves of garlic in a 12 cm wide pan. Add the bay leaf and chilli. Cover with *2 dl.* olive oil. Place the pan on low heat. As soon as the oil starts to simmer, cook slowly for about 45 minutes. The oil should not boil but only simmer. When the cloves of garlic are confit, remove from the stove but keep warm.

Use a knife to clean the oyster mushrooms. Wash with plenty of water and put them to one side on a dry tea towel.

To prepare the fried parsley Pour the oil into a *2 l.* pan or a deep fryer. Heat to 180° C. Meanwhile wash the flat-leaved parsley and dab it dry. Discard the stalks. Place the leaves in a frying basket and dip it for a few moments into the very hot oil. Drain on kitchen paper and add salt. The fried parsley needs to be used as soon as possible.

Last minute

Season the tuna with sea salt and crushed black pepper and coat them with 3 tbsp olive oil. Sauté them in a little oil in a frying pan, and finish cooking them in an oven at 160° C for 7 minutes. The fish should stay slightly pink to retain its flavour and tenderness. Let it cool down to room temperature.

Meanwhile, reduce the veal stock to concentrate the flavour and check seasoning.

Sear the oyster mushrooms for 1 minute in a pan with a knob of butter. Salt and pepper. Drain and keep hot.

To serve Take 4 pre-warmed plates. Reheat the tuna for 2 minutes in the oven. Place a small pile of oyster mushrooms in the centre of each plate, slice the tuna into 4 steaks and place a steak on each pile. Place 2 slices of bone-marrow on each piece of tuna, sprinkle with fleur de sel and add a bunch of fried parsley. Reheat the veal stock, season and incorporate the olive oil, and pour some of this sauce around the tuna slices. Decorate around the fish with confit garlic. Put the garlic-flavoured mashed potatoes in a separate dish and serve straightaway.

Alternative

Albacore tuna or swordfish can be used instead of white tuna.

Serves 4

Ingredients

800 g	White tuna dorsal fillet (without the skin and the visible blood lines)
4	Marrowbones
	Coarse sea salt
	Fleur de sel
	Table sea salt
	Freshly ground white pepper
1 tbsp	Crushed black pepper *
6 tbsp	Olive oil

Garnish

1/2 bunch	Flat-leaved parsley
4 portions	Mashed potatoes *
2 heads	New garlic
2 dl.	Olive oil
2 1/2 dl.	Milk
1	Bay leaf
1/2	Red chilli
250 g	Oyster mushrooms
20 g	Echiré butter

Veal stock

3 dl.	Veal stock *
6 tbsp	Taggiasche extra virgin olive oil

Oil for frying

1 l.	Sunflower oil

* see basic recipes

Traditional Moslem chicken biryani
with various chutneys and Rodriguan lime pickle

Recipe

To prepare the marinade Peel the ginger and garlic (removing the germ) and crush in a mortar. Peel and slice the onions up thinly. Clean the coriander leaves, remove the stalks, and chop up the leaves. Repeat for the mint.

Pour the oil into a *2 l.* pan or a deep fryer. Heat to 170º C. Fry the onions, leaving them for 4 to 5 minutes in the boiling oil. When they are golden and crisp, drain and remove from the oil with a skimmer and place them on kitchen paper. Keep the frying oil for the vegetables. Steep the saffron in half a cup of boiling water for 10 minutes.

Heat 3 tbsp ghee in a 16 cm wide pan. Sauté the garlic, ginger, cinnamon, cardamom, 2 cloves of garlic and *2¹/2* tsp cumin for a few seconds until they release a pleasant aroma. Leave them to cool down. Cut the chillies into halves, remove the seeds and slice them into very fine julienne. Cut the chicken thighs into two and place them in a dish. Add the garlic and ginger mixture to the spices, as well as the 200 g fried onions, 10 g mint leaves, 10 g coriander, the chillies, 2 tbsp of the steeped saffron, and then gradually incorporate the 250 g of yoghurt. Allow the chicken to marinate by covering with cling film and placing it in the refrigerator for at least 4 hours.

To prepare the dough Pour the flour and 3 egg whites into a bowl. Mix into a smooth paste. Add the fourth egg white if necessary. If the paste is too firm, add several teaspoons of water to soften it. Preheat the oven to 220º C.

To prepare the vegetables and rice Use a sharp knife to remove the skin from the patissons and the courgettes, and cut them into 1.5 cm cubes. Repeat for the potatoes and carrots. Heat a deep fryer to 170º C. Fry the courgettes, patissons, potatoes and carrots separately, leaving them for 4 to 5 minutes in the boiling oil. When they turn slightly golden and are half-cooked, drain and remove the vegetables from the oil with a skimmer, and place them on kitchen paper.

Shell the peas. Bring *2 l.* of water and half a handful of sea salt to the boil. Dip in the peas and then cool them straightaway in cold water.

Bring *3 l.* of water to the boil in a large pan with the cloves, 1 cinnamon stick, 1¹/2 tsp of uncrushed cumin and the salt. Wash the rice several times. Drain, add to the contents of the pan and cook for 5 minutes until it is transparent. Drain the rice and keep the cooking stock.

To make the biryani Take a thick-bottomed, 30 cm wide casserole dish with a lid. Arrange the marinated chicken in the bottom of the dish, alternating with a layer of vegetables. Sprinkle with 1¹/2 tbsp of fried onions, the coriander, mint, and peas, followed by a layer of rice. Then repeat with a further 1¹/2 tbsp of fried onions, coriander, mint, and peas, followed by another layer of rice and 1¹/2 tbsp of fried onions. Add two thirds of the rice stock and the rest of the steeped saffron.

Prepare the glaze, by mixing the egg yolks with 1 tbsp water in a bowl. Seal the casserole dish with the dough in the following way. Divide the dough into two and roll out both pieces into 2 sausages shapes, about 10 cm long, long and wide enough to go right round the casserole dish. Arrange the 2 sausage shapes around the top of the casserole dish and place the lid on top so that it forms a good seal. Brush the dough with glaze.

Last minute

Place the casserole dish in the oven and cook for 40 minutes at 220º C. Remove the dish from the oven but do not break the crust immediately. Leave it to stand at room temperature for at least 15 minutes, but no more than 30 minutes. The biryani continues to cook in the sealed casserole dish. The Rodriguan lime pickle, various chutneys and Raita sauce should be placed on the table to accompany the dish. Carry in the casserole dish: it is important to break open the crust in front of the guests, because of the aroma that comes out at that particular moment. Divide the biryani over 4 plates.

Note The success of this delicious dish relies heavily on the quality of the chicken. Grain-fed chicken, slaughtered when they are 50 to 70 days old, when their weight is between 1.2 and 1.8 kg, are best. They are better formed and their flesh is tender, firm and tastier.

Serves 4

Ingredients

1	kg	Free-range chicken thighs
8	tbsp	Ghee *
2		Cassia cinnamon sticks, 10 cm long
2	tsp	Crushed green cardamoms
50	g	Garlic
50	g	Ginger
250	g	Onions
10		Green cardamom seeds
3	tsp	Roast cumin seeds
5		Cloves
1/2	bunch	Mint
1/2	bunch	Coriander
2		Red chillies
2	g	La Mancha saffron
250	g	Plain yoghurt
350	g	Kohinoor Basmati rice, 1 year old
		Table sea salt

Vegetables

200	g	Potatoes
200	g	Carrots
100	g	Patissons (custard marrows)
50	g	Peas (shelled)
100	g	Courgettes (about 1.5 cm thick)

Oil for frying

1	l.	Peanut oil

For the dough

140	g	Flour
3 à 4		Egg whites
2		Egg yolks

Served with

4	portions	Rodriguan lime pickle *
4	portions	Various chutneys *
4	portions	Raita sauce (see recipe, page 188)

see basic recipes

Spicy cocoa crunch
with ladyfinger banana ice-cream

Recipe

To prepare the tuiles Melt the butter slowly, then remove from the stove. Mix the flour, the sifted cocoa powder, the brown sugar and the icing sugar in a basin. Pour in the orange juice and whisk. Add the melted butter and mix well. Leave the dough to stand for half an hour in the refrigerator. Preheat the oven to 170º C.

Take 4 sheets of firmish plastic, 17 cm long and 10 cm wide (the kind of plastic used as a file divider). Spread the dough onto the plastic sheets, placed on a non-stick tray. Crush the Sichuan pepper in a mixer, sift and sprinkle a few pinches over the dough. Put in the oven for 5 to 7 minutes. Remove from the oven and allow the tuiles to cool down. As soon as they are lukewarm, roll them around a 45 mm wide and 100 mm long plastic tube. Press the edges together well. Let the tuiles cool down further before removing them. Store them in an airtight tin.

To prepare the ice cream Bring the milk to the boil in a 30 cm wide pan, and then add the cream. Mix the egg yolks and the sugar, and whisk until the mixture until it turns whitish. Add the milk and the cream. Return the pan to the stove on low heat and stir continuously with a spatula until the custard starts to become smooth and even. Remove it from the stove. Peel the bananas and blend in a mixer. Weigh out 300 g of the banana purée and mix with the hot custard. Whisk and pass through a fine sieve into a bain-marie, that is a bowl within a bowl of ice. Let it cool down, then pour it into an ice-cream maker. Freeze the ice-cream when it is almost set.

To prepare the banana chips Pour the oil into a *2 l.* pan or a deep fryer. Heat to 180º C. Meanwhile peel the bananas, cut them lengthwise with a mandoline into 1 mm thick slices. Fry in batches of 10 to 15, leaving them for 3 to 4 minutes in the boiling oil. When they are golden and crisp, use a skimmer to drain and remove them from the oil. Place on kitchen paper and sprinkle generously with icing sugar.

To prepare the banana salad Peel the bananas. Dice the bananas into small pieces, put them into a bowl together with the syrup and limejuice. Chop up the pistachio nuts a little.

Last minute

Remove the ice-cream from the freezer. Use a small ladle to coat the plates with the chilled sabayon. Place a cocoa tube in the centre of each plate. Place two scoops of ice-cream in each tube. Decorate with 1 tbsp of banana salad, and stick 6 to 7 banana chips into the ice-cream. Sprinkle a few chopped pistachio nuts around the tuiles and serve.

Note For this recipe, always use ladyfinger bananas, which are very short bananas about 6 to 8 cm long. They have a smooth skin and firm flesh, with a sweet and pleasant taste.

Serves 4

Ingredients

500	g	Ladyfinger bananas (half ripe)
200	g	Pistachio-flavoured sabayon *
50	g	Finely ground pistachio nuts (green) Icing sugar

Banana salad

3		Ladyfinger bananas (half-ripe)
50	ml.	Syrup (see recipe, page 240)
		Juice of 1/2 a Meyer lemon or Tahiti lime

Tuile

125	g	Icing sugar
125	g	Brown sugar
115	g	Sifted flour
35	g	Valrhona or Van houten cocoa powder
125	ml.	Orange juice
125	g	Echiré butter
5	g	Sichuan pepper

Ice cream

300	ml.	Skimmed milk
300	ml.	Double cream
100	g	Cane sugar
6		Egg yolks
400	g	Ladyfinger bananas

Oil for frying

1	l.	Peanut oil

* see basic recipes

Mango and longan fruit salad with mildly-spiced yoghurt sorbet

Recipe

To prepare the yoghurt sorbet Bring the milk, sugar, honey, and spices to the boil in a 20 cm wide pan. Allow to stand and infuse for about 10 minutes. Add the cream and trimoline, and then the yoghurt. Whisk and strain through a conical sieve into a bain-marie, that is a bowl within a bowl of ice. Let it cool down, then put the mixture into an ice-cream maker and turn it on. When the sorbet has nearly set, place it on an ice tray and then into the freezer.

To prepare the syrup Bring the water, sugar and honey to the boil in a pan, 15 cm wide. Remove from the stove and leave it to cool down.

To prepare the mango and longan salad Wash and peel the mangoes. Cut the mangoes into sticks, 5 mm wide and 50 mm long, and put them in a bowl. Take off the shell from the longans, discard the stones, and cut the fruit into two. Blanch the almonds in boiling water and remove their skins. Cut the almonds into small sticks. Pour the syrup into a basin along with the mangoes and longans and mix them carefully together. Chill them for an hour before serving.

Last minute

Remove the sorbet from the freezer. Divide the mango and longan salad into 4 shallow dishes. Top with the syrup. Add a scoop of sorbet to each dish, sprinkle with almond julienne and currants. Serve straightaway.

Alternatives

Litchis can be used instead of longans. Choose mangoes that are ripe and not fibrous, for example Alphonso or Alphonsine, which originate from India. They melt in the mouth and have a very sweet taste.

"Trimoline" is made out of glucose, and prevents the sorbet from crystallising. Simple glucose can be used instead, or it can be omitted if the sorbet is served within 12 hours.

Serves 4

Ingredients

6		Alphonso or Tommy Atkins mangoes
24		Longans (dragon's eye fruit)
100	g	Whole almonds
100	g	Currants

Syrup

250	ml.	Water
50	g	Cane sugar
25	g	Rodriguan honey

Yoghurt sorbet

500	g	Plain yoghurt
50	g	Cane sugar
50	g	Rodriguan honey
75	ml.	Semi-skimmed milk
50	ml.	Double cream
25	g	Trimoline (optional)
1	g	Cassia cinnamon powder
5	grains	Crushed cardamom
1	g	Star anise powder

* see basic recipes

Pineapple Tatin with caramel fudge and ice-cream flavoured with oriental spices

Recipe

To prepare the base Roll out the puff pastry to a thickness of 2 mm and place on a tray covered with slightly moist greaseproof paper. Prick the pastry all over and leave it to stand for 1 hour in the refrigerator. Preheat the oven to 200º C. Then place another sheet of greaseproof paper on the pastry and a tray on top, and leave it in the oven for 15 minutes. Remove the upper tray and greaseproof paper and continue to bake for another 5 minutes, then remove from the oven.

To prepare the pineapple Peel the pineapples, cut off the ends and cut into two widthwise. Place a thick-bottomed copper pan containing 150 g of sugar and 4 tbsp water on the stove, and let it caramelise until it becomes golden, with a strong but not burnt aroma. Add 1 l. of hot water and bring to the boil. Put in the four pineapple halves and poach slowly for 30 minutes. Drain and remove the hearts from the pineapples.

Preheat the oven to 180 Cº. Caramelise 150 g of sugar and 80 g of butter in a 20 cm wide frying pan, until the mixture becomes golden. Pour the caramel into 4 cake moulds, 6 cm wide, add the pineapples and bake the Tatins in the oven for 30 minutes.

To prepare the fudge Heat 125 g sugar and 4 tbsp cold water in a thick-bottomed copper saucepan to make a caramel. Meanwhile heat the cream in another pan. As soon as the sugar acquires a golden tinge, add the hot cream, let it boil for a few moments, remove from the stove, add the butter and whisk.

To prepare the ice-cream Bring the milk to the boil in a 30 cm wide pan. Add the spices, leave them to infuse for 10 minutes and then add the cream. Mix the egg yolks and the sugar together in a bowl and whisk the mixture until it turns whitish. Gradually pour the infused milk into this mixture. Return the pan to the stove and stir continuously with a spatula until the cream starts to become smooth and even. Remove the cream from the stove and continue to stir for 10 seconds. Strain through a muslin conical sieve and leave to cool in ice. Pour into an ice-cream maker and churn. Freeze the ice-cream when it is almost set.

Last minute

Warm up the Tatins just before serving them. Cut 4 discs of puff pastry with a pastry cutter of the same size as the Tatins. Remove the Tatins from the oven and cover with the puff pastry. Place a small plate on top of each and turn them upside down. Put the caramel fudge in small greaseproof paper cones and arrange them on the plates. Place a small scoop of the spiced ice-cream on top of each Tatin. Garnish with pieces of candied pineapple.

Serves 4

Ingredients

200	g	Puff pastry *
2		Small Victoria pineapples (ripe)
150	g	Cane sugar
80	g	Echiré butter
20	pieces	Candied pineapple *

Caramel syrup

1	l.	Water
150	g	Cane sugar

Fudge caramel

125	g	Cane sugar
4	tbsp	Water
50	g	Double cream
25	g	Echiré butter

Ice cream

300	ml.	Skimmed milk
300	ml.	Crème fraîche
6		Egg yolks
100	g	Cane sugar
3	g	Oriental spices *

* see basic recipes

Crispy Grand Cru Caraque chocolate ravioli with rum-flavoured sabayon, preserved pineapple and cocoa sorbet

Recipe

Make the ravioli dough in the bowl of a food processor. Put in all the ingredients: flour, semolina flour, eggs, olive oil and cocoa. Process until the dough is smooth and even and forms a ball. Wrap the dough in cling film and refrigerate. The longer you leave it to stand, the easier it will be to roll out.

To prepare the sorbet Chop up the chocolate a little. Boil the water with the sugar for 3 minutes and add the cocoa powder. Gradually whisk the chocolate into the mixture, letting it cool down. Add the trimoline. Pass through a muslin sieve and let it cool down further in a basin in a bowl of ice (bain-marie). When the mixture is cool, pour into an ice cream maker. Freeze the sorbet, once it has set.

To prepare the chocolate cream filling (ganache) Cut the ginger into very fine brunoise. Chop up the chocolate a little and boil the cream. Gradually pour the boiling cream onto the chocolate and whisk it, to cool it down to room temperature. Put this mixture, the softened butter and the ginger brunoise into a mixing bowl and whip on second speed until it has doubled in volume. Take a piping bag with a No 9 nozzle, pipe 20 small balls the size of hazel nuts onto greaseproof paper and refrigerate.

To prepare the ravioli Roll out the dough thinly with a rolling pin or a rolling mill. Place a strip of dough on a lightly-floured work surface. Use a pastry cutter to cut circles of about 5 cm diameter. Place a ball of the ganache in the middle. Use a brush to moisten the edge of half the circle of dough with water. Holding the circle in the palm of your hand, fold one side onto the other to seal in the stuffing. Pinch the edges together to seal them. Let the ravioli dry for 10 minutes on a clean tea towel, leaving a space between them so that they do not stick together. Cover with cling film and place in the refrigerator.

To prepare the pineapple Boil up the sugar and water in a 10 cm wide pan. Peel the pineapple, cut it into four and remove the heart. Put the pineapple quarters in the syrup and cook slowly for 15 minutes. After cooking, drain and leave to cool. Then, dice the pineapple quarters into small 3 mm cubes and place them in a basin. Grate the peel of the lime on a mandoline and chop finely before mixing with the pineapple. Keep in the refrigerator.

Last minute

Pour the oil into a large 4 l. pan or a deep fryer and heat to 160º C. Take 4 plates. Place a 40 mm wide, 5 mm high plastic circle in the middle of each plate and fill it with the pineapple tartar. Remove the pastry cutter. Place a ring of sabayon around with a few traces of mango sauce. Remove the ravioli from the freezer, put them into boiling oil and fry in batches of 10, leaving them for 1 to 2 minutes in the boiling oil. When they are golden and crisp, use a skimmer to drain them and remove them from the oil. Put them on kitchen paper and sprinkle with icing sugar and cocoa powder. Remove the sorbet from the freezer, use a spoon to scoop out portions of sorbet and garnish the sorbet with a piece of candied pineapple. Place the 5 raviolis around and serve immediately.

Alternative

Coconut sorbet or ice-cream infused with ginger can be used instead of cocoa sorbet.

Serves 4

Ingredients

Chocolate ravioli dough

250	g	Semolina flour
125	g	Sifted flour
4		Eggs
40	g	Valrhona or Van houten cocoa powder
2	tbsp	Olive oil

Chocolate cream filling (ganache)

500	g	Double cream
700	g	Valrhona Caraque chocolate (contains 56% cocoa)
200	g	Echiré butter (softened)
100	g	Preserved ginger

Preserved pineapple

500	ml.	Water
100	g	Cane sugar
1/2		Victoria pineapple
1/2		Meyer lemon or Tahiti lime

Cocoa sorbet

.500	ml.	Water
100	g	Cane sugar
25	g	Trimoline (optional)
20	g	Valrhona or Van houten cocoa powder
150	g	Valrhona Caraque chocolate

Garnish

200	g	Chilled rum-flavoured sabayon *
25	ml.	Mango sauce *
4		Candied pineapple *

Oil for frying

3	l.	Peanut oil
20	g	Icing sugar
20	g	Valrhona or Van houten cocoa powder

* see basic recipes

Rodriguan honey madeleines

Recipe

Mix the flour, icing sugar and very finely ground almonds in a bowl. Melt the butter in a 10 cm wide pan until it has a nutty colour. Lightly whisk the egg whites in a second bowl; add the contents of the first bowl and whisk. When the mixture is even, incorporate the lukewarm hazelnut butter and the honey.

Allow the mixture to stand for at least 1 hour in the refrigerator before cooking it.

Last minute

Heat the oven to 180º C. Butter the baking trays and sprinkle with flour. Use a tablespoon to fill the moulds with the mixture or fill them by putting the mixture in a piping bag with a 1 cm smooth nozzle. Cook the madeleines for about 10 minutes; they must be golden when they come out of the oven. Remove the madeleines from the trays and leave them to cool down inside, standing them on the edges of the tray so that they do not cool down too quickly. Serve warm.

Note Madeleines cook better in a convection oven than in a traditional one.

To make about 20 madeleines

Ingredients

100 g	Very finely ground almonds
100 g	Sifted flour
250 g	Icing sugar
8	Egg whites
150 g	Echiré Butter
50 g	Rodriguan honey

For the baking trays

Softened butter
Flour

see basic recipes

Green Recipes

Spiced snapper on sugarcane skewers — 247

Vegetable terrine in mazavarou-flavoured Taggiasche oil with garlic crostini — 248

Green pineapple ravioli with spicy rock lobster fricassée and eucalyptus honey vinaigrette — 249

Sea bream carpaccio flavoured with green lemon and coconut — 250

Creamy watercress soup served as a cappuccino with clams and salted Grissini — 251

Creamy breadfruit soup with crispy smoked bacon — 252

Mildly-spiced camarons with pineapple and Rodriguan lime chutney — 253

Flame snapper and crayfish on vegetables simmered in dried fruit with a spicy pumpkin-flavoured sauce — 254

Pumpkin and gourd Vialone Nano risotto with crispy smoked pancetta — 255

Pot-roasted farm-raised veal rump with shii-take mushrooms and ginger-flavoured gravy — 256

Spit-roasted free-range chicken served with citronella-flavoured gravy and crispy cassava straws — 257

Crème caramel with rum-flavoured raisins — 258

Queen Victoria pineapple baked in Sichuan pepper and caramelised with cane sugar, served with citronella ice-cream — 259

Mango baked in Fragrans vanilla with diplomat cream and crispy pistachio-flavoured philo — 260

Guava jam — 261

Caramel-flavoured ladyfinger banana samossas with coconut sorbet — 262

Spiced snapper on sugarcane skewers

Recipe

To prepare the spices Heat and dry the black pepper and cumin in a small frying pan. Mix the spices together in a coffee mill and store them in an airtight jar. This spice powder will keep for one month.

To prepare the fish Ask the fishmonger to fillet the fish and remove the skin and bones. Cut the sugarcane sticks into 20 skewers, 10 cm long and 3 mm thick.

Wash the pepper leaves and cut into 3 cm squares.

To prepare the brochettes Cut the fish fillets into 3 cm chunks. Stick a piece of fish on a skewer, then a pepper leaf, a piece of fish, a pepper leaf, and finish with a piece of fish. Make up the other brochettes - 20 in all - with the rest of the ingredients. Sprinkle each brochette with the spice powder and a few drops of olive oil. Marinate for 30 minutes.

Last minute

Season the brochettes with fleur de sel. Heat the oil on moderate heat in a large non-stick pan. Add the brochettes and cook for 2 minutes, turning them so that they are golden all over. Meanwhile heat up infused ginger. Place the brochettes on a plate, sprinkle with infused ginger and serve straightaway.

Alternative

Berri blanc seems to be a fish which is close to a variety of snapper. Couch's sea bream or red sea bream are suitable alternatives. Bamboo skewers can be used if sugarcane is not available.

To make 20 brochettes

Ingredients

20	Sugarcane sticks
2	Berri blanc (snapper), each weighing 1 kg
8	Pepper leaves (optional)
20 g	Powdered turmeric
15 g	Black pepper
5 g	Grated nutmeg
10 g	Cumin
10 g	Dried ginger *
1 dl.	Olive oil
	Fleur de sel

Served with

50 cl.	Ginger sauce (see recipe, page 253)

* see basic recipes

Vegetable terrine
in mazavarou-flavoured Taggiasche oil with garlic crostini

Recipe

To prepare the vegetables Peel the red and green peppers, cut them into four and remove the seeds. Place the quarters in two shallow, oven-proof dishes, sprinkle with *1/2 dl.* Taggiasche oil, a few sprigs of thyme, garlic, salt and pepper. Cook in the oven at 90º C for about 45 minutes. Peel the aubergines, stand in coarse salt for about 30 minutes, rinse them under the tap and pat them dry. Then brown them and roast them in the oven at 120º C for about 15 minutes, until they become tender. Use a sharp knife to remove the skin of the patissons and courgettes and cook until tender in boiling salted water. Cool them down in cold water. Take the fennel and remove the outer layer, the ends and the stalks. Cut them into two lengthwise and sweat in 3 tbsp olive oil, deglaze with the vegetable stock and season with salt and pepper. Cook in the oven at 120º C for about 35 minutes.

Take a terrine, 30 cm long, 11 cm wide and 10 cm high. Line it with cling film, which must overlap the terrine by at least 7 cm on all sides, so that it covers the terrine during cooking. Place the vegetables side by side lengthwise in the terrine, placing a sheet of gelatine that has been soaked in iced water between each layer of vegetables. When arranging the vegetables, start with a layer of red peppers, followed by courgettes, patissons, green peppers and fennel. Start again with the red peppers, stop with the green peppers and finish with the aubergines and confit tomatoes. Do not forget to place a gelatine sheet between each layer of vegetables. Cook in a bain-marie (i.e. place the terrine in a dish of boiling water) at 160º C for 45 minutes. After cooking, turn over the terrine onto a press (a wooden board, 30 cm long, 2 cm thick and 11 cm wide) and leave it to stand in a refrigerator for 24 hours. Then turn out the pressed vegetables, wrap in cling film and refrigerate again.

To prepare the vegetable sauce Wash the vegetables and cut into thin mirepoix. Heat 2 tbsp olive oil in a 14 cm wide, thick-bottomed pan with a lid. Sweat the vegetable mirepoix with the spices, without browning them, for 3 minutes on moderate heat, and then deglaze with vegetable stock. Braise for 10 minutes. Mix with coriander and Savora mustard and then whip it up with Taggiasche extra virgin olive oil into a very smooth and even sauce. Check seasoning and strain through a muslin conical sieve.

To prepare the mazavarou oil Peel and chop the ginger, garlic (removing the germ) and onion. Slice the chillies. Wash the plum tomatoes and cut into cubes. Sauté the ginger, garlic and onion in 3 tbsp olive oil, add the sliced chillies, stirring all the time. Do not let them brown. Finally, add the tomato purée, the tomato cubes and the dried shrimps. Simmer for 2 minutes. Steep for 1 hour at 60º C and strain through a muslin conical sieve. Keep the oil.

To prepare the new garlic Sort through the chives, keep a few pieces for the garnish, and snip up the rest. Wash the chillies, seed and cut into fine brunoise. Chop the coriander leaves. Peel the cloves of new garlic and cut them into two to remove the germ. Put the garlic in a pan of salted cold water, bring quickly to the boil and remove after blanching for 1 minute. Repeat three times and finally rinse the garlic under cold, running water. Poach the new garlic in a pan of salted cold milk that should be brought quickly to near boiling point. Simmer very slowly for about 30 minutes; the milk must not boil. Drain the garlic as soon as it is cooked and crush it up a little with a fork. Mix all the ingredients carefully in a bowl. Check seasoning.

To prepare the crostini Cut 15 diagonal slices of bread, each about 10 cm long and 3 mm thick. Prepare a baking tray with olive oil, salt and pepper. Cook the slices at 160º C for 12 minutes, until the bread is golden and crusty.

Clean the coriander and mint, discard the stalks and chop up the leaves. Wash and drain the mizuna leaves.

Serves 15

Ingredients

1.2 kg	Red peppers
1.2 kg	Green peppers
1 dl.	Taggiasche extra virgin olive oil
32 quarters	Confit tomatoes *
1 kg	Green courgettes
1 kg	Yellow patissons (custard marrows)
700 g	Aubergine
2 tbsp	Coarse sea salt
700 g	Baby fennel bulbs
3 dl.	Vegetable stock *
10 sheets	Gelatine
1 bunch	Thyme
50 g	Garlic
4 dl.	Olive oil
	Table sea salt
	Freshly ground black pepper

Vegetable sauce

50 g	Butternut squash (peeled)
35 g	Baby fennel bulbs
30 g	Celery
3 dl.	Vegetable stock *
1 1/2 dl.	Taggiasche extra virgin olive oil
1 tbsp	Savora mustard
10 g	Coriander
1 tsp	Home-made curry powder *
1/2 tsp	Cumin powder

Mazavarou oil

20 g	Red chillies
50 g	Shrimps or dried shrimps
12 g	Ginger
12 g	Garlic
1 tsp	Tomato purée
2	Plum tomatoes (ripe)
1	Small onion
2 dl.	Taggiasche extra virgin olive oil

Crushed garlic

100 g	New garlic

Last minute

Pour a layer of sauce in the middle of each plate, place a slice of pressed vegetables, 1.5 cm thick, on top, and sprinkle with a dash of mazavarou oil. Decorate with mint, coriander and mizuna leaves and some chives. Spread crushed garlic over the crostini and arrange them on the edge of the plates. Finally, sprinkle the slices of pressed vegetables with fleur de sel. Serve straightaway.

Note Other vegetables can be used if you prefer and depending on what is available in the local market, for example adding more tomatoes or replacing one vegetable with another. Gelatine can be replaced with double the quantity of agar agar, a vegetarian substitute.

1/4 bunch	Chives
4 g	Red chillies
2 dl.	Water
6 dl.	Milk
	Table sea salt
	Freshly ground white pepper
12	Coriander leaves
6 tbsp	Taggiasche extra virgin olive oil
	Stale French stick (ficelle)

Garnish

50 g	Mizuna (green Japanese salad)
1/4 bunch	Coriander
1/4 bunch	Mint
1/4 bunch	Chives
	Fleur de sel

* see basic recipes

Green pineapple ravioli with spicy rock lobster fricassée and eucalyptus honey vinaigrette

Recipe

To poach the rock lobsters Bring the vegetable stock to the boil and add the lobsters head-first. Cook for 5 minutes after the stock returns to the boil. Then remove the pan from the stove and leave the lobsters to stand in the vegetable stock for between 30 and 60 minutes. They will continue to cook and their meat will remain tender.

Remove the lobsters from the vegetable stock and drain them thoroughly. Cut them into two lengthwise. Use the tip of a small knife to remove the intestine, which runs as a small cord through the tail. Remove the flesh from the tails and cut into slices, about 1.5 cm thick. Place the pieces of lobster in a warm dish and cover them, whilst preparing the ravioli.

To prepare the pineapple Cut off the two ends diagonally. Peel them carefully, using a very sharp knife. Then use a mandoline to cut 20 thin, almost transparent, slices. Dice the rest of the pineapple into brunoise, and place both lots of pineapple to one side.

Wash the coriander, discard the stalks, and chop up half the leaves. Sort through the bean sprouts and sweat them in 2 tbsp olive oil. Salt and pepper. Wash the chilli, cut into two, remove the seeds and slice into fine julienne.

Last minute

Put the pineapple brunoise, bean sprouts, chopped coriander leaves, red chilli julienne (keep a little for decoration), 1 tbsp of chopped ginger and the rock lobsters into a large bowl. Mix them all together with *1/2 dl.* of vinaigrette. Check seasoning. Heap the lobster fricassée in the centre of each plate, cover with thin slices of pineapple and top with the rest of the vinaigrette. Garnish with small bunches of coriander leaves, the chives, a few of the remaining sweet and sour ginger petals, the remaining slivers of red chilli and finish with a pinch of fleur de sel. Serve straightaway.

Alternative

Brittany lobster can be used instead of rock lobster.

Note Use unripe green Victoria pineapple for this recipe. It gives a nice crunchy texture and a pleasant note of acidity to the dish.

Serves 4

Ingredients

4	Rock lobsters, each weighing 500 g (live)
1	Victoria pineapple
1/2 bunch	Coriander
12	Chive leaves
12 petals	Japanese sweet and sour ginger
100 g	Bean sprouts
2 tbsp	Olive oil
1	Red chilli
1 dl.	Eucalyptus honey vinaigrette *
5 l.	Vegetable stock *
	Fleur de sel
	Table sea salt

* see basic recipes

Sea bream carpaccio flavoured with green lemon and coconut

Recipe

Ask the fishmonger to fillet the fish and remove the skin and bones. Use a sharp Sashimi knife to cut the sea bream fillets into very thin, almost transparent, slices. Carefully arrange them on 4 chilled plates, without leaving any space between them, in the shape of a circle, 18 cm wide. The middle of the plates will be empty at this stage.

Scrub the lemon under running water, remove the peel, but not the white pith, and dice the peel lengthwise into very thin brunoise.

Break the coconut open with a hammer or rolling pin, and pour out the coconut water. Use a paring knife to remove the white coconut flesh and a sharp knife to cut the flesh into thin brunoise (for the seasoning) and julienne (for the salad).

Take the chilli, remove the seeds and slice into very thin julienne. Wash the coriander, remove the stalks and chop up the leaves. Wash and dry the mizuna leaves.

Take the papaya, remove the skin, cut the papaya into two, remove the seeds and slice into julienne. Finely slice the lime leaves.

Last minute

Brush the slices of sea bream with coconut vinaigrette and sprinkle with fleur de sel. Carefully mix the papaya julienne, pieces of lime leaf, coconut and red chilli with the lime vinaigrette in a bowl. Check seasoning. Place the papaya salad in the middle of the plates that contain the fish, and decorate all over with mizuna leaves. Edge with the coconut brunoise, lemon peel, sweet and sour ginger, and coriander leaves.

Serve straightaway with warm toast melba

Alternative

Gilt-head bream (dorade Royale) can be used instead of gold-lined sea bream.

Serves

INGREDIENTS

800 g	Gueule pavé doré (Frenchman or gold-lined sea bream)
1/2 dl.	Coconut vinaigrette *
1	Meyer lemon or Tahiti lime
1/2	Red chilli
60 g	Coconut
2 g	Coriander
20 g	Mizuna (green Japanese salad)
20 g	Japanese sweet and sour ginger
	Fleur de sel
	Table sea salt

Salad

600 g	Solo papaya (semi-ripe)
1	Meyer lemon or Tahiti lime leaf (optional)
60 g	Coconut
1/2	Red chilli
4 tbsp	Lime vinaigrette *

Served with

12	Toasts melba *

* see basic recipes

Creamy watercress soup
served as a cappuccino with clams and salted Grissini

Recipe

Scrub the clams thoroughly, rinse under running water and drain in a sieve. Peel and slice the shallot and garlic (removing the germ). Heat 2 tbsp olive oil in a 28 cm casserole dish on high heat. Sweat 2 tbsp shallots (keep the rest for later), the garlic and the thyme for a few seconds and then add the clams. Boil rapidly until all the clams open. Drain in a large colander, save the clam stock, remove the clams from the shells and discard the shells. Cover the clams in a dish, whilst preparing the velouté. Strain the stock through a muslin conical sieve.

Wash the white part of the leek thoroughly and cut it up. Sweat the leek, the rest of the shallots and the black pepper in butter in a thick-bottomed pan, without browning. Add the white wine and let it evaporate and reduce to "dry". Then add the fish stock and *3 dl.* of the clam stock. Bring to the boil and allow to simmer slowly for 20 minutes. Add the cream and reduce to concentrate the flavour. Remove from the stove and whip up with butter using a hand-held mixer. Check seasoning. Pass the velouté through a muslin conical sieve and keep it hot.

Wash the bunches of cress, sort through them and drain. Save a few leaves for decorative purposes. Bring *3 l.* water, seasoned with 8 g of coarse salt, to the boil. As soon as the water boils, add the cress and boil for 4 minutes. Remove from the stove, drain and cool down immediately in cold water. Then blend it in a mixer into a very smooth purée and place it in the refrigerator.

Last minute

Bring the velouté to the boil and use a hand-held mixer to incorporate the cress purée. Process the velouté until it is frothy. Meanwhile heat the shelled clams in a knob of butter in a small pan. Add a little pepper. Share out the clams into 4 consommé dishes, pour in the frothy velouté and sprinkle generously with cress leaves. Serve straightaway, with grissini sprinkled with fleur de sel.

Alternative

Other shellfish can be used instead of clams, for example cockles or Bouchot mussels.

Serves 4

INGREDIENTS

1.5 kg	Clams
1 1/2 dl.	Dry white wine
2 pieces	Shallots
1 clove	Garlic
1	Leek
1 sprig	Thyme
200 g	Echiré butter
2 tbsp	Olive oil
100 g	Crème fraîche
4 bunches	Wild cress
4 dl.	Fish stock *
	Fleur de sel
1/2 tsp	Crushed black pepper *
8 g	Coarse sea salt
	Freshly ground white pepper

Served with

Grissini *

* *see basic recipes*

Creamy breadfruit soup with crispy smoked bacon

Recipe

Take the breadfruit. Cut off the two ends. Use a sharp knife to carefully remove all the peel. Cut the fruit into two and remove the middle part, which is not really edible. Cut the rest of the breadfruit into brunoise.

Take the white part of the leek only and wash it thoroughly. Peel the shallot. Slice the half leek and the shallot thinly. Wash the coriander leaves, discard the stalks, and keep the leaves for the dressing.

Put 50 g of butter, the leek and shallot into a 24 cm wide, thick-bottomed pan and cover for 6 minutes, to allow them to go soft. Add the breadfruit brunoise and the chicken stock. Add a little salt and pepper. Cook slowly for 25 minutes and then blend in a food mill. Bring the cream to the boil in a pan. Add the boiling cream to the soup. Add the remaining butter and mix until it is all perfectly smooth. Check seasoning, strain the soup through a muslin conical sieve and keep hot.

Remove the rind from the smoked belly and cut the bacon slices into thin cubes (lardons). Heat 2 tbsp olive oil in a 30 cm wide, non-stick pan and brown the bacon cubes until they are very crisp. Use a spatula to remove them from the pan and drain on kitchen paper.

Last minute

Bring the soup to the boil and blend it until it becomes really frothy. Pour into 4 soup plates and sprinkle with coriander leaves. Serve the crisp small bacon cubes separately.

Note Fresh breadfruit is sold in oriental grocery shops.

Serves 4

Ingredients

1	Green breadfruit, weighing 1 kg (semi-ripe)
150 g	Smoked salted pork belly, in very thin slices
2 tbsp	Olive oil
1	Shallot
1/2	Leek
200 g	Echiré butter
1 l.	White chicken stock *
100 g	Crème fraîche
1/4 bunch	Coriander
	Table sea salt
	Freshly ground white pepper

* see basic recipes

Mildly-spiced camarons with pineapple and Rodriguan lime chutney

Recipe

Give a gentle twist to the camarons, to remove the tails. Cut the shells with a pair of scissors and carefully remove the flesh.

Trim off the ends and place them flat on a dish, belly side down. Make a shallow incision, 0.5 cm long, at each end to reach the black intestinal vein. Carefully take hold of the vein and remove it. The camarons need to be kept cool.

To prepare the chutney (this can be done several days beforehand) Take the pineapple and cut off the ends. Use a sharp knife to peel them carefully and then dice the pineapple into brunoise.

Melt the sugar in a small pan, and cook until it turns amber. Add the Champagne vinegar and mix. Then add the spices, the Rodriguan lime cut into small brunoise, and the pineapple. Simmer slowly for 2 hours. Remove from the stove. This chutney will keep for several weeks in a refrigerator, in a sealed jar.

The sauce Peel and slice the shallot, celery, fennel and leek into thin mirepoix. Crush the fish shells as finely as possible using a food processor. Heat the oil in a 26 cm wide frying pan, add the crushed shells, brown them and then add the mirepoix garnishes. Stir for 30 seconds. Pour in the wine, let it evaporate and reduce to "dry". Cover the contents with water, add a pinch of salt, and simmer slowly for 30 minutes. Remove from the stove. Leave it to stand for 10 minutes before filtering the stock through a muslin conical sieve, pressing the shells firmly to extract all the liquid.

Heat a small knob of butter in a small pan and add the peeled and finely chopped ginger. Sweat briskly for 30 seconds, add the stock and reduce to concentrate the flavour. Add the cream and reduce to $2^{1/2}$ dl. Check seasoning and keep hot. Whip up into a butter and check seasoning. Add the limejuice, and then strain through a muslin conical sieve. Keep hot.

Last minute

Sprinkle the prawns with sea salt and the spice mixture. Heat the oil on moderate heat in a small 22 cm wide, non-stick pan. When it is very hot, add the prawns. Halfway through cooking, turn the prawns over, lower the heat, add a tablespoonful of butter and braise for a few seconds. Remove from the stove and place in a dish. Top the prawns with the cooking butter from the pan and sprinkle with fleur de sel. Take 4 pre-warmed plates, drain the prawns and place 2 on each plate. Place a small heap, 5 cm or so, of spiced chutney in between them, and edge the prawns with sauce. Serve straightaway.

Alternative

Langoustines or Dublin Bay prawns can be used instead of the camarons.

Serves 4

Ingredients

8	Large king-size freshwater prawns (camarons), weighing 350 g each
1 1/2 tsp	Mild spices for shellfish *
3 tbsp	Olive oil
1 tbsp	Echiré butter
	Fleur de sel

Chutney

600 g	Victoria pineapple
1 dl.	Champagne vinegar
100 g	Cane sugar
3/4	Red chilli
1 stick	Cassia cinnamon
4	Cloves
1	Rodriguan lime

Ginger sauce

40 g	Ginger
1	Shallot
1 stick	Celery
1/2	Leek
1/4	Baby fennel
2 tbsp	Olive oil
1/2 dl.	Chardonnay wine
1 dl.	Crème fraîche
120 g	Echiré butter
	Juice of 3 Rodriguan limes
	Water

* see basic recipes

Flame snapper and crayfish on vegetables simmered in dried fruit with a spicy pumpkin-flavoured sauce

Recipe

Ask the fishmonger to fillet the vivaneau and remove the skin and bones. Divide into 4 portions weighing about 140 g each. Keep in the refrigerator.

To prepare the vegetables Peel the half onion, 1 small carrot and 1 clove of garlic (removing the germ). Cook the cannelloni beans slowly, with the carrot, onion, thyme and garlic, adding a small pinch of salt, for 3 hours.

Dice the figs, apricots and prunes into thin brunoise.

Peel and wash the other 2 carrots, potato, giraumon and chou-chou, and cut them into brunoise, 1 cm thick. Keep the giraumon trimmings for the purée. Clean the coriander, remove the stalks, prepare 4 large bunches for the tempura batter, and snip up the rest. Peel and slice the shallot and half clove of garlic thinly. Warm the olive oil slowly in an 18 cm wide pan with a lid. Add the garlic and shallot, sweat rapidly for 30 seconds, then add the potatoes. Salt and pepper. Cover and cook slowly for 5 minutes. Add the chou-chou, giraumon, spices and *1 dl.* vegetable stock, and cook for another 5 minutes until the vegetables are tender. Make sure the vegetables do not brown by shaking the pan from time to time. Add the cannelloni beans and the dried fruit brunoise. Cook for another 1 to 2 minutes. Check seasoning. To finish, add half the chopped coriander.

Cut the giraumon trimmings into small cubes. Heat 2 tbsp olive oil in a 14 cm wide, thick-bottomed casserole dish, add the giraumon cubes and cover with a lid. Braise for 10 minutes. When cooked, uncover and use a mixer to blend into a smooth purée.

To prepare the sauce Wash the chilli, cut it into two, remove the seeds and dice into thin brunoise. Peel and finely slice the ginger and garlic (removing the germ). Sweat the ginger, chilli and chopped garlic in 3 tbsp olive oil, in a 16 cm wide, thick-bottomed pan. Braise for 30 seconds and deglaze with the bouillabaisse stock. Simmer slowly and reduce to concentrate the flavour. Thicken the sauce with the giraumon purée using a small hand-held mixer. Check seasoning and strain through a fine sieve. Keep hot.

To prepare the crayfish Wash the crayfish carefully. Hold the crayfish firmly in one hand lengthwise, letting only the caudal fin stick out. Take hold of the central scale of the fin and remove it very carefully by twisting it a quarter turn to the left and right. Make sure not to shorten it. Cook the crayfish for 3 minutes in the boiling vegetable stock with a pinch of Cayenne pepper. Drain and leave to cool. Shell all of them and place them in a refrigerator.

To prepare the tempura batter Place the egg yolks in a terrine and incorporate the water, a little at a time. Add the flour and stir briefly (preferably with a pair of chopsticks) without breaking down the lumps. Tempura batter ought never to be smooth and should contain flakes of dry dough. It keeps well in a refrigerator but it is better to prepare it just before using it.

Last minute

Marinate the 4 snapper fillets and the crayfish in 3 tbsp olive oil, the cumin and the turmeric.

Pour the frying oil into a *2 l.* pan or a deep fryer. Heat to 170º C. Meanwhile coat the bunches of coriander one by one in the rice flour and shake them to remove the excess flour. Then dip them in the tempura batter and drain off any excess. Fry them for 2 to 3 minutes in the boiling oil. When they are crisp, use a skimmer to drain them and remove them from the oil. Place on kitchen paper, sprinkle with salt. They need to be served as soon as possible.

Heat 3 tbsp oil on moderate heat in a small, 22 cm wide, non-stick pan. When it is very hot, add the snapper fillets. Half way through cooking, turn the fillets over, add the crayfish and the other half of the chopped coriander, 1 tbsp butter and 3 tbsp vegetable stock. Braise for a few seconds. Remove from the heat. The flesh of the fish must be opaque but still supple and moist.

Place a small bed of the vegetables in 4 pre-heated soup plates. The vegetables should be very hot. A 90 mm cutting circle or suchlike may be of help in arranging them. Place the snapper fillet and 3 crayfish tails on top of the vegetables. Coat each fillet and crayfish tail with the cooking butter from the pan and sprinkle with fleur de sel. Bring the sauce

Serves 4

Ingredients

1 kg	Vivaneau (flame snapper)
8	Red claw crayfish, each weighing 90 g
2 l.	Vegetable stock *
1 pinch	Cayenne pepper
4 g	Powdered turmeric
2 g	Powdered cumin
6 tbsp	Olive oil
1 tbsp	Echiré butter
	Fleur de sel
	Table sea salt
	Freshly ground white pepper

Vegetables

50 g	Dried cannelloni beans (soaked for 12 hours in cold water)
1	Small carrot
1/2	Onion
1 clove	Garlic
1 sprig	Thyme
2	Carrots
1/2	Giraumon (Japanese pumpkin) medium-sized
1	King Edward or Large Desiree potato
2	Chou-chou (cho-cho)
2	Dried figs
2	Dried apricots
3	Prunes
10 g	Currants
1	Shallot
1/2 clove	Garlic
1 pinch	La Mancha saffron
1 pinch	Powdered cinnamon
1 pinch	Powdered cumin
5 tbsp	Olive oil
2 dl.	Vegetable stock *
1/2 bunch	Coriander

Sauce

5 g	Ginger
1 clove	Garlic
1/2	Red chilli
4 dl.	Bouillabaisse stock (see recipe, page 213)
1/2 dl.	Taggiasche extra virgin olive oil

quickly to the boil, pour in the olive oil, whisking vigorously with a small hand-held mixer to thicken it and make it smooth. Check seasoning. Edge the fish with the sauce and add the fried coriander. Serve immediately.

ALTERNATIVE
Black cod fillet can be used instead of the snapper fish.

Tempura dough

200 g	Sifted rice flour
30 cl.	Iced water
2	Egg yolks
	Table sea salt

Oil for frying

50 g	Sifted rice flour
1 l.	Peanut oil

* *see basic recipes*

Pumpkin and gourd Vialone Nano risotto with crispy smoked pancetta

RECIPE

Peel and finely slice the shallots. Peel and chop up the garlic (removing the germ). Clean the flat-leaved parsley leaves, remove the stalks and chop up the leaves thinly. Peel the giraumon, cut into two and remove the seeds and the fibres from the heart. Dice the flesh into thin brunoise. Prepare the calabash in the same way.

Heat 3 tbsp olive oil in a 22 cm wide pan and gently fry the pumpkin brunoise for 5 minutes, with the chopped garlic, thyme, nutmeg, salt and pepper. Repeat for the calabash. Do not let them brown. Remove and drain on kitchen paper.

Heat 2 tbsp olive oil in a 30 cm wide, non-stick pan and brown the pancetta slices until they are very crisp. Remove with a spatula and drain on kitchen paper.

Heat 3 tbsp olive oil in a *4 l.* cast-iron casserole dish. Add the shallot and cook slowly for 3 minutes. Add the rice and cook for 2 minutes, stirring continuously. Add the wine. As soon as the wine has been absorbed, pour the vegetable stock into the casserole dish a little at a time, continuing to stir with a spatula. Wait for the rice to absorb all the vegetable stock each time before adding more stock. Cooking lasts about 14 to 15 minutes. The rice is then soft and the mixture should have a creamy consistency. Add the thin brunoise of giraumon and calabash, the chopped parsley, the grated parmesan, the rest of the butter and the olive oil into the risotto, stirring continuously. Check seasoning.

Take the veal stock and simmer for a few minutes after it has come to the boil. Salt and pepper. Keep hot. Chop the pistachio nuts.

LAST MINUTE

Serve the risotto in 4 soup plates, top with the veal broth, which should be very hot, and decorate with the chopped pistachios, crisp pancetta and Parmesan shavings.

ALTERNATIVE

A delicious risotto can also be made without the smoked pancetta or veal stock. It makes a tasty and balanced vegetarian meal.

Serves 4

INGREDIENTS

300 g	Ferron Vialone Nano rice
1 dl.	Dry white wine
50 g	Shallots
1 l.	Vegetable stock *
250 g	Giraumon (Japanese pumpkin)
250 g	Calabash
6 pinch	Grated nutmeg
1 clove	Garlic
2 sprig	Thyme
1 tbsp	Flat-leaved parsley
80 g	Reggiano parmesan (50 g grated and 30 g in shavings)
25 g	Echiré butter
150 cl.	Taggiasche extra virgin olive oil
3 tbsp	Pistachio nuts
8 tbsp	Veal stock *
12	Smoked pancetta
	Table sea salt
	Freshly ground white pepper

* *see basic recipes*

Pot-roasted farm-raised veal rump with shii-take mushrooms and ginger-flavoured gravy

Recipe

To prepare the dough Pour the flour and 3 egg whites into a bowl. Mix into a smooth paste. Add the fourth egg white if necessary. If the dough is too stiff, add several teaspoons of water to soften it.

To prepare the veal and the sauce Preheat the oven to 240º C. Sprinkle the veal rump with salt and pepper. Heat 3 tbsp olive oil and a knob of butter rapidly in a very hot oven-proof pan. Add the rump and cook for 3 minutes on each of the 4 sides; it will take 12 minutes altogether to brown it. Stuff the trimmings under the veal in the pan and put it into the oven. Roast for 4 minutes. Turn the rump over and roast for a further 4 minutes (total roasting time is 8 minutes). Remove the pan from the oven and place the rump into a dish. Quickly heat up the cooking juice and the trimmings. Use a spoon to remove the grease from the surface. Add the white chicken stock to deglaze, scraping the bottom of the pan to make sure nothing sticks to it. Add the veal stock. Peel the garlic and cut it into two to remove the germ. Slice the citronella, and peel and slice the ginger into julienne. Add the garlic, ginger and citronella to the stock and reduce to concentrate the flavour. Pass the stock through a fine sieve, squeezing the trimmings thoroughly to extract as much liquid as possible. At least *11/2 dl.* is needed. Lower the oven temperature to 220º C. Place the veal rump in the bottom of a casserole dish and arrange the confit shallots around it, and pour on the veal stock.

To prepare the vegetables Wash the brèdes, separating the leaves from the stalks, and twist the stalks into the shape of large petals. Take the fennel and cut off the bottom and the stems, and remove the outer layer. Shape the stems into large petals. Wash the shii-take mushrooms and cut off the stalks, which are very hard. Drain. Keep the mushrooms whole. Take an 18 cm wide pan with a lid. Add 3 tbsp olive oil, the 25 g of butter and half the vegetable stock. Heat gently. Add the fennel. Salt and pepper. Cover and cook slowly for 5 minutes. Add the brèdes and continue to cook for 2 minutes, until the vegetables are tender. Make sure the vegetables do not brown by shaking the pan from time to time. Add the shii-take mushrooms and continue to cook for 1 to 2 minutes. Salt and pepper.

To prepare the glaze Mix the egg yolks in a bowl with 1 tbsp water.

To seal the casserole dish Divide the dough into two pieces and roll them into 2 sausage shapes, 10 cm long, long and wide enough to go round the casserole dish. Put the 2 sausage-shaped pieces of dough around the edges of the dish and add the lid, making sure the dish is thoroughly sealed. Brush the dough with glaze. Put the casserole dish into the oven and roast for 15 minutes at 220º C. Remove the dish from the oven but do not open it yet. Leave it to stand at room temperature for at least 10 minutes, but no more than 30 minutes. The veal will continue cooking inside the dish.

Last minute

To serve Remove the lid, breaking the crust in front of the guests, so that they can appreciate the aroma. Place the veal on a carving board and slice it. Place the slices on 4 plates and sprinkle with fleur de sel. Surround the veal with brèdes, fennel, the shii-take mushrooms and the shimmering hot confit shallots. Meanwhile, filter the juices left over from carving the meat, add them to the gravy, heat and pour into a gravy boat. Serve straightaway.

Note The veal rump is situated in the upper part of the haunch. It is excellent for roasting and is tastier and more tender than topside or silverside.

Serves 4

Ingredients

800 g	Suckling veal rump
200 g	Veal trimmings
2 dl.	Veal stock *
1/2 dl.	White chicken stock *
25 g	Citronella (lemon grass)
10 g	Ginger
1 clove	Garlic
9	Confit shallots *
3 tbsp	Olive oil
1 tbsp	Echiré butter
	Table sea salt
	Fleur de sel
	Freshly ground white pepper

The dough

140 g	Flour
3 or 4	Egg whites
2	Egg yolks

Vegetables

20	Shii-take mushrooms
8	Brèdes Tom-Pouce (baby bok-choy)
2	Baby fennel bulbs
3 tbsp	Olive oil
25 g	Echiré butter
2 dl.	Vegetable stock *
	Table sea salt

* see basic recipes

Spit-roasted free-range chicken served with citronella-flavoured gravy and crispy cassava straws

Recipe

Peel and wash the carrot and cut it into mirepoix, as well as the celery, onion, parsley, garlic, thyme, ginger and citronella (keep a few leaves for later). Place them all in a frying pan with 3 tbsp olive oil, sauté for about 4 minutes and season with salt and pepper, then leave to cool down to room temperature.

Lift the skin from the chicken, starting from the neck and moving on to the thighs and the drumsticks. Insert the remaining citronella leaves. Salt and pepper the inside and outside of the chicken and stuff with the sautéed vegetables and herbs. Truss. Preheat the oven to 210º C. Spit roast the chicken in the oven for 35 minutes.

Baste the chicken every 5 minutes with its own juices. Check if it is cooked by sticking a needle into the thigh. If the juice that comes out is clear, the chicken is cooked.

Place the chicken on a serving dish at the mouth of the oven and leave it to stand for 10 minutes.

To make the gravy Take the chicken stock, add the citronella and ginger, and simmer for 10 minutes once it has come to the boil. Salt and pepper. Keep hot.

To prepare the cassava stalks Peel and wash the baby cassavas and then grate them into straws with a mandoline. Pour the oil into a large *4 l.* pan or a deep fryer. Heat to 180º C and fry the cassavas in batches, leaving them for 3 to 4 minutes in the boiling oil. When they are golden and crisp, drain with a skimmer, and place on kitchen paper. Season with fleur de sel and serve as soon as possible.

Last minute

Reheat the chicken for 2 minutes in the oven. Place it on a carving board, remove the 2 thighs and cut them into two. Remove the breast and slice it. Share it out over 4 plates and sprinkle with fleur de sel. At the same time, heat the sauce and add the juices from the carving, after filtering them. Pour into a gravy boat. Serve with crisp and hot cassava straws.

Alternative

Potatoes can be used instead of cassava for the straws.

Serves 4

Ingredients

1	Free-range chicken, weighing 1.8 kg without the giblets
1	Carrot
1 stick	Celery
1	Red onion
5 g	Fresh parsley
10 g	Citronella
10 g	Ginger
1 sprig	Thyme
2 cloves	Garlic
3 tbsp	Olive oil
	Fleur de sel
	Table sea salt
	Freshly ground white pepper

Citronella-flavoured gravy

2 l.	Poultry stock *
5 g	Citronella (lemon grass)
2 g	Ginger

Garnish

500 g	Baby cassava (manioc)

Oil for frying

2 l.	Peanut oil

* see basic recipes

Crème caramel with rum-flavoured raisins

Recipe

Macerate the raisins in the rum 24 hours beforehand. Put the sugar into a small pan. Add the water and bring to the boil until the syrup turns golden. Take the pan of the stove and add about 2 tbsp hot water. Return the pan to the stove and boil for a few seconds. Remove the pan again and pour the caramel into 4 moulds, 70 mm wide and 40 mm high. Leave to cool down a little before adding the macerated raisins.

To prepare the crème Pour the milk into a pan and heat. Mix the eggs and sugar in a bowl but do not whisk. Add the vanilla essence to the hot milk and pour the mixture onto the eggs. Mix well, then strain through a conical sieve. Add the mixture to the moulds, to the brim, and put them in an oven-proof bowl inside another oven-proof bowl filled with water. Put the bain-marie in the oven preheated to 150º C for 25 minutes. After baking, cover with cling film and refrigerate.

Last minute

Place a plate on top of each mould, turn it over and carefully remove the mould, letting the caramel run down the crème. A few slices of orange can be placed around the crème before serving.

Alternative

3 Fragrans vanilla pods can be used instead of the vanilla essence.

Serves 4

INGREDIENTS

Caramel

75 g	Cane sugar
50 ml.	Water

Crème

500 ml.	Milk
4	Eggs
100 g	Cane sugar
1 tbsp	Natural vanilla essence

Raisins macerated in rum

100 g	Raisins
150 ml.	10 year-old agricultural rum

Queen Victoria pineapple baked in Sichuan pepper and caramelised with cane sugar, served with citronella ice-cream

RECIPE

To prepare the ice-cream Heat the milk in a thick-bottomed pan, 10 cm wide. Wash the citronella leaves, cut them into small pieces, add them to the milk and leave to infuse for 15 minutes, away from the stove and covered with a lid. Add the cream and bring to the boil. Whisk the egg yolks and the sugar in a basin. Gradually pour the boiling liquid onto the sugar mixture, whisking continuously.

Return the mixture to the pan and cook slowly, stirring to create a custard. Remove from the stove and strain through a muslin sieve into a container placed in a tub of ice. When the mixture has cooled down, pour it into an ice-cream maker. Freeze the ice-cream as soon as it sets.

To prepare the pineapples Cut off both ends. Keep a few leaves for later. Use a large, sharp knife to peel them, removing the prickly bits from the flesh as well. Cut the pineapple crosswise into 12 slices, 12 mm thick.

Heat the ghee quickly in a large thick-bottomed frying pan. Add a layer of pineapple slices. Cook in several batches for a few minutes on each side until they are golden. Place the pineapple slices onto a dish. Discard the ghee and add a knob of butter. Return the pineapple slices to the pan. Sprinkle with cane sugar; add a generous amount of Sichuan pepper and leave to caramelise. Pour in the pineapple juice (strain it first through a muslin conical sieve). Cook on moderate heat for 10 minutes, stirring from time to time. Drain the pineapple slices and place them in a hot dish. Make a sauce out of a mixture of the cooking juices and the limejuice and keep hot.

LAST MINUTE

Re-heat the pineapple slices and place them on pre-warmed plates, 3 slices per person. Top with sauce and add a scoop of citronella ice-cream in the middle. Decorate with small pineapple leaves and the candied pineapple and serve immediately.

Note When buying a whole pineapple, make sure that it is ripe - you should be able to smell its perfume. Another method is to remove one of the leaves from the crown. If it comes out easily, the fruit is ready to eat.

Serves 4

INGREDIENTS

2	Queen Victoria pineapples (medium-sized)
50 g	Echiré butter
30 g	Ghee *
75 g	Cane sugar
1 tsp	Freshly ground Sichuan pepper
200 ml.	Victoria pineapple juice
1	Meyer lemon or Tahiti lime
12	Dried candied pineapple *

Citronella ice-cream

250 ml.	Skimmed milk
250 ml.	Double cream
6	Egg yolks
125 g	Cane sugar
100 g	Citronella leaves

see basic recipes

Mango baked in Fragrans vanilla with diplomat cream and crispy pistachio-flavoured philo

Recipe
Whip the double cream into Chantilly. Carefully stir the vanilla pastry cream and incorporate the whipped cream. Cover with cling film and refrigerate.

To prepare the philo Melt 50 g of butter in a small pan and remove from the stove. Cut out 16 discs of philo dough, 10 cm in diameter. Spread melted butter on 8 of the discs, sprinkle with icing sugar and place another disc on each of them. Place the discs on a non-stick tray, spread melted butter on top, sprinkle with icing sugar and put in the oven for 8 to 10 minutes until they are thoroughly caramelised. Remove from the oven and leave them to cool down.

Last minute
Preheat the oven to 220º C. Peel the mangoes, remove the stones and cut the mangoes into two lengthwise.

Heat the ghee in a 30 cm wide frying pan. Add the mangoes, brown them on both sides, sprinkle with cane sugar and caramelise. Split and scratch the vanilla pods and add them to the pan. Once caramelised, remove the mangoes from the pan, but keep them warm. Pour the orange juice into the pan and simmer for 30 to 40 seconds, then filter the juice through a fine sieve.

Place a spoonful of cream in the middle of each plate and put two pieces of baked mango on top. Cover with a first philo disc. Add a second spoonful of cream and put another piece of mango on top of that. Brush the remaining philo discs with honey and sprinkle with chopped pistachio nuts. Place these discs on top of the mangoes and add traces of the cooking juice and the raspberry sauce. Serve straightaway.

Alternative
To make this dessert lighter, use 0% fat "fromage blanc" instead of the double cream.

Serves 4

Ingredients

Philo pastry discs

100 g	Icing sugar
4 sheets	Philo pastry
30 g	Pistachio nuts
50 g	Rodriguan honey
50 g	Echiré butter

Diplomat cream

200 g	Vanilla pastry cream *
100 g	Double cream

Baked mango

4	Mangoes (ripe but firm)
15 g	Ghee *
60 g	Echiré butter
75 g	Cane sugar
4 pods	Fragrans vanilla
75 ml.	Orange juice

Served with

75 ml.	Raspberry sauce (coulis) *

* see basic recipes

Guava jam

Recipe

Bring *3 l.* of water to the boil in a 28 cm wide pan. Wash the jars and lids and put them in the pan, as well as a small ladle for use with the jam. Sterilise everything for at least 30 minutes and stand them to drain on a clean tea towel.

Wash the guavas and cut off the two ends. Cut them into four and put them into a *5 l.* copper preserving pan or, if none is available, a large thick-bottomed pan. Add *200 ml.* of water and cook slowly for about 30 minutes, stirring with a wooden spatula from time to time, until the tip of a knife can easily pierce the guavas. Remove from the stove and pass through a food-mill with a fine sieve.

Put the guava purée (without the seeds) into the preserving pan, add a third of the sugar and cook slowly, stirring with the spatula from the edge to the centre, to prevent the sugar from sticking to the bottom of the pan. Add in another third of the sugar after cooking for 15 minutes, stirring continuously. Skim the jam whilst cooking. Check the sugar content with a refractometre (it should measure no more than 40 brix) or take a clean spoon to taste the fruits, as they can be more or less sweet when they are ripe. Add the rest, or some of the rest, of the sugar and continue to cook and stir. As soon as the jam starts to simmer slightly, cook for about 2 to 3 minutes more.

Remove from the stove and use the sterilised ladle to fill the jars to the brim. Fit the lids and make sure the jars are tightly closed. Allow the jars to cool down, then wipe and dry them as necessary before putting them in the refrigerator.

Always keep this jam in the refrigerator or in a cool place, as the sugar content is not high enough to preserve the fruits in the traditional manner.

Alternative

This recipe can be used for any fruit. The cooking technique will be the same but, depending on the fruit, the quantity of sugar may need to be varied.

To make 4 jars, of 400 ml. each

Ingredients

1 kg	Guavas (ripe)
450 g	Cane sugar
200 ml.	Water
4	400 ml. jam jars with lids

Caramel-flavoured ladyfinger banana samossas with coconut sorbet

Recipe

To prepare the spiced caramel Mix the sugar, spices and water in a 15 cm wide pan and caramelise. As soon as the caramel begins to turn golden, remove the pan from the stove. Pour the caramel onto an oiled non-stick tray and leave it to cool down. Break up the caramel on a chopping board with a rolling pin, and keep it in an airtight tin.

To make the samossas Cut the philo pastry lengthwise into 5 cm wide strips. Melt the butter slowly. Peel the bananas, cut them into 3 cm pieces, then roll them in the spiced caramel so that the caramel sticks to the banana. Place a piece of banana on the tip of the pastry and fold in the shape of a triangle. Continue to fold, keeping the triangular shape. Brush the final fold of pastry with melted butter so that the samossas does not come unstuck. Place the samossas on a buttered non-stick tray. Brush the coat with melted butter and place in the refrigerator.

To prepare the pistachio sauce Bring the milk to the boil in a 14 cm wide saucepan and add the cream. Mix the egg yolks and sugar in a bowl and whisk until it turns whitish. Gradually pour in the milk and cream. Return the pan to the stove and stir continuously with a spatula until the sauce starts to thicken. Remove from the stove and add the pistachio paste and stir for a further 10 seconds. Strain through a muslin conical sieve and let it cool down in bain-marie, a bowl within a bowl of ice.

Crack open the coconut with a hammer or rolling pin and drain off the coconut water. Use a paring knife to remove the white flesh and a sharp knife to cut the flesh into thin shavings.

Last minute

Preheat the oven to 230º C. Just before serving, bake the samossas for 7 minutes in the oven until they are thoroughly caramelised. Remove from the oven and lightly coat with honey. Sprinkle a few chopped pistachio nuts on top.

Place 3 samossas in the middle of each plate, overlapping each other. Place a scoop of coconut sorbet next to them. Pierce the sorbet with 2 pieces of dried banana and 2 coconut shavings. Surround with streaks of pistachio sauce and serve straightaway.

Note The young coconut, whose outside colour is green or yellow, is full of a slightly sweet water that makes a refreshing drink. This water is pure and has a nutritional value that makes it ideal for convalescents. The water loses its qualities once the coconut dries out.

Serves 4

Ingredients

1/2 l.	Coconut sorbet *
50 g	Coconut
8	Dried bananas *

Samossas

2 sheets	Philo pastry
50 g	Echiré butter
50 g	Rodriguan honey
2	Ladyfinger bananas
50 g	Chopped pistachio nuts

Spiced caramel

100 g	Cane sugar
3 g	Four spices *
2 g	Powdered star anise
25 ml.	Water

Pistachio nut sauce

100 ml.	Milk
100 ml.	Double cream
50 g	Cane sugar
3	Egg yolks
10 g	Pistachio paste

see basic recipes

Basic recipes

Home-made curry powder	**265**
Garam massala	
Tandoori Massala	
Mild spices for meat	
Mild spices for shellfish	
Crushed black pepper	
Four-spices	**266**
Five-spices	
Orange or lemon peel powder	
Dried garlic, galangal or ginger	
Spicy orange powder	
Green curry paste	**267**
White chicken stock	
Poultry stock	
Veal stock	**268**
Lamb stock	
Venison stock	**269**
Cochon marron stock	
Duck stock	**270**
Fish stock (fumet)	
Shellfish consommé	**271**
Shellfish coulis	
Bouquet garni	**272**
Vegetable stock	
Royal Palm vinaigrette	
Lime vinaigrette	
Eucalyptus honey vinaigrette	**273**
Chinese vinaigrette	
Coconut vinaigrette	
Mayonnaise	
Perfumed Basmati rice	**274**
Basmati rice	
Braised giraumon	
Black lentils fricassée	**275**
Confit shallots	
New garlic confit	

Mashed potatoes	**276**
Arouille violette purée	
Coconut chutney	**277**
Cashew nut chutney	
Tomato chutney	
Cucumber chutney	**278**
Ground chillies	
Green mango pickle	
Rodriguan lime pickle	**279**
Cythera pickle	
Toasts Melba	
Confit tomatoes	**280**
Brined lemon	
Tamarind pulp	
Ghee (clarified butter)	
Oriental spices	**281**
Citrus fruit peel	
Candied dried pineapple	
Dried bananas	
Candied green apple	
Chocolate cigars	**282**
Coconut tuiles	
Vanilla pastry cream	
Puff pastry	**283**
Shortcrust pastry	**284**
Grissini dough	
Meyer lemon sorbet	
Coconut sorbet	**285**
Raspberry sauce (coulis)	
Mango sauce	
Kumquat sauce	
Cold sabayon base	
Chilled rum-flavoured sabayon	**286**
Pistachio-flavoured chilled sabayon	
Sweet potato jam	

Home-made curry powder

PREPARATION

Gently heat the mixture of spices (except the turmeric, the chillies and the paprika) on the stove in a frying pan to bring out the flavours. Then grind all the spices in a coffee mill. *

INGREDIENTS

20 g	Powdered turmeric
30 g	Green cardamom
25 g	Cumin
15 g	Black pepper
15 g	Coriander seeds
5 g	Cloves
3 g	Cayenne chillies
10 g	Paprika

Garam massala

PREPARATION

Gently heat the mixture of spices (except the nutmeg and the bay leaves) in a frying pan to bring out the flavours. Then grind all the spices in a coffee mill. *

INGREDIENTS

25 g	Cumin
75 g	Coriander seeds
40 g	Black pepper
30 g	Cardamom
15 g	Nutmeg
30 g	Cassia cinnamon
2	Bay leaves

Tandoori massala

PREPARATION

Gently heat the cumin in a frying pan to bring out the flavours. Then grind all the spices in a coffee mill. *

INGREDIENTS

25 g	Dried garlic
30 g	Dried ginger
60 g	Garam massala
25 g	Dry Cayenne chillies
15 g	Cumin
20 g	Red powdered food colouring (optional)

Mild spices for meat

PREPARATION

Heat the cumin and coriander seeds in a frying pan to bring out the flavours. Then grind them, together with the cinnamon, in a coffee mill. *

INGREDIENTS

75 g	Coriander seeds
75 g	Cumin
50 g	Casella cinnamon

Mild spices for shellfish

PREPARATION

Mix the spices and heat in a frying pan to bring out the flavours. Then grind the mixture in a coffee mill. *

INGREDIENTS

50 g	Coriander seeds
15 g	Cumin
20 g	Black pepper
20 g	Sichuan pepper
15 g	Aniseed

Crushed black pepper

PREPARATION

Heat the pepper in a frying pan to bring out the flavours. Then grind and sieve. *

INGREDIENTS

| 50 g | Black pepper |

*This preparation will keep for a month in an airtight jar, kept firmly closed.

Four-spices

PREPARATION
Mix all the spices, except the ginger, and heat them gently in a frying pan to bring out the flavours. Then grind everything together in a coffee mill. *

INGREDIENTS

80	g	Four-spices mixture
30	g	Dried ginger
25	g	Nutmeg
10	g	Garlic cloves

Five-spices

PREPARATION
Mix all the spices and heat them gently in a frying pan to bring out the flavours. Then grind everything together in a coffee mill. *

INGREDIENTS

50	g	Star anis
50	g	Sichuan pepper
25	g	Powdered Cassia cinnamon
50	g	Fennel seeds
25	g	Cloves

Orange or lemon peel powder

PREPARATION
Scrub the oranges or lemons in lukewarm water, dry then peel them and remove the white pith. Spread the strips of peel onto a baking tray, place in the oven and cook at 80° C for about 3 hours to bring out the flavours. Grind to a fine powder in a coffee mill or food processor. *

INGREDIENTS

10	Oranges or lemons (organic)

Dried garlic, galangal or ginger

PREPARATION
Peel the ginger or the galangal or the garlic. In the case of the garlic, cut the cloves into two then remove the germ. Use a mandoline to cut them into approximately 1 mm. thick slices. Spread the slices onto a baking tray, place in the oven and cook at 80°C for about 1 hour to bring out the flavours. Use a coffee mill or food processor to grind them into a fine powder. *

INGREDIENTS

250	g	Garlic (to obtain about 60 g dried garlic)
250	g	Ginger (to obtain about 50 g dried ginger)
250	g	Galangal (to obtain about 50 g dried galangal)

Spicy orange powder

PREPARATION
Heat the coriander seeds in a frying pan to bring out the flavours. Then grind them, together with the other spices, in a coffee mill. *

INGREDIENTS

80	g	Orange peel powder
60	g	Coriander seeds
60	g	Dried galangal
40	g	Cayenne chillies

This preparation will keep for a month in an airtight jar, kept firmly closed.

Green curry paste

Preparation

Heat the coriander seeds in a frying pan with the cumin and the black pepper to bring out the flavours. Leave them to cool down. Chop the chives and citronella into large pieces, peel and crush the ginger and garlic (removing the germ).
Wash the green chillies, remove the stems and the seeds, and chop them up. Remove the peel from the lime and slice finely. Squeeze the lime and put all the ingredients in the bowl of a processor. Blend until the mixture is smooth. Sprinkle with oil and add salt. Store in an airtight jar in a cool place. *

* This preparation will keep for a month in an airtight jar, kept firmly closed.

INGREDIENTS

5	g	Coriander seeds
3	g	Cumin
4		Green chillies
20	g	Citronella
90	g	Chives
25	g	Garlic
10	g	Ginger
1/2		Combava (Kaffir lime)
15	pieces	Fresh coriander roots
2	g	Black pepper
3	tsp	Dried prawn paste
6	tbsp	Olive oil
		Sea table salt

White chicken stock

To make *3 l.* of stock

Preparation

Wash, peel and halve the onions. Cut the garlic into two. Place the giblets, the carcasses and the chicken in a large pan. Cover completely with cold water and add the salt. Bring quickly to the boil. Remove the scum as necessary. Add the bouquet garni, pierce the onions with the cloves and add them, as well as the garlic, coriander seeds, mace and white pepper. Simmer for 2 hours without stirring. Leave to stand for 10 minutes before filtering through a muslin conical sieve, squeezing the carcasses thoroughly to remove all the liquid. Allow to cool down completely, cover with cling film. Keep in the refrigerator. *

INGREDIENTS

1	kg	Chicken giblets (neck, legs, and wings)
1	kg	Chicken carcasses (from a 2 kg chicken)
1		Chicken (trussed)
2		Large onions
1/2		Garlic
1		Bouquet garni
1	tsp	Coriander seeds
1/2	tsp	Freshly ground white pepper
2	pieces	Mace (dried nutmeg husks)
2		Cloves
1	tsp	Table salt

Poultry stock

To make *3/4 l.* of stock

Preparation

Wash, peel and cut the aromatic garnishes into small evenly-sized pieces (mirepoix). Cut the head of garlic into two lengthwise.
Heat 3 tbsp olive oil in a *5 l.* cast-iron casserole dish. Add the bones, chopped giblets and carcasses, and brown them. Chop up the vegetables and add them, together with the salt and pepper. Brown for 8 minutes, making sure that the vegetables do not burn. Remove the fat. Add the white chicken stock and cover with water. Add the garlic, tomato purée, and bouquet garni. Cook for 3 hours, removing the scum from time to time. Remove the giblets and carcasses with a skimmer and discard them. Strain the stock through a muslin conical sieve into a large saucepan.
Bring briskly to the boil, then reduce the heat and simmer gently, carefully removing the scum, until the stock is reduced to *3/4 l.* Remove from the stove, and leave it to cool down completely. Cover with cling film and keep in the refrigerator. *

* If you do not intend to use the stock immediately, freeze it in small portions for ease of use.

INGREDIENTS

2	kg	Poultry giblets (neck, legs and wings)
1	kg	Poultry carcasses
3	tbsp	Olive oil
1	pinch	Sea salt
1	tbsp	Tomato purée
100	g	Carrots
100	g	Shallots
50	g	Mushroom stalks (champignons de Paris)
2		Plum tomatoes
1		Bouquet garni
1	head	Garlic
1/2	tsp	Crushed black pepper
2	l.	White chicken stock

Veal stock

To make *1 l.* of stock

PREPARATION

Wash, peel and cut the aromatic garnishes into mirepoix. Cut the head of garlic into two lengthwise.
Heat the oil in a *5 l.* cast-iron casserole dish. Add the bones and the trimmings. Brown, then add the chopped vegetables, salt and pepper. Cook for 10 minutes, making sure that the vegetables do not burn. Add the white chicken stock, and then add water until it covers the contents. Add the garlic, tomato purée, and bouquet garni. Cook for 6 hours, removing the scum from time to time. Use a skimmer to remove the bones and trimmings, and discard them. Strain the stock through a muslin conical sieve into a large pan. Bring briskly to the boil, then reduce the heat and simmer gently, removing the scum carefully, until it is reduced to *1 l.* of stock. Remove from the stove and let it cool down completely. Cover with cling film and keep in the refrigerator. *

INGREDIENTS

2	kg	Crushed veal bones
1	kg	Veal trimmings (brisket)
3	tbsp	Olive oil
1	pinch	Table sea salt
1	tbsp	Tomato purée
100	g	Carrots
100	g	Shallots
50	g	Mushroom stalks
2		Plum tomatoes
1		Bouquet garni
1	head	Garlic
1/2	tsp	Crushed black pepper
2	l.	White chicken stock

Lamb stock

To make *1 l.* of stock

PREPARATION

Wash, peel and cut the aromatic garnishes into mirepoix. Cut the head of garlic into two lengthwise.
Heat 3 tbsp olive oil in a *5 l.* cast-iron casserole dish. Add the bones and trimmings. Brown, then add the chopped vegetables, salt and pepper. Cook for 5 minutes, making sure that the vegetables do not burn. Remove the fat. Add the chicken stock then top up with water to cover the ingredients. Add the bouquet garni, garlic and tomato purée. Cook for 6 hours, removing the scum from time to time. Use a skimmer to remove the bones and trimmings, and discard them. Strain the stock through a muslin conical sieve into a large pan. Bring briskly to the boil, reduce the heat and simmer gently, carefully removing the scum, until it is reduced to *1 l.* of stock. Remove from the stove and let it cool down completely. Cover with cling film and keep in the refrigerator. *

INGREDIENTS

2	kg	Crushed lamb bones
1	kg	Lamb trimmings (collar and breast)
3	tbsp	Olive oil
1	tbsp	Tomato purée
1	pinch	Table sea salt
100	g	Carrots
100	g	Shallots
50	g	Mushroom stalks
2		Plum tomatoes
1		Bouquet garni
1	head	Garlic
1/2	tsp	Crushed black pepper
2	l.	White chicken stock

* *If you do not intend to use the stock immediately, freeze it in small portions for ease of use.*

Venison stock

To make $1^{1}/_{2}$ l. of stock

Preparation

Wash, peel and cut the aromatic garnishes into mirepoix. Cut the head of garlic into two lengthwise.
Heat 3 tbsp olive oil in a *5 l.* cast-iron casserole dish. Add the bones and trimmings. Brown for 10 minutes on high heat, and then remove the fat from the casserole dish. Add the vegetables, cut into mirepoix, together with the tomato purée, bouquet garni and spices. Add a little salt and pepper. Deglaze with the wine and the port. Allow to evaporate until completely reduced. Add the poultry and veal stock, and then water to cover. Continue to simmer gently for 6 hours, removing the scum as necessary. Strain the stock through a muslin conical sieve into a pan and boil briskly, carefully removing the scum until it is reduced to $1^{1}/_{2}$ l. of stock. Remove from the stove and let it cool down completely. Cover with cellophane and keep in the refrigerator. *

INGREDIENTS

2	kg	Crushed venison bones
1	kg	Chopped venison trimmings (collar and brisket)
1		Carrot
2		Onions (medium-sized)
1	tbsp	Tomato purée
2		Vine tomatoes (ripe)
1	stick	Celery
1/2	head	Garlic
1		Bouquet garni
1	tsp	Crushed black pepper
1/2	tsp	Ground coriander seeds
		Peel of 1 orange
		Peel of 1 lemon
		Poultry stock
1/2	l.	Veal stock
1	dl.	Red Port
4	dl.	Red wine
		Table sea salt

Cochon marron stock

To make *1 l.* of stock

Preparation

Wash, peel and cut the aromatic garnishes into mirepoix. Cut the head of garlic into two lengthwise.
Heat 3 tbsp olive oil in a *5 l.* cast-iron casserole dish. Add the bones and the trimmings. Brown, then add the chopped vegetables, salt and pepper. Brown for 10 minutes, making sure that the vegetables do not burn. Add the white chicken stock and then add water to cover. Add the bouquet garni, spices, garlic and tomato purée. Cook for 6 hours, removing the scum from time to time. Remove the bones and trimmings with a skimmer and discard. Strain the stock through a muslin conical sieve into a large pan. Bring briskly to the boil, then lower the heat and simmer gently, carefully removing the scum, and reduce to *1 l.* of stock. Remove from the stove and let it cool down completely. Cover with cling film and keep in the refrigerator. *

INGREDIENTS

2	kg	Crushed cochon marron or wild boar bones
1	kg	cochon marron or wild boar trimmings (collar and belly)
3	tbsp	Olive oil
1	tbsp	Tomato purée
1	pinch	Table sea salt
100	g	Carrots
100	g	Shallots
50	g	Mushroom stalks
2		Plum tomatoes
1		Bouquet garni
1	head	Garlic
1/2	tsp	Crushed black pepper
5		Juniper berries
2	l.	White chicken stock

If you do not intend to use the stock immediately, freeze it in small portions for ease of use.

Duck stock

To make $1^{1}/_{2}$ l. of stock

Preparation

Wash, peel and cut the aromatic garnishes into mirepoix. Cut the head of garlic into two, lengthwise.
Heat 3 tbsp olive oil in a 5 l. cast-iron casserole dish. Add the wings, the carcasses and the chopped necks of the ducklings. Brown quickly for 10 minutes and then remove the fat from the dish. Add the vegetables chopped into mirepoix, tomato purée, bouquet garni and spices. Add a little salt and pepper, the poultry and veal stock, and then water to cover. Cook slowly for 3 hours, removing the scum regularly. Strain the stock through a muslin conical sieve into a large pan and bring quickly to the boil, skimming carefully, to reduce it to $1^{1/2}$ l. of concentrated stock. Remove from the stove and let it cool down completely. Cover with cellophane and keep in the refrigerator. *

INGREDIENTS

		Wings, carcasses and necks of 2 ducklings or Barbary ducks
1		Carrot
1		Onion
3	sprigs	Parsley
1	tbsp	Tomato purée
2		Plum tomatoes (ripe)
1		Bouquet garni
1/2	head	Garlic
1/2	tsp	Crushed black pepper
1/2	tsp	Ground coriander seeds
1	l.	Poultry stock
1/2	l.	Veal stock
		Table sea salt

Fish stock (fumet)

To make 1 l. of stock

Preparation

Peel and finely chop the onions, shallots, mushrooms and fennel into thin mirepoix. Chop the bones, heads and trimmings. Sweat them in the olive oil in a 35 cm frying pan on high heat, to remove all the moisture. Add the chopped vegetables and sauté them "dry", but without browning them. Add the white wine to deglaze, letting it evaporate. Add the bouquet garni, coriander seeds and white pepper. Cover with cold water and add table salt. Bring rapidly to the boil, regularly removing the scum. Simmer for 30 minutes, without stirring. Allow to stand for 10 minutes before straining through a muslin conical sieve, pressing the bones well to extract all the stock. Reduce, simmering slowly down to 1 l. of stock, so that the flavour is concentrated. Cool quickly, cover with cling film and refrigerate. *

INGREDIENTS

1 1/2	kg	Fish bones, heads (without gills) and trimmings
50	g	Onions
50	g	Shallots
50	g	Mushroom stalks
75	g	Fennel bulbs
1		Bouquet garni
1	dl.	Dry white wine
3	tbsp	Olive oil
1	tbsp	Coriander seeds
1/2	tsp	Freshly ground white pepper
1/2	tsp	Table sea salt

If you do not intend to use the stock immediately, freeze it in small portions for ease of use.

Shellfish consommé

To make *3 l.* of consommé

PREPARATION
Cut the carrots, onions, shallots and fennel into thin mirepoix. Finely crush the shells and sauté them dry in the olive oil in a 30 cm frying pan. On high heat, add the chopped vegetables and sauté them dry, without browning them. Add the tomatoes, cut into mirepoix, as well as the tomato purée, and sweat them dry. Add the cognac and white wine to deglaze, letting them evaporate. Add the bouquet garni, coriander seeds and garlic. Cover with cold water and add the salt. Bring to the boil on high heat, removing the scum frequently. Simmer for 30 minutes, stirring from time to time. Allow to stand for 10 minutes before straining the stock through a muslin conical sieve, pressing the shells well to extract all the liquid. Simmering slowly, reduce the sauce to *4 l.* to concentrate the taste. Cool down.

To clarify Peel and slice the shallots, carrots and fennel into thin mirepoix. Finely chop up the fish and shells. Whisk everything together with the egg whites. On medium heat, add the mixture to the cold shellfish sauce. Reduce, stirring frequently with a spatula, until the ingredients of the clarification float to the surface and form a sort of "frothy hat".

Lower the heat and allow to simmer, not boil, without stirring, for 30 minutes until the vegetables are well cooked. Strain what has become a consommé through a muslin conical sieve lined with damp cheesecloth, transferring it gradually with a ladle, disturbing the liquid as little as possible. Check seasoning, cool rapidly, cover with cling film and refrigerate. *

INGREDIENTS

Coulis (sauce)

2	kg	Shellfish carcasses
100	g	Onions
100	g	Shallots
150	g	Carrots
150	g	Fennel bulbs
1/2	head	Garlic
500	g	Fresh tomatoes (ripe)
100	g	Tomato purée
1		Bouquet garni
2	dl.	Dry white wine
1/2	dl.	Cognac
1	dl.	Olive oil
1	tsp	Coriander seeds
1/2	tsp	Table sea salt

Clarification

100	g	Firm white fish, such as snapper
100	g	Shellfish carcasses
5		Egg whites
25	g	Shallots
50	g	Carrots
50	g	Fennel bulbs

Shellfish coulis

To make *1½ l.* of sauce

PREPARATION
Cut the carrots, onions, shallots and fennel into thin mirepoix. Finely crush the shells, and dry them out in a 30 cm diameter frying pan on high heat in the olive oil. Add the chopped vegetables, and sauté them dry, without browning. Add the fresh tomatoes, cut into mirepoix, and the tomato purée, and sweat dry. Add the cognac and wine to deglaze, letting them evaporate. Add the bouquet garni, coriander seeds and the garlic. Cover with water and add the salt. Bring quickly to the boil, frequently removing the scum. Simmer for 30 minutes, stirring from time to time. Allow to stand for 10 minutes before filtering the stock through a muslin conical sieve, pressing the shells well to extract all the liquid.

Reduce the sauce to *1½ l.*, simmering slowly to concentrate the flavour. Cool quickly, cover with cling film and refrigerate. *

* If you do not intend to use the stock immediately, freeze it in small portions for ease of use.

INGREDIENTS

2	kg	Shellfish carcasses
100	g	Carrots
100	g	Onions
150	g	Shallots
150	g	Fennel
1/2	head	Garlic
500	g	Fresh tomatoes (ripe)
100	g	Tomato purée
1		Bouquet garni
2	dl.	Dry white wine
1/2	dl.	Cognac
1	dl.	Olive oil
1	tsp	Coriander seeds
1/2	tsp	Table sea salt

Bouquet garni

PREPARATION
Use a sharp knife to cut off the roots of the leek, level with the bulb, as well as the tips of the leaves, keeping only one part green to two parts white. Remove the outer leaf. Cut the leek into two lengthwise, wash it thoroughly under running water, separating the leaves in order to remove any soil. Also wash the celery, parsley, thyme and bay leaves.

Bunch half the leek, celery and parsley together. Add the thyme and the bay leaves. Cover with the rest of the parsley, leek and celery. Tie the bouquet together firmly, wrapping the string two or three times round the top and bottom of the bouquet, and then tie in the middle. Lightly trim the excess leaves at both ends.

INGREDIENTS
1		Large leek
6	sprigs	Flat-leaved parsley
2	sticks	Celery
2		Bay leaves
2		Thyme
		String

Vegetable stock

To make *1 l.* of stock

PREPARATION
Cut the vegetables into thin mirepoix, place in an 18 cm pan with a handle, and add the garlic, thyme, black pepper, table salt and *2 l.* water. Bring quickly to the boil, removing the scum frequently. Simmer for 15 minutes, stirring from time to time. Add the coarsely chopped herbs. Simmer for 5 minutes, stirring from time to time. Allow to stand for 10 minutes before straining through a muslin conical sieve, pressing the vegetables well to extract all their juice. Cool quickly, cover with cling film and refrigerate. *

INGREDIENTS
100	g	Carrots
75	g	Onions
50	g	Shallots
75	g	Fennel bulbs
50	g	Leek
50	g	Stick Celery
75	g	Courgettes
100	g	Fresh tomatoes (ripe)
1	clove	Garlic
1	sprig	Thyme
1/2	tsp	Table sea salt
1	sprig	Coriander
3	sprigs	Parsley
1	sprig	Tarragon
1	pinch	Crushed black pepper

Royal Palm vinaigrette

To make *3 dl.* of vinaigrette

PREPARATION
Pour the vinegar into a bowl and whisk in salt according to taste. Add the oil in a thin stream and whisk the mixture until it forms an even consistency. Mix in pepper according to taste.

INGREDIENTS
250	ml.	Extra virgin olive oil
40	cl.	Sherry vinegar
		Table sea salt
		Freshly ground white pepper

Lime vinaigrette

To make *1.7 dl.* of vinaigrette

PREPARATION
Whisk the limejuice in a bowl, adding salt to taste. Add the oils in a thin stream and whisk the mixture until it forms an even consistency. Mix in pepper according to taste.

INGREDIENTS
100	ml.	Extra virgin olive oil
25	ml.	Sunflower oil
50	ml.	Meyer lemon or Tahiti limejuice
		Table sea salt
		Freshly ground white pepper

Eucalyptus honey vinaigrette

To make *2.45 dl.* of vinaigrette

PREPARATION

Whisk the vinegar and honey in a bowl, adding salt to taste. Add the oil in a thin stream and whisk the mixture until it forms an even consistency. Mix in pepper to taste. Add the peeled and thinly chopped ginger and let it infuse for 12 hours. Strain through a muslin conical sieve and store.

INGREDIENTS

50	g	Eucalyptus honey
45	ml.	Sherry vinegar
150	ml.	Peanut oil
25	g	Ginger
		Table sea salt
		Freshly ground white pepper

Chinese vinaigrette

To make *2.45 dl.* of vinaigrette

PREPARATION

Peel and finely chop the ginger. Wash the chilli, cut it into two, remove the seeds, and cut into thin brunoise. Mix the vinegar, chilli, and ginger in a bowl. Add the oil in a thin stream and whisk the mixture into an even consistency. Mix in the soya sauce, Hoi-sin sauce and maple syrup. Let it stand and infuse for 12 hours. Strain through a muslin conical sieve and store.

INGREDIENTS

20	ml.	Sesame oil
30	ml.	Red wine vinegar
10	ml.	Kikkoman soy sauce
20	ml.	Hoi-sin sauce
20	ml.	Maple syrup
3	g	Ground ginger
1/2		Chilli

Coconut vinaigrette

To make *2.8 dl.* of vinaigrette

PREPARATION

Mix the lemon and grapefruit juice, coconut purée and fish sauce in a bowl, adding salt to taste. Add the oil in a thin stream and whisk to an even consistency. Mix in pepper according to taste.

INGREDIENTS

40	g	Extra virgin olive oil
160	g	Coconut milk (unsweetened, tinned)
60	g	Pomelo or grapefruit juice
14	g	Fish sauce
6	g	Lemon juice
		Table sea salt
		Freshly ground white pepper

Mayonnaise

To make *2 dl.* of mayonnaise

PREPARATION

Put the egg yolks in a bowl and whisk them until they thicken and become pale yellow. Beat in the mustard, and add salt and pepper. Whisk until the mixture becomes thick and smooth. Continue to whisk, adding the oil gradually, a few drops at a time, until it is well incorporated. Do not add too much oil to start with, or it will not mix smoothly. As soon as the mayonnaise begins to thicken, slowly whisk in the rest of the oil in a thin, continuous stream. Whisk in the lemon juice and check seasoning. Cover with cling film and refrigerate.

Note To make mayonnaise with olive oil, substitute a fruity extra fine virgin olive oil for the grape seed oil.

INGREDIENTS

2	dl.	Grape seed oil
2		Egg yolks (at room temperature)
1	tbsp	Dijon mustard
		Lemon juice
		Table sea salt
		Freshly ground white pepper

Perfumed Basmati rice

Serves 4

Preparation

Cut off the leek roots level with the bulb. Shorten the tips of the leaves: keep only one part green to two parts white. Remove the outer leaf. Cut the leek into two lengthwise, wash thoroughly in running water, separating the leaves to remove the soil more easily.

Dice the leeks into thin brunoise. Wash, peel and dice the carrots into thin brunoise. Sort through the coriander, wash, drain and snip up the leaves.

Wash the rice well in cold water. Bring the spices and water to the boil. Cover and leave to stand for 15 minutes, and then strain.

Melt the butter in a large *3 l.* casserole dish and slowly sauté the carrots and leeks. Add the rice and stir well together. Pour in the spiced water and the coconut milk, bring to the boil and simmer, uncovered, until the rice is cooked but still firm. Add the coriander, stirring from time to time so that the rice does not stick. Add a little water if necessary.

Serve straightaway or keep warm in a moderate oven (160° C). Break up the rice with a fork just before serving.

Note In all recipes, where Echiré butter is mentioned, any good quality butter may be used instead.

INGREDIENTS

500	g	Basmati rice
1/2	l.	Water
1/2	stick	Cassia cinnamon
1	tbsp	Cumin
5		Cardamom seeds
5		Cloves
1	tsp	Table sea salt
200	g	Carrots
200	g	Leek
25	g	Chopped coriander
1	tbsp	Echiré Butter
20	ml.	Coconut milk (unsweetened, tinned)

Basmati rice

Serves 4

Preparation

Wash and rinse the rice well in cold water. Put it in a *2¹/₂ l.* pan and add the water. There should not be more than 2 cm of water on top of the rice. Bring it the boil, add the salt, and then stir so that the rice does not stick to the bottom of the pan. Cover and cook slowly for 15 to 20 minutes. Remove from the stove, cover and leave to stand for 10 minutes. Add the butter and break up the rice with a fork just before serving.

INGREDIENTS

500	g	Kohinoor Basmati rice, one year old
1/2	l.	Water
1	tsp	Table sea salt
1	tbsp	Echiré butter

Braised giraumon

Serves 4

Preparation

Wash and peel the giraumon and dice into 1 cm cubes. Peel the ginger and garlic (removing the germ) and grind with a mortar and pestle. Peel and slice the onion. Wash the chilli, slice into two, remove the seeds and dice into thin brunoise. Wash the coriander, remove the stalks and chop up the leaves. Heat the peanut oil in a thick-bottomed 20 cm casserole dish. Add the sliced onion, ginger and chilli and sweat for 2 minutes, without browning. Add the giraumon, thyme and salt, cover and braise for 8 minutes. Remove the lid, mix in the coriander and keep warm.

INGREDIENTS

400	g	Giraumon (Japanese pumpkin)
1		Small onion
4	g	Ginger
1/4	bunch	Coriander
1		Red chilli
2	tbsp	Peanut (groundnut) oil
1	sprig	Thyme
		Table sea salt

Black lentils fricassée

Serves 4

PREPARATION

Peel the ginger and garlic (remove the germ) and grind with a mortar and pestle. Peel and slice the onions thinly. Wash the coriander, remove the stalks and chop up the leaves. Snip up the chives. Wash and cut the chillies into two, remove the seeds and dice them into thin brunoise. Wash the lentils several times in plenty of water to remove the impurities and drain them in a colander. Put the lentils into a thick-bottomed pan, cover with cold water, bring them to the boil, and then drain them again. Once the lentils have been blanched and drained, pour the olive oil into the pan. Heat slowly and add the onions, garlic and ginger. Brown slightly, then return the blanched lentils to the pan, adding the chillies, curry leaves and thyme and cover with plenty of cold water. Add salt.

Meanwhile, remove the tomato cores and bring 6 to 7 l. of water to the boil. Dip the tomatoes in the boiling water, remove them after 30 seconds and dip them immediately into cold water. Peel and quarter them and remove the seeds. Cut them into 3 mm julienne and keep cool. After cooking the lentils for 35 minutes, add the chopped tomatoes and simmer for another 10 minutes. Adjust the seasoning as necessary.

LAST MINUTE

Arrange in a serving dish and sprinkle with chopped chives and coriander.

INGREDIENTS

500	g	Black lentils
2		Onions
2	tbsp	Olive oil
3	cloves	Garlic
50	g	Ginger
5		Carri-poulé (curry) leaves
1	sprig	Thyme
2		Green chillies
6	pieces	Plum tomatoes (ripe)
1/4	bunch	Coriander
1/4	bunch	Chives
		Table sea salt

Confit Shallots

Serves 4

PREPARATION

Brown the shallots in 2 tbsp olive oil in a 15 cm saucepan. Salt and pepper. Add the butter and sugar. Cook for 5 more minutes until the sugar caramelises. Deglaze with the sherry vinegar and let it evaporate. Add the cloves, pour the white chicken stock into the pan and cook the shallots for 15 minutes until tender.

INGREDIENTS

8		Shallots (medium-sized)
2		Cloves
2	tbsp	Olive oil
1	tbsp	Cane sugar
2	tbsp	Sherry vinegar
10	g	Echiré butter
3	dl.	White chicken stock
		Table sea salt
		Freshly ground white pepper

New garlic confit

Serves 4

PREPARATION

Peel the garlic, cut the cloves into two lengthwise, removing the germ. Place the garlic cloves into a small thick-bottomed pan containing 3 dl. of water. Bring to the boil and continue boiling for 3 minutes. Strain through a colander. Put the olive oil into a small, heavy saucepan. Add the well-drained garlic cloves and brown with a pinch of cane sugar.

The garlic cloves should become pleasantly golden. Salt lightly, add pepper and deglaze with the veal stock. Simmer slowly and then store.

Note "New" garlic is the fresh crop (as in "new" potatoes).

INGREDIENTS

20	cloves	New garlic (about 2 heads)
		Water
1	tbsp	Olive oil
1	pinch	Cane sugar
1	dl.	Veal stock
		Table sea salt
		Freshly ground white pepper

Mashed potatoes

Serves 4

Preparation

The potatoes should be of about the same size. Scrub them under running water, but do not peel them. Put them into a small, shallow pan, cover with water and put on the lid. Add salt. Cook on medium heat for 20 to 25 minutes. The tip of a knife stuck into the potatoes should come out easily. Drain as soon as they are cooked. Meanwhile, pour the milk and cream into a large pan and bring quickly to the boil. Remove the pan from the stove. As soon as the potatoes are lukewarm, peel them, and mash them through a food-mill with a fine sieve into a large thick-bottomed pan. Heat slowly, stirring vigorously for a few minutes with a wooden spatula. Now gradually add 2/3 of the butter, continuing to stir to make the mashed potatoes smooth and light. Add the boiling milk and cream slowly in a thin continuous stream, mixing vigorously until the milk is completely blended into the potatoes. If the mashed potatoes seem to be a little dry and heavy, add the rest of the butter, milk and cream, mixing in the three ingredients simultaneously. Taste for seasoning and add a pinch of nutmeg. Keep warm.

Ingredients

1	kg	Potatoes (Desiree would be suitable)
30	g	Table sea salt
1	dl.	Double cream
1 1/2	dl.	Full-cream milk
100	g	Echiré butter
1	pinch	Nutmeg

Arouille violette purée

Serves 4

Preparation

Scrub the evenly-sized taro under running water, but do not peel. Put them into a small, shallow pan, with a lid, and cover with water. Add salt. Cook on medium heat for 30 to 40 minutes. When they are done, the tip of a knife stuck into the taro should come out easily. Drain as soon as they are cooked. Meanwhile, pour the milk and cream into a large saucepan and bring rapidly to boiling-point.

Remove the pan from the stove. As soon as the taro are lukewarm, peel them. Mash them through a food-mill with a fine sieve into a large thick-bottomed pan. Heat slowly to dry out the taro, stirring vigorously for a few minutes with a wooden spatula. Now start to gradually incorporate 2/3 of the butter, continuing to stir vigorously to make the purée smooth and light. Add 3/4 of the boiling milk and cream slowly in a thin continuous stream, mixing vigorously until the milk is completely blended. If the purée seems to be a little dry and heavy, add the rest of the butter, milk and cream, mixing in the three ingredients simultaneously. Check seasoning and keep warm.

Ingredients

500	g	Arouille violette (Taro)
8	g	Table sea salt
1	dl.	Full-cream milk
1/2	dl.	Double cream
50	g	Echiré butter
		Freshly ground white pepper

Coconut chutney

Serves 4

PREPARATION

Pre-heat the oven to 180° C. Open the coconut by breaking it with a hammer or with a rolling pin. Discard the coconut water. Use a paring knife to remove the coconut pulp and cut it into large pieces, using a sharp knife. Place the pieces into a shallow oven-proof dish. Dry them out in the oven for 5 minutes and then let them cool down. Clean the mint and carri-poulé, discard the stems, and chop up the leaves. Peel the garlic, removing the germ. Blend all the ingredients in a mixer until you obtain a more or less smooth paste. Check seasoning. Cover with cling film and refrigerate.

INGREDIENTS

1		Coconut
30	g	Mint
2	cloves	Garlic
3	tbsp	Tamarind pulp
1		Dried chilli
4		Carri-poulé (curry) leaves
		Table sea salt

Cashew nut chutney

Serves 4

PREPARATION

Pour the peanut oil into a large 3 l. pan or into a deep fryer. Heat to 180° C. Fry the cashew nuts, leaving them for 2 minutes in the boiling oil. When they are golden and crisp, use a skimmer to drain and remove them from the pan, place them on kitchen paper, and add salt. Clean the mint and carri-poulé leaves, discard the stems and chop up the leaves. Peel the garlic, removing the germ. Peel and slice the onion thinly. Blend all the ingredients in a mixer until you obtain a more or less smooth paste. Check seasoning. Cover with cling film and refrigerate.

INGREDIENTS

300	g	Cashew nuts
1		Onion
1		Dried chilli
1	clove	Garlic
4		Carri-poulé (curry) leaves
15	g	Mint
3	tbsp	Tamarind pulp
		Table sea salt

Oil for frying

1	l.	Peanut oil

Tomato chutney

Serves 4

PREPARATION

Take the tomatoes and remove the cores. Dip in boiling water for 30 seconds, then cool immediately in cold water, peel and cut them into quarters, removing the seeds. Cut the quarters lengthwise into thin julienne. Peel and cut the onion into thin slices. Wash the coriander, discard the stalks and snip up the leaves. Wash the chilli, cut it into two lengthwise, remove the seeds and dice into thin brunoise. Peel the garlic, removing the germ, and crush it with a mortar and pestle. Blend all the ingredients in a bowl and check seasoning.

Note This preparation needs to be made just before serving or the tomatoes will produce too much liquid.

INGREDIENTS

300	g	Vine tomatoes (ripe)
1		Onion
1	clove	Garlic
15	g	Coriander
1		Green chilli
1/2	dl.	Taggiasche extra virgin olive oil
		Table sea salt

Cucumber chutney

Serves 4

Preparation
Peel the cucumber and dice into very thin brunoise. Leave it to stand in salt. Peel and cut the onion into thin slices. Clean the mint, discard the stems, and snip up the leaves very finely. Wash the chilli, cut it into two lengthwise, remove the seeds and dice into thin brunoise. Peel the garlic, remove the germ and crush in a mortar. Mix all the ingredients in a bowl and check seasoning.

Note This preparation must be made just before serving or there will be too much liquid.

INGREDIENTS

1		Cucumber
30	g	Mint
1		Onion
4	tbsp	Extra virgin olive oil (preferably Taggiasche)
1		Green chilli
		Table sea salt

Ground chillies

Preparation
Scrub the lemon under running water; remove the peel but leave the white pith. Cut the peel lengthwise and then into thin brunoise. Stand the lemon upright and remove the pith by sliding a sharp knife from top to bottom, following the curve of the fruit. Remove the central membrane. Peel the garlic cloves and cut them into two, removing the germ. Wash the chillies and remove the seeds. Put all the ingredients in the bowl of a mixer together with the olive oil, sugar, lemon peel and sections, and the vinegar. Add salt.
Blend until the mixture forms a liquid paste. Store in an airtight jar.

Note The ground chilli will keep for a month in a refrigerator.

INGREDIENTS

125	g	Green chillies
1/2	head	Garlic
1/2		Lemon (without seeds)
1/2	tbsp	Cane sugar
1	tbsp	Ordinary vinegar
1 1/2	tbsp	Taggiasche extra virgin olive oil
		Table sea salt

Green mango pickle

Prepare at least 9 days before use

Preparation
Wash the mangoes, peel, cut them into four to remove the stones and then crush them into small pieces. Sprinkle with coarse sea salt and leave in the sun for 2 to 3 hours on a dry tea towel. Crush the mustard, fenugreek and dried chilli coarsely. Peel the garlic cloves, cut into two, removing the germ, and crush with a mortar and pestle. Cut the green chilli into two and mix it with the turmeric and the oils. Mix everything together and check seasoning. Put in an airtight jar, making sure that the mangoes are covered with oil. Leave in the sun for two days and then in the refrigerator for one week.

Note This mango pickle will keep for several months in the refrigerator.

INGREDIENTS

500	g	Green mangoes
5	cloves	Garlic
1		Dried chilli
2	tbsp	Yellow mustard seeds
1	tbsp	Fenugreek seeds
2	dl.	Mustard oil
2	dl.	Soya oil
2	tbsp	Powdered turmeric
2	tbsp	Coarse sea salt
1		Green chilli

Rodriguan lime pickle

Prepare at least 7 days before use

PREPARATION

Scrub the lemons under running water; remove the peel but not the white pith, to avoid a bitter taste. Blanch the peel in boiling water for 3 to 4 minutes, and dry in an oven at 100° C for 3 hours.

Dry out the mustard seeds in a frying pan and then crush them. Wash the chillies, cut them into two, remove the seeds and slice into thin julienne. Peel the garlic, removing the germ, and grind them in a mortar.

Sweat 2 tsp of the ground garlic in *110 ml.* of peanut oil in a 16 cm pan. Add the turmeric, crushed mustard and chillies and deglaze with 2 tbsp malt vinegar. Add the dried lemon peel and season. Let the mixture macerate for 5 to 10 minutes, stirring with a spatula. Allow it to cool down and then keep it in a refrigerator for at least 7 days before using it.

Note This lime pickle will keep for several months in a refrigerator.

INGREDIENTS

18		Organic Rodriguan limes (Ti-limon)
10	g	Mustard seeds
2		Red chillies
6	g	Powdered turmeric
5	cloves	Garlic
110	ml.	Peanut oil
2	tbsp	Malt vinegar
		Table sea salt

Cythera pickle

Prepare at least 8 days before use

PREPARATION

Peel the plums and crush with a tenderiser to remove the stones. Then crush into smaller pieces to remove the rest of the fibres. Sprinkle with coarse salt and leave in the sun for 2 to 3 hours on a dry tea towel. Wash the green chilli, cut into two and remove the seeds. Crush the mustard and fenugreek seeds and the dried chilli. Peel the garlic cloves, cut them into two, removing the germ, and grind them using a mortar and pestle. Mix with the turmeric, green chilli and two varieties of oil. Mix everything together and check seasoning. Put the pickle into airtight jars, making sure that the plums are covered with oil. Leave in the sun for one day and then in a refrigerator for one week.

Note This plum pickle will keep for several months in a refrigerator.

INGREDIENTS

500	g	Cythera plums (hog plums)
4	cloves	Garlic
1		Dried chilli
2	tbsp	Black mustard seeds
1	tsp	Fenugreek seeds
2	dl.	Mustard oil
2	dl.	Soya oil
2	tbsp	Powdered turmeric
2	tbsp	Coarse salt
1		Green chilli

Toasts melba

PREPARATION

Cut the thin baguette into diagonal slices, about 10 cm long and 2 to 3 mm thick. Spread them out on a baking tray and cook at 160° C for 12 minutes, until the bread is golden and crisp. Keep hot.

INGREDIENTS

1		Stale "ficelle" or "flute" baguette

Confit tomatoes

Makes 20 portions

Preparation

Peel the garlic, remove the germ, and chop. Clean the thyme and remove the main stems. Remove the cores from the tomatoes, bring *5 l.* of water to the boil, and dip the tomatoes in the boiling water. Remove them after half a minute and dip them at once in cold water. Peel and cut them into four, removing the seeds. Place the tomato quarters in a shallow oven-proof dish. Sprinkle with a dash of extra virgin olive oil, a few thyme leaves, the chopped garlic, fleur de sel and pepper. Cook in the oven at 90° C for about 75 minutes.

INGREDIENTS

5	Vine tomatoes (ripe)
1/2 dl.	Extra virgin olive oil
3 sprigs	Thyme
2 cloves	Garlic
	Fleur de sel
	Freshly ground white pepper

Brined lemon

Prepare at least 3 weeks before using

Preparation

Boil the water and coarse salt for 5 minutes in a saucepan, and then allow it to cool down completely. Scrub the lemons under running water. Cut the lemons into four lengthwise, except at the top (so that they are still joined together), spread them out carefully and sprinkle with table salt. Put them in the jar, wedging them tightly, and place a weight or a well-cleaned stone on top to weigh them down. Cover the lemons with the salt-water solution. Close and leave the lemons to pickle for about 3 weeks in a cool and dark place. Use only the lemon peel.

Note When you have removed one or more lemons, keep the jar in a refrigerator.

INGREDIENTS

5 à 6	Organic lemons (about 750 g)
90 g	Table sea salt

Marinade

100 g	Coarse sea salt
7 1/2 dl.	Water
	1 l. jar

Tamarind pulp

Preparation

Shell the fresh pods. Soak the pulp in hot water for 5 minutes and pass through a muslin conical sieve, pressing well to extract all the pulp. Refrigerate.

INGREDIENTS

100 g	Tamarind pods (fresh or as compressed pulp)
1 1/2 dl.	Hot water

Ghee (clarified butter)

Preparation

Cut the butter into small pieces and put it in a heat-proof dish in another dish of water (bain-marie). Heat gently. When the butter is melted, raise the heat to medium and leave the butter until it sizzles, the sign that it is beginning to fry. Remove from the stove and let the residue settle at the bottom of the pan. There must be a solid layer at the bottom and a frothy layer on top. Use a spoon to skim off the layer of froth. Line a conical muslin sieve with damp cheesecloth and pour the melted butter carefully through it to get rid of all the solid residue.

Note Keep the clarified butter in an airtight container in a refrigerator. It will keep for several weeks.

INGREDIENTS

250 g	Unsalted butter

Oriental spices

PREPARATION

Heat the cinnamon, coriander seeds and pepper in a frying pan, without adding any liquid, to dry them. Then grind the roasted spices, the grated nutmeg and mace, in a coffee mill. This powder will keep for a month in an airtight jar.

INGREDIENTS

3 cm	Cassia cinnamon
1/2 tbsp	Mace
1 pinch	Grated nutmeg
2 tbsp	Coriander seeds
1 tbsp	Jamaican pepper

Citrus fruit peel

PREPARATION

Wash the fruit thoroughly and peel with a paring knife. Place on a chopping board and remove the peel, starting from the top of the fruit to the bottom. Remove the white and bitter pith from the peel with a small sharp knife. Cut the peel into thin julienne. Bring *200 ml.* of water to the boil in a small, 15 cm diameter pan. Dip in the peel, blanch for about 10 seconds and then drain in a colander. Boil the rest of the water with the sugar. Add the peel and cook gently for about 30 minutes. Keep in a jar or container in the refrigerator.

INGREDIENTS

1	Lime, lemon, orange, pomelo or grapefruit
500 ml.	Water
150 g	Cane sugar

Candied dried pineapple

Makes about 30 pieces

PREPARATION

Preheat the oven to 90º C. Peel the pineapple and cut into very thin slices, 1 mm thick. Dry them on kitchen paper and place them on a non-stick baking tray. Sprinkle the pineapple with icing sugar and bake in the oven for 1 hour. Remove the pineapple from the oven and leave it to cool down. If it is dry enough, it should become crisp. Store in an airtight tin.

INGREDIENTS

1	Queen Victoria pineapple
4 tbsp	Icing sugar

Dried bananas

To make about 10 pieces

PREPARATION

Preheat the oven to 90º C. Peel the bananas. Use a mandoline to cut them lengthwise into thin slices, 2 mm thick. Dry on kitchen paper, then place on a non-stick baking tray. Sprinkle the banana slices with icing sugar and put in the oven for 1 hour. Remove and let them cool down. Turning crisp indicates that they are dry. Store in an airtight tin.

INGREDIENTS

2	Bananas (semi-ripe)
2 tbsp	Icing sugar

Candied green apple

To make about 30 pieces

PREPARATION

Preheat the oven to 90º C. Bring the water and sugar to the boil in a small 14 cm wide saucepan with a handle. Wash the apples and cut into very thin slices, 1 mm thick. Blanch the apples for 15 seconds, drain in a colander and place on a non-stick baking tray. Leave them in the oven for about 1 hour. Remove and let them cool down. Turning crisp indicates that they are dry. Store in an airtight tin.

INGREDIENTS

2	Granny Smith apples
500 ml.	Water
200 g	Cane sugar

Chocolate cigars

Preparation

Melt the chocolate in a bain-marie, containing hot but not boiling water. Add the cocoa butter and mix with a spatula. Spread the chocolate thinly over a non-stick tray and place in the refrigerator for 10 minutes.

Remove the tray and leave at room temperature. Then pass the blade of a large knife (about 12 cm long) or a palette knife under the chocolate at a slightly diagonal angle. As you push away from you, the chocolate will roll into cigars. Return the tray to the refrigerator to harden the cigars. Transfer the cigars to a plastic container and keep in a cool place.

INGREDIENTS

100 g	Chocolate (64% cocoa)
10 g	Cocoa butter (optional)

Coconut tuiles

Serves 4

Preparation

The first part needs to be done the day before. Put the egg and sugar into a basin. Melt the butter in a small pan. Whisk the sugar and egg together for 2 minutes, and then add the coconut and melted butter. Stir them together until the mixture is smooth and even. Cover with cling film and refrigerate.

The next day, preheat the oven to 160° C. Use a teaspoon to place small amounts of the paste onto a non-stick baking tray. Use a spatula or a tablespoon dipped in cold water to flatten them so each measures 40 mm across. Bake in the oven for 8 to 10 minutes. Remove the tray from the oven. Detach the tuiles with a spatula and mould them around a bottle or rolling pin to give them a curved shape. Store them in an airtight tin.

INGREDIENTS

1	Egg
60 g	Cane sugar
50 g	Desiccated coconut
8 g	Echiré butter

Vanilla pastry cream

To make about 800 g

Preparation

Cut the vanilla pods into two lengthwise. Put them as well as the milk into a 15 cm wide thick-bottomed pan. Bring to the boil, turn off the heat and steep for 5 minutes. Whisk the eggs and sugar in a bowl until the mixture becomes whitish. Add the custard powder and the sifted flour and blend. Sieve the vanilla-flavoured milk into a pan and return to the boil. Mix half of the milk into the egg/custard powder mixture. Pour this through a muslin sieve into the pan containing the rest of the milk. Cook slowly, whisking continuously. As soon as the mixture starts to boil, whisk in the softened butter. Remove from the stove and pour the custard into a basin. Place the basin on a bed of ice, stirring from time to time. When the cream is cold, cover with cling film and refrigerate.

INGREDIENTS

1/2 l.	Full-cream milk
2 pods	Fragrans vanilla
6	Egg yolks
125 g	Cane sugar
50 g	Custard powder
15 g	Plain flour
50 g	Echiré butter (soft)

Puff pastry

To make 1 kg of pastry (Preparation time: 6 hours)

Preparation

Sieve the flour onto a work surface. Make a hole in the middle. Put in the water, vinegar, softened butter and salt. Use the tips of your fingers to mix it gradually together, until it forms a ball. The dough should be quite soft but not sticky. Roll the dough into a flat square. Use a knife to make an X-shaped incision, no more than 2 to 3 mm deep, across the top of the dough. Wrap in greaseproof paper or in cling film. Place in the refrigerator for at least 30 minutes.

Just before removing the dough, flatten the cold butter on greaseproof paper into a 10 cm square. Ideally, the butter should have the same consistency as the dough. Lightly flour the work surface, place the dough on the surface and, with a rolling pin, roll it out into a square somewhat larger than the butter square. Place the butter in the middle of the dough and fold the edges of the dough across the top so that they meet and form a square. Use the rolling pin to press the edges firmly together, like an envelope. Make sure that the butter is thoroughly enclosed within the dough, as it must not seep out.

Flour the top of the dough lightly and roll the square into a rectangle by applying regular pressure with the rolling pin from the centre to the edges. The rectangle needs to be three times the width of the original square. It is important that the dough should be the same thickness right across. Use a pastry brush to remove any excess flour from the dough. Fold the two ends so that they join in the middle. Fold the dough in the middle like a purse. This is the first double fold. Roll slightly, put two finger marks in the middle of the dough, to indicate the first double fold, and wrap in cling film. Refrigerate.

After an hour, remove the dough from the refrigerator. Lightly flour the work surface, unwrap the dough and place it on the surface, so that the open edge is on your right. Roll, applying even pressure, backwards and forwards, to form a rectangle three times as long as it is wide. Use a pastry brush to remove any excess flour and fold in the same way as previously. Roll out slightly and mark with four finger tips. Wrap in cling film and refrigerate again, having completed the second double fold.

After another hour, repeat exactly the same operation as for the second double fold, to make the third double fold. Mark the dough with six fingers, wrap in cling film and refrigerate for half an hour.

The final fold is a single one. Remove the dough from the refrigerator. Unwrap the dough onto the lightly floured work surface, again placing the open edge on the right. Roll out the dough to make a 60 cm x 20 cm rectangle. Use a pastry brush to remove any excess flour. Fold the dough in three, by folding the third nearest you to the middle of the remainder, and then the part furthest from you over the rest. You should obtain a three-layer square. Roll out the dough slightly, wrap in cling film and refrigerate for half an hour before using. Take what you need for immediate use and cut the rest into small strips. Wrap them and freeze for when you next need puff pastry.

The best way to use the frozen dough is to leave it to defrost overnight. Roll it out the next day, refrigerate overnight again and bake the next day.

INGREDIENTS

Dough

500	g	Flour
40	g	Echiré butter (soft)
12	g	Table sea salt
220	ml.	Water
4	cl	Sherry vinegar

Butter

350	g	Butter (84% fat)

Shortcrust pastry

To make 1.5 kg of pastry

Preparation

Put the butter and sugar into a food processor and blend on the slowest setting for about 2 minutes. Add the egg and continue to mix slightly faster for a further minute. Add the sifted flour and the salt to the mixture and process further, but not too much as the flour should not turn into a ball. Remove the dough and place on a lightly floured work surface. Shape into a ball and wrap in cling film. Refrigerate for 30 minutes before using it. Some of the dough can be frozen for a subsequent occasion.

When using frozen dough, let it defrost at room temperature and roll out it with a rolling pin on a lightly floured work surface, but do not overwork it. Place it in greased moulds or cut it into the shapes you want to use. Let it stand in the refrigerator for an hour, before baking in an oven heated to between 170º C and 190º C.

Ingredients

500	g	Echiré butter
250	g	Cane sugar
1		Egg
750	g	Flour
25	g	Finely ground almonds
1	pinch	Table sea salt

Grissini dough

Preparation

Process the sifted flour, oil, sugar, yeast and improver in a mixer. Add the water and blend on the lowest setting for 3 minutes. Add the salt and blend for a further 10 minutes on the next setting. Remove the dough and let it stand in the refrigerator for at least an hour.

Double fold the dough (see the puff pastry recipe), then roll it out and let it stand again as before. Then give it a single turn, as in the puff pastry recipe, and let it stand for another 20 minutes. To make the glaze, mix the egg yolks with 1 tbsp water in a basin. Roll out the dough a final time, so that it is about 4 mm thick. Cut it into strips, 30 cm long and 1 cm wide, sprinkle with fleur de sel and let it stand in the refrigerator for another 45 to 50 minutes.

Bake at 250º C for the first 6 to 7 minutes, and then at 170º C for a further 4 to 5 minutes.

Ingredients

1	kg	Flour
4 1/2	dl.	Water
50	cl	Olive oil
50	g	Cane sugar
20	g	Fleur de sel
30	g	Echiré butter
20	g	Yeast
10	g	Improver (optional)

Glaze

2		Egg yolks

Meyer lemon sorbet

Serves 4

Preparation

Bring the water, sugar and pectin to the bowl in a 10 cm wide pan. When the mixture starts to boil, add the glucose syrup, let it dissolve and then remove the pan from the stove. Let it cool down in a tub filled with ice. After it has cooled down, add the lemon juice, strain through a muslin conical sieve and let it set in an ice-cream maker. Use a mandoline to grate the lemon peel. When the sorbet has almost set, add the peel. Churn for 30 seconds, remove the sorbet and freeze.

Ingredients

265	ml.	Meyer lemon juice
450	ml.	Water
165	g	Cane sugar
50	g	Glucose syrup
3	g	Apple pectin
1		Meyer lemon

Coconut sorbet

Serves 4

PREPARATION

Heat the milk, sugar, sanetan and coconut milk in a 20 cm wide pan, and whisk thoroughly. Add the trimoline. Remove from the stove and strain through a muslin conical sieve into a container sitting in a tub of ice. When the sorbet has cooled down, pour into an ice-cream maker. Once the sorbet has set, freeze.

INGREDIENTS

250	ml.	Skimmed milk
100	ml.	Coconut milk
50	g	Cane sugar
15	g	Trimoline or glucose (optional)
50	g	Sanetan (desiccated coconut)

Raspberry sauce (coulis)

To make *250 ml.* of sauce

PREPARATION

Wash the raspberries and crush them in a mixer with the icing sugar and lemon juice. Strain the sauce through a muslin conical sieve and refrigerate.

INGREDIENTS

250	g	Fresh raspberries
50	g	Icing sugar
1	tbsp	Lemon juice

Mango sauce

To make *300 ml.* of sauce

PREPARATION

Wash the mangoes, peel and cut into four to remove the stones. Crush in the mixer with the icing sugar and lemon juice. Strain the sauce through a muslin conical sieve and refrigerate.

INGREDIENTS

2		Mangoes, weighing 400 g in total (ripe)
1/4	dl.	Orange juice
30	g	Icing sugar
1	tbsp	Meyer lemon or Tahiti limejuice

Kumquat sauce

To make 250 g of sauce

PREPARATION

Wash the kumquats carefully, cut them into four, remove the seeds and put them into a small 10 cm wide pan. Add the orange juice and cook slowly for 15 minutes, stirring gently with a wooden spatula. Add one third of the sugar, stirring continuously and cook for another 10 minutes. Add the rest of the sugar and cook until the kumquats are tender and the sauce starts to thicken. Remove from the stove and let it cool down, before placing it in a jar or container in the refrigerator.

INGREDIENTS

150	g	Kumquats (ripe)
75	g	Cane sugar
100	ml.	Orange juice

Cold sabayon base

To make *1/2 l.*

PREPARATION

Put the egg yolks into a bowl. Bring the water and sugar to the boil in a small 10 cm wide saucepan. Pour it onto the egg yolks and whisk. Strain the mixture through a muslin conical sieve and put into a microwave-safe dish. Poach at up to 90º C, removing the bowl from time to time to whisk. Remove from the microwave oven, put the bowl into a tub filled with ice and whisk it as it cools down. Pour the contents into the bowl of a mixer, and whisk on the second lowest setting for 4 to 5 minutes. Put in a container and freeze.

INGREDIENTS

125	g	Cane sugar
1 1/2	dl.	Water
8		Egg yolks

Chilled rum-flavoured sabayon

Serves 4

PREPARATION

Use a spatula to mix the sabayon base and the rum together in a small bowl. Pour the mixture onto the whipped cream and blend carefully. Refrigerate for about 10 minutes before serving.

INGREDIENTS	
100 g	Cold sabayon base (semi freddo base)
10 g	10 year-old rum
100 g	Whipped cream)

Pistachio-flavoured chilled sabayon

Serves 4

PREPARATION

Whisk the water and pistachio paste together until the mixture is smooth. Add the sabayon base and mix well. Pour the mixture into the whipped cream and blend carefully. Refrigerate for about 10 minutes before serving.

INGREDIENTS	
100 g	Cold sabayon base
15 g	Sicilian pistachio paste
15 g	Water
100 g	Whipped cream

Sweet potato jam

To make 4 jars, each of *400 ml.* of jam

PREPARATION

Bring *3 l.* water to the boil into a 28 cm wide pan. Wash the jars and lids, together with a small ladle for handling the jam, and put them into the pan. Leave them to sterilise for at least 30 minutes, then dry them with a clean tea towel.

Scrub the reddish skin of the sweet potatoes under running water, but do not peel. Put the potatoes into a shallow pan and cover with water. Cook, covered, on moderate heat for 30 to 40 minutes. The tip of a knife stuck into a sweet potato should come out easily. Drain the potatoes as soon as they are cooked.

Crush the sweet potatoes in a food mill with a fine mesh. Put the potato purée into a copper preserving pan. Add a third of the sugar, *225 ml.* water and cook slowly, stirring with a spatula to prevent the sugar from sticking to the bottom of the pan. After 15 minutes, add another third of the sugar, still stirring from the edge of the pan to the middle.

Check the sugar content with a refractometre (or use a clean spoon to taste the jam), as the potatoes vary in sweetness. Add the rest, or part of the sugar, as necessary and continue to cook and stir. As soon as the jam starts to simmer slightly, cook for another 2 to 3 minutes. Check the sugar content again with the refractometre; its refractive index should be 35.

Remove from the stove and fill the jars to the brim using the sterilised ladle. Cover and seal the jars tightly. Let them cool down, then wipe and dry the jars before putting them in the refrigerator.

Note Always keep this jam in the refrigerator or in a very cool place, as the sugar content is not high enough to preserve in the traditional way.

INGREDIENTS	
1 kg	Violet sweet potatoes
425 g	Cane sugar
225 ml.	Water, for cooking
4	400 ml. jars with lids

Acknowledgements

I should like to thank Herbert Couacaud and Jean Pierre Chaumard for their support; my photographer friend, Christian Bossu-Picat, for his patience during the shooting of the pictures, which was always conducted good-humouredly; Tiburce Plissoneau Duquesne for his invaluable help with the editing and Toriden Chellapermal and his team for the production of the book as well as Francis Montocchio, Robert de Spéville and Marcel Masson for their encouragement.

I should also like to thank Clifford L'Etang, Nazir Hossen Dilmohammud, Didier Jacob, Tony Hoareau and Ramphul Soodarsan for their collaboration during the photograph sessions, as well as my assistants - Nanuck Alibhy, Jayedeo Sing Neerunjun, Abdool Ferose Khan, Nunkoo Mohendranath, Bisram Ramsing, Augundooa Mahen Kumar, Ramlagun Sahadeo, How Kit Chi Cheong Yim Woon, Jeetun Ghunayshyam, Poorun Dharamraj and all the kitchen staff - for all their hard work.

Lastly, I would like to thank Air Mauritius, Cathy Giraud from Macumba and all our suppliers, who have helped us in producing this book and all those others who have contributed in one way or another.

Richard Ekkebus.

Bibliography

Ile Maurice, Deux siècles de Cuisine - Jean-Claude Hein - 2001

Les Plantes et leur histoire à l'île Maurice - Guy Rouillard et Joseph Guého - 1999

Les Antilles et la Guyane à travers leur cuisine - Docteur André Nègre - Editions Desormeaux

Bonjour le rhum - J. Michel Renault - Editions du Pélican

Saveur et Splendeur des Fruits Tropicaux - D. Tate - Editions du Pacifique

© EVASION 2001

All rights reserved. No part of this publication may be reproduced, stored in retrieval systems or transmitted in any form by any means, electronic, mechanical, photocopying, recording or otherwise without the written permission of the editor.

ISBN - 99903-962-1-3
Printed in Singapore.